WITH MY
LITTLE
EYE

ALSO BY JOSHILYN JACKSON

Mother May I

Never Have I Ever

The Almost Sisters

The Opposite of Everyone

Someone Else's Love Story

A Grown-Up Kind of Pretty

Backseat Saints

The Girl Who Stopped Swimming

Between, Georgia

gods in Alabama

SHORT STORY

"My Own Miraculous"

WITH MY LITTLE EYE

A NOVEL

JOSHILYN JACKSON

WM

WILLIAM MORROW

An Imprint of HarperCollins*Publishers*

HarperCollins books may be purchased for educational, business, or sales promotional use. For information, please email the Special Markets Department at SPsales@harpercollins.com.

FIRST EDITION

Library of Congress Cataloging-in-Publication Data

Names: Jackson, Joshilyn, author.
Title: With my little eye : a novel / Joshilyn Jackson.
Identifiers: LCCN 2022035971 (print) | LCCN 2022035972 (ebook) | ISBN 9780063158658 (hardcover) | ISBN 9780063158665 (trade paperback) | ISBN 9780063297777 | ISBN 9780063158672 (ebook)
Subjects: LCGFT: Novels.
Classification: LCC PS3610.A3525 W58 2023 (print) | LCC PS3610.A3525 (ebook) | DDC 813/.6—dc23/eng/20220812
LC record available at https://lccn.loc.gov/2022035971
LC ebook record available at https://lccn.loc.gov/2022035972

ISBN 978-0-06-315865-8

23 24 25 26 27 LBC 5 4 3 2 1

For David Garber

Joshua Hearne

Adam Leslie

Lydia Netzer

Nathan Pettengill

And my favorite, Scott Winn.

Thanks for storying me through, DMs. I love alla y'all nerds.

WITH MY LITTLE EYE

July 27, 2016

Meribel Mills
c/o Liza Coombs, Creative Endeavors Agency
2122 Avenue of the Stars
Los Angeles, CA 90067

Meribel.

This isn't a fan letter. I am not your "fan," though of course I find you beautiful. Of course I love your work. I like to have you on my small screen, to freeze you and rewind you. You move for me, frame by frame, stopping when your eyes turn toward me. I can see your secret spaces. You toss your hair and cock your hip, flaunting your beauty, your cruelty, but secretly you yearn for me to take you in hand, to make you soften and open.

This letter asks a lot of you, I know. But you will not fail me. You could never. So. Look past these simple words, through the page, and see me clear like I see you. You know me already.

Can't you feel it? You can. Hold the paper to your face. Breathe in all the sweetness. We will be sweet together. I will be sweet to you when you are good.

This is, in fact, a letter from your destiny. Destiny is coming for you.

Soon.

1

I NEVER THOUGHT that I was famous enough to get murdered.

I had a small, shiny role on a popular sitcom in the nineties, some little parts in little movies, and a lot of guest spots on detective shows. That's not the kind of actress who gets Madonna-stalked. But here I was. Hunted.

It took about a year from the date of his first letter, but he drove me out of LA. Three weeks ago, I moved myself and my daughter, Honor, all the way across the country to get away from him. New phone, new email, new forwarding service. I wanted to feel safe. I wanted to do normal things, like sit here in a chichi coffeehouse so belligerently air-conditioned against August that I had ordered my Americano hot. Like chat with my new neighbor, Cooper. But all at once, I felt my spine stiffen and elongate. My mouth went dry. Cooper and I were in the middle of a deep-dive talk about our exes, a bonding point for us, when he heard me suck in sudden air. He stopped talking midsentence and cocked his head, concerned.

"What?"

I tried to make my shoulders relax. "I'm being watched."

"Really?" Cooper swiveled around, blatantly looking. He was more interested than alarmed, but all my skin was tingling and my chest felt tight.

"Really. Don't be so obvious," I said, though I was looking all around, too.

No one was looking back. Whoever was watching didn't want to get caught. My heart rate picked up. This was how I'd felt in LA, for months now. It should not be happening in Atlanta, especially here, so close to my new home. Java House was inside my actual building, on the first floor, along with a CVS, a deli, and the mailroom.

I breathed in deep, trying to calm down. Cooper was the most interesting human I'd met since moving back to Georgia. Urbane and easygoing, and I needed a friend. I made myself smile.

"How do you know?" Cooper asked.

"I can feel it," I said. "I almost always can."

"Is that an actor thing?" He liked hearing about my job.

"Yeah. I think a lot of actors have that superpower." It was true. But this? This reactive fear was not an actor thing.

Honor had a janky kind of restlessness that got into her body on hard days. She would say, "Mom, I'm full of bees," and I would rub her feet or hands with lotion until she calmed, or walk with her in circles if it was bad enough that touch made it worse. I'd assumed it was part of her autism, but ever since my stalker got dead serious, I had an inkling what she meant. Moving two thousand miles away was supposed to fix this, but I was instantly so full of bees, I could practically hear humming.

Cooper pretended to stretch so he could look behind him-self, hamming up the stealth to amuse me. I laughed, but I was surreptitiously giving closer scrutiny to every man in the place: A forty-something in line, petting his wispy goatee and reading a paperback. Two businessmen, not together, one in a red tie, one in a brown sports coat, both tapping into laptops at the tech bar. A college kid playing on his phone.

"Twenty bucks says it's him, and he's working out exactly how to make a move on you," Cooper said, tilting his head at the first businessman. "Never trust a power tie."

"You're on," I said, shaking on it, trying to mirror his playful tone, keep it light. None of the men seemed the least bit interested in me. Even so, when Cooper let go of my hand, it moved of its own volition to press my chest. One of Cooper's dark blond eyebrows quirked.

"Are you okay?" he asked.

He didn't touch me again, though. I liked this about Cooper, most of all; he clearly found me interesting and charming, but he was too hung up on his ex to try to get me into bed. I was too hung up on mine to want to go. Not now, anyway. There was a little piece of me that thought if we did become good friends, who knew where that might lead. One day. But for now, we were compatriots who'd lost in the love wars, each binding our own wounds.

"Of course," I said. *He's not here. He can't be here.*

I was trembling, though. I hid my hands in my lap, mostly from myself. I didn't want to feel this. Honor and I had fully unpacked into our midtown high-rise sublet, and our fresh start was going well. Well enough, anyway. We'd moved in such a hurry that I'd had to pick out our condo online. It was darling, as advertised, but the neighborhood was sketch. Right now, over Cooper's shoulder, I could see a homeless guy, twitchy, his skin picked open, panhandling in front of the big window. The "nearby park" was a patchy-grassed dog run full of harried adults juggling coffees and poop bags, and more than once when I walked Gumball there, I'd seen condoms and used needles by the benches.

But Honor was adjusting well to both a new school and a new therapist. The few grades she'd gotten so far were her usual As, and though there had been some bumps and a lot of stimming, she'd had zero five-star meltdowns. I was excited about my job, which was starting to feel real; I was meeting the costume designer for fittings tomorrow. I was also breathing Georgia air on the daily, calm and easy, like a normal person who didn't hate Georgia. All I needed now was a friend outside the industry; I wanted this not-a-date with Cooper to go well.

"You don't seem okay," he said.

I made myself smile and look at him instead of all around. Whoever was watching me was good at it. Hard to catch. "I'm a little nerved up. It's so strange, being home. Or back here, anyway; LA is home. I haven't set foot in Georgia for twenty years. I wouldn't even take flights that paused in the Atlanta airport."

He chuckled, but only because I'd said it as if I were kidding. I wasn't.

He said, "I get that. I'm the same way with Texas. My dad was one of those 'Hey, son, let's be extra hairy and hate our wives and go drink beer and shoot things' guys. He did not know what to do with me." Cooper talked about galleries and plays, read novels, did the *Times* crossword over coffee. Trying to picture him slogging out into the woods to murder deer in his buttery leather Mephisto loafers made me smile in spite of my nerves. He glanced around again, then added, "I don't see anyone staring."

"I'm sure it's nothing." It was absolutely something. "Anyway. Where were we?"

"Oh, yeah. So. Addie texted last night. Wants 'to talk,' she says."

I shook my head. "You know she means 'get back together,' right?" I hadn't heard from my ex, Cam. Not once. Well, I'd been pretty decisive when I broke it off.

He shrugged. "That's what she meant the last two times." They'd been on and off for a while now. "I shouldn't go. None of our problems have changed." He paused, his blue eyes flashing pain, but then he shrugged and said, "I'll probably go."

He was absolutely going to go. I could see it. Maybe it would work out for them. Maybe she and I would become friends, too. I knew she was a single mother with an only child, like me.

"How old is her daughter?"

Honor had yet to evince the slightest interest in the kids at her new middle school. On Monday, I'd told her that if she could learn the names of three classmates this week, I'd take her for ice cream. That very afternoon, she'd rattled off twenty names, last then first, in perfect alphabetical order, and ended with, "Rocky Road, please." She'd memorized her homeroom roll sheet.

"Oh, no," Cooper said, reading my intention. He smoothed the sides of his golden-brown hair. It was thick and sleek and needed zero smoothing. "Sheila's deep in the wilds of high school, and this last year it's been all boys and sneaking out. I suspect drinking. It's killing Addie, who doesn't deserve this shit. She blames Sheila's father, who hasn't called his kid in months. The stress of all this is probably why we keep breaking up. Addie's the sweetest person, but one day I bet the police will find chunks of her ex-husband in her freezer. All the chunks she doesn't eat, anyway." He smiled, wryly, but I could see he was still hurting. "Anyway. Given the givens, Sheila's not a good match for Honor-Bright."

Under the table, my foot had started jouncing. I was still being watched, and it felt stealthy and insidious. I stilled and made myself breathe slowly, in and out. I checked all the men again, starting and ending with Power Tie, the man Cooper had bet on. I didn't catch any of them staring or even looking hastily away. But I could feel eyes watching, shivery trails crawling across my skin.

I gave a quick glance behind me. The table there had been empty, last time I looked. Now, a young woman sat with her phone out, staging a mini photo shoot with her latte and her novel. She was unaware of my existence, and she looked about as dangerous as a glass of whole milk.

I turned back to Cooper, making myself smile, but a clammy, shaking piece of me felt sure that the gaze I felt skittering over me belonged to a predator. My predator.

Marker Man, Honor called him, because his envelopes came addressed in huge, jagged handwriting that glared cherry pink, or lime green, or berry blue. They stank of alcohol solvent and sickly-sweet faux fruit. I'd never let my kid read his notes, but a couple of months ago, they'd stopped coming to CEA, c/o my current agent Liza Coombs, and began showing up in the mailbox at my quadplex in LA. Honor brought the mail in most days, so there was no way for her not to notice them. The letters inside were also written in cheap, scented marker, as if I were being stalked by a ditzy teenage girl, but there was nothing innocent or fun about the things he wrote, the graphic pictures he drew.

I realized my foot was bouncing again, a jerky rhythm. I stopped it. I could still feel that palpable gaze creeping over my face, my body. I told myself I was being paranoid. I'd uprooted my daughter, left my friends, broken up with the first truly interesting man I'd dated in a decade, and traded perfect year-round weather for the sticky-hot swamp air of a state I hated, all to make us safe. I was safe. So why couldn't I stop scanning the coffeehouse, looking for— what?

I wouldn't recognize Marker Man even if he was a breath away. I'd never seen his face.

"I need to get home. I'm supposed to be reading a movie script." I was finished, actually, but I wanted a locked door between me and every other set of human eyes.

"Sure. I'm in the middle of a project, anyway," Cooper said with zero urgency. He ran his own small business designing motion graphics, but I'd gathered he also had family money. "Mind if I grab a quick refill? I need caffeine." He was already rising.

I did mind. I didn't want to sit here alone, feeling exposed. I wanted to be home, and I fought the urge to drive right to the school, snatch Honor out, and take her home, too. My rational brain knew she was safe, and she needed more independence. Last week she texted me a link to an article about helicopter parenting.

Her thirteenth birthday was coming up soon, in September— how had my kid gotten this close to teenager-hood so fast?—and her need for space was real. I wanted us to be safe enough for her to have some freedom. It was a huge part of why I'd taken a part on a show that filmed in Georgia, of all places.

Granted, it was a great part. A fat recurring role on the second season of last year's breakout hit. My character, the new lawyer at a firm that specialized in representing ghosts (because, sure, why not), had a pickup option to become a series regular, if it went well.

No way in hell, I told Liza when the offer came. Even if *The Spirit of the Thing* shot in New York or Montreal, I doubted I would've uprooted my change-averse kid from the only life she'd ever known. Then Marker Man escalated. It got very, very bad.

So here I was. Feeling a gaze brushing along my skin like bug feet, making me shudder. I told myself it wasn't him. His practiced, predatory stare was the only gaze I *couldn't* feel. After all, I'd never caught him, not once, and he'd been stalking me like I was prey for over a year.

Cooper had already put in his order. He waited beside Power Tie, who had come for a refill, and who was talking theatrically into a headset loud enough to teach the room he was important. I wanted to go upstairs. If Cooper was getting his drink to go anyway—

"I know your face, but I don't know your name," a male voice said. "It's driving me nuts."

I think if he had touched me, I would have leaped out of my chair in a panic and popped him one. As it was, I jerked and gasped, barely swallowing a shriek. He was built tall and square, looming up over me like a slab of human wall.

"Oops! Snuck up on you, there, huh?" he said, chuckling.

"A little," I said. It was the guy in the brown sports coat who'd been working at the tech bar.

"But we've met. I'm positive."

"I have one of those faces," I told him, terse.

Still, he hovered. "Wait. Do you work with Craig Philmore? At the bank?"

The question was so ordinary. Almost goofy. Half the tension ran out of my spine. He was still standing a little too close, but now, instead of a threat, I saw someone's bland ex-husband with a combover and vegan leather shoes, trying to flirt.

I smiled, feeling ridiculous, but also angry. How dare this fear follow me all the way from LA? The stalker who caused it had not. As far as I knew.

You drop out of sight, you could drop right out of his mind, the detective in charge of my case had told me. *In fact, it's your best bet.* Or maybe Detective Johnston was tired of making no progress while a psychopath edged closer, closer, closer. By then Marker Man's letters were arriving almost every day. In July, I came home from a long afternoon meeting with a casting director to find my house felt wrong. It took me an hour of prowling to realize Honor's blown-glass cat had teleported to a different shelf and the apples in the fruit bowl had swapped sides with the oranges. Hadn't they? Or had Honor moved the cat, turned the bowl? I couldn't prove that Marker Man had been there, but the house felt colder, as if his shadow had blocked the sunlight; then I saw that my thermostat was three degrees lower than my usual setting. Maybe I'd done it accidentally. Maybe Honor had felt hot. Or so I told myself.

The next day, Liza came at me with the job offer, pushing me hard to take it. The actress cast initially had dropped out at the last second, pregnant. The showrunner had worked with me before, and it was mine if I wanted it. A gift from the universe.

"We aren't exactly fighting off the offers as it stands, and you're about to hit your shelf life, babe," Liza told me. "Your income will crater when you hit four-oh, so think before you pass."

No one ever tells a male actor, *Hey, at forty, you are going stop booking jobs, or, if you're lucky, take a massive pay cut,* but I knew she was right. I agreed to consider it, but it was mostly lip service. Two days later, my favorite black bra and a picture of me and Honor in a small, silver frame disappeared. When I went to bed that night, my sheets smelled faintly of bay rum cologne. I knew then, in a way that I could not deny, he had been in the house. In my bed.

I thought, *Do I rig our bedrooms up with nanny cams? All I've gotten off the outdoor security cameras has been endless footage of Honor's feral cats fighting and mating like it's Feline Game of Thrones out there. Do I spend Honor's whole college fund on bodyguards? Never let my kid out of my sight? Or put some kind of dehumanizing finder-chip in her, as if she was my iPhone or our little dog, Gumball?*

I called Liza, never mind that it was pushing midnight. "I'll take the role," I said, and then I'd spent the night in the trundle bed in Honor's room. She had not loved that.

"It's like a sleepover. Sleepovers are fun," I told her.

"Sleepovers with Yuna are fun. Sleepovers with your mother are weird," she clarified.

My best friend, Wallace, and his husband, Paul, lived in the other upstairs unit, and after that, we slept at their place. I explained that it was too hard to live in our house while it was being packed up. That, she enjoyed. She loved Wallace as much as I did, which was saying something. He was a huge tower of a man who added another six inches with an extravagant seventies Afro. He had Sahara-dry humor and was a cat person, like my kid. Leaving him had been one of the worst parts of the whole damn ordeal.

Since we'd fled LA, I'd hired a forwarding service to send me Marker Man's abominations along with my Visa bill. Wallace picked up the bits of stray mail that came to my quadplex. He'd collected only four creepy missives, and those came soon after we left. Marker Man kept close tabs, so he knew I'd moved away. He said so in both the letters Wallace read me over the phone and the few that had been forwarded here, early on. His tone had gone querulous and pining. Then the letters stopped.

I'd gone ten days with no letter at all. Ten full days of silence. I hadn't had a break this long in months. I ought to be calming, not leaping out of my skin because some innocuous guy in a coffee shop half remembered me from TV and was taking a shot.

He'd most likely recognized me from when I played Didi on *Belinda's World.* When people couldn't quite place me, when they thought they must have met me at a party or on an airplane, it was almost always because of that old show. My actor's vanity didn't want to believe I looked that different, though I was thirty-seven now. Well, according to IMDb. Forty-two if I went strictly by things like my birth certificate and facts. I'd been fresh-faced and slight enough to claim eighteen and get cast as a high school sophomore when I did *Belinda's World*, though I'd been well into my twenties.

"We've never met," I told the man in the brown sports coat as Cooper arrived with his refill.

Cooper put two and two together and said, very flat, "It's Meribel Mills, buddy. She's famous. That's why you think you know her."

The man blinked, uncertain.

"You know—'Rah-Rah-Whatev-ah!'" I did my old catchphrase, hair flip and all, and the guy made the connection.

He flushed and his eyes got very bright. "Oh. Oh! That's you. I mean, wow! I loved that show. Wow. I should have—I'm so embarrassed!"

"No, no, this happens all the time," I assured him. Usually with fans, I tried for charming, friendly, open. I liked being remembered and recognized. But I was rattled from feeling watched, and his *Don't I know you* was a pickup line. I wasn't on the market. Not this guy's market, anyway.

Cooper picked up my vibe and stepped in close, putting one hand on my chair back and turning toward me, effectively cutting the man out of the conversation. He asked me what I wanted to do for dinner, as if we were a couple, long established. I played back, suggesting restaurants, until the brown coat evacuated.

As soon as he was gone, Cooper took his hand away to get his wallet, dropping a twenty on the table for me. "Did not see that one coming. Guy was so out of his league."

That made me smile. "Flatterer. Anyway, I was just playing. You don't have to pay—"

"Nope. I've never welshed once on a bet in my whole life. Keep it, we'll go double or nothing on some other nonsense, later." He grinned back, then took a big sip of his coffee and his nostrils flared. "This is skim milk. Or nut milk. Something awful. One more sec?

I'll get you another Americano, my treat, as penance." He was already heading back to the counter.

Cooper was one of those naturally lean men who never had to watch their weight. Not my preference. I went for scruffy and muscular, but perhaps only because most small, lithe men I knew were actors. I no longer dated actors. I wanted to tell him a second Americano was fifteen calories, which meant no butterscotch tonight, and bounce upstairs. It was true, but not the reason that I wanted to leave. The barista was already working on Cooper's order, though. I waited, restless in my body, full of bees again. I still felt watched, even though the sports coat guy was gone. I checked the room again. Nothing.

Finally, I turned my chair, putting my back toward the wall. As if that would make me safer. I stared out the plate-glass window at Tenth Avenue. Traffic was backed up, no surprise there. Rain was falling, hard enough now that the panhandler had disappeared. I peered through it—

There. My watcher. There he was.

All the way across the street. A short, stocky figure swathed in a long gray raincoat, shiny with repelled droplets. He was broad-shouldered and built thick. The second I spotted him, a gaggle of pedestrians streamed around him, blocking my view. When the last of the people passed, I saw he hadn't moved. His face was obscured by the rain and the shadow of his black umbrella, but I could feel his stare.

I heard my chair push back and bang into the wall before I realized I was standing.

I knew him. Didn't I? The shape of him was familiar, and yet, he could be anyone.

The rain picked up, making him even harder to see. I blinked and scrubbed my eyes. Could he still see me through the window, in this downpour?

"Ready?" Cooper said. I whipped around to face him, my cheeks flushing, as if he'd caught me shoplifting, or naked.

He held up his corrected drink and two more drinks in a cardboard carrier. "I got that sugar-free bubble thing for Honor-Bright. Unless she's still so mad about the move she'd throw it at you." He grinned, and I blinked, barely comprehending. "Meribel? Are you okay?"

I wasn't. I turned to peer back out the window.

Traffic. Pedestrians hurrying. Rain, falling harder. No stocky figure, anonymous in the big coat, staring in from across the street.

Well, that's a relief, I thought. Except it wasn't. I burst into tears. "Meribel?"

I was already spinning away. I ran at the door, and it swung open as if by magic. A geeky high school boy was coming in, and he'd pulled it open from the other side. I shoved past him, unheeding of his awkward stumble back, only to find myself surrounded by more big teenage boys in board shorts and T-shirts.

"What the—!" one said, and another laughed. "Whoa, lady!"

I shouldered my way through, the air thick and hot even with rain dumping down in torrents. I was trying to see over their heads, past the slow traffic, but when I finally got to the curb, there was no one standing across the street.

I stood there, soaked to the skin and yet still sweating, peering back and forth, trying to find him until I was whirling in circles. No mysterious figure in a gray coat was hustling off into the storm. The man who had been watching me was gone.

2

WHEN I WAS in the hospital, my mother told me, *You don't build a new house on a graveyard.*

She meant: *Get out of Georgia.*

I wouldn't see James. I couldn't bear to, so she kept him away. No idea how; she could be ruthless on my behalf. Maybe she even knew I'd started saving up the pain pills the nurses brought me.

I couldn't imagine a way forward, so she found one for me. *Go west.* She wrote me a check for five thousand dollars that she could hardly spare. I'd dreamed about a different life before I met James in our sophomore year at UGA. *Go have that life, now. Walk away and don't look back. Just live.*

Pack for me? I begged her. I was that weak.

The day I was released, I took my mother-loaded Civic, my wrecked heart, and my failure of a body and drove straight to LA. I fit right in with the thousands of thoroughly broken girls who had washed up in the sprawling city, all chasing the same handful of parts. I could breathe, eat, sleep again. I flushed the pills.

My mother saved me, and she handled the divorce, too. I never talked to James again.

In LA, I'd gotten very lucky, very fast, landing a part that reset me to eighteen again, as if college and my marriage and my losses had all been wiped away. I loved my job. I made friends who felt like family, notably Wallace, and friends who felt like the beloved but irritating spouses of family, notably Paul. After *Belinda's World* was canceled, I adopted Honor through the foster system. That enticed my mom to move west, too, thrilled to be Gran. I never went back to the South again. I never contacted James.

It hurt too much. I hoped James would get the sweet life we'd planned together with someone else, and I let him go. Mostly. He did, eventually. I sometimes looked at the woman he had married on social media. She sold homemade soaps on Etsy, so her feeds were all wide open.

Her name was Sarah, and she looked a lot like me: copper-blond, built like a whippet, a heart-shaped face dominated by wide-set eyes. Hers were blue and mine were green, and she overplucked her brows to an insane degree, but we were enough alike to make me wonder if that was why he picked her. At least in part.

They had three kids who looked like the babies I'd imagined having. They lived in Woodstock, a cute little town north of Atlanta. He had a beard now, which I hated. He had a lot of smile lines around his eyes, and I liked seeing that.

Now, trying to catch my breath in air so thick with heat and rain it felt like it was boiling, I remembered James owned a dark London Fog raincoat. His wife had found it on sale and modeled it herself on Insta, swamped in it, laughing. It looked a lot—a lot— like the coat worn by the man who had been watching me. That person was entirely gone, and I was sick and shivering, standing too close to the curb, when it occurred to me—had that been James?

I was still crying, shaking, but this thought brought me up short, hitching. The figure had been built short and shoulder-y and broad like James, or maybe that was the cut of the coat. I was soaked through, scared, but also wondering—did James know I was back?

I wanted the watcher to be James, so I could keep believing Marker Man was still in California. He'd gone quiet, no new letters. He must already be obsessed with some closer actress, one he could look at every day. *His kind feeds on access*, Detective Johnston had said. I'd taken that access away. I was only this afraid because fear had become a habit.

If James was watching me—well. That was interesting, not threatening. He worked downtown, so he could get here on his lunch hour. The trade mags had reported that I joined the show, no way to keep that secret. Perhaps he followed my career, and he had—

A hand came down on my shoulder and I wheeled, a small shriek escaping me.

It was Cooper, who pulled back like I was fire.

Three high school boys, still clustered under the awning outside Java House, stared at me. Two already had phones in their hands, and before I could think, I dove at Cooper and buried my rain-and-tear-slick face in his light jacket, pulling the other side over my face.

"I have to go home!" I yelled into his chest.

I wasn't so famous that TMZ would waste bandwidth on this breakdown. Maybe three seconds in the sad music part of a *What Ever Happened To . . .* compilation piece. But there were *Belinda's World* fan sites and message boards still up and active. I didn't want video evidence of this lunacy-soaked moment out there for Honor to stumble across. Not to mention all the people on set at my new job.

Cooper got it. He put a sheltering arm around me and led me, blind and snuffling into his chest, past Java House and into our building's main entrance. When I cried on men, there were usually cameras rolling, so this whole thing felt embarrassing, surreal. He kept me tucked safe while he hustled me down to the glass-walled elevator room and punched in the door code to let us in. Mercifully, the elevator door opened as soon as he pressed the up button. He took me on, half cuddling, half pushing me, the way you'd move an upset cat into a carrier. It shut behind us, and I pulled away, flushing when I saw the snot-damage I'd done to his Burberry polo. His attention was on me, however. Back in the air-conditioning, soaked through, I was shaking so hard my teeth were chattering.

"A thing I haven't mentioned, yet— I have, I had— Back in LA, I had a stalker," I told him, water dripping off my skirt and out of my hair onto the tile floor. The walls inside were mirrors, and I looked like a monster, swollen eyes lost in black pits of mascara, a smeared-lipstick mouth spilling my secrets. I hadn't brought up my stalker to Cooper even in passing, much less showed him Marker Man's notes. I'd wanted it so badly to be over. "So it can really freak me out, now. If I feel I'm being watched."

His eyebrows went up, but his eyes stayed kind. Concerned, not judging. "You think your stalker followed you to Georgia?"

"No. I don't know. I hate it here, though. I never should have come back." Humiliating, to hear the words come out in a child's broken wail. *I neh-heh-heveeeer.* He was helping me my find my keys now, opening my door and hustling me inside while I snuffled. "Oh, you left your drinks caddy. Your coffee."

He chuckled, walking me toward the kitchen. "We're past coffee, Meribel. We are now at gin. And towels." Gumball came jingling in from my room, her little nails clicking on the hardwood. She stared up at me, anxious. Cooper leaned down to pat her. "Stand down, guard dog, all is well. Where does your lady friend here keep the towels and tonic?"

I pointed him to the linen closet in the hall, and said, "I have club soda." I was trying to stop shaking, trying to pull myself together.

"That is not the same thing," he said sternly.

I scrubbed at my eyes while he went and got a towel for himself and three for me. I stayed by the door, swabbing at myself with one, then letting it fall to the floor. As he wrapped a second around my shoulders, I was imagining him talking to some other friend, saying, *Yeah. I've met Meribel Mills. More than a tablespoon of crazy in that recipe . . .*

"Please don't tell people about this." I was miserable, shivering, clutching at his sleeve.

"Of course not," he said, pulling me into a hug, so firm and calm that I believed him. Cooper smelled of clean cotton and Acqua di

Gio. He gave my back three bracing pats, as if he was burping me, and somehow that made it feel as safe as hugging Wallace. I'd missed this. Male touch with no sex in it, no threat, no expectation. It made me calmer.

I'd only met him a couple of weeks ago, at the gym inside our building; when school started, Honor and I had to push our workouts back to four. Honor was supposed to go daily because cardio helped her regulate, and I used it, too, if I didn't have a session with my trainer.

That afternoon, she'd gone on ahead while I was still changing. When I arrived, Cooper was going easy on the first treadmill, and Honor was strolling on the third. She could be prickly with strangers, but she was in friendly mode because he hadn't given her any crap for using the gym.

Honor loved rules, memorizing them, if not actually following them, and she'd seen the posted sign that said, RESIDENTS ONLY. CHILDREN UNDER 12 MUST BE ACCOMPANIED BY A PARENT OR LEGAL GUARDIAN. Honor was on the verge of turning thirteen, but she looked about ten. Two other neighbors had already tried to kick her out for being too young. When Cooper came in, she was prepped to let him have it.

He only said hello, and then he asked her the kinds of innocuous questions old people ask kids, about school and such. She felt it as an acknowledgment of her obvious maturity.

I took the only treadmill left, the one between them. He glanced over to nod hello, then blinked. "I know you. You're Didi."

Didi only appeared in about a quarter of the episodes, but it had been a plum part: Belinda's mean-girl, cheerleading nemesis, all pigtails and duck lips. I'd flounced around peeking through Aaliyah bangs and talking like the prime-time version of a nineties teenager, sneering, "as *if*" and declaring I was "totally buggin'" or that it was "time to bounce!" When Belinda went to college, the ratings started dropping. On the last season, Didi had a six-episode arc in which she admitted her viciousness had all been repressed attraction and kissed Belinda. Lesbian kisses had been appearing regularly during sweeps week for a decade by then. The bump didn't save the show.

"I go by Meribel, in real life," I told him.

Some people couldn't get over seeing me on television, but Cooper recovered near-instantly, as at ease with me as he had been with Honor. Best of all, he didn't flash that enraging, *Oh, you adopted a child with disabilities! How noble!* look when Honor accidentally reset her treadmill, losing her timer and heart rate tracker info, and she got upset enough to stim.

Maybe this was why I believed him when he said my freak-out would stay between us. I let him cover the upholstered dining chair at the head of the table with the last towel and then plop me into it. I pulled my legs up and tucked myself into a wad, watching as he banged around in my open kitchen looking for a knife, and gin, and limes.

Our furnished condo looked like the set of some family-friendly prime-time show with a laugh track. When I'd looked at pictures of this warm, colorful space online, I hadn't realized the building would be almost kid-free or that this pricey neighborhood would be so crime-y. The cheery yellow kitchen was separated from the den by a long, thin poplar dining table and chairs, the seats upholstered in a modish tangerine and cream print. My chair faced an aqua accent wall that held half a dozen brightly painted animal masks from Mexico.

Today, the show had changed to something about monsters or killers. The dark eye holes in the masks stared me down. I felt them almost the same way I felt human gazes. My skin prickled. The aqua wall itself kept going wavery, as if it were made of salty water and living things were shifting, seething, deep down under the color.

Cooper came and sat by me, pressing some sort of gin situation into my hand. I took a huge sip, sniffling and shivering.

"There's a girl, take it like medicine." He went to the bar cart to open a brand-new jar of poisonous-looking cherries that had been left there along with two kinds of stuffed olive. Gumball sat watching him, rapt, in case the jar was full of something wonderful. He dropped six or seven in his own cocktail, then got a spoon and started muddling them, turning his drink bright pink, and announced, "I'm going to shamelessly and with great confidence in my sexual identity drink this girly cocktail while you tell me why you hate Georgia."

I took another long and soothing swallow of plain gin and soda and lime. "I was married when I lived here," I said directly to the blank, judging face of the jaguar mask.

"Oh. Was it a bad marriage?" Cooper asked. He hesitated, then began, "Was he—"

"No, not at all. We were crazy about each other," I said, flatly. "We got married right out of college." I'd known then that if I wanted bio-kids, I'd have to have them early. I had such bad endometriosis that I had my first surgery at seventeen. I wasn't going to give a state-of-the-uterus speech to Cooper, though. Dating wasn't on our current table, but he was still a man. I had definitely noticed. Instead, I told him, "James grew up with three brothers and two sisters and wanted a big family. I did, too, for the exact opposite reason. I was an only child."

IVF was our best shot; thousands of dollars, injections that sent me into moody spirals, painful medical procedures. We'd shared such joy when we'd learned a little spark had landed, stuck, and started inside me. We'd waited for him with such hope. But four months in, thanks to a rain-slicked road and a tired driver racing through a red light, I'd woken up in a hospital. James was beside me with tired, red-rimmed eyes, saying, "Meribel, I'm so sorry." The spark was gone, and I was wholly changed, and there would never be another. Not for us.

I did tell Cooper about the accident, crying again, my glass already empty. Gumball walked circles around my chair, then leaped into my lap, anxious. Cooper pushed his own drink over, and I drank the bulk of that, too, even though it was thick with sugary cherries, as I wept and clutched my dog and told him things that no one knew about me. Not since Mom died. Not even Wallace. Certainly not Honor. I told this near stranger all about the life I'd let Los Angeles wipe thoroughly away, and he listened, scooting closer, but not touching me. His eyes were very kind.

"They had to take my uterus, as well. No more babies." So much for not getting grossly biological. "I wanted—"

Cooper made a *Chh* sound, sharp and fast. He manufactured a hearty grin and aimed it at the front door. "Hello, Honor."

I spun in the chair, letting Gumball down. My daughter stood in the doorframe, her small, sturdy body gone stiff and tense. Above her dark eyes, her thick, straight brows twitched toward each other. Had she heard me talk about the baby? Or was she only shocked to see me so undone, tearstained and weeping to our gym friend? I blinked, horrified. I'd lost track of time. I'd lost track of everything. This moment was unprecedented. I thought, *Honor hates new things*, and a bray of horrified laughter almost, almost escaped me. I was sick to the bone with shame.

"Your mom got caught in the storm, and she's not feeling great. Just a headache, nothing serious," Cooper said. As if Honor was five. As if we both were. "Set your backpack down, I'm going to . . ." He stopped, not sure was he was going to do, but he was rising. I was, too.

"I need to wash my face," I muttered, smiling in a way that felt plastic and purely ghastly.

Cooper gave me a fast, critical glance and said, sotto voce, "Maybe a shower."

Honor said, "Okay. Can I have screens?" Her eyebrows were still alarmed, but if she was angling for screens she must not have heard. Please, God.

I wanted my girl to look up from her endless databases of character sheets and stat blocks and her dungeon-mapping program, at least long enough to make a local friend, so we'd made a pact to limit screen time until after dinner. I hoped she cheated less than I did.

I said, "Sure," and instantly realized this was a mistake. Honor had a small, round mouth like a plum, but now it had compressed into a flat, anxious line. "I meant after dinner, of course," I amended. She hesitated, vibrating, confused. "Just—let me clean up and I'll—"

I couldn't finish that sentence any more than Cooper could. I only knew I had to stop freaking out my kid. I fled down the hall and through my bedroom to the master bath, which had a jetted shower with three heads. I peeled off my damp skirt and top and left them in a heap, then stood in the near-boiling streams, sluicing away my raccoon eyes with moisturizing foam, washing my rain-ruined hair, exfoliating my whole body with a Dead Sea salt rose scrub. I still wasn't myself, so I did my whole damn whole-body skin routine and blew my hair out. Putting on tinted moisturizer and lip balm, a little liquid blush, I felt I was rebuilding my real self, confident and easy, over all the fear and weakness that had escaped me earlier. I dressed in soft cotton leggings and an outsize keyhole T, and then I could finally look into the mirror and see the mom that Honor needed now.

I took a deep breath and stepped out of the bedroom, smiling. Honor was sitting at the dining room table, eating pizza, and whatever she saw must have reassured her, because she had no reaction. Cooper sat catty-corner, a couple of crusts on his plate. He must have ordered the food and paid for it, too, and now he was saying, "I don't know your bedtime, so I'll just trust you to 'honor' it." He chuckled at his own dreadful pun.

She snickered, too. She loved puns. "You can trust me. I'm as honest as the day is long." She also loved clichés.

He saw me in the hall then, and added, "Here's your mom. So! All's well that ends well?"

She laughed, her real, overloud bray, delighted he had picked up on her game and fired a cliché back. She asked, "*Now* can I have screens?"

Cooper made a WTH-does-that-mean face at me.

I said, "Sure. Have all the screens." She was scooting for her office nook by the fireplace before I finished the sentence. He got up and came down the hall to talk to me, his face a question. I put a finger to my lips and we went back into my room. I snicked my door closed, softly. I owed him an apology. I owed him more than that.

"I'm usually a better mother. I was going to make a healthy dinner. Pesto salmon and green beans."

"Well, it was Hawaiian pizza," he told me. "Which has fruit on it. So, that's practically a salad." His kindness almost had me misting up again, and when I apologized for that, he parroted back every excuse I'd blurted earlier: I'd been relentlessly stalked and driven from my home. I was a single mom with a new job in a city full of old pain. Of course I'd snapped. Anyone would. "Considering the history here, it's impressive that you haven't broken down before today." So kind, but even as I nodded he was saying, "I should get home. You probably want to talk to Honor . . ."

God, he was likely desperate for permission to escape. "Of course. I owe you a big favor, and I'll pay you back for the pizza."

He waved all that away. "Do you want a pot gummy? It might help you sleep."

I blinked, bewildered. "How do you know I have those?" They were hidden in my travel kit at the top of my closet. I had a prescription, so they were legal. Back home, anyway.

The question made him laugh. "I meant one of mine. Well, Addie's. She kept them at my place because of Sheila. I still have her stash."

That made me chuckle, too. "I'm good."

I showed him out, then checked in with Honor. She was building a dungeon map and typing furiously in an open chat window with Yuna while they blasted a shared playlist through their headphones. Yuna's mom let her get on screens right after school sometimes so she and Honor could work on their Dungeons and Dragons campaigns together in spite of time zones.

Honor asked for zero explanations and her gaze didn't shift off her map as she impatiently accepted my apology. I'd need to wait until earlier on a calmer day if I wanted to know whether she'd heard anything she'd need help to process. She was unwinding now.

I took Gumball on a quick walk, then put the TV on to have noise. An hour later, we all three went to bed, Gumball with me. I'd adopted the silly little thing for Honor, but she'd turned out to be team cat. Back at home, she and Wallace fed a troop of ferals, doing catch and release to get them fixed and vaccinated. Gumball was mine. I lay there for a long time with her small, hot body draped over my feet. I felt headache-y for real now, thanks to gin and pink, processed sugar.

Finally, I reached for my phone and opened my Insta, signing out of my official account and onto my looky-loo. I knew what I was going to do. It was wrong and deeply unhelpful. I did it anyway.

I had a creeping problem. While I'd been dating Cam, the Sarah-staring I'd been doing on and off for years had faded out entirely. It had started (again) when I broke up with him.

Cam had wanted to try long distance, and God, I had been tempted. But we were only a few months in when I evacuated LA. Things were so red hot and desperate between us that there was no way to know if it was anything but physical. My body kept telling my brain, *I super promise this is real*, because my body really liked him. It could not be trusted. Between our jobs and navigating Honor's schedule, we hadn't spent that much time together, and he was the quiet type. I only knew the bare bones of his history.

I'd never met his friends, his family. We'd had one dinner with Wallace and Paul. We had talked about a weekend trip. I *had* thought, *If we keep on like this, I might one day ease him into Honor's world*, but that was right after a gratuitous and glorious third orgasm. Even sunk in afterglow, the idea terrified me. Introduce Honor to a man that I was seeing? That had happened exactly never in her whole life.

I broke it off when I decided to move, and within twenty-four hours I had eaten half a pint of Ben and Jerry's and gone back to dating Sarah's Instagram feed. This was broken-heart behavior, so maybe there had been something real there. Marker Man meant that I would never know. Yet another bad turn that I owed him, but I'd get over it. I'd gotten over worse.

Still, a happy-with-her-love-life person would not be haunting her ex-husband's life via his wife's socials, now would she? Here was James looking dapper in a suit, James with his youngest riding piggyback, James and Sarah in a close-up selfie in front of some weird lizard at the zoo.

What if it had been James watching me today? Sure, half a million men in Atlanta owned dark London Fog–style raincoats, tens of thousands might be on the shorter side and built thick, but how many of them would stand in a rainstorm to stare at me?

If James was my watcher, Sarah's perky feed told me that he'd gone straight from Java House to a #datenight!!! with her. She was the kind of woman who said "squee" and "shudder-worthy," and called her dogs her "fur babies." Every time I saw that phrase, "fur baby," I inadvertently pictured a woman giving birth to a schnoodle. "Shudder-worthy" indeed.

Or I was bitter, scared, and bitchy. Her feed was cute, and in my kinder moments, I had to admit it.

This story had a red-hot sticker flashing that said, SRS RO-MANCE! above a couple of pale lavender craft cocktails and an elegant charcuterie tray. All the food she posted looked like this, little bites of things. Tapas, dim sum, sushi. Which she called "Soosh." As in, "Soosh with the hubs #datenight!!!"

I could not imagine a James who stood in the rain pining, then went home and took his wife out for "Charcoot!!!" Neither could I imagine a silent Marker Man who stopped writing letters, but then showed up on my street. The figure had been there, though. Watching.

I closed Insta and rolled over to face the wall. At some point, I must have slept. Thunder woke me, followed by the dazzling flash of lightning. I sat up, hearing rain pounding against my balcony. The clock on my nightstand said 3:02. My mouth felt coated in vile slime. I went to the bathroom and brushed my teeth, peering into the mirror. A wan and anxious Meribel peered back, wondering, worried Honor had heard me talk about the other baby. No way to tell. She was Honor, buttoned shut and long burning. If she had, it would come out of her sideways when I least expected it.

I went back into my bedroom. It was as bright and colorful as the rest of this place, with an emerald-green accent wall and puffy pillows and a fat down comforter in peacock colors, muted now in darkness. The lights from Tenth Avenue shone faintly through the sheers. I walked as if drawn toward the pair of French doors that led out to the balcony.

The watcher is there, I thought. I could feel a presence, a gaze so strong it reached through walls. He would be on the street below, staring up, oblivious to the driving rain. Keeping his vigil. James? I pushed the sheers aside and opened up both doors. It was a good-sized space, especially for Midtown, with enough room for the wrought-iron bistro table and matching chairs to be sheltered from the rain by the balcony above. I walked straight to the rail, getting misted. I peered down, seeking the exact place he'd been before, right across from Java House. I knew that I would see him. I knew it.

There he was. A dark figure swathed in the raincoat, rendered small by distance. Short and thick. Holding a black umbrella that was tilted to let him stare up. My breath caught. It was too dark and rainy, and he was too far away, for me to make out his features. I couldn't even tell if my watcher had a beard.

It might be James. It might be anyone. I wanted to scream down, *I see you!* or even go down and confront him. My body was already backing up, though, my breath ragged, my heart wild. The bedroom and the balcony were both dark. There was no way the man in the street saw me. But I felt caught.

I thought, *I'm going to call the police. Say a strange man is staring up at my bedroom.* I grabbed my phone off the nightstand, but before I dialed, I made myself step back to the railing. I made myself look down once more. To be sure.

The street was empty.

3

HE WAS FINALLY on the way to Meribel, ten days in her wake. An endless gap. He started the paperwork the second she said she was moving and broke it off with him, but even the We Pay Cash Fast people couldn't close before the eighteenth of August. That was hard, but he needed the time to get all his supplies and plans in order. He'd spent the day before at an LA campsite, but not using hookups, a dry run at what it might be like to live truly in a wilderness. It was good, he had discovered. It would work for them.

He walked past the PLEASE SEAT YOURSELF sign and took a booth, turning his mug upright for coffee. He was tired. The "seven-hour" drive from LA had taken almost nine. The camper was slow, unwieldy.

The waitress came over, finally, slopping coffee from the pot that seemed welded into her hand and saying in one bored breath, "Welcome-to-Slips-Diner-need-a-menu?"

Her gaze flicked past him to the window, then to a man waving an empty coffee cup from the counter. Her hair was the same color as Didi's from *Belinda's World*.

Rah-Rah-Whatev-ah. Except the waitress had dark roots.

"No. Grilled cheese plus bacon, and what's your soup today?" This bitch depended on his tips to live. And she wouldn't look at him?

"Chicken rice." She had a hot-pink manicure, very fresh, but there was a big chip on her index finger. Her name tag said "Callista."

"I'll have that instead of fries." She was already turning to refill the counter guy's cup when he added, "I thought this town was supposed to smell like sugar cookies."

It was why he'd pressed on even though the first leg was taking hours longer than he'd planned. When he was setting his route across the country, he'd come across an online article that said some pine tree made the air in Flagstaff, Arizona, smell like vanilla with a hint of cinnamon and clove.

That was exactly what Meribel had smelled like, the last time they were together, a bare few days before their breakup. They'd gone to Neighborhood Apothecary to pick up her prescriptions, waiting in line together, but not obvious about it. He wasn't one for chitter-chat, and she often tamped herself down when they were in public. The price of fame.

He liked to go on these little errands with her, so domestic. He liked to look at her. A lot of people did, and it bothered her, sometimes. Meribel could feel gazes. A superpower, she called it, joking, so cute. He wanted to take her hand, but then a passing paparazzi might snap them, so he stared past her, as if bored, at a display of vitamins. He kept her framed in his peripheral vision, where he could drink her in.

Those damn snoops and celeb-bloggers were what made the Roadtrek Ranger so perfect for them now. They needed to be thoroughly alone. In wilderness. She was afraid of her own feelings, and outside influences had been whispering against him. So she'd left him. Ditched him. Dumped him. Once it was only the two of them, out in the wilds, alone, they'd work it out.

At the quirky little pharmacy she favored over bland old Rite Aid, she'd leaned back, her body canting inevitably toward him. The way it always did. Her body liked him.

She was so little, he could pick her up and knot her, like a piece of string. The crown of her head had been only a few dizzying inches away, and he had breathed her in. She'd changed shampoos again—no one loved scents and products as much as Meribel—and that day, their last happy day before she left him, she'd smelled exactly like the air in Flagstaff was supposed to smell. Vanilla and smoked cinnamon, sweet and rich and ruddy. Now, on his way to win her back, he'd wanted to camp here, where the very air would be soaked in her latest scent.

"That's mostly in the summer," the waitress said. She tried to leave again.

"Hey. Wait. The sign in the window said you were hiring a dishwasher?"

It was a shit job, no doubt, but it would pay cash. He'd burned his life down the moment she said she was moving, the moment she said they had to be over because of geography. He liquidated so damn fast that he got pennies on the dollar for the house his mother had left him. He'd even pawned her jewelry. Once he and Meribel were back together, none of this would matter, though. He was strong and resourceful. For her, he could start over.

He'd spent the bulk of his cash on the Roadtrek Ranger. Even used, with a cat-piss smell in the upholstery, it had almost busted him. He hadn't realized how much gas it would guzzle, or that he would eat out so much. It made him feel close to Meribel, though, to stop at diners with real milkshakes and breakfast all day, like the Over Easy on *Belinda's World*. He liked the thick soups. He liked the buzz of conversation. But now his funds were dipping dangerously low.

The waitress finally met his gaze, but only for a second. Her eyes were wide and very green. She jerked her thumb at an older woman in a chef's coat, hulked like a Sasquatch on a stool behind the register. "Yeah. Talk to Sal if you're interested."

"I'm passing through, but if I could get a few days' work until you found somebody more suited for the job, that would be great." He chuckled, very hearty, white person to white person; dishwasher in a dump like this was a job for an illegal. "I'm camping my

way across the country. I want to see the real America. Meet real
people."

She would ask him, *Where are you headed?* now, acknowledg-
ing this job was a lark for someone like him. He might pretend to
be going the opposite way and tell her, *I got it in my head to see the
redwood trees in California.* He'd scratch at his scruff, spontaneous
and woodsy. Or he might confide, *I'm on a journey to win back the
love of my life.* Women ate shit like that up. He had learned not to
talk too much. Better to give women a hint, then let their romantic
imaginations fill a story in. Whatever she asked, he would keep his
answer short, keep her curious.

Instead, this bitch walked off. Like he hadn't been talking.

It was hard to keep his curdled smile aimed at her back, but
he managed. He stayed perfectly pleasant as he watched her trudge
between tables. She had ugly, cheap shoes but pretty legs.

When the food came, he wolfed down his sandwich and the
gooey chicken and rice. Then he went over and charmed a tryout
for the job from that fat bitch, Sal. She sent him to the back to be
"trained" by Julio, who barely spoke English. The three-sink system
was a breeze, though: wash, rinse, sterilize, and he was fast. Within
the hour, Julio left, spewing grateful Spanglish about being on since
6:00 a.m. He smiled back at Julio, low-key friendly. "De nada." He
knew how to play the game.

There was a long, thin opening between the dining room and
the kitchen for the cooks to pass the plates through. As he worked,
he could watch the waitresses moving food and order slips back and
forth. The other three were fat and tired and looked like mothers.
They called the copper-haired waitress Callie. She wore no rings.
She was younger than them, but a lot older than Didi. A little older
than Meribel. Forty, he thought. But still pretty. She would get better tips if she smiled. Her mouth stayed flat as she served egg plates
and burgers and meat-and-threes. She was Didi if Didi flunked out
of college and landed in Flagstaff, still convinced she was "all that
and a bag of chips."

Callie was nothing like real Meribel, who had adopted an au-tistic girl and who raised money for the Special Olympics. If a fan came up to Meribel on the street, she was kind and smiley. Did selfies. Signed shit.

This bitch wanted to be Meribel, but really, Meribel was her. Meribel contained Didi and every Callie ever born, every whore who spread it for pretty rich boys and looked through him and didn't blink when he asked for a job that was clearly beneath him. When he had Meribel back, when they were alone, he would own all those women, locked inside her sweetness. She would bend to him and for him; she always bent when he was near.

But first he had to get to her. Convince her leaving him was a mistake. She was scared because the thing between them—it had been so real and strong. He wouldn't say much. Just go to her. Smile. Say, "We agreed it would be over but . . . I couldn't do it."

She hadn't given him her new address, but he could find her. He knew how to look, and he had friends from his favorite message board on the dark web looking, too. He was kind of a big deal on that site. Worshipped. Buncha incels liked to read about him bag-ging an actress. They were happy to help him get her back. He'd take her someplace quiet and make her remember how it was with them. He only needed a little more cash to pay the campsites and get gas and food along his way. He scrubbed a pot, moving it through the system: wash, rinse, sanitize.

After four hours, his hands were red and chapped. Worth it, because by then, the dining room held only a couple of drunks at the counter and a table of stragglers. Only Callista was on the floor, and only Sal was in the kitchen.

Callista shooed the last customers out soon after ten, then did all the wipe-downs before coming back to the kitchen to clock out. She stomped past him like he was furniture, smelling like baby powder and fresh, female sweat. Her legs *were* good, but her ass was flat.

She kept that ass turned to him, talking to Sal. When they were back together, Meribel would not talk to some fat bitch and ignore him. She would lean in when he spoke, eyes bright, the tiniest bit breathless. She was like a hummingbird, so inquisitive and interested. So little and so fast.

When Meribel was thinking hard, she would catch her bottom lip between her white teeth and tilt her chin down and look up to make her eyes widen. The shape of Meribel's face when she was thinking was the same as Didi's, all the times she plotted to take Davie from Belinda, but sweeter. The shape of Callista's thinking face was a mystery, because God, was she a dumb whore. She picked her nails. The manicure had two chips now.

"You'll be okay?" Callista asked Sal, glancing at him. Obvious.

"Always," Sal said, and patted her own left arm. He understood then why Sal wore a chef's jacket in the heat. She was packing. Shoulder holster. He had a pistol, too, back at the camper with his rifles. His was a blunt, black Bulldog snubby.

After Callista left, he cleaned the kitchen while Sal totaled out the register, packing a fat wad of cash into a night-deposit envelope. He thought about making his move then, but she was armed and he wasn't. More importantly, he'd noticed the printed work schedule hanging on the wall beside Sal's office in the back. Eager as he was to get to Meribel, it was too good to pass up.

When he was done, Sal handed him a folded pittance that would barely fill his RV's greedy tank, for all she said he'd done good work. Of course he had. A monkey could do it. She told him he could come back the next day at four and relieve Julio again. If he wanted.

He glanced at the printed schedule, ignoring his raw hands, and said, "Happy to." He could stick it out a week.

By Saturday, he had deep, bleeding cracks in his fingers. So what. By then, he was part of the kitchen crew. Quietly friendly, helpful and easygoing, he had become invisible. Sal left right after the dinner rush, like the schedule said. Callista would close. He dawdled with the utensils until the last fry cook left, too. Just him and Callista, then. Alone, alone, alone.

It was almost eleven when she came back to the kitchen. The lights were already off out front. Her wide-set eyes flicked all around, checking that everything was spick and span, clean griddles and stainless steel prep tables, empty sink. Judging his work.

"You done? I need to lock up and go home."

The thick night-deposit envelope was in her purse, and it was for him, but that wasn't where his eyes went. He could look at her now, look at all her pieces, look anywhere he liked; they were alone. She stared at her own nails. Same manicure, but picked down to half-mast on every finger. The hands gave her age away more than the face.

He lifted out the big knife he had left in the bottom of the first sink. He hadn't brought his gun. No need. This was better. The wet blade gleamed. He turned to her, smiling, and showed her how the silver caught the low light. A few silly, stray soap bubbles clung to the edge. Quite festive.

"No. I'm not done," he told her.

She looked at him, then, all right.

4

"I'M LOVING THIS color story for you. I want you to sell this look."
Ivy Denat, the costume designer for *The Spirit of the Thing*, was a
tall, spiky Black woman, shaved bald, with a lot of piercings laddering up her ears and a perfect glossy mouth. Very LA. I liked her,
which was a good thing, because she had both her hands inside my
bra, trying to finagle cleavage out of chicken cutlets and my scant
basic materials. Last year, I finally lost my anti-facial-fillers war to
my agent, and now Liza had moved on to the battle of the boob job.
These days, she was always texting me selfies of her refurbished tits
in fancy bras, captioned, Elegant! Tasteful! Just consider it!

The actress I was replacing had C-cups and was an olive-toned
brunette to boot, so none of her stuff worked on me. Ivy was scrambling.

When she had magically wrestled me into having boobs, she
said, "Let Teddy grab a couple of pictures to text to Beck. I know
we're on the right track, but . . ." I moved past the rack full of options she'd put together and posed for her assistant. This meant setting down my phone; I'd been creeping on Sarah's Insta every time
I had a second. Unprofessional and gross to boot. But I hadn't been
able to shake the hope that my watcher had been James. Marker
Man had gone quiet. It must have been James.

This morning, Sarah had posted a picture of a cute sign shaped like an iguana that said, HACIENDAS! The caption read, New Mexican place! Should we give it a try tonight? #familydinner #Mamasnotcooking

Even pre–Marker Man, I'd never been so full-frontal naked about my dinner plans on the internet: *This is where I'm going to be tonight, if anyone with sinister intentions needs to know. PS if you think my husband is creeping out of our bed to stand under your window in the darkest small hours of morning and you want to gander back at him? Well! He'll be here, too.*

I did want to gander back, actually. The James I remembered wouldn't bounce from a nooner-stalk of his ex to #datenight with his current wife, then creep out again after she was asleep to moon under my window. That felt like an asshole move. Unless his wife was a nightmare. He hadn't been an asshole back when I was married to him, but decades had passed. He had stayed in this place where the past hung heavy. He had married my suburban doppelgänger. What had the years made of him?

I set my phone down and posed for Teddy, turning my hips, angling my shoulders. The skirt was so short, high winds felt like a danger. The jacket had a narrow, plunging V neckline that showed a hint of black bra.

I said, "This is from the Courtroom-Inappropriate Chic collection, yeah?"

Ivy laughed. "I mean, you're wearing this to represent a haunted-hotel owner who sues her ghost-slash-lover for abandonment, so . . ."

"And it's my color as a bonus." I pushed my shoulders back and smiled at Teddy like I was a confident and supernaturally gifted lawyer, certainly not a crazy person who was obsessively tracking her ex-husband's dinner plans.

"Love. You look sex-positive and smart," Ivy said, and then gave me a sly smile. "Come try this olive thing on. Try to look bilious. We have to give Beck some options that will help her pick the right ones."

As she pulled a wrap dress, I checked Sarah's post again. Repulsive,

but here I was. Now Sarah had two likes and a comment: GREAT guac,
but beware. Serious Margs!!! Her friends were also prone to exclamation points and abbreviating edible, concrete nouns. I changed into
the dress and let Teddy re-tousle my hair for more photos. All the
while, I was waiting for Sarah to answer, as if her dinner plans were a
movie plot twist. *I see dead people . . . at Haciendas!* I'd thought I was
dead to James, anyway. I'd left, I had not looked back, and James?
James hadn't followed. He'd let me go.

I wanted him to be the sidewalk lurker, though. Not for purely
pathetic, romantical reasons—although there was more of that
present than I wanted to admit—but because James was safe. He
had to be safe, right? How could married James have mailed me letters daily with LA postmarks? Letters stinking of faux banana and
tangerine and cherry, with crude, hand-drawn pictures in which I
was naked on my knees, or hog-tied on my belly, or looking up with
XX eyes and an O mouth from the bottom of a licorice-black hole.

Sarah hadn't responded by the time Ivy was happy with the
photos and let me go. I was happy with them, too. I might be distracted, but I was still doing my job. I felt good about that as I
headed out to the enormous, black Lexus SUV I had on loan from
the production company. Honor, who missed our darling sky-blue
Prius, called him Gas Dragon. I fired him up and got on the road.
It was a relief to be driving, unable to check for Instagram updates.

I got all the way back to the condo without getting my phone
out even once. Such virtue! It lasted until I was back in my office-
slash-guest quarters. The deep-cranberry room was small to be so
richly painted, but my landlord had an eye. Large, simple fabric-art
wall hangings, a wee French desk, a narrow white love seat—the
whole thing worked. I needed to answer emails, but instead I got
right back on Insta.

Sarah's answer: I could use a serious Marg. Pongo ate the dining
room rug! #puppies Do I need a rezzie if we go at six? #onedogwasplenty
#nositter

I shook my head. The exact time, even. I hurled myself onto the love seat and googled "Haciendas! Woodstock," to find the website. It was right in the middle of a long brick building full of shops, a cute space with a glass front door and a long, thin patio. I put the address into Maps, and my phone told me it would take forty minutes to get there.

I stared at the map, equal parts aghast, enticed, and disbelieving. Surely I wasn't going to drive out to Woodstock and creep on my ex-husband and his family? Because that would be wrong. And crazy. At the same time, I was thinking, *I should have borrowed a wig from Ivy*, which was the thought of a wrong and crazy person who was definitely going.

If I did go press my nose to the glass of Haciendas!, if I saw him, how would that help me? Wrong and Crazy had an immediate answer: *If you watch James with his family, you'll know if he is happy, if he loves her.*

If he did? A man in love wouldn't sneak out to moon around in front of my building in the middle of the night. Which only left—

I shuddered, and I tried to tell myself this didn't mean Marker Man had followed me. Maybe I'd seen some innocuous insomniac, moon gazing, or a neighbor had a stalker of their own. They were all the rage this season.

If I went to Woodstock and saw that James was unhappy, would it feel like permission to go to him, to ask directly? *Was it you, staring at me through the storms?* If he said yes, I'd—I couldn't think half that far ahead.

But what to do with Honor? Days-from-thirteen was plenty old enough for neurotypical kids whose mothers were not being stalked by dangerous creeps to stay home alone, but I couldn't imagine leaving her under the circumstances.

In LA, pre–Marker Man, I left her home and ran errands when Wallace or Paul was home. The only person that I might ask here was Cooper, and God, hadn't he done enough yesterday? I flushed with shame, remembering. Also, Honor might not recognize his face if he came by to check on her, much less feel comfortable enough to bang on his door and say, *Hey, the house smells like gas*, or *I hear a spooky noise*, or *I feel weird*.

This meant I couldn't go. Period.

So why was I so antsy as the dinner hour approached? I took Gumball on her walk, and then Honor did her homework while I flipped through another script Liza'd sent me. The news about my last-minute casting on *The Spirit of the Thing* had "hotted me up," as my agent put it, and Liza was exploiting the hell out of it, looking to make bank. Her note, scrawled on the front page, asked to know my level of interest in this film, *yesterday or now!* I couldn't focus, though. I was on page twenty with no idea if it was about aliens or Amish folks.

I threw the script aside and said, out loud, to my own child, "Do you want to drive out to a bookstore with me?" There was a cute indie right next to the Mexican place. I'd seen the storefront in the pictures.

"No, thank you," Honor said, and I was glad. Except I wasn't. But still, she had said no, so that was that. Except it wasn't.

"I'll make us veggie wraps to eat in the car. You can get whatever book you want. Any two books, and you can have my iPad all the way there and back, and it's a long drive, and you can still have your screen time when we get home," I promised, recklessly sweetening the pot, adding sugar after sugar until I saw her face change to a yes. But she didn't say it. I waited. Her straight, thick brows came down and her dark eyes narrowed as she looked for the catch. She couldn't find it, but I never offered extra screen time for no reason. I lifted an eyebrow. "Do you really want to look a gift iPad in the mouth?"

The cliché made her smile. "Can both books be hardbacks?"

I nodded, and she was in, no other questions, which was very Honor. She had decided to take the loot and file it under *Mom Shit*. Subheading, *Not Interesting*.

As soon as I had our car dinner ready, we left. Our place was at the end of the hall, one of the rare three-bedroom units in the building. We passed by Cooper's, a few doors down in our leg of the U-shaped layout. I almost stopped, thinking I should say hi and maybe make lunch plans, my treat, as a thanks and an apology. But traffic would be terrible at this hour. I didn't want to miss my window.

Honor didn't look up from the iPad for the whole drive. I kept thinking I would take the next exit, turn around, go home. I kept on driving, lumbering Gas Dragon through the endless stream of traffic. The sun was low by the time we pulled into the long, thin parking lot that ran the length of the brick building that housed Haciendas! and the bookstore.

As we cruised down the lot, I saw them. James. And Sarah and Rex and Beverly and Stan. They were squished together on one of the narrow patio's four-tops, alive, breathing, real. It was strange to see them as a whole. American family out to dinner. Complete. Oblivious.

"Mom," Honor said, and I startled, jerking the wheel to correct Gas Dragon a half second before I drifted into the back end of a monstrous truck jutting out of a too-small space. I backed into an open spot behind me. Now I was facing James's family, almost dead on, as if I'd come to some kind of hellish drive-in live theater. I could see them clearly under the bright patio lights, but between the waning sun and Gas Dragon's tinted windows, there was no way they could see me. My dumb heart started pounding anyway.

Not that they were looking. The two older kids had their heads bent together over—something. Sarah was trying to keep the littlest from clambering out of a booster seat. I'd come here to look at James, but my gaze would not bend that way, directly. It was so hard. I kept him peripheral, and in the soft edges of my view, he had not aged at all. The air in the car felt low on oxygen. I forced myself to turn to Honor, who was looking at Foxtale Bookshoppe's display window.

She asked, "Do they have game books?"

"Go on in and see. I need to—" I waved vaguely at a kitchen

supply store on the other side of Haciendas! "Meet me in the car in twenty minutes?"

I handed her my Visa, and she nodded and hopped out. She glanced back to see me watching her, then looked assiduously and theatrically both ways before she crossed the lot and disappeared inside the store. I sat right where I was, putting my hands on the steering wheel at ten and two, mostly to have something to hold. He was in profile. Looking down at his phone. James had a firm jaw and a nice mouth, so what was with this stupid beard? It was a close-cropped face framer, last on trend in 2008. In LA, anyway. Perhaps Atlanta ran nine years behind.

James picked up his "SRS Marg" and sipped without looking up from his screen. Sarah was busy with their stairstep children, making the older ones put away the phone they'd had under the table. Bevvy, as Sarah called her girl on Instagram, was pointing at her father's phone, clearly miffed at the injustice. Sarah shrugged, trying to get Stan to eat and not climb onto the table. The kids' hair ranged from dark auburn to copper blond, getting lighter as they got shorter. Looking at them, I felt a strange physical twanging way down low in my belly, not identifiable as an emotion. I hoped that it was shame.

James didn't feel my gaze, much less turn to meet it as if this moment was our destiny. He was now rapid-fire thumb-typing, not looking at his tired wife, either. The show at this drive-in was actually called Sad American Family. Watching them felt tawdry and unkind. The silence, the phones, the restlessness. They looked happier on Instagram. But didn't everyone?

When James was tired, his eyes seemed to slant down farther at the corners, even back when we were college kids. Now, forty feet and twenty years distant, I could see his eyes had that look. I couldn't tell if his silence and inattention indicated a hard day or actual discontent. Not from three minutes in the middle of one meal in a marriage that was a dozen years old.

This is not my James, I thought, but then he pushed his hand back through his hair, scrubbing at the back of his head, the same as he used to, exactly. When I saw that, I remembered his smell. Not the soap he used, or the cheap hair products with the kangaroo on them that he'd loved back when we were in college. The essential smell of him, his human self. The memory punched the air out of me. Did he remember me this deeply, viscerally? Had he let me go, or was he hanging on to me in ways that I could not imagine?

I knew this man, though, didn't I? Would he come to Midtown—or anywhere—to get his eyes on me? With this man, I had invented sex. Slowly. Over the course of a full year. We'd been two nervous virgins from different, uptight southern states working their way toward something, together. We'd been so innocent. Sure, he'd dated in high school. He'd mauled his share of boobs, trying to feel nipples through padded bras and shirts and sweaters. Senior prom was a big night for him; he finally saw a boob, singular, unearthed from a sea of taffeta, alive and in glorious color. A lot of color, because his date had freckles everywhere. He always was partial to redheads.

My own boobs were wholly unmauled, pre-James. I Frenched a grand total of two boys. I dry-humped, once, publicly, in a darkened school gym hung with paper lanterns while Seal sang about flowers and kisses and graves. That night, I felt something like a nose pushing into my hip bone. I was 60 percent sure it was an erection, which made me feel both thrilled and weirdly powerful.

James and I had Blue Lagooned it. This was the nineties, the internet was a fetus, and we had no easy-access porn to show us exactly how to make sex horrible for girls. I learned about men by exploring him, and he learned how to touch a woman by touching me, both of us rapt. We made out like we were doing science, if science made people breathless and euphoric. We inched our way toward sex over endless hours, drugged by kissing, entwined, pressing into each other, young wild animals swathed in layers, hands busy and roaming. I had my first orgasm fully clothed; James was kissing me and then he pulled back to look at my face, his hand down my pants, his eyes avid, pushing me to a place I'd never gotten to, even alone.

The night we finally went "all the way," as we called it in shy whispers, I'd already come twice. I was languorous, so relaxed I felt his entrance as a pressure, unpainful. Surprising and so interesting, to be filled up. Different from fingers or mouths. Instantly, all his focus turned inward to the place where his body locked to mine. It lasted all of nine seconds before he fell apart. I held him, grinning, proud to have undone him by the simple act of inviting him in.

Now, here he sat with three children that his body had made with Sarah's. No medical intervention had been required, otherwise all Insta would have known about her "fertility journey." No, he had made these three simply by doing all the things I had invented for him.

Sarah stood up abruptly, and I jerked, startled. The kids were restless. James still had half a margarita, but she was done. She waved a hand between his face and the phone, and he looked up and said something. Sheepish. Apologetic. She laughed, good humored, and bent to kiss him. I watched my ex-husband kiss his wife. It was a quick mash of mouths. A drive-by. Maybe she didn't love him. If she did, if this mother of his children loved him, then the good, dear James that I'd known would love her back. Wouldn't he? Would he let me go entirely and love her? Or would he still want to look at me? I couldn't tell.

She gathered up their brood and led them off the patio through a wrought-iron gate, heading down the sidewalk in a gaggle. I realized with a distant horror that they were going to the bookstore. Where Honor was. The idea of the child who was mine intersecting with the children who might have been—it unnerved me.

James was alone, finishing his drink. I could, if I wanted, walk over. Talk to him, if I wasn't so horrified at the idea of Honor in the bookstore with his children. Honor being Honor, she wouldn't notice them come in, but she looked about ten, the same age as

James's oldest child. What if Rex talked to her? He had glasses and freckles and an adorable dorky walk. Maybe he was a gamer, too, and they would stand side by side ogling the Dungeons and Dragons sourcebooks. She would tell anyone who showed the faintest interest all about her favorite character, a six-foot-eight paladin named Leonid. If Rex foolishly asked a game question, she would quote every rule or bit of lore on the topic. She loved to explicate why a spell required concentration, or the difference between Dragonkin and Dragonborn. Maybe they'd connect on one of the play-by-post sites where she and Yuna had multiple games going with nerds across the country.

I needed my family away from his. I texted her: I'm ready to go.

I waited for her, watching James ask for the check, helpless to do otherwise. He got his credit card back, did tip math, and rose. He headed toward the same gate his wife and kids had used to exit the patio. Now he was exactly even with my big, black vehicle.

At that moment, my passenger-side door opened, flooding the car with light. Honor clambered in waving books and talking in her loud, announcing voice. "The person said this trilogy was good, and it comes in a box set, so three was cheaper than two hardbacks." It was full dark in the lot now, and the sudden glow and Honor's voice caught his attention in a way my burning gaze had not. James looked over. Right at me.

"Close the door," I said to Honor in a strangled voice.

"It's called the Legend Trilogy." She was putting on her seat belt, leisurely, heedless of my strangled tone. "It's set in LA. But not real LA."

I was frozen. James seemed frozen, too. He stared into the car, oddly unsurprised. As if he thought, *Of course she's looking for me, at me. Of course she's following.* As if there was no way we'd ever keep eyes off each other. At last, at last, she swung her door closed. I was light-dazzled, blind in the sudden darkness. Had he recognized me? He'd only had a moment's glimpse, but I'd seen the ghost of a familiar tenseness reset the angle of his shoulders.

My vision cleared. He hadn't moved. He passed a hand over his face. Shook his head. He took one step toward me.

That broke the spell. I turned the car on, my headlights instantly blinding him, stopping him dead. I peeled out of the parking space and drove away as quickly as I could. I did not look in my rearview to see what he was doing. I didn't have to. I really did have that actor's superpower, as I'd told Cooper.

I knew when I was being watched.

5

SO WHAT DO you do? I ask him. I'm at the kind of industry house party it's easy to get into if you are young and pretty. Four sets of glass doors stand open to a huge patio with a panoramic view of the city. LA is rendered in electric pointillism, dots of bright color stretching out so far into the velvet night it seems it must go on forever.

Most people are outside in the perfect weather, forming pairs and trios and groups, jostling and reconfiguring, chatting and flirting and drinking. A jazz combo plays in the corner. I am so fresh out of Georgia that I don't fully understand that girls and boys like me are here as party favors.

I'm in the business, like everyone here, Muriel, he says. *I'm an agent.*

Meribel, I correct, and he lifts one shoulder, briefly. It's a move I'll imitate later in my successful audition to play Didi on *Belinda's World*; it is so perfectly dismissive.

I came over feeling sorry for him; he's a dad-type with a little potbelly standing alone by the staircase. Now I think, *Wow. What an asshole.* I don't notice how some other actors in the room stare at him, hungry-eyed, too nervous to approach.

He looks past me, through me, watching the front door, as if waiting for someone better to arrive. He is bored with me, his cigarette, his drink. Even breathing seems to bore him.

He says, *So, what do you do?*

The true answer is, Nothing. Yet. I'm working temp jobs and going to auditions. I'm sleeping on a couch in a walk-in closet. My five generic, broken, pretty actor roommates pretend it is a bedroom. I'm pretending, too: there is no James, there is no Georgia, there never was a baby.

I say, *I want to be an actor.*

He shrugs. *"I want to be an actor" isn't a job. It's code for "I fuck producers." And sound editors who say that they're producers.*

I can't stop my blush, but I hit back. *I only fuck sound editors who say that they're agents.*

Now I have his attention. *Oh, that's sassy. You're sassy,* he says, in an appraising way, like he's figured out what box to check on my "Type of Girl" form. *Wait, are you blushing? You are. Sassy, but there's a vulnerability there. It's nice. It works.* He looks me up and down, and all at once I feel as if I'm naked or cattle or both. *You look like a kid who stole a sexy dress from her stepmom's closet and snuck into this party, and yet, you're almost pulling it off. Sassy, vulnerable, some completely misplaced confidence. You know what? I might have something for you. Sitcom. Straight-to-series order, and the whole thing is cast, except this one part. Small, but juicy. They haven't been able to find anyone young enough who has the right mix of—* He waves a hand at me, as if my body is a bowl of ingredients that might add up to some exact, specific thing he wants to eat. *How old are you, anyway? Really. Because you look sixteen, tops. Tell me you are at least eighteen.*

I am. I'm twenty-three, but I don't say so. In case he's serious.

He can't be, though. I'm plenty buzzed on free top-shelf gin, but not so much that I don't immediately think this has to be fake, a trick, a pickup line. At the same time, my stupid heart is pounding. He was so wholly uninterested in me, until he had this thought. What if he really is an agent? What if there really is a part?

Maybe I should send you out for it, he says. *They've shot down every reasonable option in town, so they're looking for a fresh face. Let's go somewhere quiet. You can give me a quick read.* I turn for the door, but he smiles, and I think I have finally, genuinely amused him. *I'm here to meet a client. Upstairs is fine. We can duck into one of the bedrooms.*

I recoil, lip curling. How stupid does he think I am?

I'm not going upstairs alone into a bedroom with some man I just met at a party!

That was when I realized that I'd stopped my mortified remembering and gone sliding into dreaming. I could hear the soft whir of my bedroom ceiling fan and Gumball snoring on my feet, and what I really said to him that day was, *Do you have the script with you?*

He laughed. *Sure. Sure, I do. God, you are young. Don't be stupid. You can improv something,* and we went up the stairs.

I jerked myself upright, awash in humiliation, burying my face in my hands. My hair was all sweaty. I'd hardly slept after I got home from my own first mortifying foray into real-life stalking. Instead, I'd stared at the ceiling, drifting, while my brain played all of Meribel's Greatest Shame Hits on a loop. It's like that, sometimes. You lie in the dark, thinking about James peering across a parking lot, shocked, staring. You start thinking, *When have I been more humiliated?* Your brain helpfully says: *Well, that thing with your first agent at that party. Oh, and you made your mom break up with your husband for you while you fled cross-country. Maybe Insta-stalking your ex's wife is close to that cringe-y, if we look at it as cumulative.*

Cumulative and rising. I'd haunted Sarah's socials relentlessly since I broke it off with Cam. Maybe I had loved him, or was starting to, and yet I'd also felt relieved to end it while everything was so damn good between us. By which I meant the sex, and the way he made me feel so beautiful and funny and smart.

He loved to listen to me talk. He himself was so self-contained, so quiet. I knew his past in bullet points, and I enjoyed his flash-fire wicked humor, but that was all I knew of him, really. I'd never seen his house. After dates we always went to my place, and he didn't sleep over, lest Honor wake up early at Wallace's and bounce back home and find him there. Now that it was over, I'd never find out what all was deeply wrong with him. All the flaws and horrors he had been holding back to spring once I was super in it, they were moot, and I was safe. I could simply be sad.

In the throes of that sorrow, I'd let myself go back to Sarah's feeds. Now I'd moved past peering creepily at James through the lens of her life to staring at him, real, alive, in person. He'd caught me. So humiliating.

Lying in the dark, reliving my past screwups, my helpful brain added, *Don't forget snotting all over your new neighbor and spinning out in the street.* Oh, yeah. I'd felony-level overshared to Cooper. Worse, I'd let Honor see me in such a state.

I needed to make a date to paint gaming miniatures with her or hike up Stone Mountain so we could have one of our circuitous talks. It was the best way to take her emotional temperature. If she'd overheard that I'd been married, lost a child, that was big. I had no idea how to broach it. Was there a book, filed in the same section with *The Girl's Body Book?* Something that we could read and could talk about together, called *Guess What? Mommy Had a Life Before You?*

My phone's alarm started burbling. I scrubbed at my grainy eyes and stumbled out of bed. It was time to get Honor up and off to school. No matter how I felt, I couldn't let my bad day wreck hers. I faced this task like it was another acting job, as motherhood sometimes was. For everyone, I thought. When Honor was a newborn, she would scream and thrash for hours at a time. Those colicky weeks, sometimes the only thing that kept me from setting her gently down and running off into the night was imagining huge crowds seated stadium style all around us, moved to breathless tears by my unending patience.

I needed to cut myself some slack. Cooper was right; I'd been riding a rising tidal wave of stress for months. The very moment we got a thousand miles of distance from my scariest problem, I was weeping in the street and taking my child on stalking expeditions.

This was a long-overdue mini-breakdown happening because I finally felt safe enough to have one.

Right now, I had to pack it up and be a mom. A good one, like I'd had. I'm not sure anyone, James included, had ever seen me as clearly and loved me as fiercely as Mom. She was the reason I'd always wanted, so deeply, to be a mother myself. I had to channel her now and do what my kid needed. Honor's life was challenging enough with all this change.

The dresser mirror showed me a pale zombie-movie Meribel with red-rimmed freak eyes. Not what my kid needed. I took a moment to dip into the master bath and smooth on a little de-puffing eye cream and tinted moisturizer, then used a pink liquid blusher on my cheekbones and my mouth. I threw on jeans and a soft mulberry knit top to warm me up.

I went to Honor's door and tapped. "Kitty cat? Your ride to school will be here in an hour." I'd pacted with two other moms to pay for a car service, as Honor's private school lacked a bus. "Did you shower last night?" I was pretty sure she hadn't, because I had not prompted her. Honor loved the grassy smell of her own mank.

"I'm already up," she said, which was not an answer to the shower question. Which meant no.

"Greasy kitty! Get in the shower now, please," I said, so cheery.

The door eased open. Honor's sleep-creased face appeared in the cracks, her black, shiny bob sticking up in the back like a rooster tail. She still had last night's faint, guarded expression. I'd worried her, I thought. Hell. I'd worried me.

"How is your bad headache?" she asked, formal and solemn.

"Much better, thanks!" I lied. "When you get home from school, maybe we could talk some more about a birthday party." I'd brought this subject up every few days for weeks now, each time as if it were fresh, each time with zero engagement on her part. Honor would loathe it if I rented out a skate space or a laser tag arena and invited her whole class, but I wanted to mark the occasion and create an opportunity for her to make a friend or two. I decided to press a little harder. "Is there anyone at school you've noticed that seems cool? Someone you could invite for a movie, maybe?" Low key, not a lot of face time. A good introductory friend outing.

"I don't like anyone at school," Honor said. "I want extra screen time, please."

"We can do better than that!" I said, so hyper-perky it was as if I was about to explain why some all-new floor wax was a revelation. I couldn't let my kid see that I, too, felt lost. I was Honor's anchor in a sea of change, and no matter what was happening in my life, she would never turn thirteen again. I wanted it to be as big a deal as she would allow. I had one idea that I'd kept in my pocket, in case she balked at doing anything here. "What about a virtual party? We could FaceTime with Wallace and Paul. They can have cake on the porch and put out treats for the cats. Then after, you could have a lot of game time with Yuna."

That paused her. She adored Wallace, and even Paul, who was also an introvert. They liked to sit on opposite ends of a sofa and read their own books and never speak. Her eyes met mine, briefly, and then she asked, "Could we order matching cakes delivered? Caramel ones, identical. One here, and one for Wallace and Paul, and one for Yuna? And canned tuna for Worker Cat and Boomer and Clawful and any new cats, too."

She was so earnest that my smile finally felt real. "Of course we can. I love that idea."

"Okay!" she said, her dark eyes gone bright and shiny. She disappeared back into her room. I stayed where I was until I heard the shower running, then went to see about her breakfast.

We were out of Grape-Nuts. How was that possible? But I knew how. Honor ate two or three servings in the morning, along with however much fruit I could coax down her, then basically lived on love and air molecules the rest of the day. Sometimes, in the night, after I had put the bulk of her dinner in a Tupperware for my own lunch the next day, she'd get up and eat another bowlful.

While I was trying to find a fast, alternative breakfast that had fiber or protein, the shower cut out. She must have leaped in, done a quick pirouette, and was now toweling off, just as filthy as when she got in, only damper. So be it! I couldn't fight the please-use-soap battle this morning. I closed the fridge. My stomach felt so sour, I couldn't imagine cooking.

"I'm going down to grab you a croissant-sausage-roll-thingy at the coffeehouse, okay?" I called.

A small pause and then she called, "The ones from the glass cabinet?"

"Yep," I said. I'd never eaten such a thing, and neither had she.

"Yes, please!" she called back, and I heard her add, "Yay," quietly, to herself.

Pizza the other night, and now this. My pun-loving daughter called me the Vege-Tsar-us. She said I'd hide vegetables in ice cream, if I could. In fact, I had. Carrot juice, anyway. In her homemade Popsicles.

Two junky meals in the same week was practically a miracle. Fun for her, but we would both pay if I didn't rein it in soon. Simple carbs, food dyes, and preservatives made her moody and restless, unable to sleep. The more she ate healthy, unprocessed food, the better she was able to regulate. I had to get my shit together, so that by extension her shit would be together, too.

"Be right back!" I called.

I hurried down the hall to the elevator. A woman about my age was there already, pushing the down button. She was taller than me and built curvier, with broad shoulders and big boobs. Like most of the people in the building, she looked upscale-corporate in a beige-on-buff M.M.LaFleur dress and jacket combo, but she'd skipped the regulation blowout. Her hair was a mass of light brown curls.

"Hello," I said. "I'm your new neighbor, from fourteen A. Meribel Mills."

She gave me a cool smile that did not reach her eyes. "I know who you are. The actress. From that old, old show." She let me stand there for a beat too long with my hand out before she slipped the tips of her fingers into mine for a clasp both brief and limp.

Great. She was one of those people who had seen me on television and now had to make damn sure I knew that they weren't all that impressed. I once sat down on a plane by a man who did an instant double take. Instead of introducing himself, he said, "You were Didi, on TV. And here you are flying coach, huh? Well, I guess you did peak early." He spent the rest of the four-hour flight vibrating with joyful schadenfreude.

This woman was radiating that same disdainful energy. The worst vain bit of me wanted to become the haughty actress she'd invented and say, *Hey, asshole, I have forty-seven credits on IMDb.*

Instead, I forced a smile as the elevator dinged and the doors opened. We rode down together silently. In the lobby, we got into a small kerfuffle, each of us getting in each other's way as we each assumed the other was leaving the building, when really we were both going into Java House.

"Sorry!" I said, as we did our awkward little dance.

"After you," she said in a snide, knowing tone, positive that I would sweep past her, taking it as my puff-headed due. I decided right then and there I would literally die before I walked into the coffee shop before her.

"No, no, you go ahead," I said.

"No, you!" she said, equally willing to perish here.

"No, no, please!" I gestured her forward.

That was when I saw Cooper. Or rather, I saw his back. He had apparently seen me first. He was making a run for it, speed-walking out the door that led onto the street.

Bright, hot shame shot through me once again. Well, what did I expect? I'd leaped about nine intimacy levels and left him to feed my kid dinner while I had a breakdown. Now here I was, dancing in a doorway with another neighbor who hated me on sight. What the hell was I doing?

"No, you," she insisted, nostrils flared.

"Actually, I need to—" I gestured back toward the mailroom, then turned and stomped off.

I shut the mailroom door behind me, intending to lurk there until this bitch had time to get her drink and go. Waiting her out, I realized we'd forgotten to get the mail yesterday. I'd been busy falling into chunks and Honor'd been busy witnessing it and shutting down. I jammed my key into the small brass door and turned it.

It was stuck. I jerked at it. It didn't open, but a puff of smell came up and out and into me.

Alcohol solvent. Faux orange and chalky chocolate mint and the sick-sweet of hot-pink cotton candy.

I tried to pull the key out, not wanting to see, but it caught. The brass door swung open as I backed away, and a torrent of mail came spilling out to scatter on the floor. Bills. Flyers. And then the swarm of letters, all in long, pale envelopes, all covered in his bright, jagged scrawl, all stinking. Ten letters, at least. Maybe more.

My stomach clenched and cramped. I knelt to pick them up.

He hadn't stopped. His letters must have been bottlenecked at my new forwarding service. I could see the yellow stickers, redirecting them.

I wanted to scream in frustration. I wanted to sit right down on the floor and burst into public tears, again.

Instead, I straightened and starting flipping through the envelopes. They all had the forwarding stickers, thank God. Not one was addressed to this new condo. He hadn't quit, he wasn't even tapering off, but at least he didn't know exactly where I was living. Not yet.

The red circle of a postmark caught my eye. Marker Man's letters always came from LA. He dropped them off at different post offices and boxes, but always somewhere in the city.

This letter was different. My hands suddenly felt clumsy. Almost boneless. The rest of the mail fell away, shuffling itself back onto the floor in a bright, stinking scatter. This one had been stamped at a post office in Flagstaff, Arizona.

My breath stopped. I think my heart stopped, too, missing a beat.

Marker Man had been in Flagstaff—I checked the date—almost two weeks ago! Flagstaff had to be a solid seven-hour drive from LA. Seven hours east, my way. Seven hours closer. I couldn't swallow. I couldn't blink. By now he could be here.

I'd known that I was being watched. I hoped the eyes on me belonged to James. I still did. I'd even gone to Woodstock and given James a long look back. But Marker Man was on the move. How close could he have come since he mailed this letter?

But of course I knew the answer. All the way.

March 17, 2017

Meribel Mills
726 Echo Avenue, Unit A
Los Angeles, CA 90026

You know I like you least in yellow. Why do you provoke me? Still, I do enjoy watching you eat, pecking out all the seeds in your spinach salad like a pert little bird that I could hold so tight and folded in one hand, your heartbeat a flutter in my fingers. Next time, wear blue and gold for me, in Honor of your old cheerleader uniform.

No yellow. And no green. In green, you are too beautiful, too blinding to look at all at once. I want to put each perfect part of you in a separate small box, each box tied with a different color of silk ribbon. Gold. Blue. Purple. Black. Every day I'll open a piece of you up, like twelve days of Christmas. First your left foot. I'll push it into the shape of a tiptoe, like a Barbie foot, and run my tender finger down your pale, high arch.

Soon.

6

COOPER ONLY HAD one animating job this month. He was working on a rabbit, a "spokes-bunny," the client called it, for a website about hiking. The guy wanted it to look "real," but he also wanted it to do things real rabbits didn't do, like look back over its shoulder as if to say, *Hey, come on!* as it dashed off behind the woodsy logo. Real rabbits didn't crane their heads around, though, because their eyes were set on either side of their head.

Cooper cheated the eyes forward, more where human eyes would be, and the whole thing went full Uncanny Bunny Valley. Worse, its expression now read as wary and reproachful. Not on brand. Usually, he loved his creative work. He was off today.

"You are a rabbit with trust issues," he told his creation, and as soon as he said it, he recognized the rabbit's face. He'd somehow mind-screwed himself into making the animated-bunny version of Addie Portlin. Round eyes, broad cheeks, short nose, a tiny mouth shaped like a kiss. These days, it looked more like a twisted-shut, mad sphincter. Poor Ads. He should—

He deliberately stopped his mind from going down that road and spent a little time on the CoinAge Xchange. He was Verge curious, but felt he might have already missed his buy window. Nxt looked good . . . Cooper used to play the stock market, but crypto was better. He'd absolutely killed on Bitcoin, buying under a dollar and selling at thirty in 2011, eight days before the crash. Now he was looking for the next big high. In his office's huge walk-in (his unit was a two-bedroom with double masters) he had a rig set up for mining Vertcoin, but that was mild compared to buying, selling, splashing out hard, falling, recouping. Ads didn't love it that he did this. She called it gambling. Well, yes, exactly. For the record, he liked gambling, too. For the record, he was both lucky and very, very good at it.

Back on his big monitor, the sad rabbit blinked at him, ran off into the trees. Well, he was lucky when the bet was monetary. Relationships? Another story.

He shoved back from his desk. Maybe all he needed was to be out of his office. Addie had redone the room for him last year, very Restoration Hardware, with scrubbed wood furniture and a pair of modern wingbacks in taupe leather. It was meant to feel worklike, separate from the rest of his apartment, but the fact that she had made it defeated the neutral color palette and all the clean, sleek lines, made it so personal. Addie felt like a gamble he had lost, and he didn't love it. Losing. He needed caffeine.

He left the Addie-Rabbit staring disconsolately after him and went down to Java House, only to see Addie's daughter, Sheila, already in line there, skipping school, wearing a bikini top that was not sufficient unto her day (she was her mother's daughter) and Daisy Dukes. Sheila didn't see him. She was busy flirting with some yoga bro wearing Hammer pants and flip-flops. The boy was addressing his remarks almost entirely to her boobs.

Ever since they learned her dad's new wife was pregnant, Sheila had been pulling crap like this, making Addie crazy. Now the baby was here, a little boy, and her dad's infrequent visits had stopped entirely. Addie was wrecked (the new wife had started as the side piece who blew up her marriage), and Sheila—the sweet, bright kid Cooper was so fond of—had turned into a suspicious little snarler, secretive and self-destructive.

Cooper could empathize. He'd grown up in an unhappy family, with a father who kept a blatant parade of side girls who got younger and younger. Well, he kept them when he could afford them. Some months, his father couldn't afford milk. Cooper took risks, sure, but not like his father. Or maybe he just won more.

At least Cooper's dad had stuck around, unlike Sheila's. Through every feast and famine he created, he stuck, while Mom hid cash in her shoes, in the freezer, in the flour, all in the hopes of paying the electric bill. She was a homebody, but Cooper had a front-row seat for his father's life. He grew up playing the mascot at poker nights, underground casinos, the Lions Club pool hall, the track. Bill and Cooper and a girl; when Bill Hayette was winning, anyway, there was always a girl. Cooper remembered them as a collection of smells: Juicy Fruit, rum, and sweet, cheap perfume like Jean Naté or Charlie. *Aren't you cute. Aw, Bill, he's just so cute.* His dad had been a show, endless charm, endless risky decisions. Cooper learned that both those things could pay off. If you were lucky.

Sheila wasn't. But here she was, making risky decisions, skipping school with a boy, wandering Midtown nearly naked. He considered slipping out the door before she saw him. He could disappear upstairs, use his Nespresso. Addie and her kid were not his business. Then he noticed the "boy" had a Georgia Tech backpack. Well, dammit. He pushed through the door and got in line behind her.

"Hey, kid."

She startled and whirled, then flushed dull red. "Oh, hi, Cooper."

Copper pretended not to see the boy. "How is sophomore year of high school treating you?"

Obvious and awkward? Yes. Also, effective. Sheila's flush deepened, and as soon as the barista handed over an iced chai latte, the college boy zoomed off to prowl for something legal. Cooper himself had spent his twenties with an endless flow of easy, wild girls. Not like his dad, though, because Cooper had no crying wife at home, now did he? By thirty, he knew he wanted more, or better, so how was he now almost forty and single again, reduced to running some pussy-hound douchebag (probably not so different from Cooper himself at twenty) away from the teenaged daughter of his ex?

As thanks, Sheila radiated hate vibes backward at him and ordered herself a caramel cappuccino.

Worse, Cooper was thinking, *What a great excuse to go and talk to Addie* . . .

For the last six months, all Addie had done was fight with this wild kid. They stomped around the house shrieking at each other, and if he intervened, they'd both instantly turn on him. If he didn't intervene, then as soon as Sheila stormed out to do God knew what, Addie turned on him anyway.

So he and Addie would break up and make up, her a little frailer and more resentful every time, him feeling the call to do something big and bold enough to change the dynamic, pull them both into some kind of sunshine. Addie had never been more unhappy, so of course he'd started making plans. Of course he was ring shopping.

Gemma, the first woman he'd ever been serious about, had pegged it years ago, but he hadn't listened to her, had he? *I was a bad bet from the beginning, Cooper. And now? I'm not fixable, you sweet, dumb man. I'm ruined. Stop throwing good money after bad.* Kind words, to be said so flatly and coldly while he stood in the apartment that they'd shared for three years, watching moving guys tote his things down to a truck. She meant it, too, but he didn't quite believe her. Not then. He would stay, if she softened. He started to say so, but her younger kid, Maxie, came bursting in, big-eyed and teary.

Maxie was supposed to go to her friend's house after school, to miss all this, but she wanted to say goodbye. He stood there awkwardly while Gemma gave her the *Sometimes, grown-ups, even ones who love each other* . . . talk. Jesus. He hadn't kept in touch with Max. Too weird. He'd loved that kid, but what was he to her, really? Just a man who went all in, who wanted to marry her mother, but her mother had said no.

Then he met Shelley-Ann. Three and a half years later, the only thing that had changed was the number of his failed relationships. He remembered standing on a green hilltop with her, on a gorgeous, cool fall day. She kept her cardigan clutched around herself, looking like a black storm cloud, even when he dropped to one knee. Hopeful. Still. She didn't even say no. Not really. Just, "You're kidding, right? I can't . . . I can't. You know it isn't you. It's me." Flat. Finished.

So he moved to Atlanta and immediately struck up a friendship with a woman smack in the middle of a hideous divorce. Addie was the saddest, most shattered soul in a thousand-mile radius, and within a year, he was in love with her. She was smart and sweet, soft and curvy, and had great taste and wild curls, but going back to Addie now and expecting things to turn out differently was chasing an inside straight. He could work at it. He wanted to, actually. But he had learned that when you cleared away the wreckage, sometimes what was left was nothing. Nothing at all.

He should fold, call it over. It was hard, though. Their lives were so entwined. All their clothes were divided up between their units. She knew his PIN, and he'd set up her passwords. He had a copy of her car keys, because she hated to drive. She kept her illegal pot gummies at his house because she was scared this new, nightmare Sheila would find them and eat them. Or sell them. Their foundation was rotten, but the house on top of it, the doomed, doomed house, was so damn cozy, and he was the kind to leap from tile to tile as the floor fell away beneath him.

Now her daughter was digging cash out of her purse, and Cooper said, "Hey, let me get that," and pushed his card to the barista. "And a London Fog."

Sheila took her drink, a little mollified. She peeped up at him and asked in a small voice, "Are you going to tell my mom?"

Did she mean the college boy or the outfit? He should tell Addie about both. It was the right thing, and also what he wanted to do. He knew what would happen if he went to Addie and said, *I ran into Sheila, skipping school and wandering Midtown, mostly naked, picking up hairy-toed collegiate man buns . . ."*

She'd cry, he'd comfort her; he'd get pulled right back into her unhappy orbit. They would be back together, and he wanted that, too. He shook his head. No. Pulling his chips was a long-run mercy for both of them. Sheila, too.

On the other hand, Sheila was making risky choices. Cooper was a bit of expert in that field. He could see where the kid was headed, and the optimist in him thought, *Maybe I could change her path. Make Addie's life better, too.*

In the end, all he said was, "It's not my job to tattle on you, kid." This wasn't the same as saying that he wouldn't talk to Addie, but Sheila brightened.

"Thanks, Cooper." She gave him a fast squeeze. He hugged her back, of course. It felt strange to have her so out of his life, this girl he once believed would become part of his family.

Back upstairs in his office, the sad rabbit was still running on a loop, peering over its shoulder at him, then running behind the logo. He wavered between calling Addie and minding his own damn business.

The rabbit reset, beckoning him to follow, looking dour.

What if he trashed the whole thing? What if, tomorrow, he admitted that it wasn't fixable, and he began a whole new rabbit, perfect as a baby in its innocence? With a sudden mouse swipe, he did a simple drag and drop, and it was gone.

Sure, it was still on his hard drive. He could pull that broken rabbit right back out at any second, but—well. Baby steps. Maybe, tomorrow, he would empty his recycle bin and start fresh.

As he got up from his desk, it occurred to him that he had never met anything fresher than Meribel Mills. Not once. Not in his whole damn life.

7

I MET CAM Reynolds at a dog park. I was reading the script for a juicy guest spot I'd picked up on one of the venerable network police procedurals that were still creaking along. I turned out to be the murderer. It's always "Steve from *Blue's Clues*" or "The Fonz" who is the villain, in the end. Landing the murderer part meant my role on *Belinda's World* still mattered, which was a nice morale boost. I didn't have a lot of work lined up yet that year.

My agent kept telling me that forty would mean an income hit, but I wasn't forty yet. Not on paper, anyway. I was getting close, though. I could see it, and in case I couldn't, Liza kept mentioning plastic surgeons. That's a high-difficulty name drop if you want to be at all subtle, but Liza was as subtle as home Botox: "Daphne Plath, who gets all her face work done by that Dr. Myers I told you about, got the hot sister role in that indie. They still want to look at you for the repressed sister. The older one." Not. Subtle.

"Actors need working eyebrows," I told Liza. I refused to go full LA Frozen Face, but I did cold laser, which is miraculous up to a point, and leaned hard into nutrition and skin care. I believed it was enough, until Liza viciously sent me a script for the kind of fifty-something mom part that negates a female actor's sexuality forever. On the title page she scrawled, *They want you bad for this.*

Smiley face. Exclamation point. "Fifty-something" moms in movies are often barely forty. The guy already cast as the dad was deep into his sixties, which was adding insult to injury, as Honor might say.

I caved and agreed to try a little filler. A very little. Just to take the edge off.

I tried to be stealth about it, but Wallace was suspicious from the second I said I had flu. I never get sick. He kept threatening to make me soup. Him, not Paul, so it really was a threat. I put him off, claiming contagion, but when I emerged, he clocked the work immediately.

"Aaaaand she steps onto the slippery slope! Welcome! Welcome! You'll have a forehead like an egg by Christmas," he cackled. Wallace's own forehead would not be certified as virgin under any scrutiny. He was a lawyer, not an actor, but he worked in entertainment.

I got the murderer part after my first post-filler meet with a casting director who had hired me before. Liza was very *Told you so* about it, but we both had hopes this was the start of a run. There were whole chains of these procedurals. A good turn on one could lead to others. Between residuals and rent from the apartments in my quadplex, I was doing well. I'd been smart enough to buy the house outright when I was flush. But Honor's tuition and her therapy were pricey, and my paper age was about to get that dreaded four in front of it. At the dog park, I was working the script for the procedural pretty hard. I wanted to nail everything in fast, sure takes.

Gumball, outside and off her leash, romped with three big dogs, getting joyously rolled. In minutes, she had turned into a matted ball of fur, mud, and mastiff saliva. Gumball didn't really understand that she was small.

Cam Reynolds came into my life first as a shadow, darkening my pages on his way to take the other side of my bench. He sat down, a set of broad shoulders and dark hair in my peripherals. I preloaded my version of the friendly-but-cool "Nuh-uh, buddy" smile that every woman owns, but when I turned it on him, he was disarmingly attractive. Exactly my kind of thing, built low, with dark eyes and muscular arms and that kind of hawky face that's not afraid to have a nose. My own face accidentally shifted into a real smile.

He took it for the opening it was and waved a hand at the spasms of dogs. "Which one's yours?"

I pointed at Gumball. "That filthy piece of nonsense, there. Believe it or not, she's usually white. You?"

He shrugged. "I'm just here to pick up chicks."

It could have been creepy, but he nailed the tone. I laughed.

Three months later, I might not have. Back then, I'd had less than a dozen stinking mash notes from Marker Man, filed away with others that felt red-flaggy: sexual or angry or creepily off. Fear was not a blip on my horizon. It also helped that, at that exact moment, a pug dog built like a sausage link ran out of the pack and hurled itself at his feet, exhausted. Cam scratched its head while it panted and wheezed.

"I like a man who's not afraid to rock a little dog," I said.

"I don't have a dog," he repeated, serious this time. "I'm sitting for one of my partners."

"Oh. Lawyer?" I said.

He shook his head and handed me his card. It said, CAMERON REYNOLDS, SECURITY SOLUTIONS. The second I tucked it in my pocket both those names fell right out of my head.

The pug recovered and rejoined the fray. Gumball was still tearing around, so I settled in for a flirt. His chat game wasn't great. He was too quiet, but he asked me questions and actually listened to the answers, and that counts for a lot. He noticed the script and offered to help me run lines. Is it sad that I was surprised to have a man acknowledge that he'd interrupted my work? Yeah, it surprised me, as did his listening skills. LA is a town of talkers. I took him up on it.

He played both cops in all three scenes, interrogating me, catching me in a lie, and then hearing my confession. He tried to do different voices and inflections, but one cop came out super flat and the other sounded like a Muppet. He was genuinely terrible, but he was game about it. He even stood up and stalked around behind me when the script required it, and he nailed the threatening body language. I liked to watch his oiled, tight movements. He had a slick grace that struck me as a little dangerous.

It was a solid effort, but I was only flirting to keep limber. The day I met Honor at the hospital, I decided I would never let a string of random men troop through her life. I hadn't really dated in a decade. Back in LA, there was this stuntman, Barry, I called up every now and again, more friendly than romantic. He had a crazy-good body and was very sweet, but there was so much nothing happening in his head that if I yodeled up his nose, I could get a good echo going.

Cam said, "That's my cell on the card. You could text me," when I finally called my worn-out rag of a dog to me.

I smiled. "Maybe. But I should tell you, I'm kinda with somebody." I didn't mean Barry. It was just a polite way to fade.

He smiled wryly and said, "Of course you are. You likely have a waiting list."

Now, that was smooth, but he gave up too fast to be a player, and I'd been rolled by enough of them to know. LA was full of 'em, and after I signed with my first agent, I'd been easy meat for bedpost notchers and itch scratchers. In comparison, he seemed so nice, and his reluctance to talk about himself felt refreshing and a little bit mysterious. I thought, *Well, maybe I will text him*. But when I got home, I couldn't find his damn card anywhere.

Dog Park Guy, as Wallace and I called him, became a brief regret. I'd sworn not to jerk Honor around with a string of boyfriends; I'd never sworn to die alone.

Then Marker Man co-opted all my "thinking about men" headspace. His letters got more personal, more creepy, and more frequent. He started referencing restaurants where I'd had lunch or outfits I'd worn shopping. Liza wanted me to hire private security and offered to get me a meeting with "the firm that did J-Lo," but I didn't have J-Lo's budget. I read a lot of Yelp reviews and picked three security firms at random. At the first place, I got scare tactics and then a hard sell for round-the-clock surveillance teams that I couldn't afford.

Security Solutions was the second firm I visited. It was housed in a slick, generic suite in an office park with a mad amount of parking, for LA. A soothing receptionist—she could have been a voice actor for guided meditations—said, "Mr. Reynolds is ready for you," and walked me back to a small but well-appointed office.

I took one look at the man standing up to greet me and blurted, "Dog Park Guy!" then stopped short, blushing. I'd placed him so embarrassingly fast.

He made it okay by saying, "Oh, I remember you, too, Meribel. Believe it." He came out from behind his desk, smiling, holding out his hand to shake. His grip was warm and sure.

"I lost your card," I said. "This is more, 'Of all the offices in all of the etceteras . . .'"

He laughed and sat down by me in the second client chair because, he told me later, he couldn't stand to put his desk back in between us. We tried to talk business, briefly, but even with a topic as chilling as my stalker, a spark was present. Within ten minutes he straight up asked how my boyfriend waiting list was coming along. When I told him I was single, he wanted to take me out for coffee to tell me why I shouldn't hire him: He didn't date clients.

Two hours later, we were still in the coffeehouse, deep in one of those audible-click-of-chemistry situations. When he was close, I felt it in my body like a hum. When he moved, I got a sense of controlled breath and a step-slide-step-still physicality that said, *dangerous*. Not to me. Dangerous for me, maybe. Dangerous on my behalf, maybe. With Marker Man out there, I found the whole vibe sexy as hell.

We gave "going out to dinner" a try that Friday, but neither of us ate or drank much. I did most of the talking, waving my hands around, leaning in. It was easy to tell him things, even about Honor. He didn't do that Oh-you-are-a-mom thing where they glazed over or frosted up. I learned he was amicably divorced, and he had a kid, too. A son in college.

"Give me your hand; I can read palms," I said at one point.

"Really?" he asked, but obliged me, and it was a good hand, broad, with square-tipped fingers.

"Nope," I said, and kept his hand.

I'd set up a movie night with Wallace and Paul for Honor, so I invited Cam back to my place right after the entrees came. No coffee, no dessert, the bulk of our food shoved into take-home boxes. Later, in my bed, we ate the leftovers with our fingers. I watched him wolfing at cold squid ink ravioli and thought, *Sleeping with him, cool cool cool. After half a first date.* It's impossible to see a man clearly when your brain is soaked in postorgasmic chemicals. My brain was. Which was saying something, considering it was my first time with him. I thought, *I won't see the warning signs when he is inevitably mean or dumb or gaslighting me or playing games or actually still married. Except I'll never actually know any of this, because I'll never hear from him again—*

Then I stopped thinking, because he was reaching for me again. He stayed awhile longer, then didn't get pissy *or* act too happy when I asked him to go home so I could have Wallace tote my sleeping daughter from his couch to her own bed. I was too giddy and fizzy to sleep, already Pavlov's dog for him, listening for his bell.

I woke up to find that he'd already rung it: Pretend it's two days from now, and I drop this casual text: Want to hang again?

I decided not to answer for at least a day. Twenty seconds later, I sent back: Your coolness is on record. Yes, let's hang. I have to get my kid up and moving and off to school. But after?

Then I died, thinking he probably meant "Let's hang again . . .

next week." But no. He was at my place with coffee and bagels and the really good lox and capers and little minced purple onions half an hour after Honor left the house. By the time he went to work, well after lunch, I had twenty texts from Wallace, who had seen Cam arrive via the doorbell camera feed: MER!!!BEL! Is that the male person from last night? Breaching the nunnery? AGAIN?

I texted back a row of smileys, and Wallace was banging the door down seventeen seconds later, wanting to dish. From then on, Cam and I were a thing. The more we saw each other, the less I felt the pull to check out James on his wife's Insta. I didn't really notice when I stopped.

On Cam's recommendation, I hired a private eye instead of security. If the stalker could be identified, he became a person with a street address and a social security number. I could get restraining orders and injunctions. I would have some recourse. The PI came up empty, though, so Cam beefed up my home security system, adding sensors to every window. He put outdoor cameras around the house, too, because Marker Man's letters were coming directly to me by then.

Even as he escalated, I kept thinking, *This can't possibly get worse*, the way you do. Then it would.

Marker Man never mentioned Cam. Even when he talked about the restaurants where we'd gone on dates, describing the clothes I'd worn, the food I ordered, he erased Cam from the scene entirely. He wrote as if he had been the one sitting across from me, asking if I wanted a bite of his trout.

He sent more pictures: Piles of wrapped and ribboned boxes that were leaking red scrawled fluid from the bottoms. Female figures tied, or hung, or hacked into chunks. His big decision now seemed to be about where to make the cuts. The woman always had orange-and-yellow hair, so she was clearly me. It looked as if her (usually detached) head was on fire.

Every illustration had a note, sickly-sweet, faux-poem syrup with a side of violent threat.

Oh, Meribel, I am the envy of so many lesser men, such stupid men, who choose their loves less wisely. BAD THINGS HAPPEN TO BITCHES WHO CHEAT. Your sweetness, Meribel, your fidelity, is priceless. I'm so glad you never would betray me. I am so glad we are us, and that for us forever begins—soon.

I considered taking out a loan on my quadplex to pay for that round-the-clock security after all, but Marker Man never tripped the cameras. *It's only letters*, I told myself. Scary ones, but I thought, in that way that people do, *It will be okay.*

Then Liza got the offer for me to step into *The Spirit of the Thing.* I initially said no, more for Honor and my own established life than Cam, but I'd be lying if I said he wasn't a factor. I talked it over with him, rambling in anxious circles. He was quiet, supportive, but I could see how much I mattered to him. Liza stalled, pushing me hard to take it, and that was when I smelled that cheap cologne smeared in my bed.

I was done. I took the job. I moved.

Now here we were, me and Honor. New city. No Wallace, no familiar neighborhood where I was known, no Cam. My one possible friend here seemed to be ghosting me.

As soon as I got Honor off to school, I sat down at the dining table to paw through the letters that had come flooding out of my mailbox. The dates were spaced, a little. Not every day. He was slowing down? Or he was traveling toward me, so was writing less frequently. The content was very bad, ramblings about love and ownership and garish, stinking pictures of naked Meribels drawn in front of mountain ranges and rivers. Some naked. Some in pieces. Some were both.

The most recent letter had an even closer postmark—Abilene, Texas—and a picture of me on my knees. Begging forgiveness? It was captioned:

Meribel, Do you worry I am angry that you left? I am not angry. I know you are afraid. Don't be afraid of love, you silly, nervous bird. When we are alone, I will be brave enough for both of us, and wash your hair by hand in waterfalls with magnolia-scented soap. You left, but you knew there was no place too far. No way for me not to find you. Please don't worry! I am with you, always. You know this. Soon, soon, soon.

I did know this. Now. I scooped the letters up and I went straight to the police station. I knew from experience it was better to go in person than to call.

I drew Detective Avensen, a red-faced, beefy guy, blond and dimpled and wheezy. He looked like a Viking who'd been raised strictly on Pringles and box wine. Avensen really liked procedure. He flipped quickly through my stalker journal, a year's worth of meticulous records, with thick fingers and flat eyes, and then handed it back.

New city, new paperwork. I sat at his desk and we filled out forms, as if this were my first reported incident. It depressed me. The whole huge room was depressing, crowded with desks, the cinder block walls painted that industrial green color that infests schools and prisons and community centers. It must still be being remaindered from a massive avocado overorder from 1978. The precinct in LA had been almost the exact same color, but at least that place had had natural light. This precinct was housed in a walk-out basement. The windows were high slits, and the air had a mildewed tang, and Avensen was poking words into a computer that looked like a hand-me-down from an underfunded public school.

He paused to pick the letters up and flip through the envelopes, touching all over. It hardly mattered. No one was going to pass my mail to a crack team of smokin' hot forensic scientists. I'd had a guest spot on one of the lesser CSIs—I'd been the murderer there, too—and I'd also dealt with real police. I knew the difference.

I was surrounded by mostly men, mostly doing paperwork.

When Marker Man did finally cut me up and stuff my chunks in different boxes, then they would look up. It might even hit the news. *Former sitcom cheerleader vivisected and gift wrapped.* At that point, a team of probably not-smokin'-hot techs would do forensics on my corpse. I'd be too dead to feel remotely gratified.

Avensen came to the end of the stack without taking any of the letters out and said, "Those markers really stink. Whew."

"But did you see the postmarks?" I'd handed the letters to him all in order.

"Yes. There are three letters from Flagstaff. The last was postmarked Abilene," Avensen said. "So he moved. But then he stopped."

"Or paused," I said. I looked around the room, hoping to catch the eye of someone less phlegmatic. It was busy, here in Midtown. The manned desks all had citizens talking to the cops there already. There were more people waiting, lined up near a fire exit in metal folding chairs. There was only one female detective I could see, a young Black woman with her braids in a low, tight bun. She was with an elderly man who waved trembling hands as he talked. She leaned forward, as if she was listening. I wished that I'd drawn her. "He was in Flagstaff on August twenty-fifth, and the last one was mailed from Abilene on the twenty-eighth. He could easily be here by now, even if he was going Greyhound. He could have been here by the thirtieth when the man was watching me outside the coffeehouse."

"Yes," he said, looking back to his screen. "You saw a short, thick person. Wearing a hat. Under an umbrella. Across a busy road. In the rain. And again in the middle of the dark night when he was fourteen stories down. But you could tell it was the guy."

I did a slow yoga breath. "No. Of course not. I've never seen Ma—" I didn't want to use Honor's nickname for him. It was too cute. Too unthreatening. I'd picked it up for just this reason. To minimize him for her, and also help me sleep. "I've never seen my stalker," I reminded Avensen.

"So then, the person maybe watching you could have been anyone? Or even two people." He looked up, pretend-puzzled. Thoroughly unpuzzled. Trying to make me say I couldn't possibly know.

"It was the same person" was all I said. I did not mention James. He would leap at James.

"You're anxious. I get that. This has gone on awhile. Stressful. Now you get all these backlogged letters . . ."

"I saw the man watching me before the service forwarded his new letters," I reminded him. Did he think I wanted to be stalked?

"But. Well. Maybe it was someone who recognized you. From the . . ." He waved his hand at an invisible television. He'd never seen *Belinda's World*. Not his demographic. "You were on that show."

"I want that to be true. Because otherwise, my stalker knows exactly where I live," I told him.

He looked at me for a long assessing moment, and then he nodded. "You got a boyfriend?"

I sighed. I'd gone through this in LA, too. "Not really." Cam was in California. James hadn't been my boyfriend since I was a girl. Anyway, I had an easy way to know if it was James. I could ask him. That thought made my breath stop short.

James was a strategy manager (whatever that meant) at a health-benefits company called Motect. According to his wife, he traveled quite a bit, but I could call and leave a message. Maybe a receptionist would connect me to him. I could say, "Hey, you weren't by chance at Java House in Midtown the other day, were you? I thought I saw you watching me." I could even say, "I drove out to Woodstock to ask. I think you saw me, yeah?" and explain the whole Haciendas! debacle as Stalker Fear, which was true. Well, true-ish.

"An ex-boyfriend?" the detective asked.

I shook my head, vehement. "This man has been watching me in LA for over a year. The minute I move east, the postmarks start coming east."

"They were forwarded, though. If it is a stranger—and that would be unusual—he doesn't seem to have your address." He'd gone back his painstaking typing. Tap, tap, tap.

"Well, he found my house in LA pretty damn quick. How long will it take him, now that he's here?" I could hear my voice going shrill. That wasn't going to help. I was five foot nothing and blond-adjacent, which meant I had to work to help men like this listen to me. I had to stay in my lowest register. Tall shoes helped, too, but I was seated now. So I talked low and worked to keep my body still. No waving hands or anxious foot jiggles. Nothing that looked emotional. I needed him to follow up with Detective Johnston in LA, who'd been so convinced I was in danger that he had encouraged me to move. A guy like Avensen would listen to another cop. Another man.

He considered this. "Well, you can't be sure he's come past Texas . . ." I made some sort of noise then, a little whine of air in my throat, like a teakettle sound. I was about to blow. He held his hands up and admitted, "It is creepy. I'll give you that. But we still have to finish the forms. It's a process." He glanced at the envelopes, then peered back at his computer screen. Tap. Tap. Tap. "Most stalkers who eventually act out in dangerous ways know the person."

"Yes," I said. I knew the statistics. I'd taken so much comfort in the statistics, I'd probably waited far too long to move. "When he hacks me into chunks, at least I'll know that I'm quite special."

That paused him. He almost smiled. "All right, point taken. Good you came in. Good to have a record."

God, I hoped this lump was taking me seriously. I lapsed into silence and let him work. I was at square one here, but at least I'd added this to the record.

I left, still thinking about James, hoping it really had been him. Never mind his wife and the three children. Never mind I had not so much as said word one to him for decades, and that I poofed, no word, no call, no looking back, at the end of what had to be the worst week of his life, too. If he was watching me, it might be more out of curiosity or anger. I told myself, *Just call and ask. It will put your mind at ease.*

It was still well inside of business hours when I got home. I cleaned the kitchen, walked the dog, and all the while, I imagined James and his dumb beard and his tired eyes, working, with a phone close to hand. Chores done, I went back to the spare room I was using as my office. Honor found it so unfair that I had screens behind this closable door and even more inside my bedroom. A smartphone, a laptop, an iPad, a TV. All this week, she'd lobbied again for her own smartphone with a charging station by her bed, so that she could never, ever sleep again.

"Show me you can self-regulate and practice moderation with screens, and we'll talk," I said, finally. I was not worn down. With Honor, I often had to find different ways of saying no before one took. I gathered neurotypical kids were this way, too, once they hit adolescence, so Honor was a prodigy at "willfulness," among other things.

"How can I show you if you don't let me have screens in my room to show you with?" she asked, and I had to work not to laugh. This kid!

"Show me in the den," I said. "It's your screen time now. Don't take it. Instead, we'll play Bananagrams."

"But this is my screen time. Even if I had screens in my room, it would be screen time."

"Show me you can self-reg—"

But she was already up and heading across to her desk to boot up her computer, muttering, "If I had screens in my room, then I would show you."

Somehow, my own laptop screen was showing me James's office number, and here "Somehow" meant "I googled it." I could call, say his name to a real or virtual receptionist, out loud, asking for him. I wondered what that would taste like in my mouth. But I was too afraid, or maybe too ashamed, to call.

The idea nagged at me through the weekend, though, then through more wardrobe fittings, Honor's therapy appointments, more scripts to read from Liza. No more letters came from Marker Man, but I was expecting them to show up in a clump. I spent way too much time on Sarah's feeds. On Tuesday, she posted a picture of James laughing and pushing the littlest boy on a park swing. Insta life, where everyone looks happy. I myself posted nothing about being stalked, much less my own foray into stalking. My feed was about prepping to be the mom of a teenager in just a few days' time.

Wednesday was the hardest. I had no work obligations, Honor was at school, and I was fresh out of errands. Honor's three-cake long-distance birthday party was good to go for Saturday. I wasn't sure September 9 was her actual birthday, but it was close enough. All I had to do with my spare time now was wonder. I kept digging my phone out of my bag and then reburying it.

I wanted Wallace to talk me down, but when I called I got voice mail. I texted Paul, who told me Wallace was in court all day. I hadn't run into Cooper again, and it felt weird to go tap on his door. I'd let too much time pass after he'd seen me coming into Java House and practically sprinted out the other way.

I felt so terribly alone. Yes, I wanted to know if the watcher was James, but I also wanted to talk to someone who cared about me. Or who at least had cared about me once upon a time. Someone who would take me seriously.

I dug out my phone again. I had to dial the number in by hand because I'd taken it out of my contacts. But I didn't hesitate. I knew it thoroughly by heart, and this was telling, wasn't it?

It rang. Once. Twice.

"Meribel Mills," Cam Reynolds said, his voice so warm. As if he'd been waiting for this call, though weeks had passed since I moved. As if he still remembered what his bed smelled like when I was in it. He'd answered with my name, so much sweeter than hello, because it meant he'd left my number in his phone. "You'll never guess where I am."

"I wouldn't even try," I said.

"Atlanta."

My breath stopped. I thought, *Well. Join the crowd.*

8

COOPER, NORMALLY A three-times-a-week guy, had gone to the gym every afternoon for days now, even on the weekend. By Monday, Meribel still hadn't shown. As much as she worked out, this had to mean she was avoiding him. She must have seen him book it out of Java House last week.

Can you blame her, then? You fled like a little bitch, he thought, embarrassed. It hadn't been about her, not at all.

On Tuesday, he pulled on his gym clothes and headed down right at 4:00 p.m. again, hoping she'd relented. No Meribel, but Honor was there. She had the place to herself as she death-marched on a treadmill with her nose in a book. It was an oversize, flat coffee table thing with a drawing of a big, red devil on the front.

The kid wasn't moving fast enough to get her heart rate up, if that was the point, but he said, "Good for you, getting your workout in." He wasn't her parent, and he didn't need another Mills woman mad at him.

Honor grunted, absorbed in her tome. Should she be reading on a moving treadmill? Even one set to "Trudge"? He took the machine next to her, planning to catch her if she lost control and went (very slowly) flying backward. He set his treadmill to a faster setting, but not by much. It was hard to truly push himself the way he did when Meribel was here, too, being savage about it.

He asked Honor how school had gone ("Fine, thank you") and what she had learned ("Math") before deciding there was no easing this self-contained little person into a conversation. He bluntly turned the topic to her mother.

"Is your mom feeling better? Since she, um, her headache?"

Honor said, "She's fine, thank you."

Her impeccable manners, combined with her flat, dismissive tone, amused him. He got the sense that Honor had no idea if Meribel was ill, much less ill with him. He wasn't positive that Honor recognized him. He tried one more time, holding the rail so he could bend and peer at her book. The monster looked like Satan in a loincloth, one massive hand fisted around an upset Barbie in a gold-plated bikini. Near the bottom, a tiny knight and some idiot in a blue bathrobe were attacking it.

"Who's the big red guy?" he asked.

"An archdevil. Moloch. But I hate this cover. It's the original," Honor said, not looking up. "The original *Player's Handbook* cover is worse, though, because there's no girl at all. The man who invented Dungeons and Dragons said that it's not *for* girls." Honor didn't often have a lot of tone with him, but this was withering. "Actually, girls play it much better. We play 5E better, anyway."

"Is that so?" he said, amused. He stepped off onto the sides of the treadmill so he could tilt his head and read the title. *"Dungeon Master's Guide.* Is it fun? How do you play?"

She brightened. More than that. She came alive. Twenty minutes later, she'd spewed a lot of information about character classes, which made almost no sense to him, and game play in and out of combat, which more than made sense. It sounded interesting. So much of it was based on what the dice said, very appealing. You took risks, the bigger and more creative the better, and then the dice decided whether they'd pay off—or kill you.

By then she was giving him a winding account of everything that had happened so far in her favorite game. She was animated, even bubbly, the book propped on the treadmill's screen so she could wave her hands around.

"It's set in ancient Greece, with classic gods and monsters. My character killed Medusa, and he has a Pegasus named Frank. Me and Yuna, that's my DM, are obsessed with Greek and Roman mythology." It was true. Meribel said the kid had already read Robert Graves, *The Iliad*, *The Odyssey*, and Seneca's *The Trojan Women*. She was, what, twelve? "He's a paladin. That's a knight bound to a god. Mine serves the Moirae. Spin! Measure! Cut!"

He worried again she would fall off as she pantomimed these actions, but he didn't want to crush the vibrancy spilling out of this otherwise very contained small person. When she finally paused to breathe, he asked who Moirae was.

She peeped at him sideways, as if he'd asked how to work a toilet or what refrigerators did. "The three Fates. They decide all of life, the destinies of other gods, even. Clotho spins out years, Lachesis measures for each mortal, and when you're out of time, Atropos takes her shiny, inexorable scissors, and she snips. The end."

"Inexorable, huh?" he said, amused all over again, but she nodded, wholly earnest. "So when your time has run its course that's it? That seems pretty true to life. The Fates, now, I only know from that Disney movie about Hercules. Old women, sharing an eye . . ." Sheila had loved that DVD, back when she was twelve and sweet and he and Addie were falling for each other.

"No! Disney conflated the Fates with the Gray Sisters. They—" She was aghast, but midexplanation, her timer chimed. She looked to the controls, suddenly quiet, and powered down the treadmill. She seemed to power down, too, as she stepped off it. "Anyway, they're different. I'm done. Bye."

"Tell your mother I said hello," he called after her, but she trudged out as if he hadn't spoken.

He did a half-hearted circuit around the weight machines,

thinking about Meribel Mills. Meribel was stressed right now. On the edge in many ways. But she wasn't broken. Her last relationship had ended friendly, and it had been new, anyway. Her marriage had died years ago, and to circumstance, not cruelty. She and Honor got along. Hell, they actually liked each other. Well, Honor was a likable kid. Wikipedia had told him Meribel was thirty-seven to his thirty-nine, and that was different, too. Once he'd stopped whoring around, his serious relationships had all been with older women. If he wanted to stop repeating his mistakes, he should play a different game altogether.

By the time he was on the hanging leg raise, abs burning, he'd decided he should go and see her tomorrow. Take a risk. Knock on the door and say, *I'm not getting back with Addie. What if you and I said 'Screw it' and went out to dinner?* Or even better, he could deploy his secret weapon. It was this: He cooked.

His mother'd taught him, saying women loved to see a fella with a saucepan. His own father wouldn't have recognized the implement, so he wasn't sure how she knew, but she'd been right. With Addie, cooking dinner (especially since he cleaned up after himself) guaranteed that she'd get flirty and hustle him back to his place the second Sheila went to bed. If he could find some unique or clever way to help Addie to stop being so focused on her ex and her current misery with Sheila— He stopped. He turned his mind deliberately away from that. That was finished.

As he flipped through his battered Julia Child book (butter, butter, butter), he realized his talent was likely wasted on Meribel. She survived on leaves and bits of fish and strong black coffee.

He'd taken her a bottle of wine as a welcome-to-the-building after they'd met in the gym, and when she invited him to help her drink it, she said, "All I have on hand is Grape-Nuts, gin, and six kinds of sparkling water. Oh, maybe some microwave popcorn. I think it's sea salt flavor?" Sea salt was not a flavor. Garlic butter and fresh-grated parm, now that was flavor. Her fridge was a wasteland with a packed produce drawer.

That night, they chatted and watched an episode of *Black Mirror*. It wasn't kid appropriate, but Honor was at her computer desk with her back to them, cycling through about fifty open browsers, building a complicated labyrinth and talking in a chat window and reading dense blocks of text on multiple forums. She had on headphones and didn't clock that another live person was in the room, much less the show.

Halfway through, Meribel suddenly straightened and said, "Crap! I never did my crunches."

He said, "We could do them now," joking, but the next thing he knew, they were both on yoga mats, knocking them out. Dating Meribel Mills could be deeply improving in a hundred ways. If he survived it.

He closed the Julia Child and took his laptop to the white marble breakfast bar and googled "Low Carb Casseroles." He scrolled, and they all sounded terrible. Some garbage monster had invented quiche without a crust. Why? He'd trade five years off the back end, years of being old and frail and bitching about his knees, for one right now with cream and bacon. He did a Publix run for mushrooms, fresh spinach, many cheeses; bending to buy 2 percent milk instead of half-and-half. Addie had taught him this (abominable) substitution, saying he had the metabolism of a coked-up ferret, reviling her own extra pounds, no matter how often he told her she looked good.

The next day, whisking eggs and grinding fresh nutmeg, he knew he had to let this break be real. Time to stop toying around with various scenarios, trying for the high-return, small-chance outcome that would let him create peace for Addie.

He decided to take the quiche over straight out of the oven, before Honor got home from school. He hoped Meribel would invite him in to hang. Casual. Cooper hated dating. Back when he was a young asshole, a date was a way to get over. He ran plays and percentages, learning what worked on this kind of girl, on that one. He wasn't that guy anymore.

Cooking for her might help them skip the bullshit, get to something nice. Dinner. Conversation. *How was your day.* He liked waking up with the same warm person, comfortable with each other's morning breath. He missed those dumb, quiet nights playing Yahtzee or streaming old sitcoms with Addie and Sheila. He had to remember that those nights were no longer possible. Addie cried all the time, and Sheila cussed them both out and looked like—well. The kind of girl his father used to run around with. If he dared to ask, *Did you finish your homework,* she'd snarl at him, *You're not my dad.* She was doing all kinds of risky things without weighing the odds.

He should stay out of it. Bet on something new. Not just personally. Movies, television, now that was some high-risk shit. He had a fat bankroll tucked away, part of his Bitcoin coup, waiting for the right wild wave to ride. Meribel might teach him how to get in that game . . . Change would do him good.

He thought that he was resolute in this decision, but as he stepped out of his condo with the quiche, he saw Addie herself coming around the corner into his hallway. He froze, fighting a cowardly urge to duck back inside his door. It would be undignified and pointless. Their eyes had already met, and she had frozen, too.

Then she did it. She leaped back around the corner.

He wanted to laugh, but it was so sad.

"Addie . . ." he called.

She peeked around. "Sorry. That was ridiculous." She walked toward him, her face pink.

He could feel the serious heat of the fresh-out-of-the-oven pie pan through his oven mitts, but he wished he wasn't wearing them. They were silly, puppet-y things, fashioned to look like chickens. Sheila had given them to him last Christmas.

She said, "I was actually coming to see you."

"Oh. Why? I mean—" He sounded so hearty and fake. He swallowed. Addie looked good. She was wearing a fitted ivory-colored dress and her hair was up the way he liked, all those crazy little tendrils hanging down around her pretty face.

"Should I not?" she asked. Her eyes were locked on his, so sad they made his own eyeballs feel oddly sweaty.

"Probably not," he said, and her face fell. He tried for casual. "You're off work early."

She smiled, but her eyes stayed sad. "I had a dentist appointment." She started to say something else, but by then, her gaze had locked on the pie pan. Her eyes narrowed. "Cooper, are you seeing someone?"

It was none of her business, but he had to work to keep from getting defensive. He should say yes, even though he wasn't. Technically. Meribel was a light on his horizon, and walking toward that light didn't make him a cheater. Even back when he was man-whoring, he never cheated. Anyway, he and Addie were flat over. Why did he feel guilty? Why had Addie gone so hollow-eyed and silent? God, he was ridiculous, holding his hot pan in his stupid chicken mittens.

"Addie. Why were you coming to see me?"

She shifted her weight from foot to foot, still eyeing the pan, her mouth pressed flat. She didn't answer the question directly. Instead, she told him, "We were supposed to go to Wild Waves, remember? We talked about it all year. You bought tickets, even, and now it's going to close down for the season."

His eyebrows went up. "You came to talk about the water park?"

Addie's little mouth bunched into a sad wad. She swallowed and looked away. "What if we went? What if we tried, and it was fun. Cooper, I feel like I'm losing Sheila. I've lost you. I need . . . something."

That was all it took for him to waver. He felt it like a wave, pushing him toward her, and the thought held so much joy. What if he could make it all be so much better? He loved her. He should risk it. There were still so many things that he could try. He was patient. He was smart.

A wiser part of him understood that they were things that he had tried before. He couldn't think of a single option that hadn't failed already. With Gemma. With Shelley-Ann.

He said, "If we walk away, right now, we could be friends—"

"Oh, bullshit, we could." She flushed, glancing from his idiotic chicken mitts to the hot pan again, and then down the hall to Meribel's. She knew who Meribel was. Addie'd been so excited when they heard this actor from a show she loved was moving into the building. "Is that a quiche?" She took his flushed face as an answer. "A quiche for the actress. I know that you two have been hanging out. Or whatever."

He said, "It's crustless." As if the lack of pastry rendered cooking for another woman blameless.

"Mm." She folded her arms protectively across her chest.

He forced a smile, tried to get his voice to be hearty. "I'll give you the tickets to Wild Waves. You can take Sheila and one of her friends."

Addie pressed her lips together. "If she had friends, she wouldn't be so wrecked about you disappearing, now would she?"

Sheila was more upset about her *father* disappearing; it was shitty to put this on him, but he bit back every angry answer he felt building. He stood silent, trying to wait her out, loath to head over to Meribel's place while she watched.

Finally he said, "Did you need something else? This pan is hot."

She snorted. "Doesn't she have a kid, too? Maybe you three can use the tickets. I hope you have a great time. Playing house. With our replacements."

His smile became a grimace, his hands sweating inside the chickens. "I told you, you can have them. I'll slide them in your mail slot."

"Oh, will you? Will you slide them in my mail slot? God! Cooper! You star-fucker. She's not even that famous!" Addie said, and then she finally wheeled away and stomped off.

He waited until she was all the way around the corner. Waited longer, until the sound of her angry footsteps faded out. He took a deep breath. Letting it all go. If he needed further proof that this was best . . . He turned back to Meribel's door.

There was a cheery, pale blue basket sitting on her welcome mat. Like an Easter basket. Instead of eggs and candy, it was heaped with half a dozen wrapped presents, each tied with a silk bow. They were so small and gaudy. There was a plain white card on a plastic stick, the kind that came with floral arrangements, but this one was jammed into the presents. He hadn't noticed it before because Addie had appeared around the corner.

A word was scrawled on the card in hot pink, as bright as the various wrappings and ribbons, but looked too short to be "Meribel." Maybe the sender signed it? Four or five letters. Perhaps "James"? That was the ex-husband, he remembered. He was curious, as anyone would be. If the sender wanted to be discreet, they would have used an envelope, not this little stock card. As he bent to look, he realized the card itself had a smell, oversweet and chemical, like the cotton candy lip gloss he'd gotten Sheila for her last birthday. She'd said, "Oh. I loved this stuff. When I was in middle school."

It wasn't a signature, though. It wasn't a name at all. The card said: *Soon.*

9

CAM REYNOLDS WAS in the city, and my heart was pounding so hard I could feel the pulse in my hands, my feet. Everywhere.

"Where?"

"Omni Hotel. The downtown one."

Cam Reynolds was at most ten minutes away from me, even in Atlanta traffic. I couldn't swallow right. I had the phone pressed so tight to my ear. It made his voice sound closer. Then I realized, his voice was two thousand actual miles closer, which was exciting and wrong and strange. "So, you're here on some kind of work trip?" I was trying to sound casual. It came out strangled, a little.

"Sure, Meribel, this is a coincidence," he said, deadpan, and I laughed. An awkward pause, and then in what was clearly a confession, he added, "It's a research trip. To see if a permanent move to Atlanta is feasible." He flopped it right on out there. I realized that I'd sat down on my bed.

"Oh," I said, trying for neutral and landing on very, very loud. I didn't realize how much I had missed the rumble of his voice until I had it in my ear. Hearing it again, I could almost smell him. He used a soap or a shampoo with bergamot and lime, and under that, he was like woodsmoke and black tea. After I broke it off, the ghost of that scent haunted my bed; I cried the day I washed him off my linens.

He chuckled. "You said no to long distance. So . . ."

I had said no. But I'd been pretty broken up about it.

"You are going to move," I said, slow and ponderous, as if testing how the words might taste in my mouth. "Move here."

He said a few more words, and I had to lean in to make sense of them, that's how floored I was. "I'd say I'm exploring it."

"Without talking to me?" This was a little too invested, wasn't it? Or maybe Marker Man had broken my sense of what people did when they liked another person. I didn't want Cam coming clandestinely across a whole country to my city, but, perversely, I wanted his body in the room with my body. I loved that body, so dense, so compact. A soldier's body, scarred and tough.

A few years back, I'd done a war movie for cable, playing a nurse. My lover, the main character's brother, died in the middle. There was a short, brutal scene where I screamed over his body, wailing and rocking. After a really good take, the one where we knew we had it, my dead lover winked at me and went to craft services, and I took a nap in a temperature-controlled, quiet trailer. They edited in bombs and gunfire later.

Cam had really been in war. He'd been army, an airborne Ranger, stationed in Afghanistan. He'd been shot, twice. Once over there and once in California on a bodyguard job. I'd traced the scars with my fingertip.

We'd never spent a night together. But after sex, before I sent him home, I liked to doze on the inside of my bed, near the wall. I'd push him on his side, facing away, loving the feel of this thick, muscular animal turning easily under my hand. I would be the big spoon, curled into his broad back. This way, all his most threatening pieces pointed out, away from me, at the world. Tucked behind him felt like the safest place that I could ever be.

There was some truth to that feeling. He knew how to fight, and he had killed people, in war. He didn't talk about it, not in detail, but I knew he was capable—and dangerous. He was dangerous in other ways, for me. He might break my heart, or worse, Honor's, if I let him all the way into our lives. Now he had come here on his own recognizance. But he wasn't mine, I wasn't his, and now that I'd seen proof that Marker Man had also come charging across the country after me, I was hypersensitive to anything from men that felt overinvested.

Into the silence that had fallen, I said again, more sternly, "Without talking to me."

"Yes. Without talking to you. Since I'm the one currently considering upending my life." He was teasing, his tone light. I had an actor's centering ego, that was true. "I came to explore the idea, the city, decide if it was feasible on my end, and then I planned to talk to you." He was calm, but by the end he sounded a little uncertain. He blew out all his breath and added, "Fair to say, I miss you, Mer. I think about you all the time."

Had I missed him? I'd decided that I couldn't have him, so I tried not to think about it. When he came up in my mind, I got busy, deliberately turned to other things. Usually Sarah's Instagram feed, which was—ugh, just so super healthy.

I tried to make my voice match his. Soft. "I wish I'd known that you were here." I was holding my phone so hard my joints hurt.

"I thought, Why bring it up, until I see if there's anything for me here besides Meribel," he said. "When your name came up on my phone screen, it felt creepy to be in your city and not answer."

The difference between stalking and courtship is so thin, I thought then. *It all depends on if the person likes you back.*

Out loud I said, "Okay, well, you know this is batshit crazy," but it came out so damn sweet. I did. I liked him back. Crap.

"Since you know I'm here, should we—can I see you?" he asked.

"Yes," I said, instantly. No thought behind it. Even if it reopened a box I'd closed. Even if it cracked my heart all over again. I couldn't have him this close and not pull him closer. "To talk. Everybody keeps their pants on."

"Sure," he said. "I brought pants."

I put him on speaker so I could open up a browser and go to my aesthetician's website, booking myself for a quick facial and a blowout in the morning. I told myself there was nothing wrong with wanting to look good when your former bona fide was inbound. It was harder to explain away scrolling down the service menu to *Waxing*, but I booked that, too.

Into the silence, he asked me, "Are you panicking?"

I said, truthfully, "I might be panicking," but it went up at the end. Like a question.

I'd forgotten how much I liked his low, rumbly laughter. "I get it. Moving feels serious. To you. But my kid is grown up, and I'd be moving closer to him, anyway. I'm going to drive over and see him, while I'm here." Marco was currently studying environmental science at Clemson.

I said, "It feels risky. For you. Who knows how long I'll live here. If the series fails, or if my character doesn't catch on, I could be back in LA in half a year."

"If things are good with us, I'll move back with you. We'll know by then. Meribel, changing cities isn't a big deal."

That made me blink. Relocating cross-country had been pure upheaval for me and especially Honor, but the army had moved Cam around his whole adult life. In and out of the country. Into war zones, even. The four years he'd lived in LA since his military retirement was the longest he'd stayed in one place since he graduated college.

I had to ask. "What do you think about Atlanta? So far. I mean, do you like it?"

That blowing-out breath again. "It's a great little city, and my partners in LA would buy me out, no question." The doorbell rang, then, but I didn't think he heard it over his own answer. I wasn't expecting anyone, and these days, this was enough to push my heart rate higher. Gumball was snoozing on the sofa, and her ears didn't even twitch. Some guard dog. Cam was still talking, telling me, "Don't freak, though. This isn't a way-too-soon proposal, or pressure, or— All I know is, it's stupid to like a person this much and suffer the geography."

I headed for the door, my hand tight on the phone. "Okay. What if we had lunch. Tomorrow."

"Good. A restaurant. Shirts, shoes, service, pants, the whole thing."

I stood on tiptoe to see out my wide-angle peephole. There was Cooper on my doorstep, wearing big, fluffy oven mitts that looked like they had faces, holding a round Pyrex baking dish. He had also brought a gift basket. I could see it resting on the floor beside his feet. I was relieved to see him. Not only because strangers at my door made me anxious these days, but because this looked like an overture. I pulled the door open wide, putting a finger to my lip in a silent, *Shhh*, and pointing at the phone.

I said, "I can get us a table at South City Kitchen." The manager there loved *Belinda's World* and would squeeze me in, even if they were solid booked. Then, to Cooper, I mouthed, "Cam Reynolds." His eyebrows went up, and he took a step back. I pulled the door wide, motioning him in, and I left the phone on speaker. It felt odd to talk to Cam and have Cooper in the room. Not that anything even romance-adjacent had happened with Cooper. If I was being honest, though, I had thought of him as a possibility, which made turning off speakerphone feel weirdly too meaningful. We were almost finished anyway. I left it on and asked Cam, "Want me to pick you up tomorrow? We can drive over together."

Cooper mouthed, "He's in town?" When I nodded, one eyebrow lofted and his eyes narrowed.

He came in, though, carrying his hot dish, stepping over the gift basket he'd set on the stoop. It was made of pale, flimsy wicker with clear cellophane grass in the bottom, like a baby's Easter basket. It was full of tiny presents. The fact that he'd brought food and the basket made it weird. Was I supposed to open all those little gifts in front of him, like a miniature Christmas? We didn't know each other "pile of presents and a dinner" well. It was an overcorrect, after a week of our paths not crossing.

"One o'clock?" Cam said.

"Sure." I'd be done at the salon by eleven.

"Are you—" Cooper mouthed, then stopped, looking away, embarrassed.

"It's just lunch," I said, for both of them, very stern. Now I wished I had closed the speaker. I added, "Sitting upright in public."

"Absolutely," Cam said. But I heard undertones.

Cooper must have heard them as well, because he turned away, fast, and went to set the Pyrex dish down on the table. He stripped off the silly mitts and threw them down, as well.

I meant it, though. Probably. The waxing was just in very most unlikely accidental case. Sex would muddle things up. Considering that I'd driven across town to stalk my ex-husband last week, considering that I'd only called Cam to stop myself from calling married James, more muddling was the last thing that I needed. I turned my back to Cooper and spoke softly.

"I'm serious. We need to think how it would work." There was a small, buoyant pause as we both realized I'd said *how.* "I mean *if,*" I corrected, immediately, but I'd said what I had said. I glanced back. Cooper had not gone to get his basket, and he'd left the door hanging wide open, as if he expected me to go collect it for him. Unless—it wasn't from him?

I asked Cam, "Did you send me something? A gift basket?"

Even as he said, "Nope," I realized Cam couldn't have sent it. He didn't have this address. I looked to Cooper, but he shrugged and shook his head. Not his, either. I felt the small hairs on the back of my neck, even on my arms, start trying to stand up, as if a low-level electric current was now running through me. I hurried toward the open front door.

Cam said, "Call my cell from the car tomorrow, and I'll come down. Save you the parking."

"Perfect," I said, and bent to pick the basket up.

I smelled the marker ink before I saw it. Cotton candy flavored, sickly sweet.

Soon, the card said, each letter thick and wobbly, as if the word had been traced over and over, one *Soon* on top of another, until the card stock was almost soaked through. I recognized the hand-writing, even though it was only a single word. I recoiled, almost leaping back, and Cam heard me gasp.

"Mer?"

I was wheeling toward Cooper. "Was this in a box? Is it from the mailroom? Did you bring it up, or open it, or—" The words came out fast and harsh.

"Who are you talking to?" Cam said, and his voice dropped, colder and more serious. I was now with the soldier. That danger-ous physicality that he kept coiled inside his body was leaking out. I could feel it, even through the phone.

"Of course not. It was sitting there when I arrived," Cooper told me.

"Mer. Who the hell is that?"

"It's fine. I'm fine. It's my neighbor Cooper, dropping by with some food." My voice was shaking. "Cam, someone left me a basket. No, not someone. He did it. Him. I see his writing on the card. Je-sus, he was here. In my hallway! He was right outside my house." I was dizzy. I couldn't bring myself to touch it. Cooper came toward me, concerned.

"Tell me your address," Cam said, from very far away.

"The stalker?" asked Cooper.

"Meribel!" Cam said. Tight. Urgent. I heard him walking, heard a door opening. "I want to come over. Now."

"Hang up," Cooper said.

"I need to think," I said to both of them, then to Cam alone, "I'll call you back."

I could hear Cam saying my name again. I hung up.

I didn't want to touch the basket, but more than that, I didn't want to stand here with my door wide open feeling exposed. Marker Man had been here. On my doorstep.

I snatched the basket up by its twee, babyish handle and slammed the door shut between me and the world, locking it. I didn't want to keep on touching it. I went to my long table and set it down as if it were as hot as Cooper's dish. I put my phone beside it. Cam was already calling back, but I turned the phone facedown. I'd let voice mail handle it. The basket was all I could think about.

I had not heard from Marker Man, not since the great pile of held-back letters had come pouring out with postmarks stretching east across the country toward me. I'd called my forwarding service and spent twenty minutes on hold, waiting for a real person so I could eat their liver. I'd been coldly, blackly furious, but by the fourth time I'd heard what sounded like, hand to God, a Muzak version of Nirvana's "Come As You Are," I'd calmed enough to realize tearing the head off a minimum-wage customer service rep would do no good.

The girl who finally came on the line was in charge of exactly nothing, including my personal mail. Based on the fuzzy sound quality, I doubted she was even in the country. I explained that the service was letting my things pile up and then sending batches. I was paying for my mail to be forwarded each day. She'd apologized, clearly reading a script written for this exact scenario, explaining that this sometimes happened with new accounts, but that it should not continue. And yet, after that initial flood, I'd gotten no more mail from him.

Maybe because he was here.

I turned to Cooper. "When you came over, was anybody in the hall? A man? A stranger?"

"No. I was bringing you this quiche, as an apology." He saw the question on my face and flushed, faintly. "I did see you at Java House when I booked it, but that wasn't about you."

As an actor, I probably didn't hear or even think those words often enough. Another time, it would be a nice relief to know Cooper hadn't been avoiding me. Right now, I was too busy panicking.

"I'm glad. Just—distracted."

"Of course you are. I'm getting the impression that this stalker might be more than an overzealous fan on Twitter, huh? I didn't see anyone—well, not any strangers, in the hall." He stared at the basket. "Should we open one?" He sounded both interested and repelled. I liked the "we," though. As if I was not alone in this.

I started pulling the bright, beribboned packages out of the little basket. Each one had the same soft, crinkly give, as if whatever was inside had been wrapped in tissue paper. I didn't like touching them, even to sort them into sizes. I set them out in a row: One round. One square. A rectangle. Eight slim short ones. It was all grossly familiar. I teetered on the brink of understanding, and then I physically blanched.

"Meribel?" Cooper said.

The packages were like a puzzle. I didn't want to see the picture they were making, but I already had. My hands began laying them out in the correct order. I didn't want to be right. But I was. I had the right number, the right shapes and sizes to mimic the way Marker Man's "presents" to himself had been set up in the drawings he had sent me. From far away, I heard myself saying, "I think it's parts. Body parts."

"As in, *fingers*?" Cooper asked with genuine horror and stepped toward me.

"No. I mean, God, I hope not." I shook my head. That was worse than what I thought, and it shook me back into myself. "Doll parts. Like a Barbie. He drew this a couple of times, me cut into pieces, each piece of me wrapped in a separate box, a different-colored ribbon, all presents for him, from him. These are the right size to be doll parts." I remembered the line about running his finger down the arch of my dead, free-floating foot, and shuddered. Barbie had a high arch, her foot perma-molded into high-heel shape.

"We shouldn't touch them?" Cooper asked, his voice canting up at the end in a question. "Forensics."

That made me laugh, a dry, scared sound. "I've been on that show, but that's not how it works in real life. No one is going to dust my Barbie corpse Easter basket for prints."

By then, I'd placed the round package that had to be Barbie's head at the top, then laid out the rectangle and the square as her torso and her hips. The eight longer, slimmer rectangles were all the same size. I used two each to make jointed arms and legs. When I was done, she was complete, and there were no packages left.

"Jesus. That's about the size for a Barbie," he said.

"If he wanted to be realistic, it'd be a Skipper doll," I said, smiling tightly and indicating my opposite-of-Barbie figure.

A startled chuckle escaped Cooper. "That's some gallows humor, Meribel."

I heard admiration in his tone. He thought I was tough. I wasn't. I was terrified, sick with it. His reaction heartened me, let me lean into my anger instead of my fear.

My lip curled. "It's pathetic. Not to mention, deeply unoriginal."

I'd seen so many TV shows and movies with cut-up dolls and Barbie parts. Even more shows where they skipped the symbolism and simply showed hacked-up girls. Not only in slasher films, either, where every character but Final Girl dies gruesomely. I'd personally been murdered three times on network TV and twice on cable. I'd spent hours in makeup getting custom mutilations. There were a lot of parts like that available for girls, especially young, thin, white ones. Even for older, thin, white ones who got facial fillers.

It was one of the things Liza had said to me to convince me to get some work done: *You never want to look too old to be credibly sex-murdered.* This was back when Marker Man was just the author of a few creepy letters, casually tossed in a box with other suspect mailings. Liza's line had been funny to me, then. Now, it made me angry, and I was glad. Angry was better than paralyzed, numb with horror. Angry was better than helpless.

I picked up one of the "feet" and tore the paper off to find red, Christmassy tissue paper. It was wadded and soft from use, almost waxy. Recycled. Touched and crumpled again and again. The idea that his hands had done this made touching it upsetting. I unraveled it quickly, and found I didn't have Barbie's lower leg and foot, after all. I had a mini Twix bar, like what Honor got from neighbors, trick-or-treating.

"Candy?" Cooper said. "Are you kidding me?"

I snatched up another, larger package, the one I'd assumed was Barbie's trunk. I tore it open and found more touched-all-over re-used red tissue paper that unraveled to show me a mini Snickers.

Cooper blew out a big breath. "Well, that's a relief!"

"No," I said. "It isn't. This is worse." It did not ease my sense of violation or encroachment. It only left me furious. "This is some bullshit. A cut-up doll would at least register with the police as ominous. This is smarter and creepier than that. He knows I'll understand it, but to anyone else, it's like—a regular gift."

I could see it dawning on his face, an understanding of how creepy this was, how much worse than doll parts, craftier and more clever, but also harder for those outside my situation to take seriously.

What was I supposed to do, take this to my brand-new, square-one detective and complain that an anonymous person had sent me candy? As if the largest threat Marker Man posed was to my low-sugar diet. Avensen, with his love of protocol and forms and literalness, would not be moved by this. All at once I was swaying, and I felt my knees start to go out. Cooper half caught me and then drag-walked me to the sofa. Had I almost fainted? I was not a fainter, but I realized I'd had my knees locked, and I'd stopped breathing. I bent over to put my head down, and he splayed his warm palm on my back.

"Breathe," he said, calm and certain.

"How did he find me?" I asked the floor. Still angry, but also near tears at his kindness.

"Just breathe," he repeated.

As soon as it was clear I wasn't going to pass out, he stood up, going to my kitchen. I heard him banging drawers open, and water running, and then he was back with a fresh dishrag, cold and wet, to drape on the back of my neck.

"You should eat something," he insisted. "You might be in shock. I brought quiche. But you need carbs. I don't suppose you own a cookie?"

I shook my head. "I can't eat. But I'd love coffee."

"Good. Caffeine is good."

He went back to the kitchen to make it. After a minute, hearing the Keurig grind and burble, I wanted coffee bad enough to stand. I got up and walked on shaky fawn legs to my dining room table. He brought a steaming mug over, then went to make himself one as I sipped and tried to figure out my options.

"I should take pictures of the basket and the presents, anyway," I told him. Document everything, as Detective Johnston back in LA had advised. Cooper sat down by me, his own coffee pale with oat milk, and I got my phone out and did a mini-shoot of the basket and the gifts, wrapped and unwrapped. "Should I put the packages back in and stage it on the mat? To show where I found it?"

He made a thinking face, but before he could decide, my doorbell chimed again. My gaze flew to his in instant panic. He stood abruptly, his chair scraping back. Honor was due soon, but she had keys. I set my coffee down with a thump and got up, too, hurrying to the door.

Cooper followed, saying, "Wait. Wait! Let me open it," very low, but urgent.

"I'm just looking," I whispered, and put my eye to the peephole. I sucked in my breath. I could feel Cooper hovering behind me, close and tense. But—no.

"It's Cam," I told Cooper, breathless, like I'd put my eye up to the peephole and beheld a wonder. Cam Reynolds on my doorstep.

I was already turning the dead bolt when Cooper's hand pressed the door, his arm stretched over my shoulder to keep it shut. I looked back to see his face so close, eyes intense, his mouth turning downward in a scowl as he whispered, "Did you ever give him your address?"

I was already pushing at his arm, trying to move him so I could open the door. I couldn't budge him. Cooper was built slim, and his wiry strength surprised me. After half a heartbeat, he let me shove his arm out of the way. He stepped back a few feet, but his whole body was tense, his face set in a warning, and the question he had asked me finally landed.

No. I had not given my address to Cam. He had found me anyway. Found me and showed up exactly when I needed him the most. Cooper read the answer off my face and threw his hands up, his mouth almost silently shaping my name. "Meribel!"

I turned away and pulled the door wide.

There he was. We stared at each other for less than a second. It was long enough for me to take in the broad power of his body, the blunt features of his face, all set to grim. Cooper's reaction had registered, but I couldn't care. Not with Cam right, really, here. He'd found me, and he'd come to so fast because he'd heard the fear in my voice. Not for a more sinister reason. Cooper didn't know Cam like I did, or maybe he was jealous.

As he came inside, I hurled myself at the living wall of his thick body. His arms closed around me, lifting me off my feet, holding me tight against him. I tucked my face into his neck, and the smell of him was—well, it was exactly as I remembered.

"Cam," I said into his skin. "Cam, I'm scared."

"I know," he said. I lifted my face, wanting to see him, and I wouldn't want to be the person who'd given him that expression. Once, a man tried to snatch one of his clients right off the street. He'd broken the guy's arm and dislocated both his shoulders.

"Of course you are," said Cooper from behind me, overloud and taut.

A pause. Cam set me down, but he didn't let me go. He turned me, instead, tucking me under one arm, shutting the door behind us with the other. "I'm Cameron Reynolds. And you are?"

"This is Cooper," I said, and that was enough with introductions, now. "Cam, I want you to look at this basket." Threat assessment was part of his job. He'd know exactly how seriously to take this.

Cooper said, "You got here fast. Weirdly fast."

There was no smile in his voice, and Cam's body stilled. Cooper stopped blinking. Their gazes became fixed, intense. Two male animals eye-stabbing each other across the room. My nostrils flared. All I cared about was the basket, the idea of Marker Man coming down my hall on soft feet, pressing his ear against my door. This was the last thing I needed.

"Stop it," I said. I meant to sound dismissive or stern. It came out shrill. The air between them had thickened, gone electric. Even Gumball felt it. She was up, standing stiff on the sofa with her little legs braced.

Cooper looked to the basket, back to Cam. "Seriously. How did you know where to find her? On the same day this stalker got her address, you have it, too."

I boggled. He could not be suggesting—

Cam's arm dropped from around me, his head tilting in a way that seemed weirdly inhuman. Birdlike, almost, but nothing small and backyard friendly. Something with a big wingspan and talons. Raptor.

"Who exactly is this guy?" Cam asked me.

"I'm her neighbor, and I'm not the problem here," Cooper said. He stepped forward.

Cam's voice was low and quiet, but dangerous for all that. "This neighbor who showed up at the same time as your nasty little present, there." He was talking to me, but even as he spoke, he was moving forward, too.

10

I GOT BETWEEN them.

"Stop it. Stop this stupid shit, right now!" It came out too high, almost a squeak. Not the tone I wanted. I held both my arms out, and I felt so small. "This isn't helping." I hated the shake in my voice, but it registered with both of them. Cooper eased backward. Cam's shoulders came down a fraction.

Back in my office, we all heard the small French cuckoo clock chime once. It was three thirty.

I blinked like a person waking up from a bad dream. "Honor is due home. We have to—my kid does not need to walk into whatever the hell this is." The air between them stayed thick with suspicion, and I waved my hand as if I was trying to manually disperse it. Honor never seemed to notice tension overtly, but it got into her, anyway. She soaked it up into her body, and it would have to come out later.

I turned to Cam. "You have to go." They were both so bristled up. So many hackles.

"Me?" he said, calm but disbelieving, eyeing Cooper. Cooper, to his credit, stayed neutral. No body language telegraphing triumph, or it might have gone much worse.

"I don't want Honor to meet you this way," I told him. There was truth to this. "She needs prep time for new people, and—" I cut off abruptly, conscious of Cooper. But I wanted to say it. Even in the middle of this testosterone-fueled ugliness, I was telling the truth when I added, "I want you and Honor to like each other." It was a feeling left over from when we were dating. This would be their first time meeting, and it was not—not at all—how I'd imagined it.

Cam pushed air out. Flashed a small, grim smile. "I'll evacuate. But I'm not going far." He was looking at the basket again, the stinking note with its single, pink-scrawled word. "I'm not leaving the building."

"Fine." I wanted him to stay close, actually. I wanted him to come back soon. This was Cam. Any building felt safer with him in it. Even so, I had a ton of questions, starting with Cooper's. How had he gotten my address? "What about the stairwell? It's down the hall. I'll text you to come back."

Cam gave me a sharp nod and let me bustle him out. Already I could breathe better, as clouds of freaking man pheromones dispersed with every inch that separated them. I watched him walk down to the fire door and go inside. As soon as he was out of sight, and therefore out of earshot, I closed the door and whirled on Cooper.

"You shouldn't have said that to him." My voice was tight.

"Of course I should have." Cooper was moving in short, tense strides, first to the bar cart for the gin and rocks glasses, then back to the kitchen. It felt like a good call. "You haven't thought it through, Meribel." I wanted to protest, but he was talking. "Look at the timeline. You start getting letters from this overinterested fan. A month or so later, you *happen* to meet Cam Reynolds, and he makes a play." He was now at the fridge, getting ice and club soda. "You shoot him down, and not long after, your stalker starts to escalate. He keeps getting scarier. Until you are scared enough."

"Enough?" I said. My eyes were drawn back to the basket. Marker Man was not trying to push me into the red on some fear-o-meter. I didn't think he ever thought about what I might actually be feeling at all. He invented everything he wanted me to feel and taped it onto his idea of me. "Scared enough for what?"

"To need a bodyguard. So you make the rounds of security companies, and oh, hey, one of them is owned by none other than that guy you met, the one who wants to date you." He was making my drink the way I liked it: Gin. Lime. Soda.

"That's paranoid," I told him. "That's as crazy as Cam saying you're Mar—my stalker. Like you planned to drive me out of LA so I would move into your exact building in Atlanta."

"Is it?" Cooper said. Rhetorical.

"Yes! It wasn't like I met Cam, and the next day, boom, I had a fresh new stalker." I knew Cam was down the hall, on the other side of a fire door, and I also knew that Cooper had to be wrong, he had to be—and yet my voice had dropped to a whisper.

"Right. You get a stalker, and then you 'happen' to meet a private security expert, the perfect person to protect you, at a dog park. Doesn't even have a dog." Cooper made it sound so sinister, as if our respectable meet-cute was actually a plot.

I shook my head, emphatic. "Okay. Okay. But there are a million private security firms. Cam had no way to rig it so that out of all the offices in all of La La Land, I'd walk into his."

He'd turned his own drink shamelessly bright pink again with maraschino cherries and juice. He brought mine over. I took a sip, and it was poisonously strong. Good. He took a pull of his, too, eyeing me over the rim of his glass. Not like he was thinking. More like, he'd already thought, and was trying to figure out how to say it to me. "How did you pick which security companies to visit? Was his on someone's recommendation or—"

The ones Liza recommended were A-list. So expensive. "No. I googled and I checked the Yelp reviews, then I picked three. It was random. Actual nefarious plans can't rely on luck."

"Random? He gave you his business card—"

"Which I lost!" I interrupted, but he kept right on talking over me, less afraid of volume than I was.

"—and maybe you lost it, but it's also possible the name of the firm was stuck in your subconscious mind, so picking his company wasn't nearly as random as you think. And then—he puts up cameras for you, cameras that somehow never caught this guy—"

That shut me up. I swallowed. Was it possible? I shook my head. I didn't want it to be possible. Anyway, I knew Cam. Sure, he was a closed person, not easy to read, and we hadn't dated long, but if Cam was Marker Man, surely I'd have sensed it. "Cam says he likely scaled a wall and got into my place from the roof."

Cooper lofted an eyebrow. "Oh, is that what Cam says?"

I kept talking over him. "Cam couldn't guarantee that I would come to his firm. Or any firm!"

"Of course not," said Cooper. "But the fact is, you did. If you hadn't, then I bet the stalker would have escalated until you did, or you would have had another 'accidental' run-in where he appeared at your pharmacy, say. With no prescription."

I glared at him. "It was his partner's dog."

He said nothing, and the silence stretched. I drank most of my drink so fast I felt a cold spike in my brain and had to press my hand against my eye.

Cooper started to speak, but at that moment, we both heard keys jangling in the lock. I was instantly moving, shoving the weird presents back in the basket and then setting it down in a chair, which I wedged under the table. We stayed silent as Honor came banging in. Her backpack looked half as big as she was, stuffed full of textbooks.

"Hey, kitty cat. You remember Cooper." I was working hard not to look at the basket, mostly hidden under the table. This close to her birthday, Honor would assume it was for her. I didn't want her thinking about it at all.

"Hello. I hope you are having a nice day." Her voice was casual, and she gave him a small smile. Honor was polite and had many scripts for how to talk to adults. Grown-ups often didn't realize she was on the spectrum when they first met her. Then she added, "There's a creepy man in the stairwell."

Immediately my heart was pounding, but Cooper rolled his eyes and muttered, "Damn right, there is." Oh. Honor meant Cam. So did Cooper. Then he shot a guilty look at me and said to my daughter, "I mean, darn. Darn right."

I was waving that away even as Honor told him with great earnestness, "'Damn' is not a bad word, Cooper." I was freaking out, but it still registered with me that she knew his name. After I'd told her I was having coffee with the guy we met in the gym, she'd called him "new Wallace," with such disdain that it clearly meant "subpar replacement Wallace." Never mind that Cooper was short, straight, white, wiry, and Wallace was tall, gay, black, built. She'd warmed up to Cooper now, though. Pizza was a miracle worker. "They say 'damn' in PG. If it's bad, you can't say it in PG."

"Well, okay, then. Daaaaaamn right," he said.

Honor cackled. He was really good with her. If he kept this up, Honor might even learn his last name. I relaxed, just a tick, and polished off my gin, five o'clock rule be—darned. It had been a day.

He chuckled with my kid and started picking mashed carcinogenic cherries from his ice and eating them.

"Is that candies?" Honor asked.

I startled, but she meant the cherries, even though Gumball had now disappeared under the table and was sniffing at the basket like a hairy little CANDY HERE! sign. Chocolate was bad for dogs, but Gumball and Honor could both smell Twix bars from space. These particular bars could be drugged. Or poisoned. Or full of razors. Even if the best scientists on earth tested them and declared them pure, I would not accept any sweetness from that source. I didn't want an object Marker Man had so much as looked at touching my child.

"It's a fruit," Cooper said. "People are supposed to have five a day."

"That is not officially a fruit," I said in quelling tones, before

Honor could ask for the jar and a spoon. "What were you doing in the stairwell?"

"Coming up the stairs," she said, giving me eyebrows like *Duh, Mom*. She said no more. Sometimes, these days, it was hard to tell what was autism and what was age-appropriate behavior.

"Why the stairs instead of the elevator?" I asked her, patient, patient.

She flirted up one shoulder in a tweener shrug. "I always come up the stairs after school."

That was news. "Every day after school you walk up fourteen flights?" Not skeptical, because my kid was bad at telling me direct lies. It was just that, as much as she loved to share information, it was rarely the information I needed.

"You like me to get my heart rate up," she said. Oh, so pious!

I narrowed my eyes. Getting this girl to the gym required maternal wheedling, a high level of sulk-tolerance, and sometimes what felt like the direct and benevolent intervention of a small and sweaty deity from one of Honor's games. If I got her to go three days out of seven, she slept better, regulated well, and I called the week a win.

Exercise was great for her, but I didn't love the idea of Honor stomping up through dim stairwells alone. Not while baskets of candy that were stand-ins for my own dismembered body parts were getting hand-delivered.

The doorbell chimed. Early. I had yet to mention Cam. Honor took this as a great excuse to change the subject. "I need a giant snack because I'm starving." She went to dump the heavy backpack in her room, then came back through, heading for the kitchen as I went to open the door.

Cam looked sheepish. He'd seen pictures of Honor, so of course he'd recognized her. He started to tell me, softly, "She came up the—"

"I know."

I hadn't moved out of the doorway, though. He stood on one side, me on the other. He tilted his head slightly left, cut his eyes.

Asking if I wanted to slip out and talk for a sec. His dark gaze was so open. It clearly had not occurred to him that I would be suspicious of him simply because Cooper was. With him this close, Cooper's accusations seemed so much less credible. Stupid body, louder than my brain. I stepped aside so he could enter, then locked the door behind him and put the chain on.

"Honor, this is Cameron Reynolds. You can call him Cam. Or Mr. Reynolds. But Cam is fine." Repeating names for her was habit.

Her lips pressed together, and then she said, "That's him. From the stairs."

I was impressed with the facial recognition; he must have really creeped her out. Cooper lifted his glass and rattled the ice in an ironic salute.

"Cam is a friend from California. He's staying for dinner." I wanted him to do more than that. I wanted him to sleep on the sofa. Just as soon as I had pulled it over to block the front door.

Her head cocked, interested. "What is dinner?"

Well, that was my kid, bouncing immediately to the most Honor-relevant information.

When Honor was six, our downstairs renter's toddler became entranced with her and started following her around.

"Where did that baby come from?" she asked me.

I'd been waiting for this. I had a whole big talk scripted and rehearsed, plus a book to give her, after. I was warm but very matter-of-fact, like a PSA with a pulse. I used the correct, medical terms, but kept it light on the mechanical details, and was super positive about the whole thing. Honestly? I crushed it. A+ first sex talk. I was mentally patting my own back for not causing extra therapy while I waited for her follow-up questions.

She regarded me with her dark, serious eyes. "Okay. But where did *that* baby come from? It dumped out Worker Cat's food bowl."

Honor had not noticed Terry swelling up over the course of months, or disappearing for three days, or coming home with a small, squirming, mewling something in a sling. Terry's baby simply did not exist until it was being a pain in Honor's ass, and I'd explained sex to a kid who had zero interest in that information.

I'd learned it was best to answer the questions she actually asked, not the questions I was worried about. I left the Cam seed planted but unwatered and said, "Buddha bowls."

"With tuna?"

"Yes."

I waited, but she asked nothing else, so I pushed. A little. "Cam is a bodyguard."

She swallowed, and her shoulders went tense. That, she understood. She came two steps closer to look at him more thoroughly. Over the past year, we'd had a lot of talks about strangers, my job, fan overinterest, and what to watch out for. She knew I'd considered a bodyguard before.

She said, quite bitter and hard, "Because of Marker Man."

Cooper looked over, quizzical. I shrugged. I hadn't used that name with him, and maybe I should have. Maybe then he would have known from the pink-scrawled card that something was up with the basket and thought to check the other halls.

"Yes. We need to be careful for a while, okay?"

Her eyebrows came together. "But we moved. We moved to not have a bodyguard. We moved from Worker Cat and Wallace and Paul and Yuna and my house. Why do we have one?"

I could feel her small body filling up with storm. I looked to Cooper, and then Cam, and they both saw it, too. There was nothing on Cooper's face but empathy for her. Cam was more stoic, harder to read, but he radiated zero pity.

So many people got this wrong, going insta-moist and hand-patty and sorry for me when they realized Honor was on the spectrum. It never failed to enrage me. Honor was by far the most interesting, intense, and amazing little person, and autism was part of who she was. Anyone who felt sorry for her—or me—because she had her challenges could fuck right off. I was grateful neither of these men had let that kind of energy into the room. I would know.

I was good at reading feelings. Case in point, I could practically taste the bad energy bristling the air between them. I could feel sinister intent leaking like miasma from the basket.

"I know, sweetheart. It's not fair, but he hasn't stopped. I don't want you climbing in the stairwell by yourself."

Honor looked back at Cam and asked him, bluntly, "Do you own a gun?"

"Yes," he said, at the same moment I said, "Of course not."

He looked from her to me, and he went still again. Cam had a way of being still that was 50 percent stiller than other living people. When he spoke again, his voice was thick with patience. "Of course I own guns. I'm a bodyguard." The patience was for me. Then to Honor, "I also have a concealed-carry license and a lot of training. If you want to see a gun sometime, I'll show you. You can touch it. We can take it apart. Whatever you want, but only together."

Honor asked, very intense, "Can I shoot it?"

"If your mo—" Cam started, but I talked over him.

"No." I sounded a little testy, which was good, considering I felt extremely testy.

"I want a gun, Mom. My own gun. For if Marker Man comes in the house." Even more intense now. She was right on the brink.

"Please excuse us?" I said to Cam and Cooper. Honor was processing a lot. She needed a minute, and strangers or near strangers in the room made everything much harder for her. "Come on. Let's go change into gym clothes." She needed privacy, and then hopefully a hard fast hour on a treadmill. Movement always helped.

"Why? I'm already sweaty in these clothes. From coming up the stairs. I can gym in my school top. I can gym in khaki pants." She sounded querulous.

"Let's go." I was walking toward her, reaching, but she turned in that catlike way she had, staying out of my reach as she stomped into her room. I went with her, not sure she understood how deeply furious she was. Honor had a hard time knowing what she was feeling until she saw what she did. If she fell thoroughly apart, kicking and roiling and hitting at herself, then after, when she was calm, we could talk it through, and she would know. She would say, *I am very angry,* or maybe *grieved,* or *scared.*

I closed the door behind us, then went to her white, plain dresser and got out a pair of clean yoga pants and a dice-covered THIS IS HOW I ROLL T-shirt that she loved. "Do you have a question?"

She snatched the clothes. "Are you going to make the tuna for the Buddha bowls seared on the edge but raw inside?"

She wasn't asking about fish. I knew how she liked her fish cooked. She was asking if any more changes were coming. "Yes. I'm going to cook it exactly like that."

"With edamame. But not any tomato. At all. Because sometimes you let tomato in the salad and then pick it out, and I know because it has juices. I can taste it when those juices touched my fish." Very accusing tone.

"I won't let your salad touch any tomato," I promised.

She stood holding the clothes, her body still braced, her brow still lowered. "I want you to turn your back."

I made myself not react. This was new, and honestly a little silly. I knew her body like I knew my own. She still had a curve to her spine, a little sway to her belly. Her breasts were barely buds. Not to mention, she had on a training bra and the floppy cotton granny-panties that were the only style of underwear she'd tolerate. Her underthings covered more than her bathing suits. I turned, though, giving her the privacy she asked for. Her body was her body, I'd been telling her since before she had words. She got to say who touched it, who saw it.

She was still on edge, but coming down. I could hear it in the stomp and rustle as she changed. "I do want a very big snack."

"I already made you an almond butter sandwich. It's in the kitchen." She'd been coming home asking for big snacks all week, then still eating some of dinner. New, for my little cereal hound, like this privacy thing. She was getting ready for a growth spurt.

Getting ready to grow in all kinds of terrifying, lovely ways I likely was not prepared to handle.

"And I want grapes." Very demanding.

"I got a nice, fat bag of green ones." We were out of red, and they were her favorite, but she wasn't going to break apart over the grape color. Forty seconds ago, she might have. If she went to the gym and worked out hard, the whole storm might be averted.

"Did you order my birthday cakes already? The all three exactly the same caramel birthday cakes for my party online with Wallace and Paul and Yuna?"

"Yes," I said, not sure where she was going.

"Is that my only party?" She was very casual. A request for information. But my breath caught.

"It doesn't have to be. Do you want another party?" It was hard to not sound eager or mom-pushy, hard to tamp down on the excitement that infused my body and act as if what Honor was asking for was normal. Because, of course, it was. Just not for her. "What kind of party?"

"I don't know. I can ask my friend for a suggest."

"That's a good idea," I said, casual, but my chill was all an acting job. Inside, I'd gone hopeful and tense and delighted. "We could do a movie party. Skating, bowling, whatever you guys like. What's your friend's name?"

"I don't know," she said.

I heard her bedroom door reopening, so I turned around. She was already gone, heading for the kitchen, the sandwich. I followed her back to find the air in the den still felt electric. Cam quirked an eyebrow at me, cutting his eyes at Cooper, like, *This guy*. Cooper looked flushed and belligerent.

Men. I had zero energy for this nonsense—not with Marker Man leaving gifts on my very doorstep and Honor on the cusp of something. I followed my kid, who was beelining to collect her snack.

"Is the friend a boy or a girl? Is this a your-age person, from school?" I said. With Honor, it could be our eighty-year-old neighbor from 14G. Hell, the friend could be Cooper. He had given her pizza, she knew his name, and she was more comfortable with grown-ups.

"She's a teenager. Like I will be," Honor said, and crammed four grapes in her mouth. She'd taken a huge handful, and she picked up the sandwich, too. As worried as I was that Marker Man had followed me, had been in my building, on my very hall, I could still feel joy. Honor had a friend. A girl. Her age or close to it. She added, "Maybe I have two friends. I'm not sure. I'll have to let you know."

"One is fine. Two is fine," I said, voice casual, heart soaring. "You can invite as many friends as you want, to whatever kind of party sounds fun."

She looked at Cam, thinking, and then said, "We could go shoot the gun for my birthday party. Me and my friend. Or to the movie place with the good popcorn."

That took a little wind out of my joy-sails. Cooper cleared his throat.

"Sure," I said. Meaning movie place.

"I'm down," Cam said, meaning—guns? Theater? Both? He wanted to take me and my daughter and her possible friends to a movie, or shooting? Boyfriend or bodyguard? Bodyguard or—that question didn't bear finishing.

"Thank you, Cam," Honor said. This was very fast for her to remember a name. She'd probably learn his last name instantly, if I let him give her a bazooka.

"Great! Maybe stick with a movie, because her parents likely won't let her shoot guns," I said, thinking, *And your parent will not let you*. She looked at me with mild exasperation, storm gone past. Now I was being the most unreasonable, silly mother on the planet. I followed her to the front door. "You want to eat before you—"

"I'll eat on the way. I'm fast at eating."

Not a thing to encourage, but I took the win. Honor had made a friend, or possibly two, and gotten herself past meeting a new person and the big, scary truth that Marker Man had not yet left our lives. "Take the elevator. I don't want you going up and down the stairs alone, okay? Promise."

She thought about that, and I feared that I had set her worry back in motion. But no. She spoke in a matter-of-fact singsong. "I promise I won't go up and down the stairs alone." Honor was the world's worst liar, but excellent at obfuscation. When she said it so directly, I relaxed. About the stairs, anyway. Off she went.

I turned back to Cam and Cooper. I was torqued off, but most of my fury was for Marker Man, so I took a deep cleansing breath. As soon as I had myself in hand, I told Cam, "You shouldn't have told her you own guns. She isn't going to see them. I will not have guns in my house."

He went still, again. So very still. I'm a kinetic person. I have never once in my whole life gone still the way that Cam did then. "Meribel. There's a gun in your house right now." He flipped his jacket back and showed me his shoulder holster.

"Holy shit!" Cooper said, looking to me. In his head, Cam was the best candidate for my stalker, and I had let him come into my apartment, armed.

I felt my eyes go wide. "Cam! How did you get a gun here from California?"

He chuckled, low in his throat. "I checked it, like anyone with a concealed-carry license and a job like mine. Meribel. Come on. I know you can shoot. How many hours have you put in at the range?"

A couple years back, I'd had a small but juicy part in a crime-caper movie called *Bad Gambit*. Not a blockbuster, but it was produced by the Weinsteins and distributed by Metro-Goldwyn-Mayer with a wide release. I played Becca Tart, a woman who loved guns so much that she owned five with names. She was in the end-scene shoot-out and had a scene at a range with the main character. I'd wanted the character to look like she thought shooting guns was better than sex and chocolate cake combined; *that* had taken some real acting. And training. And practice.

"I would never shoot a gun for real, in real life, Cam."

"Is that what you plan to tell Marker Man?" Cam spread his hands. "'I won't shoot when you come to kill me because I have a kid and a strict rule'?"

When he put it that way . . . I looked to Cooper, who shook his head and shrugged.

Cam said, "Your kid is curious. Let me demystify guns for her, and she won't need to mess with one alone. Not that she could get her hands on this one. This gun stays on my body. I even sleep in my rig when I'm on a job."

On a job. That paused me. Made the danger rise up so real again. "Does that mean—am I hiring you?"

Cam's eyes flicked to Cooper, but then he shrugged and looked right at me, as if Cooper and his freaked-out, suspicious glare weren't in the room.

He said, "You're not a job, Meribel."

I felt the words like smoke, a spicy warmth curling and pluming through me. My body liked his body. My body wanted me to trust him.

He smiled wryly and said, "Do you want to hire me? Would you be happier if—no pressure. I don't—" He looked at Cooper, grim-mouthed and not going anywhere, and shut up.

Cooper picked up the bottle and blatantly splashed more raw gin into his pink ice. He was watching me as if I were a frozen deer and Cam were headlights, and he could witness something awful happening, but saw no way to stop it.

He said, "So. Dog Park Guy. I want to know, how did you find her condo? So fast. On this day of all days."

He meant that Marker Man had found me today, too. He'd come right to my door to leave me chocolate-covered metaphors. Last week, someone in a dark raincoat had been watching me have coffee, and then again, standing on the street, staring up at my window. I still hoped it was James, but—I blamed Cooper for my next thought; James and Cam were built a lot alike.

I swallowed. So, I had a type. Even so, I said to Cam, "It's not a bad question." I wasn't accusing him of anything, but I did sound uncertain.

Cam agreed, though. "It's a great question. We need to talk about that." That put me more at ease, until he added, "Do you know someone named Addie Portlin?"

I couldn't place the name, until I heard Cooper blowing all his air out. "Oh. I never met her, but I know the name. She's Cooper's ex."

Cam's eyebrows lowered. "Your ex lives in the building?"

"No," I said, and at the same time Cooper said, "Yes."

I turned to stare at him. "She what?"

He shook his head, confused. "You know that. I told you she and I started dating when I moved here."

"Here to Atlanta!" I said back. He shrugged, and I scrubbed at my face. "You meant here, here?"

"Yeah. She's fourteen J."

I could feel cartoon surprise face taking over my features, my jaw unhinging, eyes going wide. "She lives on our floor?" When he nodded, I put it all together with a sharp, internal click. I held up a hand to Cam, as if to say, *Just a second.* "Is she tall and heavyset with curly hair?"

"I wouldn't say she's heavyset," Cooper said, defensive. "Maybe by LA standards."

The curvy woman who had been such a thorough bitch to me at the elevator! *That* was his ex. No wonder he had bounced so fast from Java House. I'd assumed it was about me. I was an actor, and we tended to assume things were. But no, he'd been fleeing from Addie Portlin. He really was still so hung up on her. I also thought that he was way too hot for her. Hotter and younger, because Elevator Bitch was midforties, maybe older. She must have one hell of a winning personality, for all she hadn't used it on me.

Cam looked back and forth between us, picking up the weird vibe and then dismissing it near instantly. He got right down to business. "After you hung up, I tried to call you back. When you didn't answer, I got on Google, and I found your address in two searches."

Now he had my full attention. "My home address is on the internet? We have to get it taken down." I said it even though the cat had clearly left the bag. Hell, the bag had blown away in a tsunami. "God, that explains so much." I gave Cam a fast rundown—the Watcher in his gray raincoat across the street, under my window. I wanted it to be James, but—"You think that was Marker Man? He got here a week ago?"

Cam gave me a half-smile, lofting an eyebrow. "Yep. Anyone could find you, thanks to Addie Portlin. She's the one who posted your location."

I couldn't help throwing a speaking glance at Cooper. We'd worked out together three or four times at the gym by then. Plenty of people in the building had seen us, and the word had gotten back; I'd been lifting weights with her ex-boyfriend, and in return, she'd told my stalker exactly where to find me.

11

HONOR FIRST NOTICED Red Bear Girl because she was a teenager person.

In this building, the people were mostly white and suit-wearing age. No one had a hat or huge tattoos or braids or a distinctive shape. The men either had beards or not beards. The women, even the Black ones, had the same straight hair with the bottom half curled into shapes Honor called doody-rolls. "Hipsters, Business Casual edition," her mom called the neighbors, and said that choosing a place online was a mistake. The nearby park was only for dogs. There were no stray cats she ever saw. There were homeless people, instead.

In the LA quad house, she knew everyone's face and name and apartment and hobbies. Wallace and Paul were best, and had the other upstairs unit. Terry and Luis and their baby lived under. The baby was bothersome, but Luis and Terry both played a lot of kinds of instruments and both called her Twinkie and both had long, dark, raggedy hair and were always together. Under Wallace and Paul was ancient Mrs. Chin, who could pat a little ball of meat and scallions into a dumpling wrapper and then fold it into a perfect shape, very fast, the same every time. She would give Honor six in a straw basket, and Honor wished her stomach was big enough to fit in twelve.

At the quad house she had Worker Cat and also other strays. Worker Cat would let her sit close when he came out from under the porch to stare at her with his yellow lamp eyes and crunch his food. Once he touched his black nose to the very tip of her finger. Here all they had was Gumball. Gumball was hers, for therapy, Mom said, but Gumball liked Mom better than Honor and had to be walked to poop. Gumball was objectively terrible.

Honor could always recognize Red Bear Girl. Her shapes and colors were distinctive. She had big, slouchy bear shoulders and enormous boobs and her hair was tall and very red and very curly. Honor recognized Red Bear Girl even when she pulled the hair into a puff on top of her head.

They'd met more than a week ago, when she saw a teenager person disappearing through the heavy door that led to the stairs. No one took the stairs because they were hot and dirty and dark and only for if there was a fire. Honor was supposed to be going to the gym, alone, because Mom already did a session with her trainer, but she stood in the hall, thinking, then went into the stairwell to see what the teenager was doing.

Red Bear Girl was not in view, but Honor smelled misty sweetness—pineapple?—drifting up. She went down one flight and around the corner, and Red Bear Girl leaped up from her seat on the next landing. She was leaking steam from her mouth.

She laughed when she saw Honor and flopped back down. "God, I thought you were my mom!" She took a big suck off her e-cigarette. It was the new kind, called a Juul. The pineapple smell was sweet and good. "Hey, are you in fourteen A?"

Honor nodded. "I'm Honor Mills."

Red Bear Girl said her name too, but Honor didn't know then that they would be friends soon so she didn't carefully remember it. Then Red Bear Girl said, "Your mom is that TV actor, yeah? I bet you think you're so damn cool because you're from LA."

Honor shrugged. She wasn't cool, but LA was cooler than Atlanta. So it was hard to answer.

"Can I have a suck off that pineapple?" She'd never vaped before, though the lacrosse girls at her middle school had discovered Juul and now the second-floor-south girl's bathroom always smelled like old dessert.

"It's mango flavor, dumbass. Juul doesn't even come in pineapple."

Honor didn't much care what it was. "Can I have a suck off that mango?"

Red Bear Girl blinked and her top lip curled back to make her teeth show. "You know, Cooper used to live with us, almost. Now all he does is hang around your mom and French her ass, and he and my mom—meh. Your mom isn't even that famous, but she took him. So, I mean, sure. Why not hit my Juul, too."

"Thanks," Honor said, and reached for it. Red Bear Girl said Cooper, so maybe she meant Mom's New Wallace, who was shorter and white and straight and inferior, like everything in Atlanta. But not terrible. Honor had decided to remember his real name was Cooper and call him Cooper.

Red Bear Girl pulled it back. "That was complete sarcasm. Do you not get sarcasm?"

Honor shrugged. She kept her hand out.

After a moment, the girl passed her the device. Honor wasn't sure how to do it, though. She turned it this way and that.

Red Bear Girl finally said, "You have to—" She made some incomprehensible face shapes and gestures, and then stomped up a step and showed her.

Honor took a small mouthful, almost like a sip, but of air. It was sweet and fruity. A mist. It didn't make her cough. She took a second, deeper sip, and it did make her cough. After another few seconds she felt dizzy, her heartbeat throbbing in her face.

"I feel weird."

"Nicotine," Red Bear Girl said. "It's super addictive. You're probably addicted now."

"Probably," Honor agreed, and the girl laughed.

"Not literally," Red Bear Girl said. "Jesus. What are you, autistic?"

"Yes," Honor said. "Are you in high school?"

The girl went silent for a moment and blinked at her, then said, "Yes. Do you have to take meds for that?"

"Not right now," Honor said, handing back the Juul. "I go to the gym for it. I can't have food dye or hardly any sugar and I go to therapy, which my mom calls Floor Time, which is stupid because it isn't on the floor."

"That's weird," Red Bear Girl said.

Not to Honor. "In LA, everyone goes to therapy."

"I have ADHD," Red Bear Girl said. "I can just take pills for it." She considered Honor another moment, sucking—no. Hitting, the girl said. Hitting on her Juul. "You are a weird kid. What are you, like, a fifth grader?"

"Seventh," Honor said.

"No way. You're shitting me." That was when Honor began liking her. Honor liked people who said exactly everything that they were thinking. Red Bear Girl seemed mean and very truthful.

"I'm about to be thirteen." It was irritating to keep having to tell people, but Honor liked having no breasts and no period and no new smells. Even really sweaty, she could put her nose into her armpit and it smelled green in there, like cut grass. Most girls in her grade had started to have smells after PE. Yuna had her period, and even her familiar Yuna-smell got coppery and odd on those days. She also had little boobs. She said they hurt and itched. Honor wasn't looking forward to any of that. "Cooper guessed fourth grade."

That was at the gym, the first time he made her have one of the five conversations that grown-ups make kids have. She liked those conversations; she'd had them many times, and she knew every possible path. She made them fun by trying to fit in as many clichés as possible. Her record in one talk was eleven. She liked Cooper because he'd understood that there was a game, and he'd played it with her.

Red Bear Girl quit arguing then and passed Honor the Juul again, freeing her hands to thumb-text fast into her phone. "So, I'm texting this guy. Rodrigo, isn't that name dead sexy?"

"Is he your boyfriend?" Honor asked with interest. She took another tiny sip of mist. Held it in her mouth.

The girl shrugged. "We're talking. I'm not actually allowed to have a boyfriend until I'm sixteen." She rolled her eyes. "Anyway, he's not the only boy I'm talking to." Then she told Honor a lot of things about boys that Honor had never suspected. For example: "Talking to" was an official thing you did with boys before they were your boyfriend. That was *slang.*

Once Red Bear Girl knew she was almost a teenager person, she liked Honor back. They'd met up three times, every day Mom had her trainer, to "hang," which meant walk around the streets. Hanging took up Honor's gym time, so Red Bear Girl had the smart idea to use the stairs. It was hot in the stairwell, so Honor came home out of breath and very sweaty, and Mom never said, "Honor, were you at the gym, or 'hanging' and learning how to cuss good with a teenager?"

Today, their fourth time to meet, Mom made Honor late.

Cooper waved goodbye and said, "Godspeed, Honor. Or treadmill speed anyway."

This was a joke. Wordplay. Cooper was turning out to be a pretty good New Wallace. Honor was carrying the sandwich and grapes, so she couldn't wave back. She nodded goodbye instead, to him and Mom, but not the bodyguard. (Cam. Cam who has a gun. Cam.) She went immediately right into the stairs because Red Bear Girl was going to meet her there, so this was not lying or disobeying. She'd told Mom she would not go in the stairs alone.

"I was about to leave you. There was some creepy guy coming out of the door when I got here. I thought he'd run you off," the girl said. She had a can of Sprite and a packet of Oreo cookies because her mom kept normal food around.

"What's your name?" Honor asked.

"Um, Sheila?" Red B—Sheila said. Sheila. Sheila. Sheila. "How do you not—God, you're weird. Let's go to Walgreens."

Red B—Sheila had a plan to get more hair dye. Under her very red curls, pale brown was coming in at the roots. Honor worried it would become harder to find Sheila if she stopped having red hair, but now Sheila said she had decided on blue, so actually that would make it easier.

They went very rapidly with their four feet making clop-clop sounds, sometimes together like a trot, sometimes one-two-three-four fast in a row like a gallop. In LA, when she was little, she'd had riding therapy on Poohbear, who was yellow and fat and nice. She got so good, Mom said she didn't need a certified therapy horse anymore. In LA she'd been learning jumping on Trouble, who was black and glossy and fast. She would have riding lessons here, too, soon. Mom had found a place and signed her up.

"I want to have a birthday party with you," she said to Sheila. "Would you come?"

Sheila thought about it as they went down and down. "Where?"

"Probably a movie," Honor said. Sheila didn't answer, and it didn't feel good, so she said, "Or to shoot guns. I don't need a present."

Sheila shrugged. "When?"

Honor said, "This weekend. I have a cake birthday with my California friends on Saturday. It could be Sunday."

Sheila said, "Mom is trying to make me go to Wild Waves with her then. She's got a thing about it, but God, like, the two of us all day trying to—ugh."

The stairwell was very hot, and she was already sweaty, which was excellent. Honor said, "I could pick Wild Waves for the birthday party. I like swimming okay."

Sheila eyed her. "It isn't just swimming. It's actually pretty cool, just, not, like, if you have to go with your mom. They have a wave pool and a million slides and a lazy river and rafting rides. They have a flume ride through a haunted castle, and a big blue dragon head breathes water spray on you at the top of the last hill."

Honor's interest perked. "My mom said that I could pick whatever. I could pick that."

That made Sheila's mouth press hard and then turn up. "Okay. If you pick that, I'll come."

At the bottom of the stairs was a small, hot space with two doors. One door went into the glass-enclosed elevator place. They went through the other, into a dark hallway full of storage closets that came with the units. They had cheap, slatted wooden doors more like gates, so Honor could see what all the people had. Mostly what they had was boxes.

"It's so creepy down here," Sheila said.

They hurried to the fire exit at the end of the hall. This door opened onto a small alley. When they pushed it open, it made a fast shriek of terrible bells that lasted until it closed behind them. Now they were locked out, but here was Xena Warrior Princess, leaning on the wall waiting for them.

"Hello, Xena Warrior Princess," Honor said. She remembered Xena's name because she liked streaming that show. Xena always wore black and gray in layers, even though it was warm. This made her easy to find, plus she smelled musty and had a black cavity like a dark sore in one of her dog teeth.

Xena Warrior Princess might be her second friend, but it was hard to know, because she was a homeless person. Maybe Mom would allow it, because she was a very young homeless person. Older than Sheila, but not much. Maybe not, because Xena told her last time that if any pieces of her short, dark hair ever bothered her, she hacked them off with her big knife. That meant she had a big knife, which might make Mom disqualify her as a friend.

The first homeless person Honor tried to feed was an old man who was wandering up the sidewalk outside their building on a day the car service was late or she was early. She was waiting inside, but she saw him going by with his cup for change. His sign said HUN-GRY, but it was hanging down in his hand, not held up to read. She was very full of cereal, so she darted out and tried to hand him her brown-bag lunch. He didn't take it.

He said, "They're gonna kill me and eat my eyes, and they'll do you that way, too." He had a lot of foamy spit collected in his lips-corners, and when he bent down and talked at her it flew off and some speckled on her face. She wanted to run back inside, but he was coming close, so fast. She backed away down the sidewalk instead, and he kept coming, saying, "Pull your eyes right out and eat them, pop like grapes, pop and swallow. Grapes."

There were grapes in her lunch and somehow that made it scar-ier. She backed up more then, very fast, and maybe that made him chase. Cats were that way. Worker was that way. She was part ac-tually scared and part interested, but the farther she got from the door into her building the more it seemed like actually scared.

She was almost to the corner of the building when Xena stepped out of the alley, and she barked at him. She literally made a mean sound like a bark and then said, "Shoo, shoo, shoo!" He did.

He went back the other way, and Xena said, "He's not so bad. He's just, like, off his meds." Xena looked young but also dirty and in layers and with a very definite smell.

Honor said, "I wanted him to have my lunch for being home-less. I feed cats back at my house in LA, but no cats live here." Then she held out her lunch as a test for if Xena was homeless, and Xena took it and immediately started rummaging to see what all there was, which was what a homeless person would do.

Also she laughed and said, "Well, I'm Xena, and I'm sure as hell not a cat, but I'll take any lunches you ain't using."

Now Sheila was feeding her, too, and she thought that Xena was cool. She thought Honor was cool for finding her. If Xena Warrior Princess was her friend, maybe the three of them could play D&D, tabletop. Honor could DM and teach them. They each handed over the food they had brought, and Xena kept the grapes out to eat right now, but put the rest in her big coat pockets, even the sandwich. She always ate the fresh things first, so now Honor asked for fruit or carrots, which made Mom happy. Honor would eat Oreos first, if she was homeless, or if she had Oreos.

"These are really good," Xena said with her mouth full. For her it was normal to get food from strangers, and Honor or Sheila or both had to come every day now.

If you start feeding something, at a certain point, you're obligated to keep on. Wallace told her this, after Worker Cat got used to her. Once Worker depended on her, he might not have another idea of where he could get dinner. Honor brought food to Xena now on gym time or when she would go get the mail. Her mom didn't like for her to get the mail, but Honor said, "I know Marker Man is sending letters. Not getting the mail doesn't make me not know." In LA, the first time she saw one of his letters, the address was purple and smelled like grape.

"Let's go to Walgreens," Sheila said.

There was a CVS in the building, but neighbors were in there a lot. They didn't want to see neighbors, who might mention they were hanging to the mothers, and Honor was supposed to be at gym. They also had to pass Java House. Sheila went around the corner and peeked in. She didn't see any neighbors, so they scuttled past very quickly and went down the block. While they walked, Xena got the sandwich out.

Honor liked to watch Xena eat the sandwich very fast, in small neat bites, even though it made her homesick. At home she liked so much watching Worker Cat eat, but he wouldn't let Honor pet him. She would like a petting cat. Worker was hers, though. Wallace had promised to take care of him, and he still texted her pictures, so Wallace had not forgotten her, at least. Yet.

"Where do you sleep?" Sheila asked. She liked to ask Xena things about being homeless.

Xena said, "Different places. On days I get twelve dollars and line up, I can get in the shelter. But I don't always get twelve dollars."

"That's hard-core cool," Sheila said. Honor thought it was very terrible. Mom said Honor liked to be dirty, but the thought of being this dirty, her clothes all dark and layered with filth and hot and not knowing where she would sleep—it made her stomach feel sick.

"It can be scary. At night. For girls, especially." Xena looked at Honor and stopped talking, like Honor was a kid. Honor knew what she meant, though. Then Xena looked up at the gray, dark sky. "And rain sucks."

At the Walgreens Sheila looked at blue hair dye, but decided not to. She and her mom had already had a bunch of fights about the red, which her mom called McDonald's hair. Honor handed a twenty-dollar bill to Xena. Honor had a lot of money. She always got allowance and birthday money and good-grades money, but then Mom bought her stuff, too. In her pig, she had almost seven hundred dollars.

Xena folded the money away into a pocket and Sheila said, "Are you gonna buy the Juulpods?"

Xena said, "Yeah. Calm your tits."

It was a cool thing to say. Honor wanted someone to get upset so she could say it, too. Xena got in line and bought the pods and a pack of generic cigarettes. She had to show ID, so she was at least eighteen. She was like a college person, but homeless instead of at college. Xena kept all the change and the cigarettes.

Honor got M&M's with another twenty, but only ate a couple. If she ate them all her mom would know, because sugar made her impossible. Her mom said, "It makes everyone impossible, really. It's a drug." Which was stupid. It was a food. Honor wished it was a drug. Maybe her new therapist would prescribe it, then.

"Did you get twelve dollars today?" Sheila asked, as they walked back. Xena shook her head. Honor had change from her other twenty, but then Sheila said, "You should sleep in the storage part of the building. No one would know. Ours has the old sofa in it, even. Just move the boxes."

It was a good idea. When it stormed, Worker could always go under the house, into the crawl space, and be safe. Xena didn't have a place like that.

Xena darted her eyes around. Finally she asked, "How would I get in?"

"We could let you in," Sheila said.

"Now?" When Sheila nodded, Xena said, "I can't now. I have shit to do. I'd need to get in later." They walked on, and then Xena asked, "Do you have an extra key to that alley door?"

They didn't. No one who lived there had a key to that fire door. If Xena had a phone she could text them to let her in, but she didn't.

Sheila said, "If we had duck tape, we could put a piece over that thing in the door, so it wouldn't lock. Then when you were tired, or if it rained, you could come in and peel off the tape and be safe."

"Duct tape," Honor said. They both looked at her and waited. "Duct. Not duck."

Xena turned back to Sheila. "You would do that?"

"Sure," Sheila said. "Like, who would even notice? Only us and you would know the door wasn't really latched."

Honor said, "We can get duct tape from the Walgreens next time we go. I bet they have it."

She pictured Xena safe, hidden under the building where Honor could always feed her. It sounded like a good idea to her.

12

"YOUR EX *DOXED* me," I said to Cooper. I couldn't get my head around the pettiness.

Cooper flushed and swallowed, and I could see how much he hated this. "She's jealous. This is my fault."

Cam was reading off his phone, "Not defending her, but she posted on a private Facebook group called Midtown Moms." It says they 'share support, hive-mind advice, and resources. A space to ask about everything from surrogates to sitters, breastfeeding to birth control—for you or your teen daughter. Be aware, MM is a judgment-free zone.'"

I snorted. "Free of even good judgment, if the mods let her post my home address. Closed group or not, that's low."

"Here. Look," He brought his phone over, and sat down close so I could see. His leg pressing mine was a distraction even in the middle of my temper. Cooper came and leaned over the back of the sofa to look, too. Addie's post was dated August 17, the very day after I'd met Cooper in the gym.

My whole building is buzzing like bees with no hives-or-lives because some F-list aging starlet moved onto my floor. Rah, Rah, Whatevahhhh. I wish my neighbors would talk about something else!

I laughed, but it was a small, sharp sound. "I ought to be too upset about the actual danger to clock the 'F-list' and the 'aging starlet' parts, but nope, as it happens, I have the emotional range to be furious and also scared and also want to bitch-slap Addie Portlin."

Cooper got a little bit defensive. "She didn't actually post the address. Or even your name."

I spun back to glare at him. "Like hell she didn't. The catch-phrase makes it obvious!"

He was flushed. He nodded, miserable. "No, you're right."

"It was enough," Cam agreed. He backed out of the picture, and I saw we were looking at a screen cap, not the actual post. Some other member of "Midtown Moms" had reposted Addie's complaint the very next day, tagging it in a category dedicated to cast news on the *Belinda's World* subreddit.

Holy cats, this is from my mom group! OF COURSE I immediately went back and read all of this sour broad's other posts. I think Meribel Mills lives in a condo over a coffee place that's literally a few blocks from me! Didi is practically my neighbor. Java House is too hipster chic for me—I'm a Starbucks Basic Biyotch, for real—but I know where I'm gonna be getting my skinny vanillas for the next few months. Can you say STALKER? ~BooBear1212

"I can. I can say stalker," I said bitterly. I touched Cam's screen, scrolling down a slew of replies telling BooBear1212 that I was sweet as pie about meeting fans and doing selfies. Several had pictures of me with them attached.

Cooper pushed off the sofa and went into the kitchen to refill his rocks glass, with sparkling water this time. He stayed there for a moment, his back to us, processing.

"Maybe I *should* hire you," I said to Cam, very soft. I could feel my hip pressing into his. With Cam this close, his dark eyes kindled, it was almost impossible to take Cooper's suspicions seriously. Almost.

He shook his head. "I don't have equipment here, or contacts, or employees, or resources. To do a job right, you need the basic tools."

"I have you, basic tool," I said, sugar-sweet.

"Oof, Mer, painful." His eyes lit up. He knew that I was flirting. Dammit.

I was always flirting with him when I was at my meanest. Back when we were dating, I'd say the most awful things, and the next second he'd have me pinned against the wall with his hand down my pants, just as I'd intended. The trick was tone, and saying mean things that were the opposite of truth. Cam was not a tool, there was nothing basic about him, and his swagger said he knew it. That contained, relentless confidence was so attractive to me; I was baiting him. As if I wanted him to come right at me.

If Cooper weren't twenty feet away in my kitchen, if Honor weren't due back from the gym soon, Cam's grin was telling me I'd be in trouble. The little niggling voice of doubt that Cooper had let loose into my head was asking, *Yeah, but what kind of trouble?*

God, how could I be so scared, so stressed, with a tinge of bleak suspicion running through me, and also furious enough to go Full Metal Freezer in a cold war with a neighbor, and also just a little bit turned on? Okay, more than a little bit. This physical pull between us was a mind-twister; the reconnection was immediate and strong. Now that Cam was physically here, charging the scant space between us, I realized how much energy I'd dedicated to not thinking about him. I breathed in the warm smell of him, looked at the way the corners of his eyes crinkled when he smiled at me. Being without him was like visiting Denver, where the elevation wasn't enough to kill me, but every breath took work. Now a thousand green flowers were uncurling on a vine in me, carbonating my blood with oxygen, even in the midst of all this stress and fear. Or, perhaps, because of it.

"Dammit, Cam," I breathed.

"Dammit, Meribel," he whispered back.

I thought he was going to say more, but Cooper spoke from the kitchen. "It was a shit move on Addie's part. I'm really sorry." It felt good that Cooper had landed on my side, as hung up on her as he was.

Cam leaned back and switched gears. "Are you going to move again?"

Cooper turned back toward us, clearly thinking I would, also clearly not happy about it. That felt good, too.

The thought of Marker Man knowing where I slept was a weight, but one that I'd lived under now for months. I shook my head. "I've already moved thousands of miles because this psycho had my home address in LA. It bought us, what? A couple weeks of near peace? Not to mention, I have a kid who needs stability to thrive. I can't keep dragging her to new apartments that he'll find instantly, anyway, because as soon as I start filming, those locations are on the internet and he can follow me right to my next place. And the next. This could go on for years and years and years, letters and candy and veiled threats and watching."

Cooper said, almost a mutter, "Or he could come at you tomorrow. Really hurt you. It's a dice toss. I love a gamble as much as the next guy, Meribel, but these are some high stakes."

"I know." I threw my hands up. There was no way to know what was paranoid and what was smart. Not until I spent my life savings on protection, and nothing happened. Not until I gave up all I'd worked for and hid for years. Not until I did none of these things, and he climbed right into bed with me and killed me. What was I supposed to do with that? "I won't go cower on some cold Canadian island with a new nose and a new name. I don't want to give up my career to wear a mackintosh and throw my phone off a dock and then stare wistfully out to sea like a discount Meryl Streep."

"Changing apartments is worthless," Cam agreed. "I do want to beef up your security here, while I'm in town."

"Oh, *you're* going to do that," Cooper said, with a speaking glance. Like I was asking Mr. Fox to change the lock on the henhouse and keep himself a copy of the key.

Cam, oblivious to the undertones, thought he was being asked for his credentials. "Yeah. I run a small security firm, back home."

I was working not to be pissed at Cooper; Addie was to blame

here. It was hard to remember that, though, when he was also bristling up at Cam, who was only trying to help. I stood up, and I
made my tone soft as I walked over to Cooper. "Could you go talk
to Addie? Get her to take that post down, anyway."

A tense beat, and then he said, "Sure. Sure, Meribel."

I looked back at Cam and thought, *And then we'll be alone.* I
turned away before I said it out loud. I softened my tone further.
"Thank you, Cooper. I know it's a lot to ask." He'd been working so
hard to avoid her.

Cooper nodded, but gravity had come into his lithe, light body.
"I'll go see her tomorrow, okay? We already had a run-in today. I
can't—" He stopped himself, then rubbed at his eyes. "Tomorrow.
I'll sort it out. I want to go home right now and take a couple three
ibuprofen." I put my hand on his shoulder and nodded. What did
another day matter? Marker Man knew where I was. He put his
hand over mine for a moment and squeezed it. "You're okay here?"
he asked me softly.

Alone with Cam, he meant. "Sure," I said. I was almost sure.
Mostly sure.

I walked him to the door, and the last thing he said, quietly,
just to me, was "I like it that you'll gamble. I like it that you're so
damn bold. If it comes up snake-eyes for you, though, then, well.
You have my number."

Cooper walked off down the hall. As he disappeared around
the corner, Cam spoke very softly, almost in my ear. I almost came
out of my skin. I hadn't heard him following.

"The only way to stop this is to find him. I'm going to install a
doorbell camera. If Marker Man comes back, if we get a good view
of his face, it could lead us to a name."

"With a name, I can at least get a restraining order," I said. It
was smart, but I still felt bitter. "That will make him easier to pros-
ecute. The DA can offer him a deal if he tells them where to find
all of my pieces."

Cam was already examining my dead bolt and lock, but when

I spoke, he straightened up and looked at me. His mouth was grim and serious. "Meribel. If we get a name? If I find him? A restraining order will be the least of this guy's problems."

That made me feel both worse and better. He asked for pen and paper, and we went back inside so I could dig a long, thin notepad with a cat on every page out of the junk drawer. He started taking notes, narrating as he made himself a list. "Do your elevator cameras work, or are they theater?" I didn't know. "I'll find out. Also, your lock is bad. I want to put in a grade-one dead bolt. I'd like to check out the whole building, see what we can do to make it more secure before I go."

"Back to the hotel?" I sounded dismayed.

"I meant home," he said, and that was worse. "I'm supposed to drive to Clemson day after tomorrow and spend the weekend with Marco. Then back here to catch my flight home."

I couldn't ask him to stand over me while I slept for the rest of his natural-born life any more than I could go hide in a hole and never poke my nose out again. I plopped back on the sofa while Cam went room to room, taking notes and thinking. I was thinking, too.

He came out of my bedroom, and when I looked up, he said, very abruptly, "Are you seeing that guy?" My eyebrows went up, and he flushed faintly. "I mean. None of my business." A pause. "But are you?"

I shook my head, no. Just, no. I didn't say that I'd thought about it, nor did I mention my ongoing, foolish, hopeful-hope that James had been the person in the rain who had been watching. And that his gaze had been kind. Here we were, alone. Cooper thought this was dangerous, and it was, but not in the ways that he was thinking. Cam was looking at me, so intensely that I dropped my gaze and finished my drink in one long swallow.

"Honor should be back by now," I said, my voice a little shaky, reminding myself as much as him. Then it occurred to me, she really should be. Honor was a minimal-cardio person. "I'm going to pop down to the third-floor gym and check on her, okay?" I was already up and moving, and the air felt cooler and less charged with every step I took away from him.

When I opened the front door, Cam close in my wake, I saw my girl coming down the hall toward me already, her hair sweaty. There was a tall, very curvy older girl with her. Her pile of Crayola-red curls made her even taller. I lifted my hand in a wave, and even before Honor spoke, a horrible prescience made me know what she was going to say.

"Mom. This is my friend. For the birthday. Her name is Sheila Portlin."

Crap on a cracker, as my mother used to say. This was the child of Cooper's ex, Addie, who was both my elevator bitch and the woman who had doxed me.

"Wonderful," I said. Not wonderful, but Honor's face was so bright and happy. I hadn't seen this version of her smile since we left LA.

"Sheila and me want to go to Wild Waves Adventure Park on Sunday. For the birthday. Can we do that?" Honor said.

Older. Troubled. Mom who hated me, and whom I had good reason to hate. Neat. But smiling Honor knew this new friend's name.

"Of course we can," I said.

13

CAM SLEPT OVER, Cooper's suspicions be damned. I wanted his body (and his gun) between my family and my front door.

I did a lot of Making Up a Bed on the Sofa theatre for Honor: *Here is a blanket! Here is a pillow! Mommy surely isn't having bed-time man friends over that you might have to interact with in long-term father-figure ways that could upset your life!*

The idea of her mother having a boyfriend or even plain old sex was probably less awful than needing a bodyguard to not be murdered, but with Honor it was hard to read reactions in real time. Her stress manifested sideways and later, sometimes so unconnected to the source that I couldn't trace it. Part of this was autism, but my online parenting group assured me another part was standard-issue teenage girl.

I slept restlessly, cognizant of Cam just a thin wall away. Cognizant of Honor, too, our inadvertent chaperone. I woke up early, just past six, in a literal cold sweat. I'd been dreaming that Cam pulled off his face to show me that he had a second one, wet-mouthed and avid-eyed, kept under.

Ridiculous, I told my pounding heart. *If he was Marker Man, you'd know. Can a person get this close to dangerously crazy and not know?*

People could, though. People did, all the time. I'd read the news stories: The nice, quiet retired guy who had a freezer full of human heads. That high school football coach who'd been abusing all his players. Back home, a renowned surgeon in Palo Alto had kept a trafficked woman in his basement for five years. All successful people with jobs, friends, and family, hiding the fact that they were predators under their smiles. No one spotted them. I drifted in and out of sleep, my dreams telling me I had locked myself in with the very thing I feared the most, my waking mind telling me, *Impossible. Impossible.* I got up, finally, took a quick shower, and then put myself together. I felt better with a little makeup and my hair freshly blown out.

Atlanta's dog days had extended into September, so I threw on a leaf-green cashmere tank top and some boho floral silk pants that weighed exactly nothing. When I came out of my room for coffee and I saw Cam—scruffy and tousled and sexy as all hell—my late-night fears seemed far away and stupid. I wished, in fact, I'd set my shower colder.

I turned my attention to getting Honor fed and off to school, trying not to laugh when she dourly shouldered her heavy backpack and slogged off, saying, "Hump day."

Honor loved puns, but she would not get that one. I sure as hell wasn't going to explain it. Not when I could feel Cam watching me, amused, over the rim of his coffee mug.

I'd never spent the night with him. Never seen morning Cam scramble himself some eggs, rubbing at his eyes. I wanted to know what it would feel like if I pressed my mouth against the corner of his neck and shoulder, but instead, I sat down with my phone and kept busy cleaning out my inbox while Cam borrowed my bathroom.

He came out dressed in yesterday's dark jeans and wine-colored shirt, unshaven, a light jacket hiding the gun. Instead of rubbing my face into his scruff, I dragged him out of the apartment to do the building tour, in part because there was a low, low chance of staying vertical if I was alone with him. He got down to business, taking notes: secure, not secure, fixable, not fixable. He wanted to add the doorbell camera and install another on my balcony.

"I'm on the fourteenth floor," I told him as we rode down in the elevator. "You think I'm being stalked by Peter Parker?"

"The camera I want up there is a serious piece of equipment. I texted Jake to overnight me one from the office, and I'll angle it at the street, in case Marker Man comes back to moon up at your bedroom again."

I nodded, asking myself, *What if the camera catches James?* Well, then I'd know. Again I felt that strange, sad yearning for the girl I was when I lived in Georgia, for the man she'd loved. This, now. This could get my mind off Cam and up out of the gutter; I wanted my watcher to be James. Side benefit: It would absolve my guilt over watching him at dinner with his Mrs. and their spawns. We'd be even.

"I don't love the first-floor shops," Cam said, and I startled, pulled out of my own head and my past as we left the glass-walled elevator lobby. "They give anyone an excuse to be in your building." The elevator cameras were fake, which irked him. "I want to talk to your management company and the condo association head and pressure them to put real ones in. They could have caught this asshole dropping off the candy basket. Text me their numbers. At the very least, I want the lobby door code changed."

He wanted to see every entrance and exit, so we went through the heavy door that led to the storage units. Through the slatted gates, we could see boxes and bits of decaying furniture as we made our way to a heavy metal fire door. Cam checked each one, working his way all the way down the hall to the fire door, making sure every gate had a padlock on it. He grunted approval, then pointed at the sign that said EMERGENCY EXIT, ALARM WILL SOUND.

"Is that true?" he asked.

"How would I know? I'm a rules follower," I said, with modest, downcast eyes, and he laughed out loud. "Seriously, I'm never down here. The storage units are—Cam!"

I'd interrupted myself because he'd taken one big hand and shoved the bar, pushing the door open. Immediately, a shrill, obnoxious bell shrieked. Loud. Insistent. He let the door bang shut, and the noise cut out.

"I don't think it's attached to anything. It doesn't call the cops or—" He pushed it open again, and my anxiety jacked higher. Maybe I *was* a rules follower. It opened into an outdoor alcove, deep and big enough for both of us to stand. We stepped out and let the heavy door clang shut behind us to make the ringing stop. The alcove dumped into a narrow alley that ran between my building and the next. Even lined with dumpsters, it was wide enough to scoot a car through.

I stepped out into the alley and looked up and down. There were other alcoves, I saw, likely back exits for the shops. To our right, the alley ended in Tenth Avenue; cars moving quickly past. Quickly for Atlanta, anyway. Left led to a T intersection with another alley.

I stepped back toward Cam, who was inspecting the outside lock, just as he straightened and turned in to me. All at once, he was close enough for me to feel heat rising off his body. My breath stopped, and his face changed. Apex predator. Interested head tilt.

I blinked. He didn't. I turned away, fast, walking back into the alley and toward the next alcove. I couldn't hear him moving, but I could feel his eyes on my body and I knew he was close behind me. We were so alone. More alone than when we were in my apartment, which felt full of Honor even when she was at school.

You happen to meet a guy at a dog park. And he has no dog, said Cooper in the back of my head.

Shut up, Cooper.

"Meribel," Cam said.

I turned back, and he came at me. Fast. I almost screamed. Adrenaline dumped into my bloodstream. At the same time, my traitorous hands were reaching for him. He muscled me across the alley, pressing me up against the brick wall of the other building, one thigh easing between mine, his hand catching my head to save it from a bang into the bricks. Breath I didn't know I had been holding came out of me, and my flash of fear transformed into a different kind of energy. God, but this was such a bedroom move. There was a pause, like a question. I tilted my face up to him. An answer. The last bit of breath I owned pressed out of me, and there was no air in the world that could replace it until he kissed me, until I breathed him in. His other hand found the small of my back and pulled me into him.

My arms were around him, pulling him so close, and was my leg going up to wrap around him, too? Yes. Yes it was.

It was only a kiss. But an animal piece of me was thinking, *Here. Now. Let's go. Against the bricks, shaded from the morning sunshine, and why did I wear pants when I own at least a hundred little flippy skirts, a thousand swingy dresses?* His body against mine pressed out all of my suspicions. If anything, my more cerebral self was thinking, *Dumbass, you live here. Drag him back upstairs before you end up arrested or having alley sex on YouTube.* I broke the kiss to tell him we should go up, and then I froze.

We were being watched. He felt me stiffen and go cold. He pulled back, his hand falling away from my ass, his face a question.

"Eyes on us," I said. I knew it. I knew it.

He didn't question me. He'd seen me do this trick twenty times. He was turning, looking all around, hawkish and alert. I thought about his grim mouth when he'd said, *If I find him? A restraining order will be the least of this guy's problems.* The gun was in his shoulder holster. I had felt it when he pulled me urgently against him.

It could be anyone, though. Anyone. I felt gazes, not identities. But. What if Marker Man was here? Me and Marker Man. Cam and a gun. I could feel my pounding heartbeat like a whole-body pulse. I peered up and down the narrow road, but I saw no one.

Cam started up the alley toward Tenth Avenue, me sticking

behind him, close. I looked back over my shoulder and—there. Movement. Just a flash. A figure jerking back into the center alcove. Someone had peeked out. I grabbed his arm and he stopped. I pointed at the place.

He eased a hand into his jacket and I heard the soft click as he unsnapped the gun from the holster. I dry-swallowed, scared, but did not stop him. He didn't take the gun out, but his hand stayed close.

He pointed for me to go out to Tenth, where cars were streaming by and the occasional pedestrian passed, hurrying down the sidewalk. I shook my head. Pointed at the alcove, emphatic. He splayed one big hand on my chest and pressed me back into the bricks, like, *Stay here, then.*

All at once, I was the dumb girl in a movie. TSTL, "too stupid to live," we called that girl, and she showed up in so damn many scripts. She ran directly into the exact trouble that a smart man in the scene immediately preceding had pointed out, doing exactly what he told her not to do. While this man fought to the death for her, she made big-eyed terror face for flash-fire cuts instead of picking up a baseball bat and helping.

I tried not to take those parts. I wanted to play women who were stronger, smarter, more complex. Women I would be proud to show my daughter. Was I playing her now? Because this had to be a movie. It felt so fake and bright and awful. Me pressed against a wall, heart pounding. Someone in the alley watching. A broad-shouldered man, compact and dangerous, moving deftly down the street with such tight, coiled grace it hurt my heart and scared me. My hand on my mouth. Waiting for the hero to—

Fuck that. I started after him. If this was a movie, it was mine. If it was real—and it was real—it was still my scene, my life, my stalker. Cam felt or heard me behind him. He looked back and gave me a sharp nod, like, *Okay, then.*

He paused to the side of the alcove, met my eyes. When I nodded he turned in a rush of sudden movement, so fast he blurred for me. I heard a short, sharp scream like a bark, and I think I screamed, too, same way, in a burst. My whole body froze. Cam was already catapulting backward, pulling his hand away from his jacket. It was empty. No gun. He almost banged into the wall, his hands up.

"Okay," he said, so calm and soft. "Okay, okay."

"I will end you, you piece of shit!" The voice was loud and female, young and furious and scared. I found that I could move again.

Cam, still with his hands up, repeated, "It's okay. I'm not here to hurt you."

I moved to him, putting my back to the wall as well, so I could see into the alcove.

"Don't you touch me!" She was flattened against a fire door, a can of Mace held out in front of her with stiff, shaking arms. She was pressing and pressing at the trigger. She was young, high school aged, or maybe college. Her dark hair was cropped in crazy pieces, and her eyes were wild. Under her layers of dark, musty clothing, I could see her chest rising and falling; she was breathing so fast and hard. The canister shook in her hands.

"Hey, now," I said. My heart was still pounding, slow to get the memo we were mostly safe. "Hey."

She registered my presence and a little of the wildness went out of her eyes. Her gaze shifted back and forth between us, and she stopped pressing at the trigger. She lowered the can a few inches.

A ratty blanket on the ground behind her held a red leather journal, some colored ink pens, and a black trash bag stuffed with what looked like more dark, musty clothing. She was homeless? This child? The poor thing. I wondered how she'd gotten here. Drugs, or mental illness, or a bad home life, or all of these. I started fumbling in my purse, and she raised the can back up, eyes rolling.

"How old is your Mace? The mechanism's broken," Cam said, still so calm. "I'm glad, or I'd be rolling on the ground right now."

He sounded almost admiring, and I felt it, too. At the crucial moment, my own body had frozen instead of picking fight or flight.
This girl had done her best to fight. Maybe, if my life were more
like hers, my body would pick fight, too. When I thought of it that
way, her valor made me desperately sad.

"Here," I said, holding out three twenties. It was all the cash I
had on me.

She lowered her arms, then threw the Mace can sideways into
the wall with a disgusted sound. She looked at the money, then to
Cam, then to me.

"What does he want for that?" She was talking to me. Negoti-
ating. It took me three long seconds to understand what the child
meant.

"Oh, honey, no," I said. "No, no. Just take it. Get some lunch.
Get a room." Or drugs. Whatever. I could not control what the girl
did with the money. All I could do was give it or not.

It took another three seconds, her crafty eyes shifting back
and forth, and then she darted forward and snatched the bills. Her
cheeks were very red.

"Sorry I scared you," Cam said, lowering his hands, slow and
careful. I started to pull him away, but he resisted, and then he dug
in his jacket pocket and came out with a can of his own. "Pepper
spray. New. This one will work, if you flip the safety off, so be careful where you aim it. It's gel, so you have less chance of blowback."
He pointed to the safety, and then held it out. Her eyes narrowed
again. She stayed back, and after a second, he set it down at his feet
and turned to leave.

This time, I balked. She was very pale, but sloe-eyed in a way that
reminded me of Honor. She made my heart hurt, and the fact that
he had so matter-of-factly armed her made my mind go to all the
reasons she might need a weapon.

"Can I help you? In some way?" Her eyes squinted with disdain
at the question. "Could I call somebody for you?"

She snorted. "Call my mom," she said. "Tell her I said hey." The sarcasm was so thick, even Honor would have clocked it.

"Come on," Cam said. This time, I let him pull me away.

We headed back toward Tenth. When I looked back, the canister was gone, and she was out of sight. "God, maybe I *should* move." We kept going. I said, "I don't think she was the person I felt watching. You surprised her, and my skin is crawling, still. Although that could be residual."

My heart had certainly not stopped banging around like it was trying to escape my chest. I could feel my pulse in my hands and my face, the thumping residue of panic. We stepped out onto Tenth and looked around at the few pedestrians. They all seemed to be hurrying off to somewhere, not watching me at all.

I walked to Java House's big plate-glass window, and I cupped my hands near the glass to peer inside. This time of day, it was packed. Three big groups of college kids clustered around the larger tables. The others held mommy singles and duos with strollers and the latest book club picks.

No one stared back at me. No one was waiting by the bathrooms, alone. The only males in the whole place were three of the regular baristas and the college boys and a gay couple sharing a slice of pound cake at a two-top.

Cam stepped up, his reflection appearing behind the translucent me caught in the glass.

"Let's go back to your place," he said.

I could feel his heat, steady at my back. I looked at the two of us, together. The way he loomed over and around me, taller, wider. More dangerous. More armed.

"Cooper thinks you're Marker Man," I told him.

His reflected face was serious, unsurprised. "What do you think?"

I met his eyes, and my bad dreams, my lingering doubts, all dissipated. Cooper was wrong. The man I had seen oozing down that alley with his hand on a gun wasn't Marker Man. The man in that alley was bent on unleashing violence against my stalker.

"You're not. I know you're not. But—" I scanned the tables again. No lone men that I could see. No men dawdling on the street, sneaking glances at me in the reflection. "But he was here, Cam. It was him." I could feel it in a way that I could not explain.

Marker Man was watching us.

14

HE SAT QUIET, his breath gone shallow and hot, trying to feel Meribel's gaze passing over him. He knew she could feel people watching her. He knew everything about her. She'd talked about her "actor's superpower" in at least four interviews. Now he tried to channel it, make it his own. If it belonged to her, then it was his.

Yes! A sweep of heat across his shoulders. So intense. A burning. She was on the other side of Java House's big window, looking for him, urgent, urgent. Was her nose pressed to the glass? Yes. Was she leaving little eager, sweaty handprints? She was. He could feel that, too.

He didn't turn around or meet her eyes, though he was so tempted. They hadn't been this physically close since the breakup. She must by now be desperate for him, full of sweet regret. But he wouldn't show himself. Not with the poaching a-hole standing there, too. His presence would taint their reunion.

What an unpleasant surprise to see him here, in their new city, pawing at Meribel like an animal, grinding her into a wall. Disgusting.

He'd thought about striding over, fast and quiet, pulling the pistol out of the small of his back and pressing it to the side of that guy's head. Pop. The end. He could almost see the blood arcing out to spatter on her pretty face, like red freckles. Her relief to have that ape's dead hands fall off her body. Her smile to see him.

He'd walked past the alley twice, trying to decide. Usually, he would look past her at a tree, a dog, some lesser bitch, keeping her at the far edge of his peripheral vision so she wouldn't feel his gaze, but today, he had stared openly. Usually, if someone stared at her so directly, she would sense it instantly. Her head would go up and on the swivel, her nostrils flaring. She was so repulsed by the mauling the California asshole was subjecting her to, it had taken a minute.

She'd felt him, though, in the end. Love was like that. As soon as he saw her pushing the ape away, he'd hurried past and slipped into Java House. There he plopped down into a chair, back to the window, at the largest table, which was already holding half a dozen nerdy college boys. He'd leaned back and announced, "I'm waiting for my drink, here."

They'd all said, "Sure, man," and "Whatever."

That's right, you stupid jackasses. I didn't ask. I told you. He hadn't even ordered a drink. He had only that second burst in, but not one of these dorks had the stones to challenge him. *Eat balls, book nerds. I sit where I want.*

He was panting as if he'd been running, filled with a black fury at seeing another man put hands on Meribel. He needed to calm down.

He didn't blame her. They were like Ross and Rachel. On a break. That was another good sitcom. He liked a lot of the old ones, but *Belinda's World* was best. He'd picked Didi to be his, and she had been, and she would be again. Soon.

He imagined standing, turning to face the window, smiling, seeing her eyes light up with love and recognition. When they were truly reunited, she would be so happy. He knew what she wanted, better than she did.

He felt her gaze drop, felt her moving away with the asshole. This guy was so damn vulture-y and low! His rage made the air taste hot, even scorched. Someone needed to teach him not to poach.

That thought got him up and moving, out and then down Tenth, to a little side street where he'd parked. The Roadtrek Ranger was too cumbersome for city driving, so he'd picked up an old Honda motorbike on the cheap at a flea market in Arkansas. The cash-fat night-deposit bag from the diner in Flagstaff stretched to cover it, but barely. Now the Ranger was at a campsite way out west of the city, and he used the bike to zip invisibly through traffic. Meribel liked motorcycles. She'd learned to ride one doing an indie film called *Worn Hearts*. Her best sex scene. If he froze it just right, there were a few frames where she flashed her little tits.

He got on and started the engine. He liked the roar of the bike waking up. In an interview, Meribel once said, "Not to be a walking cliché, but I felt powerful and sexy on that Kawasaki. Maybe because it's stupid dangerous, and dangerous things are always a little sexy. Whatever. Let's agree that I'm at least a cliché that can pop wheelies."

He headed out of town, thinking, *Powerful and sexy*. He wanted her to see him, straddling this bike. He'd let her get on and cling to him, riding bitch, pressing up so close, panting and trembling. He could almost feel her. Soon.

His preparations were close to complete. He'd taken another shit job, at a diner on the ATL Perimeter, nowhere near the campsite, just last week. He'd kept it through the weekend, until the waitress he liked best was closing. Alone. Everyone called her Molly, but her name tag said "Margaret." Her bright hair had dark roots. That Monday night-deposit bag hadn't been crazy fat like the Saturday night one he got in Flagstaff.

He wondered whatever happened to that Flagstaff waitress. Callista. The little bitch with the good legs. He liked to remember the way she said, "Please," when he pulled the gleaming knife out of the sink. So clean, which he thought was polite. That made him grin. A mannerly knifing. He remembered turning the blade back and forth in the light for her, wondering what it would it feel like to stick it in her.

She held out the bank bag. "Take it. You can take it."

"Aren't you scared I'm going to rape you?" he asked, curious.

As soon as he said it, she was. Maybe she was relieved, too. Maybe excited. Maybe lying down under him was what she secretly wanted, and that's why she ignored him so hard. The knife was an excuse, so she could grunt and sweat and writhe like a piglet and still pretend that she was not a whore. Even Meribel played this game, sometimes. Women were that way.

"Please," she said again, and big, fat tears came spilling down her cheeks. He stepped forward and held his hand out for the thick deposit bag. "Give it."

She was happy to give it to him, stepping in so obediently to pass it over, then her eyes went wide and wild when he shoved the knife into her abdomen anyway.

He'd had to really push. Stabbing was hard. People were so thick and meaty. Still, she was more surprised than him. She'd been thinking about taking her dress off, showing him her parts, and when he jerked the knife back out of her middle, she stood for a second with blood in a fast bloom soaking her uniform. She was slow to crumple, clutching her core, and her dress flipped up. Her underpants were old and faded. Whore. Just because he and Meribel were on a break didn't mean that *he* would not be faithful. He took her phone and left the waitress in a heap. He liked remembering her bleeding on the tile floor, making that little whistling breath. So shocked.

He was still doing searches for "Callista" and "Flagstaff" and "Slips Diner" online, to see if she was dead, but it was hard because of paywalls. As if he would pay for the shit local paper just to see if he had offed some bitch.

That's how he said it on the message board, when he asked if anyone lived there and had access. He told those incels he liked to keep a right count of his dead mouthy bitches. That got them excited, yip-yapping and bouncing, wanting details. He had fed 'em, the pussies. Not a one of them had ever put a knife right in like that. Like he had done, now. He liked to remember pushing through her gristle.

No one had found a story about a woman stabbed dead in a diner, though, so maybe she'd lived. He preferred to think she'd died. Maybe there was no story because no one cared too much. She was just a waitress.

Rocketing back toward his campsite, he felt—not mad, not at Meribel—disappointed that she wasn't being as faithful, not fully waiting for him. She must have gotten his candy basket. She must know he was ready to make up. She would have to apologize for straying, beg and cry at his feet. In the end, he would forgive her and save his grudge for the squatty, dead-eyed jerk who manhandled his girl right in front of him. The guy was shorter than him, and square, with a craggy, weather-beaten face like a leathery, mean dog.

He needed to get Meribel alone, so he needed another really good deposit envelope. He had to stock up on supplies before he and Meribel came back together. He wanted to take her out into the real wilds. No people. No other campers. Just the two of them, alone, for a long, long time.

He turned into the campsite and slowed down, so as not to call attention to himself. The Ranger was in the older part, empty except for him because it had no sewer hookups, but he had to pass through the new part, full of hippies and families. Now that he was close, his stomach buzzed and fizzed. He hadn't meant to be away this long.

He was worried for nothing, though. His campsite was all very quiet and correct as he pulled up. He took his helmet off and pulled a couple of Tums out of his pocket, enjoying the chalky crunch.

He chained his bike up, and then he went inside to fix himself a chicken noodle cup. This kind had powdered milk in it. He added water and put it in the microwave. He liked to use less water than it said. That was how his mom, who was dead now, fixed it. She would sing, *Mac-a-chee, mac-a-chee, what's your dinner going to be*, when she cooked pasta, even if it was spaghetti. When she did make real mac-a-chee, she liked to put in chunked ham and canned mushrooms and call it Fancy Dinner. She had bad taste in men and she drank, but he missed her whispery-soft voice. She never gave him too much shit. It was sad that she was dead.

While his food got hot and soft in the water, he got out paper and his markers and set them on the kitchenette's work counter. He drew Meribel in profile, flat on a bench, naked. Hot pink nipples that smelled like Frankenberry cereal. Orange hair, curtains to match the carpet. He drew the bench propped up by two human heads instead of legs. The man-ape's leathery frown face held up one end. The head at the other end had a sweep of light brown hair, yellow streaked, and blue eyes as round and blank as marbles behind hipster glasses. The neighbor he'd seen Meribel canoodling with at Java House.

Meribel had been missing him that day. She had run out of the coffeehouse into the rain, very tearful, and the neighbor had followed. That guy had been so eager to get arms around her. Cooper Hayette. His name was on his mailbox, along with his apartment number, which was very close to Meribel's. Predatory, all these men.

"Don't think I've forgotten you, ya fuck. I know where you live," he said, scrawling cherry-scented blood burping out of Cooper Hayette's mouth, red-staining his smug, dead face.

Then he sat on the bed to eat his creamy noodles. The bed was custom, a built-in double. The front half was a storage chest, and the back half also had a rough storage space he could access from a hatch outside the camper. That one was empty. He planned to fill it with jugged water and rations, so he and Meribel could live off the grid a good long while.

So many things could be hidden in this clever camper; it had no wasted spaces. The inside chest, underneath the bed where he was sitting, was already full. He liked sitting here. The mattress was thin. He could feel soft thumps and vibrations under his haunches as he ate. He liked that even more.

When he was full, he stood up and threw his Styrofoam noodle cup away and then pushed back the mattress to reveal the hinged lid of the storage chest. He unlocked it, worked the latch, and lifted it.

Last time he looked, she had eyes like a raccoon from crying. Now her eyes were bare and red and swollen. Her waitress skirt had rucked up on her legs so high he could see a bit of ugly cotton flower panties like his mother used to wear. Maybe she'd been kicking with her bound legs at the lid. That was bad to do. He'd told her not to be loud. The smell of urine and the snot crusting her nose made her seem like a toddler, though she was at least thirty-five. Too young for those underpants. When he was working at her diner, her hair looked good, gleaming pale red gold. From this angle, though, her dark roots were obvious.

He should take the gag off and give her a drink of water if he wanted to keep her much longer. She'd cried so much she had no water to make tears left. Her mouth worked around the gag, so dry he heard the click. He took his pistol out and showed it to her, reminding her he had it. He turned the weapon back and forth, pointing at her, and away, at her, and away, tracking up and down her body, to be sure she understood how good she needed to be if he ungagged her. If she begged nice enough, she'd maybe get a drink.

Oh, hey. She had more tears inside her after all.

15

CAM CRASHED ON my couch again after a long day installing cameras, upgrading my alarm system, and hounding the building's management company and the president of our co-op board about whole-building security issues. First, though, we revisited the precinct together, taking the basket. I wasn't sure if the escalation made Avensen sit up tall and pay attention, or if it was simply Cam's male and military presence, but at least he seemed to take things much more seriously. I left it all with him, glad to have the horrible thing gone from my house. Cam didn't have time to go to the hotel and get his toothbrush. He grabbed a new one at the drugstore downstairs, along with three-packs of boxers, white Hanes T-shirts, and new socks.

I lay wide awake in my own bed, thinking about Cam and Marker Man. They had only one thing in common: both were willing to cross the country in pursuit of me. Oh, the difference one small word could make, if that word was "yes." Marker Man hadn't asked the question. In his eyes, I didn't have opinions or ideas or even a soul. I was only his idea of me. Cam saw me whole. He'd come to Atlanta, and he'd decided what he wanted. Now he was asking me if I wanted it, too.

Yes meant I would walk down a road toward something real with him. Did I love him? Or did I feel so strongly because he was a shield from danger, or because the sex was so damn good? *Yes* meant I would not call James, and I'd stop wishing James would call me. I didn't know how to stop wanting that.

At the same time, I was hyper-aware of Cam's body sprawled out warm and sleepy on my sofa, one thin wall away. Too thin a wall, considering my child was tucked up snug behind another. I didn't open my door and whisper him to my bed, but God, that was a thing I wanted. I wasn't ready to say, *Yes, forever,* or even *Yes, let's try,* but I really wanted to say, *Yes, tonight.* So much so that it almost felt inappropriate.

Why? I was single and human. I was a mother, not dead.

It was habit. Until Cam, the best sex of my life had been two decades in the past. It hurt to remember how careful James and I were about birth control, back when we were college sophomores. We worked so hard to *not* be pregnant. Cam was one wall away, but sometimes James felt closer, even with twenty years, thirty miles, four kids, and one wife standing between us. The history ran so deep. It all felt so unfinished.

When I moved to LA, James was the only person I had ever been with. Then I went to a regulation LA party, and met an agent, and followed him upstairs, and got bent over a leather recliner. That encounter felt so separate from me that it was almost second person. It had felt second person in the moment, too.

Because—if you're not absolute hot garbage—how do you find yourself listening to the downstairs hum of party conversation and a jazz combo's generic background version of "Summertime" while your dress is rucked up to your hips so some middle-aged asshole who might or might not be a big-time agent can have sex with you? Two minutes before, you watched him pick up the guest-room phone and make a call, ostensibly to book you an audition. In your hand, you hold a yellow Post-it note from a pad he picked up off the bedside table. There's an address and a name and a time on it. The adhesive feels tacky on your fingers, and you think, *It's all BS. He can't really be an agent? Can he? If he is . . .*

When he grabs your neck, you freeze. It's fast and surprising when he turns you, pushes you. You bend. You feel your dress ruck up, feel your underwear shoved aside. He's physically insistent and not asking and anyway, what does it matter? Even if you're dry and it hurts and you don't like him and he's old enough to be the dad you never knew. You let it happen. You're drunk. You left James without a word, and he must hate you, and you deserve his hate, and you hate you, and you can't make babies, so what's the risk here? You heard the crinkle of the condom, his hands leaving your hips briefly to roll it on. You could have straightened then, but no. You stayed bent, legs straight, face pushed into the leather upholstery, holding the shape he pressed you into. Maybe you think, *They took out all the parts that made me female, so what is this guy fucking, really?* Maybe you think, *This is what my body deserves.*

My body *had* failed. It had failed at all the things.

I almost didn't go to the address on that Post-it. Showing was a straight-up act of masochism; I was sure I would find a parking garage or a vacant lot. But no, there was really an audition. Not a casting call, but the real thing. Me with a script and a screen test and five important people at the table, paying attention, liking what I was putting down. One of them was the actual casting director. One of them was the showrunner.

The offer to play Didi, when it came, went through the agent who had set it up in the first place. He had to ask the casting director for my contact information so he could offer me the job. He thought it was funny that he hadn't bothered to ask even my last name at the party, and then I'd landed the part.

"I really do have quite good instincts for these things," he told me on the phone. "I should have trusted myself and gotten a number, but here we are. Amazing, yes? Your life is going to change. I smell a hit."

The next time I saw him was in a fishbowl glass conference room at CEA, watching his partners and assistants bustling about as I signed whatever he put in front of me. I had no understanding of how excellent the terms he'd negotiated were, but he was very good at his job. From then on, it was strictly business between us. He behaved as if there never was a leather chair or bad jazz or a girl with no uterus who had to steal her roommate's pads for two days after, and he stayed my agent for four years.

I remembered, though. Every time I took his calls, that ninety seconds I'd spent bent over a chair was with me. He hadn't finished because his phone buzzed and he said, *Oh, my client's here.* He stepped back and put himself away, zipped up, and went right back to the party, leaving me there to put myself back together. I wasn't sure I had yet. Even now.

When he left for another agency, I stayed with his former assistant, Liza. He was torqued, but for me it was a relief. After a bitchy snit, he was professional about it. For years after, until he did me the favor of dropping dead of a heart attack in the middle of a luncheon, I'd run into him at premieres or other industry events, where we were friendly. *Air-kiss, air-kiss, Hello, Hello.*

While I was working on *Belinda's World*, I'd had a lot of sex. Why not? I'd been rewound to eighteen again, and I was on a hot show; everyone wanted a piece. Who cared if I partied? I played the bitch, not the ingénue. I got a little bit into coke culture, but I was smart enough or lucky enough or had been loved well enough by Mom to tap out before it ruined me.

As *Belinda's World* lost momentum, so did my love life, such as it was. I got in therapy (everyone in LA is in therapy), and I realized I was neither happy nor having fun. I still wanted, more than anything, a family.

Wallace encouraged me to adopt, a thing I spoke of with both longing and a lot of fear. I was unsure how to start, even, but Wallace hooked me up with a lawyer who walked me through my options, then fast-tracked the process. Once I had Honor, well, I wasn't wholly celibate, but Wallace called me "celibate-adjacent." That was pretty damn accurate.

Until this man. With Cam sprawled on my sofa, I couldn't stop remembering that I liked sex. I liked sex with him, anyway. He made it about me in such excellent ways. The last time I'd had sex that truly felt like it was for me was on the other side of the accident that had changed my life entirely. I didn't sneak out and drag Cam back into my lair and have my way with him, though. Even though he'd made it very plain that he was game. No, I'd cast myself as Sensible Mother.

What I learned: Sensible Mothers don't get laid, and they probably don't sleep well, either.

In the morning, I was showered and made-up and fully dressed before I poked my nose out of my room. Fitted black pants, a cami, and a sheer floral tunic wrap thing that was all complicated ties and windings and flutter sleeves. I worked myself into it like I was putting on a whole-body chastity belt. Cam had done what he could to make my apartment more secure, and today he planned to drive up to Clemson to see his son for a few days. *It would take that long to get me out of this stupid outfit*, I thought as I searched for the hole the first tie went through.

When I stepped out, he was still asleep. He had on one of the plain white T-shirts that made his tan skin seem darker, almost golden. He'd pushed the sheet down around his waist, and I could see the waistband of his navy boxers. I stood there trying to remember how to swallow until a small curl of a smile told me he was with me.

He said, without so much as cracking an eyeball, "I can feel you looking. Is there coffee?"

I scuttled away to the kitchen, flushed, feeling caught, and brought him back a mug. Splash of milk, no sugar. It felt intimate to know that this was how he liked it. He thanked me and went back into my room to take a shower in my triple-jetted stall. I started making breakfast and thinking a little too hard about exactly what that might look like when Honor threw her door open, like *Ta-da!* She was vibrating with happy energy, very pleased. I was scrambling eggs with the veggies left over from a stir-fry, but she went right for her cereal.

"I might be thirteen right now," she announced, pouring a big bowlful.

"You might!" It was true. "Do you want to be?"

She shook her head. "I want to be thirteen on the flume ride, Sunday. I'll go through the haunted castle part still being twelve and turn teenager at the very top, when the water dragon breathes on me, and then whoosh down all new. With Sheila."

"That sounds perfect," I told her. She liked choosing the moment when she clicked into a brand-new age. I'd made that fun for her, because we were never going to know her exact birthday. Not for sure.

Honor was left in a laundry basket at a fire station on September 10, 2004. She'd been a week old, give or take a couple days, which made today, the eighth, perfectly possible. A note on torn, lined paper pinned onto her blanket said, *Heres my heart and on my honor Id of kept her if I could.* I had that note stored safely for her in an envelope in my jewelry chest. I had the blanket, too, pink with elephants all over and a cigarette burn in one corner.

I'd shown her these things when she first started asking about her bio-mom, telling her that her gorgeous dark eyes and her smile and her first name and our life together were all gifts from that unknown lady, who had clearly loved her. I'd also gotten her DNA analyzed, hoping to one day help her explore and connect to her heritage; there was no telling what Honor was by simply looking at her. The results? My child had ancestors from four continents and a host of countries: Ireland, England, Senegal, Scotland, Mali. She was 8 percent Polynesian, and 6 percent Indigenous, and nothing more than 10 percent. In short, my girl was an American.

Newborn Honor had olive skin and a shock of flossy hair that stood up straight like jet-black wheat. Her eyes were that murky newborn color, and she was so fresh her fringe of dark lashes were still crumpled and fine, nearly invisible. God, I'd fallen so hard, the second I saw her.

The lawyer was a straight-up shark who careened me fast into motherhood around all obstacles and corners, as Wallace promised he could. Honor was placed with me as her foster mom, adoption track, while she was still in the hospital being treated for jaundice and cocaine and nicotine withdrawal. I could empathize with every part of that but jaundice. We walked the hospital hallways and rocked in a nursing chair, her crying, me crooning, exhausted but bonding. I took her home and waited, sweating it out with my screaming darling, so in love with her already that I worried I would die if the bio-mother changed her mind and showed within the window. Now here she was, eating her cereal, swinging her legs. Thirteen. Give or take a day or three.

"Can I have some of that egg scramble, to take with me?" She really was setting up for a growth spurt. I put some into a wrap with a little cheese and then rolled it in tinfoil. She slung her backpack up onto her shoulders.

"Is he coming to the birthday?" She was looking at Cam's abandoned bedding on the sofa.

"No. He's leaving town today." I watched carefully, but her reaction was as neutral as the question, simply soliciting information. I suspected she had zero thought that Cam might be important in my life. She was asking if I thought we needed more protection at her birthday party. My answer set her more at ease.

I handed her the wrap and let her go. She hated for me to walk her down to the car service, which was developmentally correct. She was pushing at me in all the right ways, and my fear of Marker Man couldn't stop her from wanting to grow up. Our compromise was for her to wait in the lobby until she saw the car pull up, then text me once she was in. Today, though, feeling anxious, I went out on the balcony to watch her get safely off to school.

When the car service SUV appeared, she came out of the alley, not the door. My eyebrows came together. She'd promised not to go into the stairs alone. Almost before I could complete the thought, Sheila came out behind her. That child of mine! Letter of the law, not the spirit, always. I shook my head, rueful and amused, and waited until I saw her safely loaded. Sheila kept on walking up the street.

When I came back in the room, Cam was leaning in the doorway to the master bath wearing his dark jeans and his drugstore finds. Wet hair. Fresh shave.

"I need to go to my hotel and pack."

"I'll drive you," I said immediately, because I am a masochist.

He didn't object, and we headed down silently together. We stopped in the lobby so I could hit the mailroom and collect some flyers and two more letters drenched in stinking marker. One postmarked here in Georgia only yesterday. God, he must be close. I met Cam's eyes and shook my head, mouth pressed. I shoved them unopened into my bag.

I started to stalk out of the cramped space, but he took my arm, halting me. "Meribel. Do you want me to stay?" His dark eyes were serious, his mouth set. "I can push back with Marco, delay my flight . . ."

I did want that. So bad.

I shook my head, no. "I wish I could write Marker Man a letter of my own. I'd ask him to please break into my house while you're here so you could beat him into a paste and send him off to prison. But this could go on months. Years, even. You can't sleep on my sofa until you die of old age, waiting."

"Yeah," he agreed. Even so, his eyes were saying that he might, if I asked.

I wanted to ask. My body wanted me to ask. But fear, even layered over with good sex, was a terrible foundation for commitment. I couldn't ask this man to upend his life and move here, to James's city. Not if I was still hoping, every other minute, that James was watching me with kinder eyes than Marker Man. I couldn't see a future with Cam in this city that was so soaked in my past.

"You have a life, Cam. Go see your kid, and then go back to it. Nothing has changed since we broke up in LA."

He looked like he wanted to say something. He even started to, twice. Not much of a talker, Cam. Whatever it was, he swallowed it and nodded. His eyes were so sad then, sad and tired.

We went down to the garage in silence and got into my car. The worst of morning rush hour was on the wane, and it was a fast two miles to get him back to his hotel. Within minutes I could see it down the road, tall and looming. It was like the building was coming at us. In three minutes I'd pull in, and let him out, and he would go inside, and then he would be gone.

"Meribel," he said. Just my name.

I kept my eyes on the road. "You can't move all the way across the country because I'm scared." I didn't say, *I can't stop thinking about a different man, and you deserve to be someone's first, best choice.* Instead, I told him something just as true: "If you moved here to protect me, it would feel too much like using you. For you to uproot your whole life—it has to be more than that."

A moment's pause, and then he said, softly, "For me, it's more than that."

I swallowed. "Cam. I have no way to know. We have to call this thing. We have to be done with one another."

I pulled into the turnaround, but he didn't get out. He waited until I put us into park and then he looked me dead in the eye.

"So this is how we say goodbye? Like last time. You say we're done, and we're done? I'm good with that. That's the best way. Don't kiss me goodbye. Don't come upstairs with me. I don't want you to." His hand reached out and took mine, though. His was warm and callused. He had a half-smile, and his eyes had gone all dark, and he was blatantly, blatantly lying.

I felt my whole face flush red. I turned and eased my car into the valet line.

16

WE BARELY MADE it to his room. Truthfully, we started in the elevator, and it was a mercy that we had it to ourselves. Upstairs, as soon as the door slammed behind us, he picked me straight up with one arm around my waist, my legs already twining up to wrap him, and he kissed me. His arms, his smell, his cotton shirt—even the room felt like a turn-on. Hotels always did. The little soaps and anonymity.

He bulled me backward toward the bed so fast the room blurred, or my eyes wouldn't focus. I didn't care. This was goodbye, and we were going to make it count. The weird wrap shirt that had been so hard to get on was helpless against him. He pulled a string, a bow unraveled, and then it was drooping off my shoulders. He tossed me back onto the bed, then knelt, tugging at my jeans until I was wearing just the cami. My hands fisted in his dark hair, his head between my legs, and I fell into it and let it happen, made it happen, all the things we liked, pulling him up to me, into me, and it was not enough, it couldn't be. I was desperate for him, missing him even as we did it all again.

After, we lay side by side in the crumpled ice-white bedding, staring blankly and peacefully at the ceiling like exhausted idiots. The clock would not stop moving, though. After a little, he reached for his phone. I was so drugged with it that I fell asleep listening to him tell the car rental people he was going to be late, and to hold his car. Hard, fast asleep. I felt so safe here by him in a tall, tall building with hundreds of rooms, all the same, and no way for anyone but Cam to know which one held me.

I woke up to the shrill yell of a telephone. He'd set a wake-up call, and I saw that I had half an hour to get home before Honor's carpool service dropped her off. Cam was gone, bag and all, but I had a note from him. He'd paid for another night, so I could sleep. He'd also left me a steel lockbox on the pillow.

> The code is 7644. It's loaded, and it's unregistered. You know how to use it. You should keep it.

That's all. No goodbye. We'd already said it, or maybe he didn't want to. I sat up, half angry, half scared. I knew what was in the box. I did know how, thanks to my safety training and range practice to play Becca Tart. *Loaded*, his note said. *Unregistered*. Cam could be a little shady. I thought of texting him, immediately, angrily, saying, *Turn around, drive back, and get this damn gun.*

I didn't. Instead, I put the heavy box inside the hotel's plastic laundry bag and carried it out with me. I think it felt heavier than it actually was. I needed to think this through, later, when I was not so simultaneously sated and sad and furious.

I hit traffic on the way back. The gun had thrown me, and getting my stupid tunic thing back on had been a struggle. I burst into the condo ten minutes too late, calling, "Sorry! Sorry!"

I knew immediately that Honor wasn't there, though. The apartment had that dead-air empty feeling. I stopped in the doorway.

My heart rate jacked, and my fingers tightened on the plastic-wrapped metal box in my arms. In that moment, I knew I was keeping the gun. I wanted it. I wanted to get it out and run with it, drawn, to find my kid and shoot any stranger I saw looming near her.

I tried to suck some air into my screwed-shut lungs. She was only a few minutes late. That fact didn't change my death grip on the gun safe, nor did it slow my heart rate. I wasn't sure if I was being the s'mother or the right amount of cautious. I set the gun box down and texted her.

Where are ya, kiddo?

Instantly, I saw those dots that told me she was texting back, and all my airways opened. Her answer made me smile: I am in the building. Talking to my friend.

Her *friend*. I rubbed at my eyes. It had been a day. I had big emotional whiplash from goodbyes and guns, and a small, bonus whiplash from a flash of fear and then joy for my child. I decided I should lean in and take the joy while I had some available.

Granted, Sheila was older and troubled, and her doxing mother had an enormous butt-stick about me jammed in deep, deep, deep—but still. Honor's *friend*. I hid the gun box deep in the big roll-out drawer that held the pots and pans, and then I started making the after-school snack she always seemed to want these days. My pleasure lasted until my daughter stomped in a few minutes later. I looked up, smiling, only to find her thick, straight brows were thunderously lowered and her walk was extra-stompy.

"Sheila's mom says she can't come," Honor said. She slammed the door and then hurled herself down on the sofa. "So not a birthday." Her whole small body was as clenched as a fist.

I kept my own shoulders loose and my voice light. "Do they already have plans? We could pick another day." I was filling up with murder on the inside, where it counted, but outside I stayed warm and cheery.

Honor shrugged, uncomforted. "Sheila says her mother doesn't know you, at all, so she can't ride off in some car with you to who knows where." This was a quote. I could hear it in the intonations. "Sheila says her mother is a—" she stopped abruptly.

I'd already filled in that blank. *I am with you, Sheila*, I thought.

"Don't despair," I said. If not knowing me was the problem, well, Addie Portlin was about to get a damn crash course. Did the bitch need my résumé? Letters of recommendation from former employers and some therapists? Hey, maybe a blood sample? Why not. "You should have snack and do gym, and tonight, when she's home from work, I'll walk down and have a talk with her."

Honor looked at me, almost alarmed. She wasn't great at reading a room, but she knew my moods and could be sensitive to them. "Are you going to yell?"

"Of course not! I will be a sugar-rabbit, a baby deer, a tiny, furry lemming. You can draw more flies with honey than bazookas," I told her as I handed over a nut butter and banana sandwich. Not even my messed-up cliché could make her smile. That made me feel more bazooka than ever. Sheila's mother was a bug-eyed fly, rubbing its hands together on a pile of offal like Queen Shit of Turd Mountain, as my mom used to say. She was exercising power over my kid to get at me. What the hell had Honor ever done? What had I done, for that matter, other than go to the gym and have coffee with her ex?

I waited until seven thirty, but the time gap didn't improve my temper. I put our supper dishes in the sink and told Honor that she could have her screen time, if she wanted. I was going to speak to Addie Portlin. I yanked the door open and went sailing down the hall. Honor, for a wonder, decided that this particular human interaction held more interest than her maps and games. She trailed me, pushing air out in a nervous little puff.

Good, I thought. *It'll be harder to go right to violence in front of witnesses.* I was mostly joking. Mostly. I actually thought it would be harder for Addie to hold her unreasonable "no to birthdays and joy" stance in the face of adolescent suffering.

I rapped smartly at the door, and Honor stayed to the side, leaning, tense and stiff, against the wall. I heard footsteps coming, then a pause. Addie must have looked through the peephole, because it was another long, long thirty seconds before the door opened. She was still in her work clothes, another festival of well-cut, layered neutrals. Her shoes were off, and even her toenails were painted some taupe-adjacent non-color. Her face was unreadable.

"Hi! I'm Meribel Mills." Bright friendly tone. Warm eyes, even. Never let it be said that I don't put the work in. "From fourteen A."

"I know who you are," she said, talking over me before I got half of my name out. "I suppose you're here for an apology." Very tight. Almost angry. "I'm sorry my post caused you trouble. I was saying private things, I thought in private, but as Cooper pointed out, there's no such thing as private on the internet. I took it down."

I felt a flush of gratitude that Cooper *had* talked to her. That must have been hard. He really was my friend. Addie, finished with her flat apology, made to shut the door, but I stepped in closer, fast.

"Let's forget about it," I said, so perky. I kept showing her all my actor's teeth, straightened and veneered. "I actually wanted to talk to you about our kids. We're new here, and it's Honor's birthday, and your daughter is the only friend she's made so far. I understand that you have some concerns about the party. I was hoping to set your mind at ease, so Sheila can attend."

"Honor is the little dark-haired child? How old is she?" There was no pause for me to answer her questions before she turned back and called, "Sheila? Sheila!"

"I'm a teenager, not a child," said Honor loudly. She was out of Addie's sight, but now she pushed off the wall and came into view. Addie's whole face changed, first to surprise, and then to something almost human.

"Oh. I didn't realize you were here," she said.

Sheila came up behind her mother, and when she saw me standing there, her eyes went wide and she sucked her lips into her mouth.

Addie glanced doubtfully from her daughter to my own, and then she asked Honor, "You're a teenager?"

Honor, looking like baby thunder in her ratty shorts and outsize T-shirt, said, "Almost. The party is for me turning thirteen."

Addie crossed her arms, but it did look like she was reassessing. I got it. Fifteen and ten was weird and creepy in a way fifteen and thirteen wasn't. She turned to Sheila. "You guys are friends?"

Honor answered first, overloud and very flat. "Yes. Sheila is my friend."

"We hang out," Sheila said, not correcting so much as refining.

Actors are good at reading people. Especially film and TV actors. On the stage, you go big. You have to. But for camerawork, micro-expressions matter. I saw Addie have a run of all the same feelings I'd had when I first saw Honor and Sheila together: irked that her kid liked my kid, worried about the age gap, but also hopeful that her child might be connecting. I remembered Cooper telling me Sheila was troubled . . . It didn't soften me, exactly, but I understood how isolated the poor girl must be, for her mom to mirror all my feelings so exactly. It made my heart go out to Sheila, and it also set me slightly at ease. "Troubled" meaning "outcast and friendless" was better than "in deep with drug-addled hordes of sex-crazed juvenile delinquents."

Addie Portlin hated her child's loneliness. I saw it, and it made me like her better, at least until she said, "Well, we already had long-standing family plans to go to the water park. Me, and Sheila, and Cooper. You know that I am back with Cooper, right?"

Her eyes were hard as agates, and she gave me a bland, cool smile. She knew damn well that I had no idea, and she expected that the news would hurt me.

I added a thousand megawatts of sunshine to my own smile. "Well, that's fantastic! Since we're all going, we can just combine. I assumed the teenagers would want to roam about on their own, and I'd be stuck all by myself most of the day. It would be nice to have some grown-up company."

Her eyes narrowed, and the bland-bitch smile wobbled, uncertain. "You want us all to go. Together."

I flirted up one shoulder. "I'd love it. Cooper and I are friends— well, friendly acquaintances, and here's my chance to get to know another neighbor better. Another mom."

She weighed my words, trying to read my expression. She really

did believe I'd dated him, which made her territorial bullshit a little less abrasive. A very little.

"I suppose that makes sense," Addie said. I could see curiosity
dawning. She wanted to see us together, me and Cooper. Lord, the
suspicion!

Behind her, Sheila muttered, "If you break up again before Sunday, it doesn't mean you get to follow me and Honor around all day."
She tried and failed to exchange an eye roll with my daughter, who
was radiating pleasure. Honor was oblivious to the fraught inner
workings of personal relationships that were on ugly display here.
She didn't yet feel the basic undesirability of having mothers along
on a teenager's birthday outing.

Addie put a pinching hand on her daughter's shoulder. "Don't
be rude. Ms. Mills already said that you could run around and do
kid things." Then to me, "There's supposedly a beer tent where the
grown-ups can collapse."

I would need an IV morphine tent, but hey, better than nothing. "Super. I'll order us a car service, so we won't have to worry
about driving if we want to have a couple."

Addie's eyes widened. "You really don't live like the rest of us,
do you." Not a question.

I laughed, embarrassed. Sometimes I forgot that normal things
for me were not a part of regular life. The convenience even my
small amount of fame afforded was an easy thing to take for granted.

"Perk of the job," I said. "And please, call me Meribel."

Judging by the expressions in this hallway as I turned and
stalked off home, the only fully happy person on the road to Wild
Waves day after tomorrow would be Honor.

17

SATURDAY NIGHT, XENA waited in the alley way too late, hoping Sheila or Honor had gotten the duct tape, finally. Weekends were hard, because all the grown-ups didn't go to work. That morning, Sheila came down and gave her a bag lunch and promised she would get the tape later on. Xena wanted to be inside, so bad. In this building. Alone. She wanted to be snuck into this building and hidden under it. If it finally happened, she'd be able to think clearly, make some plans. Out here, she was scared all the time. Even at the shelter, it was hard to think or plan. Last time, someone stole her socks, and that mustache person tried to touch her.

Honor was probably asleep, and it was obvious that Sheila had forgotten or couldn't escape her mother, but Xena waited anyway. She was sitting with her back to the wall, leaning on her Hefty bag. Her eyes were so grainy, so heavy, and the next thing she knew it was deep night and the Monster Talker was standing over her in the dim security light over the door. Close.

He was big, built like a grizzly, and he had huge, rolling eyes, the lower lids gapped and saggy. He leaned down and talked at her face, but not to her. He talked to monsters. He told the monsters, no.

"No, monsters! I will not hurt that girl. I will not. No, monsters,

I won't lean down and bite her face to see if blood is sallllllty. No, monsters, I won't grab her leg and drag her—"

By then she was up and running, as fast as she could with her bag slung up over her shoulder, sleep-drool still wet on her face, already crying. He followed, loudly refusing in detail to do what the monsters wanted. They wanted such bad things.

Xena had the pepper spray gel and a knife in her bag. She didn't stop and turn and fight him, though. She already knew she wouldn't. She'd been in Atlanta almost two weeks now, and she'd failed to be brave even once, so far.

She thought, before she left her mom, she would do heroic things and be amazing. It was that way in the books she read. In books, girls who lost or ditched their mothers brought murderers to justice or got revenge or became magic. Real life wasn't that way. It was safer to be in and out of shelters and by-the-week hotels with an addict mom than being for-real all-the-way homeless by herself. This was an awful thing to know, but it was true.

She was faster than the Monster Talker, even with her bag, but long after she lost him, she was too scared to go back to her alley. Too scared to sleep again, anywhere, while it was still dark. She walked and walked, circling around this quiet block and then that one. Right before dawn, in the charcoal start of Sunday, it rained, a sudden hard fall that slapped at her and soaked her through. She felt so moldy now, and pathetic to be standing in the alley waiting for Honor or Sheila, hoping to be given breakfast like one of Honor's ferals. Hoping to be finally allowed *inside*.

Nothing ever goes right, not one thing. I need one thing. If I had one thing go perfect I could be amazing. I could be like Katniss, or Lisbeth Salander, or the real Xena. I could be. I only need one thing—

The shrill bells screamed. Sheila opened the door; she had a big paper bag in one hand. In the other, she had the duct tape. She really had it. She'd remembered.

"Hurry, come in," she said over the bells.

Xena dashed in, so they could let it shut and stop the clanging. This had to be a miracle, or magic. All that waiting, all that wanting in, and now the roll of tape was in her hand. Like she'd willed it to happen. She was inside and she could tape the lock and come in or go out anytime she wanted.

"Come on, we have to hurry. I'm supposed to be getting my mom a latte," Sheila said. "I'll show you which storage place is ours." They hustled down the dark hall, and Sheila stopped in front of one of the gates. Xena could see piled boxes and the promised sofa through the slats. The gate was padlocked, but Sheila said, "The code is 3636."

They opened it up and worked together to move boxes off the sofa. It was covered in a dark blue nubbled fabric, soft and dry, with a lot of extra cushions. Inside the bag Sheila brought was a whole sleeve of Fig Newtons, an orange, a heavy flashlight, and a pack of batteries.

"Won't your mom notice?" Xena asked. She meant the batteries. It was eight big C-cells.

"Fuck my mom," Sheila answered, very casual, so, okay then. Xena was feeling really good about it. Really good. Then Sheila said, "I wish you could come to the birthday thing with me and Honor."

It hit Xena wrong. She had a weird moment that was like being ripped in half. She wasn't a hero, or a detective, or a warrior princess. She wasn't forged in the heat of anything, and she hadn't magicked Sheila into finally bringing the tape. She was just a girl who sat in alleyways and panhandled and ran and hid and took sandwiches and fruit and cookies from a weird little kid and this girl. When Xena was maybe Honor's age, before her mom picked the wrong boyfriend and then got into oxy, Xena got to go to birthdays at theme parks or skate rinks. She would bring a present in a gift bag from Target, maybe lip glosses or cute, funny socks. Now, she was not that girl. Now she was this one—no longer birthday party material.

Xena said, "Well, this is cool, though. Anyway, I was going to work on my book today."

"You're writing a book?" Sheila said, perking. She was a reader, too.

Xena, left out of the birthday, felt her interest like a flash of power. She said, "Not the kind you read. I'm trying to write something, like, real. About how life is, really."

"I like real stuff," Sheila protested, like Xena had insulted her. Which, she had. Kinda. Just a little. "I read *The Book Thief*, and I liked it. I read *Slaughterhouse-Five* like fourteen times."

Xena shook her head. "Not like history and Nazis. This is about now." It felt good to push a little, to leave Sheila out of a thing, too. Now that she was inside.

Sheila cocked her hip, challenging. "So what's it about then?"

Xena told her. "Okay, so there's this girl. She lives kinda out in the country, but not totally. There's stores she can get to. There's a highway near her house. She's got a swim hole she goes to every day in summer, with a tree and a rope. The water is all green and murky, but familiar and hers. So she isn't scared. She doesn't even think about it.

"One day she goes and swings out on the rope and flips and dives right in, headfirst, and someone has swerved a big old ancient Chrysler off the highway. It went right in, bloop, and sunk nose-first and lodged. Too deep in the murk for her to see it. She smacks right into the trunk, face-first. So hard. It snaps her neck, right at the brain stem. She dies so fast it's like a light switch. Click. On. Off. She doesn't even know."

Xena stopped talking and waited for Sheila to ask what happened next. She would, probably. Xena was good at stories.

"Oh, my God," Sheila said, her eyes wide. She was impressed, a little, which made Xena feel even better. Sure enough, Sheila took the bait. "What happens after that?"

It felt very good to shrug like a real hardcase and say, "Nothing, that's the end. That's *real*."

Sheila blinked and looked discomfited, and Xena had to work hard not to smile. Good. Sheila didn't believe the story really ended that way because Sheila thought that she was safe. She wasn't safe.

Not in her nice apartment. Not anywhere. You never knew what was under the water, did you? You could be the kind of girl who went to birthday parties, but then your sister died and your mom started oxy and lost her job and then lost the house and had more bad boyfriends, one after another. All those girls in books who do the hero shit, they leave their families, but leaving Mom hadn't helped her be anything but scareder. It was bad to be a girl who knew what real was. Real was, any second, you could leap into a pool you thought you knew, a pool that had been safe a thousand times, and then you smack face-first into a Chrysler with a vanity plate that says BIG STUD, and that was it. Click. No one would save you or avenge you. You would just die.

Sheila said, "Well, anyway. I have to go." She shifted from one foot to another, side-eyeing the exit, eager to go to her party while Xena was trying to help her see how the world was. Sheila wasn't going to listen to a girl who smelled like musty thrift store clothing and armpit and Morning Breeze Lysol because last time Xena dumpster dove, she found a can with some juice left. This morning she'd aimed at her pits and crotch and hosed her clothes down with it.

Xena felt bleak and red and abandoned, watching her go.

She wanted inside, and she was, but now it only made her feel more helpless. Why was *that* the wish that worked? She willed things all the time, more important ones, and couldn't make them happen. Xena was always telling herself she would be brave and strong and make her life better, but then all she did was run and hope for tape. She wasn't magic. She was weak. She was going to lock herself in a storage closet and eat fig cookies and call this progress. It hurt to know that she was weak. But it did not surprise her. Nothing surprised her very much these days, truthfully.

By now Sheila was meeting Honor at the front to be driven to the birthday. Maybe Xena should tape the door so she could get back in and stomp out of the alley. March right up to the car and say hello. She pictured all their faces, shocked in different ways. Not birthday material. Whose fault was that? Not hers. She imagined a chakram in her hand, imagined sending it spinning, bladed, after them in their fine car.

She had to be braver.

18

COOPER STOOD ON the sidewalk watching weekend traffic winding down Tenth Avenue, waiting for the car service. With his hand in Addie's, he felt thoroughly at ease.

Addie, less so. She fidgeted and fretted and peered back at the coffeehouse, again. It was already doing a brisk business. Sheila had gone down half an hour ago to get lattes, and she was just now near the front of a good-size line. He and Addie were the only ones waiting on the sidewalk in front of the building.

Addie leaned into him and said, "We need black paper plates and cups with curly fire letters that say 'Hell for the Grown-Ups,' instead of 'Happy Birthday.'"

He chuckled. "Next you'll want a cake made out of molded dog shit, covered in vanilla buttercream."

"Cooper, I'm not kidding," she said, grumpy, but he was buoyant enough for both of them. He lifted her hand to his mouth and kissed at it with big, goofy smacking sounds until she was fighting a smile. Her eyes stayed worried, though. She glanced again at the coffeehouse, then said to him, very fast and low, "I know you didn't sleep with her, but—" When he started to protest, she pressed his arm and spoke over him. "I believe you. I do. But. Are you sure *she* didn't think that you were dating?"

He waved all that away, so at ease. He'd covered this. "I told you, she's as hung up on her ex as I was. As I am."

She pressed, though. "It's okay if you were, like, comforting each other. In whatever way. If you just tell me."

"Meribel Mills is not my type," Cooper assured her, and that was true.

It was also true that before that creepy California asshole showed, Cooper had decided *not my type* was exactly what he needed. He'd never tell Addie that he'd planned to start something with Meribel, much less that he'd sensed Meribel was open to it. She'd picked Cam, and he was fine with it.

Well, perhaps he hadn't been as sanguine in the moment . . .

He'd waited a day to confront Addie about the doxing, just as he'd told Meribel he would. He'd felt that it was like a coin toss. This woman, or that. Some new Cooper, or the one he'd been for ten years now. Money bets were mostly about fleecing chumps; the house won in the end, always. Gambling on people, that was heady stuff, to hurl human hearts and bodies, his included, right into the arms of Fate.

There was more than one fate, though, he remembered. Spin. Measure. Cut. Okay, the Fates then. He had waited, interested, alert, his future up and spinning, to see if Meribel would tell the sketchy creep from Cali to eff off and take a risk on Cooper. If she had, he really would have given up Addie.

When she didn't call, he went to Addie's knowing they'd get back together . . . Tails it was. He didn't care if she ever took the post down. The damage was done. Still, Addie was predictably upset to hear a stalker had used her post to get to Meribel. She really was a sweet person, at her core. He'd comforted her, hugged her, and she'd clutched him so tight, tilting up her face. So easy then to kiss her, to fall back into her bed, back into their shared life.

Whatever happened now, he was at peace with it. More than that, he was happy. This was the beginning of a high-stakes human gamble, and oh, he loved it. Standing on the street with her hand in his, he was all bubbling pleasure.

Finally the coffeehouse door opened and disgorged Sheila with two iced lattes. She was wearing a very short yellow sundress with glow stick bracelets laddering up both arms and looped through her Ronald McDonald hair, while he and Addie were in swim shorts and T-shirts. The kid looked ready for a rave, not a water park. She and Addie had already fought about it. As the door swung shut behind her, they could both see a man, fully thirty, if not older, blatantly staring at her ass. Addie shut her mouth with an angry pop, but Cooper was in such a good mood, he didn't even go punch the guy in the face.

Hard to blame the guy. Sheila, dressed like this, looked much older than fifteen. She reminded him again of someone his father would have run around with. Like someone his father did run around with, in fact. She reminded him of Barely.

Her real name had been Beverly something, but his father called her Barely as a joke. As in "barely legal." She had huge boobs, a wasp waist, a big round butt, long legs, a smoky laugh. Cooper was twelve that summer, and Barely was around from when school let out all the way to August. That was longer than most girls lasted, but his dad was on a winning streak.

Cooper wanted to hate Barely for his mom's sake, but she was so cheery. She joked with him, ruffled his hair, called him "Little Man" and "Cutie." She'd come up behind him so her big breasts brushed his neck and put her hands on his shoulders and tussle him around.

He had dreams about her. In one, his mother was crying again, and he knew why. He got his father's pistol and he walked into a meadow where Barely was in her bikini lying down in all the flowers. He shot her and shot her, a bunch of times, to make his mother stop crying, but Barely didn't mind. She liked it. As bullets hit her, she squirmed and laughed and her big boobs wobbled. He woke up sticky. It was hard to look at her for a few days after that one, as if she might see into his brain and know.

One weekend near the end of summer, his dad took Cooper and Barely down to Mobile to meet up with a bunch of friends at the dog tracks. They rented a glass-enclosed balcony upstairs, and his dad ordered baskets of chicken wings and pizza rolls. The air was thick with cigarette and cigar smoke. Barely gave Cooper her beer, almost full, because it "got too warm." He drank it, very fast, while his dad and the friends laughed and cheered him. He felt woozy after, and his body kept moving over to where Barely's body was. She shared her tip sheet, let him pick dogs and made two-dollar bets for him. Win, place, or show. She smelled like roses, and Cooper won and won and then kept winning, almost every race. The wins each felt so good. Even though he hated Barely, he liked it when he won and she hugged him and jumped up and down with him.

Dad's friend Boomer said, so loud, "Uh-oh, Junior popped a li'l woody," and they all laughed.

He flushed, but Barely punched Boomer in the shoulder and said, "Jealous, much? The kid can't hardly lose, ya sour old goot," and then Cooper felt okay. He picked a dog called Sage's Ready Rocket to win, and he had Barely put down every bit of money he'd accumulated so far with his little bets. Eighteen dollars. Boomer told him he was dumb and put a thou on some trifecta thing and lost big. Cooper's dog smoked them all at three-to-one, and Barely danced him about yelling, "Ha, ha suck it, Boomer," and he loved her and hated her and hated Boomer and he hated his shit dad and he loved the win and it was such a sharp, sour high.

Now, as Addie seethed and Sheila put a sway in her hips for the creeper watching, he took Addie's hand. He had that good feeling, like when the ball was whirling and the wheel was spinning, that last open moment when bets could still be placed. He had the inside line. He could push things in the right direction for Addie. His life would be more interesting, now, and her life would get better.

"I should have made her put on shorts. Or her ski suit." Addie's mouth was bunched up tight, and whose fault was that? Inside the coffeehouse, Sheila had added bright red lipstick and another coat

of shitty attitude to her ensemble. As she passed her mom one of
the drinks, Addie asked her, "Makeup? At a water park? And those
bracelets won't show up in the daytime."

Sheila shrugged, slurping at the latte he'd sprung for, one hip
cocked sideways. "They look cool underwater."

He ignored the tension and told them both, "We're going down
Poseidon's Plunge, I hope you know. All three of us." It was the
tallest slide in the park, over a hundred feet.

"Good luck getting me on that!" Addie said. She was gamely
trying to match his mood, but she didn't quite get there. "Assuming
we actually go. Your actress is late to her own kid's birthday party."

His watch said 9:02, but this was not his first jealous-girlfriend
rodeo. He made a disapproving click noise with his mouth.

Addie dug in the big beach bag he was carrying for them all
and unearthed the gallon bag of trail mix he'd made yesterday. He
had done it the way Sheila liked it: hand-roasted macadamias and
pecans with brown sugar and smoked paprika, buttered and baked
Chex cereal and sesame sticks, then scoops of gummy bears and
M&M's. He'd decided to join this family; when Cooper went in on
something, he went in all the way. Addie pulled out a handful, stress
eating. As she chewed, a sleek, black Lincoln SUV pulled over to
the curb near the front doors. It put its hazards on and idled there.

Cooper whistled. "Pretty swank."

"Super swank," Addie acknowledged, but her mouth turned
down. "She's kind of an entitled person, isn't she? She basically
told a car service to block off a lane of Tenth Avenue, and now she's
late."

This early on a Sunday, the light traffic had no problem streaming around it, but Cooper repeated his disapproving click noise,
just as Meribel and Honor came bustling out the front door. Honor
looked of a set with him and Addie, wearing flip-flops and a cov-
er-up with a cartoon cat on it. The cat had a giant bouffant hairdo
made of snakes, and underneath, in rainbow font, it said MEOW-DUSA!

Meribel, on the other hand, was rocking a filmy sarong situation,

Chanel shades, and an enormous sun hat. Leading Lady Beachwear. Addie nudged Cooper, giving him a tiny eye roll. He quirked an eyebrow back and didn't point out that Meribel might be extra, but she looked a thousand times more water park appropriate than Addie's kid.

Meribel was beelining toward them, calling, "Sorry, sorry, sorry! That's our car!"

Most of his attention was on the building. No Cam. Cooper's eyes narrowed as the Mills family joined them. He asked Meribel, "Is this all of us?"

Meribel said, "Yep." A little tight.

Addie said, "Oh. Cooper thought your boyfriend would be coming."

Meribel's gaze went instantly to Honor, but Honor was off to the side. She had her phone out and was blatting loudly about water-slides at Sheila.

"I don't have a boyfriend," Meribel said, firm and quiet. She caught Cooper's eye and added, "If you mean Cam, he left town."

That might have been interesting, before. But for Cooper, the coin had landed. He squeezed Addie's hand, and made his face radiate mild sympathy for Meribel as she held up a finger to the driver, asking him to wait a minute. She turned to her daughter.

"What are you guys looking at?"

"It's an interactive map of the park," Honor said, flashing the screen at all of them. "If we want to minimize waiting, we need a methodology." God, her vocabulary killed him. She looked like a fourth grader, but she talked like a forty-year-old classics professor. Being around her, so bright and well-mannered and sweet to her mother, made Cooper mourn the girl that Sheila used to be. He would not mourn this current version.

"We could start at the gate and go to the first attraction we see . . ." Cooper said, and Honor looked up at him, almost pitying. He held for a beat. Then, "After all, a slide in the hand is worth two in the next section."

She cackled, patronizingly relieved that he was playing clichés instead of being stupid. She hit back with "Only line time will tell."

Sheila said, "A wait in line, saves nine?"

They all cracked up, Meribel, too. Only Addie looked sour, so he put an arm around her. Part of making this work was trying to smooth over these little moments, concentrate on reshaping the family in the larger sense. Sheila was being almost sweet with him today, for whatever reason. Girls were moody. Cooper suspected she was doing it for contrast, because she was being an absolute bitch to her mother.

Meribel turned to the car and opened the passenger door. "Hiya, Antony, don't you dare get out into that traffic. You'll be smashed flat, and we're more than capable of working our own doors. Everyone, this is Antony."

Cooper waved to the driver, and then he popped open the back door on this side, bowing the girls toward it, mock chivalrous.

"Thanks," Sheila said, then turned to Honor and said, "This is cool. Is this a limo?" as she got in and slithered all the way across the back bench seat.

"No, just a car service," Honor said, less impressed, scooching in behind her.

He got in after the girls because Meribel was shooting an amused glance at him and Addie was watching like a hawk to see if he'd return it. That left the captain's chairs in the middle row for Addie and Meribel. They got in and buckled up, eyeing each other, Addie wary, Meribel smiling.

"So, what do you do, Addie?" Her tone was friendly, interested.

"VP, human resources," said Addie, tightly. Full stop.

Meribel grinned. "So, you're a people person." Ouch. That landed. The car pulled smoothly into traffic, and Meribel called back, "Girls, you buckled?"

"Who wants trail mix?" Addie chimed in, making her own voice bright.

Meribel eyed the big bag doubtfully, then said, "We just had breakfast. Did you not have time to eat?"

Addie shrugged, flushing, shooting Cooper a look. She was sensitive to anything that might be a reference to her weight.

"Can I have some later?" Honor asked. The map was interesting, but not so very that she missed the offer that included candy. "It's my birthday."

Meribel blew air out her nose. "You'll be eating theme park trash all day." Honor said nothing, but her mouth turned down, and Meribel relented—or at least deferred. "You can have a little. Later."

Addie was wide-eyed and incredulous, but Honor agreed with good cheer.

"Why don't I make the girls each their own serving," Cooper said. He knew about Meribel and sugar; he'd planned for this. He got out his stash of Ziploc snack size bags from the big beach tote between his feet, and Addie passed the trail mix back. When Meribel craned around in her seat, he gave her a reassuring look, like, *I got this*. Under her watchful eye, he cherry-picked an Honor serving, heavy on the nuts and sesame sticks with a sprinkle of the cereal. He added three or four M&M's and one lone bear, a microserving of sugars floating in a sea of fats and proteins.

Meribel gave him a grateful look as Honor tucked the snack into her waterproof fanny pack, satisfied, and then she called out with forced, sharp gaiety, "Hey, let's have music! Do you have a good, fun playlist, Addie? Antony will put it on for us."

Addie said, "We could put on Sheila's. Would you like that, hon?"

"Whatever," Sheila said, snotty, but she did dig out her phone.

While they were busy picking music, it was easy for Cooper to pocket the second, empty snack bag and instead hand Sheila the one he had prepared at home. It was much the same as Honor's, more nuts than candy. The main difference was, three of the gummy bears in this bag were from Addie's stash of California edibles. Ten milligrams of THC in each.

Honor was a rulesy little person. He thought she would listen to her mother and stick to her own bag. If she didn't, well, everybody paid their money and they took their chances. The odds were with Honor. Anyway, small side risks were an added tingle. As Sheila put her own snack away, his mood got even brighter.

A little chaos in the world. A ripple in the water. What would happen when she ate them? Cooper was a curious person. Maybe nothing. A bust. Sheila was probably stoned half the time anyway these days; she might simply enjoy it. The safe bet was that Addie would realize Sheila was high. She'd never believe her daughter hadn't dosed herself, especially since Addie had just last month caught Sheila clearly buzzed and watering the vodka down. Sheila had denied, denied, denied in a slurry little voice. Sheila getting caught high, Cooper thought, would be a good return on his investment. This was a seeder bet, anyway.

These little wins would wedge into the gap that was already there between them; it would make things so much easier on Addie, later. It was also possible that that much pot could press Sheila right into psychosis. She was on some medications for ADHD and he thought a little something for depression; there was an off chance at some interesting interactions.

The big long shot? A side bet for the real players? If Cooper hit it on the flop, the girl could drown. It was also possible that she'd forget the snack, lose it, get it wet, throw it in the trash. So be it.

He didn't mind a long game. When his last girlfriend's daughter had grown into a problem child, just like this—curves and lies and boys—he'd broken Lizzie's EpiPen. Every time Lizzie made her mother cry, he'd put a drop or two of nut oil on a random cookie, or swirl it into a leftover serving of pasta primavera. He had eight long but interesting months, watching her mom or one of her brothers hoover up these little bombs. Honestly, what a run of luck the girl had! Then one day, the world tipped perfect for him, as it often did: an isolated hike with two other families. A sleight-of-hand swap for a different kid's brownie that had walnuts in it. Fin.

Shelley-Ann left him, anyway, six months later. She took the boys and moved back to Canada to live with her mother. He'd been heartbroken, of course, but he'd left Shell better off than he'd found her, so that was a comfort. He knew it might end that way. Gemma, much like Shelley-Ann, with her own bad divorce, her own rebellious eldest daughter, had already told him, *I was a bad bet from the beginning, Cooper.*

He'd read that the stress of losing a child destroyed half of all relationships and made the other half much stronger. His last two had been broken by it, and a less experienced gambler would think, *Well, so now the odds are in my favor.* They'd be wrong. Fifty-fifty, straight up, every time. He'd set some wheels spinning, flip some cards, and see. Even if he lost Addie in the end, he knew from Lizzie, and from Gemma's daughter Ruby, the game itself had savor.

Meribel had passed Sheila's phone up to Antony, and now Taylor Swift's iconic voice filled the car, singing "Shake It Off." A little on the nose, Cooper thought, but Meribel said, "Crank it!"

From the safety of the back seat, he let his gaze slide over her bright hair. She felt it. Felt him looking, and she turned and tossed him a smile over her shoulder. He should definitely keep this friendship, even work to help her get along with Addie. He liked Meribel. He got along fine with Honor, who was cute as a button and just as sweet as Sheila had been. Once.

When Sheila was gone, he bet everything would be much better for his current lady. Addie would be forever. And if not? Well, win some, lose some. Meribel would be there, a queen of hearts tucked in his sleeve. Cooper settled back in the leather seat and smiled. No matter how it all came out, it was going to be an interesting day.

19

"MOM, KEEP UP," Honor hollered at me. The girls had done a round of slides, lapping the whole park, while Cooper and Addie sunbathed and I had tucked myself into a corner in the shade, reading. I reapplied Shiseido UV protection as we headed for the flume ride, even though I'd yet to get wet. Nothing aged skin faster than the sun.

We'd saved the Dragon Drop, since a lot of people had had the "go right to the best ride first" idea, and the line had been so long.

Honor beelined for the ride entrance at a high knee trot. Sheila followed, not as fast, trying to be cool. Honor, being Honor, was oblivious to coolness.

For me, it was unnerving to be at an amusement park at all, especially now that I was up out of my shady corner, moving through the crowds. I hadn't considered or noticed all the ways my world had gotten smaller as Marker Man loomed larger in my life. It was a glorious September day, hot and bright, not humid, and the park was very full. As we threaded our way through couples and families and roving packs of teenagers toward the Dragon Drop, I realized how long I'd been avoiding places where throngs of people surged this way and that, brushing me with a thousand passing glances. It kept all my skin in such a prickle that if there was a single, steady gaze on me, I could not feel it.

Honor strained ahead, galloping and then running back to announce, "I am going to suddenly turn thirteen when the dragon breathes on me. Then me and Sheila are going off alone again, but this time as two teenagers."

"Are we going to stay split up all day?" Addie asked, balking at the entrance to the line, her mouth compressed. "Can't we all—" She looked at her child's horrified reaction and petered out.

We entered the switchback queue, followed by an older couple and a tall, gawky teenager. He had a sad wisp of facial hair that marked him as an upperclassman. His shoulders were hunched and he hurried ahead of his parental units, trying to widen the space between. I wanted to point him out to Addie, let her see how normal separation behaviors were at Sheila's age, but when we caught up to the bevy of college-aged kids ahead of us, he stopped short, easing back quite close to his parents. Strange behavior—until I clocked how his gaze skittered past us grown-ups to Sheila in her sundress, curvy and bare-legged and pretty.

"I spy flirting, three o'clock," I said to the girls, grinning, much too quiet for him to hear.

It took a sec for that to land with Sheila. When she realized what I meant she said, "Oh, my God!" She was blushing, but she also fought a smile.

Addie turned a suspicious glare on her daughter. "Do you know that boy?"

Eye roll. "God, Mom, no."

Behind us, the older couple argued exuberantly about which Property Brother was cast on *Dancing with the Stars*, and the weedy would-be suitor-of-Sheila slouched silently, trying for casual, no doubt wishing he was an orphan.

Addie started to speak again, but Sheila interrupted her. "Hey, you know what would be neat? If our log careened out of the shunt thing and we all died before my mom said even one more word about it."

Honor let out an abrupt bray of laughter, and now she was

looking back at him, too, open-mouthed and curious, subtle as a hammer blow.

I said, "Honor, look away, be chill."

The line moved, and Sheila grabbed Honor and dragged her forward. I let them create a little space, and Addie took the opportunity to turn cold eyes on me. "Ha ha." She wasn't laughing, only saying the words, flat. "If you want your daughter picking up strange boys who look old enough to drive, great, but leave mine out of it."

I felt color rise in my cheeks until I was as red as Sheila. "I wasn't suggesting she—I thought she'd find it flattering."

"That some boy finds her pretty? Is that the Hollywood route to self-esteem?" Addie turned away, and I shot Cooper a look like, "*This* bitch." He stayed as neutral as Switzerland, though, watching riders ahead of us load onto the boats. Correct boyfriend behavior, I had to give him that.

The line was moving again, and Addie thrust herself ahead of me, closer to her kid, driving Sheila farther from the gawky kid, as if every college boy in the whole gaggle ahead wasn't ogling at her backward. Sheila had the kind of body that called male attention, even when she was looking at a video on Honor's phone, not flirting back, oblivious. I let Cooper go ahead of me as well and dropped out of the conversation.

The whole half hour we were shuffling toward the ride's loading zone, my own mood was swinging up and down. I kept flashing back to the afternoon I'd spent with Cam, having little stomach drops before I was even on the ride. Each of those brief euphorias was followed by a sink; Cam was gone, and we were really done this time.

The two girls were whispering, intense. Cooper and Addie were looking at some app together, and here I was, alone. All I had to remember Cam by was a loaded gun and some security cameras. I tried to put him out of my mind by people-watching or toying with my phone, only to have another sex flashback. It was a relief in more ways than one when we got close to the head of the line.

Cooper put his phone away in their waterproof beach bag. "I was checking the weather. There was a chance of thundershowers, but I think we're in the clear."

Honor whirled abruptly our way. "Will the thundershowers go to Midtown now, instead?" She grabbed Sheila's arm, spinning her and looking her urgently right in the eye.

My maternal secret-smelling thing awoke. A flume ride with a dragon head and turning thirteen was a breath away, and she was freaking about distant rain? It was fine for Honor to have privacy. All kids needed it, but Sheila was older, and troubled, and might have secrets that were actively unsafe for someone Honor's age.

"Why does it matter if it rains in Midtown?" I asked, so casual.

Honor's gaze slid over to me, and I could see anxious little wheels turning. Her gaze dropped and she confessed, "Mom. Me and Sheila have been feeding a stray."

My hackles went down. In fact, that made me smile. Trust Honor to find the one feral cat who had survived the Midtown traffic. "Oh, that's fine. That's fun. I know you've been missing Worker and the others. Don't worry about him, though. He'll know a dry place to go if the weather gets bad."

"It's a girl," Honor said. "Me and Sheila were supposed to make a place for her. But we didn't do it yet. If the rain comes—"

Before I could reassure her, Sheila interrupted, oddly terse. "I did it. This morning."

"You did?" Honor asked, clearly pleased.

Sheila nodded, her face flushed. "Yeah. I went down early this morning and set it up. I saw her. She's fine."

"You made a cat shelter in the alley? Like a fort?" I was imagining a cardboard box type situation by a dumpster. Well, this explained what the two of them had been doing before school. I smiled. It was so sweet.

Sheila shrugged. "Kinda. I had to buy some duck tape, though."

"Duct tape," Honor corrected. "Our stray is named Xena Warrior Princess and she has a gray coat and is young and seems cool."

Sheila was still being weird, eyes down, which I couldn't under-stand until Addie said, strident, "Is that what took so long with the lattes? You went all alone into an alley to fart around with trash and duct tape while I believed that you were getting coffee?"

It was physical work not to roll my eyes. If this was Sheila's big rebellion, Addie ought to be writing checks to cat shelters as a thank-you to the universe.

Cooper put a calming hand on her arm. "I think it's cute. A nice shared project for the girls." I agreed with him. Age appropriate, and it showed a lot of empathy. "Maybe we can catch this cat, get it spayed and vaccinated, and—"

Sheila snorted with laughter, though I didn't see the joke. Be-fore I could ask, she turned away, stepping up to the loading zone.

I wanted to ride with Honor, but the boats only sat two; Honor wanted to turn into a teenager with Sheila. Developmentally ap-propriate, no matter how much it squeezed my mother's heart. When she looked back at me, I smiled and waved her on. Addie and Cooper clambered into the next small boat.

The attendant said, "Lone rider?" and the failed-flirt boy got the same question. They slotted him in behind me, where he sat stiff with mortification. I held my hat and glasses while the ride chugged us dutifully up hills and dropped us down little runs like waterfalls inside the haunted castle. It was like a discount, medieval Pirates of the Caribbean, with animatronic knights jousting and feasting, a princess waiving a hanky, a Robin Hood type climbing in a window. The inside drops were mild, and neither I nor the boy behind me screamed or hooted or held our hands up, even when we plummeted down the last big hill, out into the sunlight, where a huge white dragon head blasted us with icy spray. I wished again I was with Honor. She must be overjoyed.

By the time I got unloaded, she was galloping down the exit ramp toward a hutch where more college kids were hawking the pictures taken during the final drop. Honor made us pause to watch the pics cycle through until ours came up. There was my girl, eyes shut, mouth clamped, clinging to the boat like a limpet as the dragon breathed its water blast into her face. Behind her, Sheila was in midscream, both hands lifted, but she wasn't interested, even in her own picture. She stared off down the street a little slack-jawed. Maybe woolgathering.

The next shot showed Cooper grinning, Addie shrieking. Then me, my eyes were closed as if in supplication to an angry god; the kid behind me looked ready to puke right down my back.

"I want to buy mine," Honor said, enraptured. "That's me turning thirteen."

Autism can come with both price tags and weird gifts, and this was both; as my child joyfully plunged through her chosen milestone moment, she had no idea that the mothers at this birthday kinda wanted to stab each other. I bought all three of the overpriced, god-awful pictures. Maybe I could get a friendly effects guy to Photoshop me in over Sheila. A prettier me, actually, why use the real picture at all? I'd get the damned things framed, both versions: truth for Honor, enhanced reality for me.

The line was even shorter now, and the girls wanted to go again. This time, I insisted on riding with my kid to get a real picture. Sheila rode with a blond sorority girl who had come in a trio with two equally blond friends. After the second ride, Sheila was looking glassy with fatigue. Addie and Cooper were off a little way, to the side, talking in low tones. Watching them, I felt a low-key prickle starting all over my skin. Was I being watched, or were they talking about me?

"Maybe we break for lunch?" I suggested loudly, suddenly wanting walls around me.

Honor instantly protested. "We ate our snack mix right before we met you! We aren't even hungry yet. We can eat by ourselves, later, because the lines for slides will be so short while all the other people eat."

Sheila lagged a little, staring off, not really following. Honor nudged her, and she jerked and then said, "Yep."

Honor said, "We're teenagers. We want to talk about teenager things with no adult supervision."

That made Sheila laugh, abrupt and high. "God, you're weird."

Honor released her own abrupt laugh and said, "You're weirder."

They really were friends. Two years wasn't a big age gap by midcollege, but between thirteen and fifteen were some big, important changes. I would have to supervise them closely, but Honor had made a connection here. That was too rare and valuable a thing to be discounted.

"Give your creaky old mom a hug, teenager girl."

Honor obliged me. She smelled grassy and sweet and young. And chlorinated. Sheila stared past us, through the trees, down at the wave pool, mesmerized.

Addie came over. "Are we splitting up again?"

I nodded and told Honor, "Text me every hour or if you get tired. We can go home whenever. Antony is standing by. When you do want lunch, have the chicken Caesar salad, okay?" I'd looked over the menu on the website earlier this morning.

Addie shot me a startled look and Honor's eyes narrowed as she said, "They have vegetable pizza."

I'd seen this option, and she'd walked right into the very compromise I'd plotted. "Thin crust, and you have a deal," I said. We shook on it. Honor grabbed Sheila and pulled at her until the girl startled into life. They walked away.

Addie said, sotto voce. "You're policing her birthday lunch? Wow. I guess her big present this year will be bulimia."

Cooper stepped up to join us just in time to hear that. He wheeled and canted left, suddenly very busy finding that interactive theme park map on his own phone. Smart fella. I was working hard to bite back the meanest words I knew. I didn't owe Addie an explanation. I felt more like I owed her a smack. But my kid liked her kid, and her kid seemed to like mine back, so I gave her one anyway.

"Honor's on the spectrum. Simple carbs and crowds are a fast train to a meltdown and a tearful, early exit."

She blew past that. "Sheila's ADHD, and I am, too. You think because I let her pick her own damn lunch, which I can tell you right now will be a burger, I'm hurting my kid? You think I want to make her fat and dumpy like her mother?" She said all this very fast and low, her face expressionless. Addie's cruel assessment of my opinions and her own body both surprised me.

"It's a burger, not meth. You aren't—" She wasn't listening. She was tracking the girls as they went threading away through the crowds. Honor was steering Sheila like a barge. The girl seemed loose to me, her walk oddly disjointed. I said, "Sheila's beautiful." She was. Bright eyes, a scatter of pale freckles, a turned-up nose, a wide smile. "You know she is. And she's a godsend for me, for Honor. Honor doesn't make friends easily. I'm very—I'm grateful you all came." It was all true, but—if I hadn't been with the kid for the last hour, I might have wondered if Sheila had been drinking. Just then, a youth group in matching T-shirts surged out of a souvenir shop, blocking my view. I turned to Addie. "Sheila seems a little off to me." I worked hard to make it not sound critical.

Addie said, "She's fine. We had a fight," but she was already puffing back up. Ready to come at me.

I didn't want to get back into it, so I ignored the little mother-spider tingle at my center. After all, they were teenagers at a family friendly water park. There were moms and dads and young cute staff in blue-and-yellow-striped suits all over the place.

Considering Marker Man, they were probably safer here than in our own building.

20

THERE WAS A very grown-up thing, true and secret, that Honor did all day long at the water park: Honor carried the Juul. This was because her mom got her a waist pack that the water couldn't get in, even in a pool, but still, she liked having it on her person. Also, they stayed mostly together, no parents very much. After Honor became a real teenager, though, Sheila got much slower.

Sheila said, "I don't feel right. I think I'm sleepy."

Honor said, "You need to do more slides."

She dragged Sheila, but Sheila stood quieter and quieter, staring. Honor attached to her and pulled her into lines, up stairs, down slides. She carried Sheila's mats. Even sliding down, Sheila was waterlogged and dismal. In line for the Power Plunge again, she balked and wouldn't walk at all, even though they were almost to the stairs.

She took Honor's hand. "Listen. Listen. Xena is writing a book. A sad and awful novel." Sheila rolled her eyes and then stamped one foot, then the other, the way that black horse back in LA, Trouble, did when she was considering a sly side kick at Honor. Her instructor, Mr. Jim, told her that mares were moody. It was easier to know a horse mood than a person mood, but Sheila had foamy spittle in the corners of her mouth like Trouble did sometimes. She was being *intense*. This was bad.

"Is Xena not okay?" Honor asked. "Did you really see her?"

Some boy behind them said, "Uh, the line is moving?"

Honor said, "Go around." Stupid boy. "What did she say?"

Sheila grabbed at Honor's arms right below her shoulders and then squeezed. Honor didn't love it. It made it hard to listen.

Sheila said, "I gave her duck tape."

Honor said, "Duct tape. We have to go up now. We should slide." Honor grabbed two mats off the pile and pushed back into the line, dragging Sheila upward.

Sheila whispered, "The book made me so sad, but her life is worse than the book, even. When I think about her sleeping in an alley and nobody loved her, I think I might fall up. Like off the earth. I might throw up food if I had any food. I want to hold onto some grass. Like, if I could throw up, and then if there was long grass, very strong, and I got very flat on it, that would be good. I feel weird. Am I acting weird?"

"Yes," said Honor. They were through the roped-off back-and-forth part of the line and now they had to go up. "Do you have a stomach flu?"

That would be terrible. It would ruin the birthday. At the same time, Sheila was her friend. If Sheila had to be sick and ruin the birthday, Honor would be so supportive. She imagined going to get the mothers and Cooper. She could say, *I think Sheila is sick and needs to go home, and I came and told you, even though it ruins my birthday.* She already turned thirteen and got breathed on by the water dragon, which were the most important parts. Also, maybe her mom would be so impressed with her maturity, she would let Honor have a replacement party. It could be shooting guns. Mom said guns did not solve anything, ever, but Honor thought they might solve how to make up for a ruined birthday party.

They were at the top. Honor said, "You have to get on the mat and go whooshing down. Now." Sheila's weirdness made her be upset. She pushed her friend onto the mat and down she went. Then Honor went, too, and she barely enjoyed it. Usually she loved how her stomach dropped on slides. She loved to put her hands up and let gravity have her. Sliding felt good, even when the pool water went up her nose at the end, but not when Sheila was acting so wrong and weird.

Honor sloshed up after she landed, and Sheila was still down under the water.

The attendant said, "Clear the landing! Hey, hey, get your friend! You're holding up the line."

Honor reached down and grabbed Sheila's arm and pulled her up. They waded out and Honor put their mats on the return stack and pulled her onward, hoping Sheila would be regular now.

She wasn't. "Look. I need to be cradled. I want to get in the wave pool."

They were back near the front of the park by the huge pool that made waves like the ocean, and Sheila stopped dead, staring out at it. Honor hadn't wanted to go in it before, at all, because it was crowded and looked sloshy and terrible.

"I want to go into that wave pool," Sheila said again, slower. She blinked.

"Okay," Honor said, because the wave pool was almost empty and very flat right now. The pool went on and off, and there was a big timer ticking down by the speakers that said when the waves would come on next. It would be off for twelve more minutes. No waves, and the music was low. All this seemed good.

"What if we went out there on floats, while it was off. I'll tell you how to play Dungeons and Dragons?"

Sheila nodded, emphatic. "That would be so good. If you talked a lot. I want to listen to nice things. Tell me how to play."

There were stacks of floats by the edge. Sheila got a pink one, Honor got a green one, and they waded out and then kicked toward the middle. It was deep and blue and peaceful, but Sheila was not peaceful.

"I need you to talk now. Don't stop talking. I'll come off the earth. I'll die. I'll die. I am going to be killed. Do you hear me? This is real! I may be being killed."

Honor held on to Sheila's float and started talking, louder, over Sheila, until Sheila stopped and listened. Honor started with character creation, telling Sheila about every race and class, and Sheila put her face down and listened, saying, *Mm-hm. Mm-hm.* Sheila seemed okay as long as Honor was talking, which was easy. She could talk about Dungeons and Dragons for a long time.

It started to be nice to lie crosswise on their floats with their feet in the water, facing each other. Maybe later they could really play. Honor was so interested in teaching the rules that she barely noticed people were now coming in around them. By the time she saw, there was a long blue float too close by with three teenager girls clutching on it. A country-like man with a baseball cap and a beard had come in too close the other way, hanging on to the float of a lady wearing jean shorts. Honor began to feel like bees might get into her, buzz her blood, and people kept on wading out, pushing everyone together, blocking them in. More floats crowded closer. Some mothers. Some children. A dad and a boy. Four more dads. They all pushed in. Then the music went up very loud and the pool started to slosh them, back and forth, back and forth, and they were surrounded. People and waves.

Honor had been in the real ocean, a lot. She said to Sheila, "It will be okay. I've been in the real ocean. It was very great."

It wasn't like that. Not really very great at all. In the real ocean there was wind and surf noises and not a lot of people pressed so close and no speakers blaring "Achy Breaky Heart." Here, people sang and hooted. So many of them. Some legs she didn't know touched her legs. Half her blood was made of bees now.

Sheila said, "You can't stop talking. Are we moving? I am going to vomit. I might fly."

Honor wanted to fly. That would be so good. Her paladin could manifest wings once a day. She wanted that. She wanted to flap up and out and deep into the quiet sky away from all the people and sloshing and jostling and shrieks and song.

She put Sheila's hand on her float and said, "Grip this. Really hard."

When Sheila seemed clipped on, Honor let go of Sheila's float and sat up tall, straddling, the way she would sit if the float were a horse. She kept her hands free so she could flap them, flap some bees out, while she was looking for a path or hole that she could kick through and drag them back to the shallow part where the fat babies were in the little waves with mothers. If they could go toward the babies it would be shallower and shallower like a real shore and they could walk out. She could hardly even see that place, though, not over the people and churning and terrible music. Now it was "Macarena."

Honor felt a buzz all in herself, and she began to float up into the top of her head. Bees first, then this floating; these things often happened right before things got real bad. She saw the shore when the waves pushed her up, but not a way to get there. It was hard to breathe. She rocked and flopped but couldn't feel that she was moving with the wave pool sloshing her so much.

She thought, very calmly in a quiet place way up high in her head, *If I could hit myself in my face very hard a lot of times, I could think*. It was true. But people would be upset and put their hands on her and she would have to bite them. There would be no choice.

"Can you help me?" she asked Sheila, but Sheila wasn't there.

There were a lot of boys on separate floats wrestling and splashing instead. When she looked harder, she saw Sheila's pink pool float was on the other side of all the boys. Empty. Sheila had let go, and the wave pool had sloshed those boys closer. She craned up tall again, as tall as she could and tried to see if Sheila had moved onto another float with this boy or that one. She might have done that. Sheila liked boys. But no. But no. And no.

Every bit of pool was covered in floats and children and couples and people, but none of the people were Sheila.

Honor needed everyone to stop. Honor needed the pool and the music to stop, too. Her teeth chattered even though the sun was hot. She had to wait. That was all. When the waves stopped the people would leave. She had to cling on and not scream or hit herself, and when the waves stopped, she would go get her mom and Mom would find Sheila.

Sheila's pink float bobbed. What if, when her mom went to look for Sheila, Sheila was sunk under all the floats down where a lifeguard didn't see her. What if she was there for the whole time they were looking. Honor's body wanted to thrash and hit itself, but up in the floating part of her real mind, she wanted to be a teenager and brave. A paladin. She held her nose and went under to look.

It was terrible, under. So many stranger legs waving. So much slosh. Muted screams and shrieks and music distorted into moaning whale song. Her body moving when she didn't move it. Chlorine stung her eyes. She peered all around, and she did see Sheila. Sheila was deep. So deep, and paddling in a weird spin, her head pointed toward the bottom.

Siren song! Don't listen! Honor tried to say, but it was bubbles. Sheila should have tied herself to the float. Honor was pretty good at swimming, though, or at least she was when she didn't need to scream so bad. Her mom said she was part fish. She tried to be part fish now, and she dove down, kicking strong, to grab her friend. Honor pulled, trying to spin Sheila so her head was pointing the right way. Then she could find a gap in all the legs and floats and drag her to the air. Sheila grabbed her back, though. Sheila was so strong and bigger. She spun Honor, instead, and yoinked her down more. Honor saw her friend's mouth was open, screaming slow bubbles.

Honor shoved and kicked, but they were caught in the surge and sway. Sheila's hands on her gripped hard enough to bruise. Was it a fight? Sheila's body thrashed and so did Honor's. Bubbles and clutching. Were they trying to climb each other? Honor wanted free. Sheila didn't seem to know which way up was, and

Honor couldn't find anything to push against. Honor needed to breathe. She needed to breathe and scream, breathe and scream, very, very badly. Sheila burbled and clutched. They tumbled with each other, thrashing under all the floats and people, under all the legs, into the kick and churn. They were lost and spinning into blue. Down and down and under, deep, where nobody could see.

21

ACTORS ARE EGOCENTRIC, and we can be touchy. There are always competitive games happening in my industry, but I was feeling shame pings to find myself so deep in one with Addie. Still, did I not have good reason? She'd Mean Girled me, a stranger, at the elevator, then she'd pointed a flaming arrow at my door for Marker Man. The tension between us was 100 percent on her.

Or so I told myself, pious as Honor when she was being so strictly, literally truthful that the facts were obfuscated. Yes, she started it, but I had gotten on the ride, and I'd stayed on even after I knew it was really about Cooper. I didn't love being so at odds with a neighbor, and women cat-scratching over a man was so damn cringe-y. I loved it less and less the longer I stayed in it. If I didn't end it, it would never end; the only way to win Bitch Game is not to play.

I girded my loins, got out my phone, and opened the interactive map Honor had found, looking for an olive branch. By which I meant gin. There was a restaurant by the entrance, a real one, with sit-down table service and a full bar. It wasn't hard to get Addie and Cooper to agree to throw in our literal towels and spend the afternoon in the shade, daytime drinking.

We had to wait for a patio table under the fans, in the deep shade, but it was worth it. As far as I was concerned, the girls could go slide themselves mad all afternoon. I was done. I ordered gin and soda, extra lime, and Cooper got a beer. Addie asked primly for water.

I said, very friendly, "Oh, come on, Addie! Do not let Antony sit in the parking lot waiting to drive us home for zero reason."

She shrugged, looking at Cooper, not me, and when he gave her a charming WTH smile, she asked the waiter for a margarita. As soon as the young man left, she said, "On your head be it. This is way too early to start drinking. You think these girls will really want to leave at five? The park stays open until sunset."

I didn't care what the girls wanted. Trash food, excitement, crowds—Honor would have a meltdown at some point. It was the price for this day, this memory, and I was willing for us both to pay it. But I didn't want it to be so big and awful that it ended up overshadowing all the good. I especially didn't want it to happen here.

I told Addie this, and she seemed to take it at face value. Once our drinks arrived, I went Full-Frontal Actress, launching a charm offensive, asking her all about her job, her hobbies, how long she'd been in Atlanta, where Sheila went to school, if she liked it. I got terse answers, at first, but I took them with an open smile and kept on, ruthlessly friendly. The margarita helped her get more comfortable, more chatty. I learned what a human resources executive did (well, sort of), and that Sheila was in a different private school than Honor, one I might want to look into for high school.

Halfway through the second drink, she'd thawed enough to ask me about Cam.

Cooper answered before I could. "The guy's a creep. I'm glad you didn't get back with him. Did he leave town?"

I ignored his opinions and stuck to the question. "Yeah, he fled Atlanta."

Addie made the most sympathetic face I'd seen from her yet. "Oh, sorry. Did he get off okay?"

I quipped, "Twice, actually," without thinking, and Addie's eyes widened. She had to work to stop an actual spit take.

As soon as she could swallow, she let out a bark of startled laughter, then lifted up her cup. "Mazel tov!"

I clinked my plastic cup against hers, to zero sound effect.

I said, "It's over, though. Really." I made myself sound brisk, like I was fine with it. Pro, but I could feel an inner chasm stretched out wide between my tone and what I felt about it, really.

Cooper chimed in, "It was the smart call. I mean, right? Considering?"

He was still thinking Cam was Marker Man. I knew better, but I wasn't going to argue with him. "We should order food. We don't want to be dead drunk to meet the girls."

When Addie ordered a burger, I said that I would have the same, like a peace offering. Cooper ordered a horrifying chili cheese fry situation that came in a huge mound. It looked like dog food and smelled like heaven. Drinks and junk food fueled more unfraught chat about our jobs, the girls.

Addie said, "They really do seem to get along. Sheila used to have a small herd of friends, but, ugh. Sometimes I think the divorce was like—she doesn't want to trust anyone now. She lost interest in her clubs, spends all her free time with books or on Snapchat with boys she barely knows. Honor is good for her, I think. I hope that she won't end up being bad for Honor. We need to keep a close eye—the age difference."

I agreed, and it felt good to have her on the same page. Safer for Honor. "I'm grateful for Sheila. Honor's slow to make friends. Maybe you and I could become actually, really friends, too."

Her eyes met mine. "Sure," she said, meaning no.

"Because of Cooper?" I said. Oh, gin! The man was sitting right there.

She misunderstood me, either deliberately or courtesy of the third margarita she was sipping. "Sheila and Cooper are close, but with our breakups, she's pulled back. She expects him to be gone in the next second."

"I'm not going anywhere," said Cooper, with his mouth full. "I'm in. No matter what happens with Sheila. I hope you know that."

Addie looked back and forth between us as he said it. Then she said to me, "You never went out on even one date, did you." She was pretty buzzed. Before I could answer, she said, "I know you're tight, though. Not going to lie. It's a problem for me. But if this friendship between our girls is going to happen, you and I have to find a way to be—"

He made an uncomfortable noise and said, "Exit stage left to the men's room, pursued by a bear." He straight-up fled.

I was on my third cocktail, too, and I'd ignored the bun and tried to stay out of the fries. The gin had me all chatty. I said, "Cooper and I were never a thing." That was true, but then I added, "There was never a chance we would be." That was a lot less true, but I'm a good, good liar. It came with the job. I had considered Cooper. From more than one angle. The truest thing of all, though, was that if I said this to Addie, she'd be a bitch to me forever. I needed an alliance, here. "All he ever talked about was you, and I talked about Cam, and my ex-husband." I saw her surprise. "Yeah. I was married. My ex lives here, and that has complicated every-thing. My history here in Georgia is why Cam and I broke up, not Cooper." That was true. I wish that I'd stopped there, but gin is truthful stuff, and it kept talking. "I think it's really over with Cam, and it may have been a bad mistake. I might be in love with him."

She looked at me with a tentative softness. "Okay. Well, then, that would suck."

We smiled at each other, wary, but I was leaning into friendly. I suspected that it wasn't only gin, or even only acting.

22

XENA WARRIOR PRINCESS spent most of the day in the storage room under Sheila and Honor's building, calming her own damn tits. She was inside, finally. She knew she should work on a plan, but for the moment, it felt good to check this box. Inside! Plus, Sheila's mom had stashed six boxes of old books here, and XWP was a reader.

Most were full of Sheila's ancient, torn kiddy shit with Crayola scribble-scrabbles and Sheila's mom's old bodice rippers. The last box was fully fantastic, though. Sci-fi, dystopian, fantasy, horror. She spent most of the day immersed in an old Stephen King she hadn't read before. *Firestarter*. About a girl who could burn crap up with her head. She wished she was that girl. Or Black Widow from the Avengers. Or the real Xena Warrior Princess.

She'd told Sheila and Honor that her name was Xena, just Xena, but Honor sometimes called her the whole thing, which was weird, but also cool. Her mom had owned the show on tape, like actual VHS tapes from when she was a baby. When they lost the house, they couldn't take a VCR or all those box sets of tapes. They couldn't take much at all, just what she could carry. First, she packed all books and toys. God, kids were dumb. Her mom made her repack, mostly clothes and food and stuff for hygiene. She had taken her sister's old stuffed bear, Vita.

Here's what she had left from the house: One of poor, disinte-grated Vita's plastic eyes. Her sister's old copy of *Watership Down*. An old key chain with four keys-to-nothing on it.

What now? She needed a plan, but all she had was a fake leather journal from a CVS with a handwritten story in it. The story was so sad that Sheila hadn't even asked to read it. She got up and stood in the cool, dim hallway, listening. Nothing. She was really alone, which was the safest thing she could be. She thought about Sheila and Honor having fun at the park, screaming down the slides when they ought to both be screaming all the time, just at the world.

When she finished the book, she knew she should try to think of something good to do that mattered or would help her, but she was hungry. She left, pausing to put the duct tape over the latch. The bells clanged, but any kid who ever snuck out of their middle school to smoke knew bells like that were not connected to a damn thing. She went outside and hurried around to the front of the building and went in. She passed the indoor coffee shop entrance and the locked glass lobby with the apartment elevators, heading to the deli.

She had money, and since she ordered food, the deli had to let her use the toilet. She spent a good while in there, washing up in the sink with the pink liquid soap. She changed her underpants and washed out both her spare pairs. Someone did come and knock, so she yelled, "I am pooping!" They stopped and went away. She came out feeling cleaner than she had in a while.

Both her sandwiches were ready, and she bought two Cokes and one bag of Cheetos and three soft cookies with nuts and white chips. She still had even more money from Honor's mom, so she went to the drugstore and got a new toothbrush for a dollar and toothpaste and floss and a pack of breakfast bars and a big-size bag of candy corn and deodorant, too. She could smell the good sand-wich smell because she'd gotten them toasted. She wanted to go back to the storage unit and eat one while it was warm.

She started trotting back, to go *inside*, and she loved Sheila and

Honor then. It made her feel wise now and not mad to think of them at the water park, screaming at the fake danger of slides, as if that was the thing that made a person scream. She hurried around the corner and down the alley. When she got to the duct-taped door, she stopped. She had a bad thought, and it was this: What if someone had found the door taped open? A bad person, like the man who said no to the monsters, or someone even worse, one who had monsters and didn't say no. The world was full of them. What if a person like that got in ahead of her? What if they were inside right now, hidden, waiting, and when she went in and the door clanged shut behind her, she would not be alone?

She peered at the seam. She'd done a good job of lining up the tape with the edge, and not a hint of silver duct tape showed. It didn't look like a door that a person could simply pull open. Also, the door itself was set back in an alcove in a dumpster alley. How many had even passed it by, much less tried it out, in the hour she'd been gone?

The chances seemed very, very small that someone had found it and gone in ahead of her and was now waiting in the dim, fusty hall. To get her.

Unless someone had watched her do it to begin with. It was hot out, but still she shivered.

She stood there, almost frozen for a moment, but out here in the muggy heat, the musty smell in her clothes came alive and rose like steam around her.

Fuck it, she thought. *I am Xena Warrior Princess. Or I will be, anyway. Tomorrow. Or later. Soon.*

She went inside. Brief bells, shrill, like a scream, like a warning. She ripped the tape away, and the door clanged shut behind her.

23

SOMETHING HAD HONOR. Bands around her. Tight, constricting. Her scream came out in bubbles, her breath knowing better than she did which way up was. She was almost empty before she understood the thing that had her was a person. He jerked and tugged at her. She screamed her last air out into his face.

The boy was very strong. She wanted to fight him, but she couldn't. She wanted to keep screaming, but all her air had gone away up in the water. Sheila had her, too. Hands. They all three flopped and thrashed. The boy spun, twisting all three of them upright in a clot, and then he put his huge big gross bare foot on Sheila's face and shoved her, extending his whole leg, ripping Honor free. Sheila's hands scratched at her skin, but the boy tore Honor loose. Instantly, he thrust Honor up, up, and she went, kicking hard, her lungs so empty they felt like they had twisted shut. She fought through the water, up to a small square of space between some floats, and then her head burst out. She sucked in breath so fast and big it hurt her throat. Some water got in, and she coughed. She wanted to scream more. She couldn't. She had to shove the water out fast and suck in more air, new.

She dashed at her burning eyes, kicking, and saw the empty pink float off to her left. It was Sheila's, but she paddled over and grabbed it anyway and clung. By the time she got her breath enough to scream, the boy burst through to the surface, dragging Sheila. Her friend coughed, pushing at him weakly. Her red hair hung in her face in wet draggles and rings, the glow sticks looking plain plastic and yellow in the sun.

One of four dads on a four-dad float said, "Hey. Hey! You kids all right?"

The boy, who was a stranger, answered, "Yeah. Yeah. We were playing. Just wrestling."

Honor was almost sure this was a lie. But only almost. Had Sheila been playing? Had the boy?

The dad looked at Honor and she showed him teeth. Made a thumbs-up. Coughed.

He ignored her and only talked to the boy, "Well, you be careful roughhousing. Those are girls."

Sheila laughed then, but it wasn't her regular laugh. It was a short, hard noise, like a bark. Honor clung to the float. Miserable. Honor was not playing at all. She said to the boy, "I want out. I want this over. I want out."

It was like a chant. The boy said, "Hang on," and then he toted them, swimming strong and pulling the float. He was a good swimmer. He kicked his long legs and pushed other floats, made a path happen, and, ignoring the surge and slosh, shoved a way through all the people.

After a few feet, Honor thought, *I am being rescued like some damsel*, and she started kicking, too, helping save them, helping him get Sheila into the shallows. The boy was tallest, the first who could put his feet down and wade them out. Sheila was next tallest, but she clung to the float, eyes closed, moaning. Then Honor could touch and she pulled with him and soon Sheila was sitting on her bottom in the shallow surf near some babies.

They helped her up. The boy put an arm around her like she was his girlfriend. He walked her, Honor trailing, to a shade pavilion over to the side. It was pretty empty now, and he took Sheila back to a lounge chair in a corner. She slumped down, moaning faint soft moans while Honor sat on a different lounge near and waited to see what would happen next. That whole thing in the pool, the part where they were under, it was over. Working to get her breath back, and all the kicking, had quieted the bees. Now that it was over, it seemed pretend. She didn't want to think of it.

Sheila said to the boy, "You were in line. At Dragon Flume. The flirt boy." She put her hand right on his face and slid it down and laughed.

Honor said, "What?" She didn't know this boy. She looked at his face, trying to recognize the pieces. He was tall and skinny and had some wispy face hair that wanted to be a mustache. Nothing about the shape of him was interesting or familiar.

The boy laughed, though. "Your friend is tripping balls, huh?" he asked Honor.

Honor had no idea what that meant. She said, "I left my green float loose out in the wave pool."

There was a sign telling you not to do that. You were supposed to take the floats and put them back when you were done, but the boy said, "Fuck that float. You almost drowned." Honor liked to hear that, that they had almost drowned. That was what she thought. It felt good to know what was true, and that no one had been playing. He turned back to Sheila. "Hey. What did you take, huh?" He looked at her hard, but she stared back and then shrugged, very slow. He said, "Well, maybe don't go in a pool. Lie down. Sleep it off."

Honor was mouthing, *Fuck that float.* It was a cool thing to say.

She didn't need to scream now. She was okay. They had been in peril. That was interesting, and even though the boy had rescued them, she kicked along and helped at the end. She went down deep after Sheila even though she was upset and stimming. It wasn't as heroic as what Xena Warrior Princess would do, or a paladin, but it was some pretty good sidekick stuff. Good enough for Gabrielle. That was cool.

The boy hung around some, trying to talk to them, but Sheila only wanted to lie there with her eyes shut. That was good. Honor had the 5e Player's Handbook on her phone. She opened it and read, even though she knew every word inside of it. It was good to read a thing you knew, and see it was the same. After a little, she looked at the talking boy and said, "I want now really to be very quiet, and alone. Okay?" She crunched down on her chair and read more. When she looked up again, he'd left. Honor pulled her lounge chair over closer to Sheila, who looked like she was sleeping. Good. That made her be quiet, too.

A lot later on, when Honor didn't mind it if she talked, Sheila said, "Oh, God. Don't tell my mom."

Honor nodded. Almost drowning and talking to a boy was a secret from mothers. Obviously. She said, "Do you want me to tell you more things about how to play D&D?" and Sheila did. It was good to do this. After the wave pool, she didn't want to go back in the water. She liked it, here, in the shade, talking to her quiet friend.

Her mom had texted a lot of times by now to ask how it was going. Honor didn't lie. Not once. She texted back things like: We went in the wave pool. True. We rode the Plunge twice in a row. True.

Now Sheila opened her eyes and said she needed a Coke. Even though it was so late for lunch they were actually close to needing dinner, Honor looked at the map, then walked to the closest food stand and got two veggie pizzas and a Coke for Sheila. She got herself a water because her mom said she might as well huff glue as drink a soda. Also, the bees still felt close. Out of her, but close. If she drank even a little soda, they might come.

Sheila was better after she ate. She apologized. "I think I got sick. I still feel so slow and weird. I'm really sorry. Are you going to tell my mom?"

Honor said, "Tell your mom what?"

Sheila got tears in her eyes and hugged Honor, which Honor didn't love, but it meant that they were really friends so she made herself be still until the hug was over. By then it was almost time to go.

Mom texted, Meet us at the gate, now. I hope you had fun, but we need to get home.

She texted back, We are near the front right now. True.

We'll wait here. True.

Thank you, because this was mostly a good birthday party. True.

Honor worried that the grown-ups would ask questions. Sheila was scared, too. They didn't want to tell about any of the teenager business, but both the mothers were chatty with each other and loud.

Only Cooper seemed to be noticing Sheila. "You feeling okay?" he asked, leaning in.

"We want to sleep in the van and be quiet," Honor told him, sternly. She and Sheila piled in the back and Sheila slumped, leaning her head on the window, closing her eyes. Cooper sat in back with them again, but when he tried to talk to Sheila, Honor said, "I told you. We have to be quiet now and maybe sleep. I said."

Her mom spun back and said, "It's okay. That's fine. Sometimes after a long, fun day, it's good to be quiet. Let's have some peaceful music and decompress." She had Antony put on Honor's nighttime playlist, which was mostly just Regina Spektor with singing and piano. Nice.

There was a wreck, and getting home was slow, almost twice as long as going there had taken. It got darker and Honor listened to songs and played on her phone. Sheila was asleep again, she thought. Maybe the mothers also fell asleep, because it was very quiet in the car. Maybe she did, too.

Some sharp noise, maybe a cuss or yell, woke Honor up. They were almost home. She recognized her street and the buildings on the block before their place. Up ahead, Honor saw a host of flashing lights. Emergency vehicles. She heard her mother suck her breath in, waking up, too, and at that sound, Honor found her own spine was getting very, very straight.

Cooper said, "Are they at our building?" They were.

One lane had been blocked off entirely, and Honor counted three police cars and a fire truck. The sidewalk had a lot of people, some in uniform, some just plain, milling around.

Was Mom crying? That made Honor go very still and sit up even taller. Even Sheila woke up, scrubbing at her face. Cooper leaned forward past them, sticking his head between the seats. Mom was saying something hushed and unhappy.

"You don't know that it's him," Cooper said, loud, and Honor understood then.

"Yes. I do," Mom said. "I do know. I feel it."

"Marker Man. Marker Man got in our building," she told Sheila. Sheila's eyes got big.

"Who?" Addie asked.

"Maybe all those cop cars mean they caught him?" Cooper said.

Her mother laughed, but it wasn't her real, happy one. "I hope so. We have to all hope that."

Honor crossed all her fingers. It was hard to swallow around all that hope. All that hope her mother said they all had to feel now.

Cooper asked, "But how could he get in? We all got that memo, not to buzz up anyone we don't know. The code got changed. How could he get in the building?"

Honor felt a pinch on her hand and looked over. Sheila was sitting up now, too, very tall.

"Xena," she mouthed.

Honor blinked. The door. The duct tape. That was a way in, and they had made it. Her body started rocking, faintly, and she felt the hum and buzz again. They had made a way inside and then gone off to have the birthday.

Sheila grabbed her arm, and Honor didn't love that, but right now, she almost did. She clutched Sheila's arm back, because on the heels of this awful thought, a worse one came. Marker Man and his letters. His pictures she had seen. She had seen one that was just a naked lady cut in half, with cherry blood spilled out all over, stinking. The picture was of her mother, but her mother lived upstairs. To get upstairs, to get to Mom's room, he had to go right past all the storage places.

They had opened a door for him, and let him into the quiet underneath part. Where Xena was. Alone.

24

I TOLD ANTONY to pull up to the curb, as close to the building as we could get, given the cop cars and the fire trucks that were already there. No sirens, but they sure were putting on a light show. I felt my spine elongating and my hands clenching. A young cop with medium-brown skin and a serious expression came toward us, motioning for us to move along. Antony put on his hazards, and I pushed the lever to send my window scrolling down and called to him, "What happened?"

"Ma'am, you need to—"

"We live here. We live here!" Cooper said, leaning forward between our seats.

The officer asked for a license, and Cooper had his wallet out before I could dig my ID out of my beach tote. He passed it up, and I gave it to the cop. He looked at it pretty carefully, and then his eyebrows knit.

He handed it back, saying, "Mr. Hayette, there was a break-in—" I knew what his next words would be, knew down in my bones, knew even though there was no breath between them. Time slowed for me, so much so that I could have gotten in ahead of the cop and said them first. "—on the fourteenth floor."

"Shit," said Cooper, eyes gone wide. Addie turned to me and mouthed, *The stalker?* She looked guilty. Stricken with it.

Marker Man had found a crack, in spite of the boosted security. He slithered through, again. The thought of him back inside our most personal spaces started me shivering, as if the temperature had dropped a sudden twenty degrees. I hated to think of his hands, rearranging the fruit in my bowl, fondling Honor's glass cat, drifting through my clothes, maybe stealing another bra. I hated his body, rolling in my bed to mark it with his scent.

My mind went to every horror movie I had ever seen or been in. What if he was still inside? As soon as I asked myself the question, I was dead certain that he was. He would be hidden cleverly in a vent or up inside a ceiling. As soon as the cops left, as soon as I was dumb enough to sleep, he would be on me.

The cop said, "Why don't you pull in and park? I'll take you to the officer in charge."

Honor piped up from the back seat, her tone belligerent, which I read as scared. "Why is there a fire truck?" It was a good question.

The cop said, "There was a small fire. No one was hurt, and it didn't spread to any other units."

All at once this cop, his car, the other officers somewhere in my building, even the fire truck made me furious. Rape threats, abduction threats, death threats, and I got forms and tutting and sad jazz hands. One tiny, contained arson, and here the cops were, all over. I should have set my house on fire months ago and told them it was him.

I looked back to see Honor had shrunk, pressing herself into the upholstery, disappearing beside a wide-eyed Sheila. Addie looked positively sick with guilt.

The fire was so confusing, muddling my rage and fear. Was he trying to burn me out? All the furniture was rental stuff, not even mine. Then I remembered my storage boxes in the guest-room closet that held all of Honor's best artwork, her old report cards, her school pictures. Another was full of photo albums holding paper pictures of my mother and baby me. Honor's baby book. Polaroids of young Wallace and my friends on the set of *Belinda's World*. In my own closet was the jewelry chest that held Honor's baby blanket and the note her bio-mom had written. These were all my most precious belongings. *Would he burn these things?* I wondered. Of course he would. He wanted to take away anything I cared about, until only my invented, nonexistent love for him was left.

The young officer wasn't finished, though. He leaned down closer, looking back and forth between us and then into the back seat. "Who all lives in unit D?"

I blinked, and my certainty that the fire was set by Marker Man deserted me. Honor and I lived in Unit A. Unit D? D was Cooper.

"Just me." Cooper's voice had gone high with surprise. "Someone set *my* place on fire?"

The officer hesitated, and his lack of concrete answer was a yes. "If you're ready, I can take you up." He stepped back, lifting his radio to his mouth and talking low.

Cooper cursed softly. I wanted to yell to Antony to peel out and gun it down the street. In that moment, I could happily abandon everything we owned here to stay uncertain that this was my fault. Maybe it wasn't. It could be random, some firebug burglars happening by. Ridiculous, and yet I wanted to believe it. If I ran, I'd never have to know.

It was futile. Where could I go? He followed.

I grabbed my beach bag. My purse was down in there, hidden under a towel. I dug out a tip for Antony and thanked him, and I remembered I'd stuffed the most recent envelopes from Marker Man down in here, too, unopened. Unread. His letters always said the same damn things in different words, anyway. If this was some dumb TV show, I could dissect the letters word for word like some hot version of Miss Marple, and I'd find an obscure literary reference that led us right to him. In real life, I made copies and took them to the police, who filed them for just in case he killed me, later. Then it would be serious. Then someone would find his ass and get him into prison. It would make a great Lifetime movie, with a purely fictional, leggy lady cop as the necessary strong, female protagonist. And me? I'd be playing the dead girl, once again.

The smell of the envelopes made me sick and anxious, but I owed it to Cooper and my other loved ones to see if Marker Man had decided that my friends were targets now. I let all three in the back seat pile out after Addie. Sheila, especially, was very slow, so I had time to look at the envelopes. The most recent was postmarked the seventh, and it had taken only two days to arrive because it hadn't had to make its way through my service. He'd mailed it directly to my condo, postmarked in Georgia.

I ripped it open. Inside was yet another drawing of me naked, tied spread-eagled, prone, and helpless. Instead of a bed frame, the mattress I lay on was supported by two cherry-blooded human heads. Now, that was new. One head had brown hair, a sad mouth, and Xs for eyes. *Cam,* I thought. The other had blue eyes, and round glasses, and hair in a double-colored scribble-scrabble that stank of chocolate and fake banana. It was Cooper.

Marker Man must have seen us together. When had we been in public? We'd hung out mostly at the gym inside the building or my condo. The only place we'd been out together was the coffeehouse. I had a sick heart-drop feeling, then. I thought of the squat, bulky figure standing in the rain across the street . . .

I so badly wanted that to be James. But the postmarks on the letters, the basket, now this attack . . . I climbed out of the SUV and hurried to catch up. The girls were anxiously following close on the cop's heels, Addie and Cooper holding hands tightly and walking just behind them. I wordlessly handed them the drawing. Licorice-black words written heavily underneath it said, YOU ARE NOT FOR THEM.

He whispered. "Shit, that looks like— Is that me?"

Addie said, "You think Meribel's stalker is after you now?"

I had no good answers. Was I supposed to explain to them what the cops kept patiently explaining to me? *Oh, this kind of stalker almost never escalates.*

Tell that to the guy whose apartment had been set on fire. We'd reached the glass elevator lobby, and I pulled ahead to put in the fresh-changed, useless code. Honor bustled past me, still child enough to want to push the button for the elevator. I couldn't stay here in the lobby, hiding from the truth, forever. I had to go upstairs now, to see what all had been lost or ruined or taken.

25

HONOR LIKED SHEILA'S house. It was very brown and plain with tan walls. The art was brown, like old-timey photos, and the carpet was another brown, and the curtains. It even smelled brown, because Sheila's mom lit up a soy candle called Warm & Woodsy as soon as they walked in, then went to change out of her bathing suit. Honor and Sheila were dry from sitting in the pavilion chairs all afternoon, so instead of changing, she said quietly to Sheila, "We have to go get Xena Warrior Princess."

"I know," Sheila said. Her eyes were wide and weird, still. But she was talking more regular and like herself.

Honor was banished to here while her mom secretly told the cops that Marker Man set Cooper's house on fire and that meant he was coming after her friends, now, too. Honor was not supposed to understand this. This was to help her not worry. Which would work, if she was stupid.

She knew it had to have been Marker Man, and she expected this to be confirmed the next time Mom was on the phone with Wallace and thought Honor had music blasting in her headset instead of nothing. It was usually nothing, because Honor liked to type entries on her play-by-post D&D games while designing maps with

Yuna and typing chat with Yuna and cocking her quiet headphones to hear what happened next on *Orphan Black*, which she was not allowed to watch. Honor liked to do a lot of things at once, which meant she often got to hear things Mom wouldn't tell her because of her being still a kid. It was good to know those things. Especially when a person wants to kill your mom or take her or hurt her. It was important to know what was happening.

She wanted to be down the hall with Mom and Cooper, wearing headphones so no one talked to her, pretending to hear music but instead listening as they told the police things. Mom would give over the footage from the doorbell. Honor wanted to know if the doorbell had showed what Marker Man looked like. If a person wanted to take your mom, and you could remember their shapes or colors or their face, that made it easy. You looked for that person, and if you saw them, then if you were a kid, you ran for help, or if you were a paladin, you fought them.

She said to Sheila, "Marker Man could be anyone at all." It made her pace to think this. Her body would not sit down on the brown leather couch or any chair. It was too full of bees to sit.

"That's so true. It could be anyone." Sheila was better than she had been in the wave pool, but the mothers had noticed she was weird. *Shock*, they guessed, instead of *trippin' balls*, and they wanted her to eat food. Maybe trippin' balls *was* shock from almost drowning. "What if one day you were in line at the grocery store and you reach for gum and someone else reaches for gum and they touch you with their sweaty gross hand and it's the stalker and you don't know. I would freak. I would die."

Honor shrugged. This was not upsetting to think about, because now she was going up into the back of her head. She was already buzzing, but now she felt that slither and shift, as the thinking parts of her crawled up and backward to press against the very top back of her skull in a calm, flat pancake. Her body walked back and forth, back and forth, trying to jostle her back down, but her thinking parts kept floating up anyway.

Sheila's mom came back in and leaned on the brown couch and said, "What if I scrambled you girls some eggs?"

"Yes, ma'am," Honor said, because she didn't know the mom's name. Then her eyebrow beetled up, suspicious, and she asked, "Are you going to put vegetables in?" When her own mom offered eggs she always tucked in a bunch of scallions and mushrooms and spinach leaves. Sometimes her mom put in shredded carrots, as if that was the same as the best cheese because it was orange. It was not the same. At all.

"I can," Sheila's mom said, but did not go toward the kitchen. She stayed looking at Honor. "So how long has this been happening? To your mother. The stalker."

Honor said, "A year." The mom still stood there for a while looking, but when Honor said, "When will you make the eggs?" she finally left.

As soon as the mom was cooking with music coming out of her phone, Honor went all the way to the window as far from the mom as she could go. Sheila came with her, and Honor got close enough to smell chlorine in her hair and say, "We need to go down there and know what happened, really. Because of Xena Warr—because of Cat. We should call her Cat now. In case someone hears."

If Xena Warrior Princess was Cat, then Honor was allowed to keep her. Helping Cat was teenager business. If Mom guessed Xena Warrior Princess was a homeless person, and that Honor and Sheila had let in Marker Man and he had maybe killed Xena, there would be all kinds of nose poking.

Sheila shivered. "We have to check on Cat," which Honor had already told her. "He went right past her to get up here."

From the kitchen, Sheila's mom called, "Has he ever hurt anyone, this stalker?"

Honor started to answer, but Sheila talked before Honor could answer. "God, Mom, you are so not subtle. I am not in danger and you are not. He is obsessed with Honor's mom, not us, and anyway, he just writes letters."

A small silence. Then the mom said, "And burns up her friends' beds."

Honor started to talk again, but Sheila was staring at her mom and breathing hard and her fists were clenched, so Honor had to wait. Finally, Sheila said, very loud, "Well, that's so cool how you made it about *you*."

The mom got stiff and they stared at each other from all the way across the whole apartment like this was a game of Blink. Sheila won, and her mom was also very red now in her face. Honor tried to be patient while they did this, but her thinking parts kept floating up and she was so worried about Cat.

Finally when the mom went back to making eggs, Honor said, "Do you think Marker Man did sex to Cat or killed Cat?" Honor was not supposed to see the pictures Marker Man made, but she took letters for herself from the mail sometimes, to see. In the pictures, her mom was naked or tied or scribble-scrabbled red with blood or in pieces or down a hole or all these things. That's what he drew, nakedness and killing. No one Honor knew was ever killed. At her school, a girl named Debbie had done sex with her high school boyfriend. People talking loud in homeroom said she had, anyway. Sex sounded gross to Honor, and if Xena didn't want him to do sex to her, then that was worse, and killed was worst of all. She had to think, *It is a cat, some wild cat under the house, not even Worker Cat, just any.*

Sheila's eyes were big and her head shook in a little no. "Do you think he would have hurt her?"

Honor nodded. She did think it. Marker Man had bad ideas. It was bad when a cat who was really a cat died or was very hurt. All hers and Wallace's were feral, so they lived dangerous lives. Sometimes they went missing and one time she herself found a stripy one named Limpy in the road dead from a car. Very still and smashed. Very wet and red and flat and not alive. All the energy was out of Limpy.

What if they went down and checked on Cat and it wasn't a

cat but a girl ripped all open or strewn or ruined. Like Limpy, but worse. Like Marker Man's pictures of her mom. Those were things he thought about. Those were things he wanted to do. She thought seeing a dead, ruined person would be worse than seeing Limpy.

Sheila whispered, "We let him get in."

Sheila clutched at Honor's arm with her hand, even though this was exactly the time that Honor did not want to be clutched with anything. You had to let friends do this, though. She had to be still now and get clutched, which meant she could not pace. Inside her skull, her real self, the thinking parts of her, climbed higher, got flatter.

Honor rocked harder, trying to jostle back down into her anxious body. So many bees. She had to know if Cat was dead and strewn or safe, and then she would calm down.

She said very loud to Sheila's mom, "We have to go down real quick and check on Cat, our cat, though."

"The cat is fine," Sheila's mom said, stirring eggs, not turning around.

It was hard to rock enough while being clutched. She had to move. Her hand was clammy and she patted the clutch hand off and once she could pace it was better.

"What if Marker Man got Cat, though?" she asked, so loud, for the mom to hear.

Sheila's mom said, "Feral cats are very smart and they hide."

That was true. Maybe their Cat was smart and good at hiding, too? Sheila said, real mad, "Mom! We have to check."

Sheila's mom got that kind of flat and hard parent voice that meant really no and said, "We are not going outside to stomp around in a dark alley right now here in the night. I will take you to check on the cat tomorrow."

Honor and Sheila met eyes and Sheila made a bunch of faces and blinks that could mean anything. Sheila's mom thought the cat was outside. They were not going to be allowed to go, and if they did get to go, even tomorrow, the mom would come with them to the alley where they would call for a cat who didn't exist. They would not actually get to look for Cat who was inside and maybe . . . peeled. It was all impossible and ruined.

"Come have your eggs, and then you can watch television, if you want." Sheila's mom put down plates with eggs that were not cooked enough and gross and also toast that had raisins, which was disgusting. They sat and Honor put four bites of eggs in and swallowed the slime of them fast like pills, to be compliant. This was how adults worked. If you were compliant in one thing, then they would sometimes give you another.

Honor said, "Can we at least go down to the storage locker you have?"

"Why on earth—" the mom started, but Sheila interrupted.

"That idea is great! I have books down there that I said Honor could have, and Honor's not really supposed to watch TV."

"TV is a screen," Honor said piously.

"You have a ton of books up here," said the mom. "None of us are leaving this apartment."

Sheila said, "But Mom!" and her mom said, "Sheila!" and then it was just spatting. Honor got up and paced and thought and next time she paid attention, the mom was stomping away loud into her room. That meant the conversation was over.

Sheila said, "Okay, so new plan. Do you know how to make yourself throw up?" Honor shook her head. "Jam a finger in the back of your throat. Puke first thing in the morning, and then we both have to stay home from school."

That was a true rule. Anyone who puked could not go in a school for twenty-four hours. It was a good plan except Honor couldn't stand to throw up even for Cat. Also, with this plan, they still had to sleep all night not knowing if Cat was in pieces.

"Mm," said Honor.

Even with the pacing, she could not stop flattening and rising. Now she was not really in her buzzing body. She liked that, liked to be up out of it, flattened and cool. She was so calm here above the body. This is what her mom didn't understand, how very calm and smart she was, how she had good ideas and observations when she was back up here. Like she had a plan for Cat now. A calm good plan she made. She couldn't say it, though. She needed to get down inside her body so she could say things, say her good new plan for Cat. Her hands started slapping at her head to try to push down.

"What are you doing?" Sheila said, very loud like shrieking. "Stop it, stop, now, stop!"

Honor ignored her friend because she really had to keep hitting at her head and face while her mouth made sounds. Her body had to do these things.

Sheila tackled her and wrestled her to try to make her be still, but Honor could not be still, and then the mom came out and saw them rolling and ran away out the door into the hall yelling, "Meribel! Meribel!" She was very loud about it.

Then Mom was there, smelling that fresh kind of sweaty that was all salt. Mom was holding her now, not Sheila. Mom wrestled her body and made it stop hitting her head and face, but the body had to move and Mom knew that. Mom pinned Honor's flailing arms in a bear hug so very squeezed and that was good and Mom rocked her very hard and that was good. Her mom said a lot of words at her over and over like, *Baby, it is fine, hush now, stop now, you are safe,* and also a lot of words at Sheila's mom like, *No, do not touch us, she is fine, please get ice, I have her, she is fine.*

Mom was right. Honor was fine and not upset or unsafe at all. She was fine and calm and now she unpeeled from the top of her skull and came down into her whole head to be behind her eyes again, which was where she was most of the time. In a book she read she learned that Aristotle told the Greeks to think the heart was most important. He said people lived in their chests, in their hearts. Sometimes, like when she rode a horse, she thought he might be right, but mostly she thought he was dumb. You were your brain, really.

Honor said, "Can we go home?" and her mom knew it was okay

to let her arms go and help her up. Mom had an ice pack now, and she pressed it to Honor's face so Honor couldn't see if she nodded, but she must have, because she said to the other mom, "Thank you for getting me. I'm taking her home. The police were done with me, mostly, anyway."

Honor felt good and stretchy. She pushed at her mother and took the ice to press on her own, rolling it back and forth across her face. "I want only air on me." Sometimes after her body did this, all her skin got extra alive and she needed soft pajamas and no sheets or blankets, even her weighted one she loved, and no hands. Mom stepped away.

Sheila's mom said, "Are you okay, sweetie?"

"Yes." Maybe the "sweetie" meant that Honor could still be friends with Sheila even though Honor had had an upsetting fit.

Sheila came over close. Too close. But Honor let her because maybe Sheila wanted to whisper about Cat. But Sheila only said, "*Are* you okay?"

"I had a meltdown," Honor said, very loud. "I am autistic. Sometimes this happens." Very loud like theatre she said it. "Tomorrow I won't go to school even though I didn't throw up. I need to be quiet and left completely alone tomorrow."

Sheila stared at her and then said, "Okay, ya big freak." But she must have understood that this was Honor's plan to not throw up and still go check on Cat, because she mouthed, no sound, but just the shape of it, one word at Honor: "Baller."

Sheila's mom said, "Sheila! Apologize!" very loud, too.

A lot of kids got weird and didn't like her after she melted down, but *Baller*, according to Sheila, was the best thing you could be. So Honor made her mouth smile and said, "Nah, you're the freak."

Mom said, "It's fine, Addie. It's—affectionate. They say that to each other."

Honor wished she had thought to say *Calm your tits* to Sheila's mother. That would have been the right time to say the cool thing Cat taught her, and now she'd missed her chance and Cat might—no.

They had a plan. Sheila would throw up and stay home, too, and in the morning, Sheila's mom would go to work and Honor's mom would leave her alone if she said she needed quiet and space. She could sneak out. They could go down alone and check on Cat.

It would be hard to wait until the morning to see if Cat was dead or gone or hurt, but they had to. Because of how mothers were.

26

I STAYED WITH Honor in her room, not touching her, encouraging her to keep pressing the ice pack on her poor face. She was going to have at least one shiner, though. Maybe a double.

Once, after a particularly trying spring with multiple melt-downs, some *helpful* neighbor (who never bothered to come talk to us) called Child Protective Services to report "frequent facial bruising." It had taken multiple calls with Honor's therapists and forms and conferences to get that sorted out. Now, we were in a new city, at a new school. I'd brought the school counselor letters from her therapists and the relevant bits of her medical records. Even so, I'd have to call tomorrow and talk it through with them. I felt ashamed, almost as if I *had* hit her.

I had her nighttime music going, both to calm her and cover the low voices of Cooper and the police still talking in my den, which meant I couldn't hear her breathing. Was she awake? Hard to tell. She could be so very still. "Hey, kitty cat, are you sleeping?"

"Yes," she said, and I couldn't help but chuckle. She added, "Almost."

She pushed her mostly melted ice pack away and said, "I don't want it to touch me anymore," so I picked it up and pressed it against my own eyes for a moment. I needed to do instead of think. If doing failed, I would think a thousand things before I'd allow myself to feel. I was standing on the edge of a tall cliff. Any little breeze could set me teetering. Any little push and I might plummet.

I wanted Cam, wanted his trained, strong body—and his gun—between me and Honor and my front door, between us and the world. I'd broken it off with him in part because here in Georgia, James felt so real. My past felt so close. But if I started crying or yelling now, how could I stop? Who would hold me down like I'd held Honor? I was scared, and furious, and, as if I needed more, my stupid, fickle heart felt like it was breaking.

I stayed another few minutes, until I heard the faint sounds of the policemen leaving and I was positive that Honor was asleep.

Cooper was still there, sitting on my sofa. He smiled at me, rueful. "I thought I'd wait and check on you and see how she was doing before I . . ." He gestured down the hall.

We'd talked to the cops here and he was going to stay with Addie because his mattress had been set on fire. It was thoroughly ruined, even though it hadn't caught well. No accelerant. It was an incompetent but brutal and very intimate destruction. On top of that, his glassware and dishes were shattered, his art defaced. His bedroom walls and carpet were smeared with human waste, and in every other room, Marker Man had found his paints and used up all the red, writing the same message over and over, the words drooling down the walls in crimson:

Stay away from her! Stay away from her! Stay away from her!

"We're fine," I said, but tears started up in my eyes at his kindness. "I hope you know that I am going to pay for the damages."

He waved that away. "I have insurance. I'm worried about you."

I would be more worried about safety, were it me. I would be sprinting as far away from the actress with the stalker as I could, if my whole house stank of feces and burned foam. He would have to take the bedroom down to studs and replace the drywall and the carpet to get the smell out.

"I'm at least going to cover the deductible."

"Stop," Cooper said. "You didn't do anything. Addie and I were talking over cohabitating anyway. This will be a nice practice run." He quirked one shoulder up in a shrug. "Unless we break up again, and then, you know, I'm coming right here to claim your sofa."

I smiled like he was joking, though it seemed a likely outcome, actually. They weren't the most stable couple, and this was a stressful way to test-drive living together. I wouldn't mind having him, if it came to that. I owed him, and I'd feel safer.

He asked, "Should you stay here?"

"I honestly don't know," I said. "Tonight me and my kid are both too damn exhausted for me to do much about it."

I could never leave Honor in this place by herself, now. I'd have to put her in an after-school program when filming began, but school was a lot of people time for her already. She wanted to be at home in the afternoons, in her room or on the sofa with a book, decompressing, but she couldn't be alone. Safety in institutions.

He stood, preparing to go, and said, "Well, we're right down the hall." He started for the door, and then he paused and turned back to me. His voice went fierce. "You never told this whack job to get obsessed with you. You asked for none of this. I can't imagine the stress . . ."

I had to work again to not start crying. It was lovely of him to think of how I must be feeling, when he was the one with the ruined condo. I felt so grateful for his kindness, and even more grateful that he was not blaming me for what Marker Man had done.

I blamed me, though, a little. Meribel Mills, center stage always, opinionated, animated, dressing in jewel tones, calling eyes to me, getting fillers and Botox to keep my face fresh, hiring a personal trainer and limiting carbs to keep my body lithe, all this work to stay some kind of fuckable so I could keep the job I loved. So far,

I had stayed young enough, thin enough, pretty enough to be em-
ployed, and because of this, part of me believed that maybe I *had*
asked for this. Women with any fame, even my small dram, learn it
is better not to self-google, but of course we do. Liza told me not to
all the time, and then added, "When you do it anyway, even though
you honestly know better, you must never, never, never read the
comments." Well, of course I had.

*She has egg eyes. I'd like to set her on my lap and spin her like a
top. She looks like a frog. I'd bend her over and just wreck her. Is she
pregnant or fat or does she just have a food baby. Wow, did she get old!
Her tits are too small. Her ass is too flat. She's too pale. She looks like
she'd give good head if she'd ever shut up talking. I wouldn't hit that
skank with someone else's dick.*

I had read all these things about myself and much, much
worse. People talked about actresses as if we were objects, and the
excuse—the reason?—was always the same: *She put herself out there.
She asked for this, she asked for this, she asked for this.* People talked
about women who got stalked or raped or killed or beaten the same
way. *What was she wearing, what did she say, how much did she have
to drink, why didn't she leave, why didn't she call out for help. When
there were people. Right downstairs. She asked for it, whatever she got.
She called it to her.*

Cooper was saying to me, *No, you didn't.*

I wasn't a weepy person. Usually. Tonight, though, I was spend-
ing every other minute welling up and pressing a desperate hand to
my lips to keep a sob in. I went to him by the door and hugged him,
really tight. "Thank you" was all that I could manage.

"It's fine," he told me, patting at my back. "We're friends. If you
need anything . . ."

I stepped back, wiping my eyes. "Same. If you need anything
at all. To be honest, I would like to show you something? If you'll
come into the kitchen for a minute?"

He did. Once there, I opened up the pots-and-pans drawer by
the stove. It was the last place in the house that Honor would go

digging through. I took Cam's lockbox out from underneath the Dutch oven.

Cooper recognized it instantly. "That's a gun safe."

I knew he'd grown up in Texas, had probably been hunting a time or two, but that was rifle stuff. I asked, "Do you know how to use a pistol?"

"Of course," he said. "My dad had me on the shooting range before I could walk. But."

I beeped in the little four-tone code, *boop, beep, bah, bah,* and swung open the lid. The gun was dark gray and squared off. Even though I kept it, the matte gleam of the metal struck me as sinister. "It's loaded."

He cocked an eyebrow. "Every gun is always loaded, even if someone says it's empty. It's good you have the manual safety on." He reached out with one finger to touch the little lever, then ran it down over the words "SIG Sauer" on the handle.

"I don't want Honor knowing it's in the house. I am going to sleep with this box, but if I'm not home, you can find it in this drawer. I'm going to give you my spare key, okay? You know where it is, if—if you need it." Marker Man had destroyed Cooper's house. I worried next time he might go after the man himself.

"Where did you get this?" He read the answer off my face and his nostrils flared. "That guy is sketch."

"I told you, it's over," I said. I'd traded Cam for James. Not even James. For his memory. For the idea of a man who would stand in the rain or under my window, but with only good intentions. I clicked the box shut and showed him the code again, *boop, beep, bah, bah.* "Memorize it, because I am not writing that PIN down anywhere."

"I got it. You want me to stay?"

I chuckled. "I'm sure Addie would love that!"

He grinned, too, shaking his head. "Obviously I'd text her to join us."

"It's okay," I said. "She and I got onto better footing today. I really want us to be friends, so let's not push it."

We said our good nights, and I showed him out, but then he paused again in the hall.

"I hesitate to bring it up. I know friends are a struggle for Honor, but I have to say this. Watch out for how much time she spends with Sheila? I hate to talk shit about my girlfriend's daughter, and I love Sheila, but I know she's sneaking around with boys. Older ones." He took a deep breath and then added, with so much regret my respect for him rose up another notch, "I think Sheila might be experimenting with drugs."

I had a big emotional reaction to that. Honor's only friend. "What kind of drugs?"

"I don't know. But at the park did she seem—off to you?" He mimed holding a joint to his lips, sucking on it, and a lightbulb went off. She had seemed off, and in a way that damn well ought to look familiar. Everybody in the business, hell, half of California, had "anxiety" and a prescription, me included. "Addie is not fully open to seeing how deeply troubled Sheila is. I worry they are heading for—well, anyway. If Sheila's using pot at a water park with her mom right there, what's she doing on her own?"

It was a valid question. I thanked him and closed the door. This was serious, and could have an impact on my kid, but it wasn't a thing I could begin to tackle tonight. My plate was full enough, and I wasn't sure at all what was the best approach. I needed sleep, and Wallace's counsel, and most of all, for Marker Man to be in jail.

I went back to my room, toting the gun in its box. Once I was alone, it was hard not to give in to instant masochism, open my computer, and watch Marker Man walking down my hallway on an endless loop. Cam had set the doorbell up so all the footage sent itself to both of us immediately. When I'd pulled it up for the cops, I saw Cam had turned off his access before he left me at the hotel. If I watched it, I would be the only one.

I went through my bedtime regimen instead, which always calmed me. Skin care, hair care, body lotion, soft pajamas. But once I was in bed, in the dark, alone, I could not resist. I sat up and pulled my laptop off the bedside table.

I opened up my doorbell app and called up the footage. Cam had set the camera's sensitivity to "hair trigger." It had started filming when the door to the stairwell clanged open, telling me that Marker Man was careful enough to walk up fourteen flights in case the elevators had security cameras. They didn't yet, as it happened, but it was telling that he hadn't taken the risk.

The video was decent quality, but the hall lighting was low. The collar of his dark coat was pulled up, and he had a black fisherman's cap pulled way, way down. He was bulky, built low and wide and shouldery. I could see exactly none of his face. No hair. Not even a slice of neck. He didn't come toward my door at all. He didn't even look my way, the camera-conscious bastard. No, he walked decisively the other way, right to Cooper's place. Just as he turned toward Cooper's door, the camera clicked off. He had stepped out of range.

That stocky body, short and wide. Dark pants and what looked like black combat or steel-toe boots. This figure in its long gray London Fog was undeniably the same person I had seen standing in the rain, watching me have coffee with Cooper. I'd seen this exact person again on the street in the middle of the night, staring up at my floor. And me? I'd stood out on my balcony like Juliet, pining like a stupid innocent for love, when only death was waiting in the garden.

27

I ADDED HONOR'S poor, bruised face to Marker Man's extensive tab when she finally came out of her room. It was well after nine the next morning, but she was still in her soft, knit pajamas. She was sluggish and quiet as she flopped down into a chair at the dining table, her right eye puffed and already turning spectacular shades of deep purple. A smaller half-moon of violet had formed under her left.

I listened to coffee burbling and Honor crunching cereal. She had her D&D *Monster Manual* and *Bullfinch's Mythology* both open, cross-checking something.

Marker Man felt close. So very, very close, and James felt far, and Cam felt gone. Who did I have now? Cops. Sure, they were taking it more seriously now, but they weren't here.

"How are you doing?" I asked my girl when she looked up from the books to pour herself a second bowl of Grape-Nuts. Her swollen eyes broke my heart right into pieces.

"Not good," she said in a petulant, small voice. "My paladin serves the Fates, the *three* Fates, but now Yuna says I have to pick one." She turned the book to show me a picture of the young beauty spinning at the wheel, the tired mother measuring out thread, the crone wielding her scissors.

I asked, "Which one is best?"

Wrong question. Her brows came down. "All three together is best. It takes all three Fates to make a god. With one, my paladin is serving a chunk of a collective!"

"Hm. I see the problem." I didn't, fully; she was so exacting. Her character was Lawful Good, meaning a morally upright sort who liked rules, order, systems. *Sure, Honor. Your* character *is that way*, I thought, and then I realized, since she *was* so like her paladin, I should simply ask her. "Is your friend doing drugs? Sheila?"

"No, that's dumb," Honor said, immediately and with zero tension. She didn't even look up from the book. "Unless I pick Lachesis I can't cast Raise Dead, but I don't like her best at all."

I worked hard not to smile. Deciding what Fate to pick was such a simple, lovely, childish problem that it reassured me. If Sheila had done drugs in front of her, Honor would have told me. Her head was in her game, even with Marker Man breaching our very building.

"What does the rule book say?" With Honor this was almost always a good question, but now she glared at me like I was the dumbest person ever born.

"Mom. It's homebrew." I held up my hands in surrender, and she added in way that sounded like the start of a fight or a threat, "I can't go to school today. I will throw up. I will." As if Greek mythology and D&D and skipping school and gastric distress were all related.

I smiled, calm and sure. This was normal in the wake of the kind of meltdown she'd been through yesterday. "Of course you're staying home. I do want you to take some time to read and hopefully nap, but we can go to summer rules for screens today, all right?" She needed downtime, and disappearing into her gaming forums and map programs was good stress relief. Let her reset. Let her pull back and breathe.

Not even summer limits made her eyebrows unknit, but she said a tight, fast "Thanks," before she gathered her books and her phone to go back to her room. I could hear her dictating what had to be a text for Yuna as she went. "So now my paladin is supposed to say, 'Evil beware! I serve a chunk of a collective god and can't raise dead!'"

I got up and made myself another cup of strong, black coffee. This morning my mirror had shown me a tired, middle-aged face trying to swim up under my fillers. Fine. In fact, if Yuna told me that I had to pick one Fate to serve, I might take the Crone, whichever that one was. No one stalks the Crone.

I felt so powerless. My kid's watershed birthday had been tainted, and her only friend might be a danger. Her stress levels were skyscraper high, as were mine, and there was nothing I could do to shake my stalker's avid interest. It wasn't even about me, though Marker Man would say it was. I was a shape to him, the outline of an object, filled in by him, interpreted by him. Not a person. I couldn't stop him from coming after me, my friends, my family, because he stayed hidden, watching me, inventing me. I wasn't good at patience, but my whole life was now reduced to waiting. He was the watcher. He had the power. The watcher always has the power.

I reached for my phone to distract myself with Instagram, and instantly got hit with a humiliated guilt pang. Hadn't I done all these same things to James? I'd sneaked and spied and put eyes on him. Before that, I'd been watching him on the sly through screens like this for years.

Love or stalking. Yes or no. Toy or person. I was tired of being played with like I was a doll or a deck of cards—woman as entertainment—but hadn't I invented a yes from James when I'd told myself that it was him under my balcony? It was not all that different from the way Marker Man told himself that I adored him. They were stories, as much mythology as what Honor was reading. I'd liked my story so much, I'd traded Cam for it. Cam, who was real and solid and had been here when I needed him. The minute I said no, he had gone silent. When someone says no, a decent person honors that.

Now, with a gun hidden amid the Le Creuset, with Cooper's

bed burned and human feces and threats streaked down his walls, I didn't want to be a person who would do anything remotely like what Marker Man was doing. I owed James an apology. Which meant I had to contact him. Directly. The very thought made me sick, but not so sick that I could fool myself into thinking that this was not the right thing to do.

I couldn't call James from the living room, where Honor might overhear us, and certainly not from my bedroom. That felt way too intimate.

I took my coffee and my phone through the master and out onto my balcony. It was a gorgeous fall morning, soft with sunshine, but not yet hot. Much too pretty a scene to match the soundtrack I was hearing: strained violins, my heart a bad drumbeat.

I started to close the French doors, but I was tired of feeling trapped. The day was gorgeous. I decided to leave them open the way we did at home, my real home, until the day got too hot. I liked traffic and bird noises, the smells of the city coming in. I sat down at the bistro table, and it was the work of seconds to get James's office number pulled up. I'd already visited the website, flipped to the contact page, considered touching the number. I'd considered it multiple times, actually, but for wrong and selfish reasons. Now, at last, I dialed it for the right one.

When a pleasant-voiced receptionist answered, I said, "James Whelan's office, please." She put me on hold, and I listened to two bars of what sounded like, so help me God, Muzak Coldplay before it started ringing again. My heart rate jacked even higher. My chest felt squeezed. I wasn't sure what happened next. I couldn't picture James at his job. My idea of office jobs came from workplace sitcoms. I was not attached to real life, much, was I? Did people still have secretaries? I imagined a woman with boufy hair and lacquered nails, straight out of *Mad Men*. She'd ask who was calling, and I'd say, *Why, this James's possibly secret ex-wife, Meribel Mills.* Or I might say, *A scared and sorry person who's been creeping on him, hard.*

James answered his own phone, though. He said his name into my ear, and the voice, his singular pitch and timbre, was familiar and memory-faded at the same time. When I said nothing, he repeated, "James Whelan. Hello?" His southern accent had faded quite a bit. It was all I could do to not hang up, or worse, pitch the phone right off the balcony and into traffic. I could hear myself panting like a pervert, and he said, soft and certain, "Meribel."

This much later, he knew me by my breath.

"Hi, James."

I sounded uncertain, almost shy. Like my true young self, the one I barely remembered. I'd been a sophomore in college, trying not to get caught scoping out the cute guy in world history, when James fell for me. In my twenties, I reset myself to eighteen and became confident, strident "Rah, Rah, Whatevahhhh," Didi. She was all id, relentless and willful, and so was I. In LA, I abnegated my old sweetness, my uncertainty. I abnegated all my years with James.

"So that *was* you," he said. "In the parking lot."

"Yes," I admitted. I could feel how hot my cheeks were. "I'm very sorry about that."

"No, no, it's—" He didn't say it was okay. He took longer and thought more. "It makes sense. If I'd known where to find you, I might have done the same thing. Just to see you." If he was half the Google-sniper I was, he could have found me, thanks to Addie. "I knew you'd moved here to film that lawyer show. I mean, I follow your career. A little." There was a brief pause and then he said, "Not in a creepy way."

He said it with no irony, but I blushed anyway. "Sure. Like I drove out to your town and lurked in my car watching your family eat guacamole 'not in a creepy way.'"

He chuckled. "Hey, I've been jumpy ever since I realized you were moving back, wondering if I would hear from you. Part of me thought I hallucinated you sitting in that car, imagined it because I wanted to see you. Or I wanted you to want to see me." He trailed off. A normal person would have called him that day instead. I should have. The gap had felt too big, too impossible to cross so simply. Then he surprised me. "I'd still like to see you. Not to—I don't know. I want to see you."

I heard myself say, "I want that, too."

Another pause. My knuckles were white on the phone.

"Is there a reason why we shouldn't, then?" he asked.

Oh, just my kid, who only knows me as Mom, not as a person with a history and a broken heart. Just your wife. Just three more kids who look like the ones I dreamed of having.

"None I can think of," I lied. "I live in Midtown, so it would be easy. Your job is maybe ten minutes away."

I obviously knew where he worked, since I had called his office, but this was an inadvertent admission that I'd also mapped out the distance in between us. Either he didn't catch it or he took it in stride. He'd already admitted he followed my career, but to be fair, my job was much more public.

He said, "I'm in a meeting until ten thirty. Maybe we could get together at eleven."

My breath stopped. I had to push it out to make a single word. "Today?" That was so very immediate. I wanted it, though. I wanted it to happen. Sooner was better. Talking to James felt like opening the door to a room I hadn't visited in decades, one I could not see from here. I wanted to see that space again. Maybe walk through. Maybe even close that door behind me. But. Honor. "I can't today. My kid is home from school. Not feeling great."

He was already backing down, a little sheepish. "Oh, sure, yeah. You must be busy. I'm being ridiculous. I mean, it's been years. We both—" He was going to get off the phone. I felt it. Or I knew him well enough to read it. I could not bear one uncertainty more, I realized, so I talked fast, over him, before he could hang up.

"Unless you want to come here? There's a coffeehouse right downstairs. Inside my building. I could slip down and see you." This would work. Honor needed solitude and quiet to recharge, and I'd be close enough to get to her in two minutes if she did call for me.

"That would be great." He sounded relieved.

I gave him the address and told him where to park, and then a silence stretched between us. It got awkward, but hanging up would end a contact that was twenty years past due. I made myself say, "I better let you get back to work."

"Yeah, okay. I'll see you soon."

We hung up. My coffee had gone cold. I didn't mind it. I scrolled to Cooper's contact info and texted him.

Could you maybe come over to my place at eleven and work here, just for an hour or less? I have a meeting down at Java House. Honor'll likely stay 100 percent in her room, but I'd feel better knowing you could call me if she did come out or wanted me.

I didn't think she would. A meltdown like the one last night often acted as a whole, hard system reboot. She'd spend the day holed up with books and screens and silence.

Sure, Cooper texted back. Sheila stayed home from school, too—stomach flu, but I think it's stress. It might be nice for us to have a break from each other.

I half hoped it was stomach flu, because that explained why she'd been so disconnected at Wild Waves. Not high, just off because she was getting sick. I texted back, Friend, I owe you one.

I got up, and there behind me was the new security camera, looking over my shoulder and past the rail, down to the street. Cam had installed it, but he had removed his access when I broke up with him. When I came out here and sat down, he hadn't gotten an alert. He hadn't poured a cup of coffee of his own and sat down to watch me talk to the ghost I'd chosen over him, and that told me something.

I could trust Cam Reynolds to respect a person's privacy more than I could trust, well, me.

28

HONOR, SCRUNCHED UP in her bed, phone in hand, reveling in Summer Rules, was texting with Sheila about their secret *Save Cat!* plans. Sheila had stuck a finger down her throat and urped up her whole breakfast and was at home streaming whatever she wanted on her mom's iPad. Her mom had gone to work, so she could go to the storage rooms at any time. Lucky.

Sheila sent: But I have to get past Cooper. Still, he is easier than mom. You could say you want to go to the gym? We can even go by the gym. If you want. Sheila knew Honor wasn't good at lying.

Honor texted back: Mom loves gym. If I say that, she might come with me.

Maybe she could make a hump in the bed with pillows like an asleep Honor puppet and slip out? She was thumb-typing in this plan for Sheila when her mom tapped at the door. She called, "What?" Mom popped only her head in, which meant it would be short. Good.

It was better than short, though; it was useful. Mom wanted to know if Honor minded if she went downstairs to have an early lunch meeting in the coffeehouse. "It shouldn't be too long. And I'd have my phone."

Honor was more than okay. Honor was great. She said so while thumb-typing, My mom is going to the coffeehouse at eleven. WE GO

THEN! WAIT FOR ME AND DO NOT GO WITHOUT ME. It could be dangerous or bad. Cat was their shared friend or project, and they should both help her together, or it was too scary.

Her mom said, "Okay, good. Cooper is going to come work here, in my office, if you need anything. Plus I'll be right downstairs."

Sheila: I won't. I'm scared to go by myself.

Honor texted, Why? And told her mother, "I don't need Cooper to sit me. I'm a teenager."

Sheila: What if HE is down there. Hidden. Marker Man.

Honor hadn't thought of that. That was worst of all, even worse than if Cat was hurt or missing or dead. She had dreamed it all night. A girl body. Xena. Ruined, like the drawings. Like Limpy the real cat in the road. But him, downstairs, with Xena or with her body, that was scarier. In Honor's imagination, even in all of her bad dreams last night, Marker Man had come in the taped door, hurt Cat a lot, ruined Cooper's apartment, and then left.

Mom said, "He's going to be working, baby. He won't bother you. Are you texting Yuna?"

Honor texted: The police would've found him if he was down there. Out loud, she very carefully did not lie to her mother. "Yuna is being unreasonable and still says I have to pick one Fate." True.

Sheila: What if he is in our storage unit, hiding in the boxes with the lock on? I gave Xena the combination. He could have made her tell. So when the cops were there, the storage rooms were all locked. With padlocks. They check the hall, maybe peer in the slatted doors. They don't see him. Marker Man is way too sly. He's buried in crates with only his eyes up, like a crocodile. And then we go down and—blammo.

Honor shifted, her body starting to buzz a little bit as she imagined this. She sat up, but her mom had slipped out, closing the door quietly behind her. Not that she would have told her mom. This was teenager business. Even Cat was a teenager, nineteen, the oldest teenager possible, like Honor was the youngest. Also, this particular Cat was really Xena Warrior Princess and a homeless girl and might be down in the storage room dead or harmed or captured. No adult would let them check, but they had to. It was their responsibility.

My mom has a gun. Should I bring it?

Last night, when she was not sleeping, she heard her mom and Cooper talking in the kitchen. It sounded very soft and secret, so she'd slipped out and down the hall and crouched at the corner, listening. She'd peeked around and seen her mom hiding the gun box down in the big low kitchen drawer.

Sheila: Do you know how to shoot a gun?

Honor thought about it. Did she? Well, didn't anyone? She'd seen a lot of people, her mom included, shoot them on TV or in movies. It isn't hard.

Sheila: Baller. Hell, yeah! Bring the gun.

Honor nested way down deep in all the covers. That made her less scared. If she had the gun, everything would be fine. She opened a browser to check her play-by-post games, but none had updates, so she browsed around, reading old campaigns. She wanted music, but needed her ears free. She had to hear it when her mom left. Then they would go down.

29

A FEW MINUTES before eleven, I stood outside of Honor's door, breathing quietly and listening. Nothing. I peeked in, and she was in the bed, an unmoving hump beneath her weighted blanket, one foot sticking out. That foot was always out. Even when she was a baby, it would fight its way free of any coverlet. She didn't move, and her phone was beside her, screen facing the ceiling, so she was likely asleep. Yesterday had worn her out. What a way to come of age.

I closed the door gently and headed down to the coffee shop, wearing leggings and an outsize aqua tunic with a long belt wrapped twice around myself to make a waist. Tinted moisturizer, a little liquid blush, pale lip gloss, brown mascara. This was wardrobe and makeup for Young Meribel, smelling like Ivory soap and wisteria shampoo, hopeful and unbroken, a page from the look book of the girl who had belonged to James.

Java House was nearly empty. A pair of kids, probably from nearby Georgia Tech, studying together. Three adults, each alone, each peering into a laptop. If this was LA, they would all be writing screenplays, but here, it might be novels or dissertations or emails. Two were women, but the last one was a man. I was in the habit of pausing and studying any man I saw alone in my spaces, but this guy was pushing seventy.

No James, yet. I'd come down a couple of minutes early to grab a table in the short leg of the L-shaped room, out of view of the big storefront windows. I didn't want Marker Man to see James with me. I wouldn't make him a target. I dumped my bag onto a two-top all the way at the end of that short leg, then went and ordered myself an Americano and their lightest roast with a big splash of half-and-half. All these years later, I still remembered how he took his coffee.

I was almost back to the secluded table with the drinks when I heard James say, "Meribel."

He was coming around the corner wearing khakis and a navy blazer: standard American male office worker. He hadn't had time to cast himself as anything else, but those were his eyes, down-tilted, his slightly crooked nose, his thick eyebrows. Both his un-flattering beard and his dark brown hair had some gray now, but I could still make out the boy I'd loved.

I went straight to him, and to me, it felt like a slo-mo dash through a rainbow-draped meadow that would somehow end with me in his arms. I couldn't blink. I barely breathed. In reality, it was the calm, measured step of a woman with two very full cups moving toward a man she hadn't seen in twenty years. He seemed calm, too, almost stern. Maybe he was only feeling serious. My mouth was dry, my hands trembling so hard I could see it in the surface of the coffees. I held out his mug, and he took it.

"Meribel," he said, again. His voice cracked deep.

"Hello, James." I'd stepped in close enough to know that he smelled different. My James had worn Cool Water, a fresh, young smell, minty and clean. Now he had on something woodsy and spicy, altogether darker. I didn't like it. I couldn't smell the person who was James under it, and I knew, I just knew, his wife had picked it out. I wanted to step in closer, go on tiptoes, put my nose into his neck, and remember him. I shifted my weight, foot to foot. "You want to sit?"

"Sure."

As we threaded our way through some empty tables and sat down across from each other, I felt wary, hopeful, guilty, and a thousand other feelings in a swirl. Too many to parse. Was this how Honor felt when she tried to recognize the emotions that blew through her, unnamed and uncontrolled? I leaned in like a camera on a dolly coming in for an extreme close-up, staring at his face with such intensity I saw every eyelash, every pore, every micro-expression. I was too focused on him to feel any other gazes. The last time we'd been in the same room, it was a cold cube in a hospital. I'd felt ruined, finished with life. He'd hovered, silent and sad, unable to help. What could I possibly say to him now?

I did know where to start, at least. There were words I had long owed him, words I'd wanted to say for decades: "I'm sorry."

We both knew it was inadequate. He smiled, taking it in the spirit I had offered it, both as owed and not enough. He must have wanted those words at some point, but I saw he didn't need them now.

He shrugged, helplessly, and spread his hands. "Hey. It all worked out."

"It did?" I asked. He was looking back, so intensely that I had to break the moment. I buried my face in my coffee cup, scalding my tongue. Good. My stupid mouth was forming questions that were not my business. *Do you love your wife*, for example. Or *Are you happy*.

"You look the same," he said, not answering my question. Almost any woman in America would know I'd put a lot of money, time, and medical effort into making these words more true than they usually were, but men could be blind about these things.

"So do you," I said. He didn't, but I wasn't lying or acting. I meant that I could see the boy I'd loved inside this middle-aged man with his little craft-beer belly and his tired eyes, even if I couldn't smell him. "Are you happy?"

"Yes," he said, soft and sure. "Are you?"

"Yes," I said. That was true. Stalker and stress aside, I really was.

I heard how true it was in his voice and then mine, and somehow that made it okay to say, "Tell me about your kids. Got pictures?"

"Oh, well," he said, stalling, looking at me from under his eyebrows to see if it was really all right to show me these children who looked like they could be ours. I got my phone out and showed him first.

"This is my girl," I said. "This is Honor. Only child. I thought about adopting a brother or a sister for her, but she was so against it. As soon as she had words to tell me her opinion—and believe me, my girl had opinions before she had words—she was adamant about not wanting a baby brother or sister."

That made him laugh. "My own girl is that way. Strong-willed? Whew. Believe it. Middle child."

Once we started, it got easier. The words came fast and thick. "Maybe Honor would have liked a sibling once she had one, but the possibility made her so threatened and thundery. When she was four, we were reading a book called *I Love You Like Crazy Cakes*, and she asked me, 'Can two people be a family?' When I told her yes, of course, I realized it was true." I paused, and we looked helplessly at each other. We'd both wanted a big family when we were married. "She's enough. More than. Show me yours?"

It was a good half hour. Sweet and solid. I told him about Honor's love of cliché, her near eidetic memory, her obsession with Greek mythology and D&D. His oldest was into D&D now, too.

"Total nerd, like his dad. His group doesn't use the Greek gods or myths though. I wish. I mean, that at least touches on classic lit." He'd been so impressed to hear that Honor was reading *Antigone*. "Instead of Fates and Furies, I hear weird crap about icy archdevils named Levistus and fifteen ways to kill an orc." The other two were both into soccer. "Bev, especially, is actually cool. Weird, huh? Her mom's influence."

That paused me. He'd been careful to keep the conversation centered on the kids. This was the first time he had directly said a thing about his wife. I quirked an eyebrow, trying not to make it flirty when I told him, "You were cool enough to land me."

"I have a knack for dating above my pay grade," he said lightly, trying to power through the awkwardness. I had sounded flirty. Just a little. "But you were alterno-theatre-chick cool. Sarah's more mainstream. She was in a sorority." He said it like he meant she was from outer space. That had not been our crowd in college. Not at all. "Now she's in the Junior League and all the other moms copy her haircut." His tone was amused and admiring, not disparaging, and I was glad. I hated men who talked shit about their wives to other women. Never mind that it also felt like a twisty little stab in the gut.

A question rose in my mind, perhaps the only question that mattered. *Does your wife know you are here?* Even thinking this, I couldn't meet his eyes. I looked down, and I noticed he had yet to touch his coffee. It was cold now, while my cup held jet-black dregs. Back when we were married, my own coffees were half milk and full of sugar. I would no more drink that now than I would chug rat poison. But I'd expected James to still drink his this way.

I said, "You take your coffee different now."

He looked up, confused, and then smiled and said, "Oh, yeah. We're off dairy."

My head filled with white noise and his outline wavered. Now, I didn't need to ask the question, *Does your wife know you are here?*

Of course she did. It was right there in the "We." *We* are off dairy. She owned this guy with his dumb beard, the three kids. She knew he drank his coffee black. Or with soy milk. Some mysterious way. She picked out his spicy cologne, and she understood his office job, and he loved her. Maybe sometimes he looked at his phone at dinner, but he loved his wife.

I knew then, finally and for sure, that I was not in love with this man. I didn't even know this man. I hadn't come here to see this James at all. I had come to see my past, look at the life I'd fled, and see how deep regret ran. I looked at this familiar stranger, and I wouldn't trade my *now*, my family, even with Marker Man, for anything I'd lost, even the baby that never got to be. I loved my life. I loved Honor, so charming and difficult and gifted and complicated. I loved my satisfying work, and Wallace, and my other friends. James, this James, didn't fit the woman I'd grown into. This James liked how his life was going, too.

"I'm really glad you're happy," I told him, and I meant it. He nodded, glad for me right back. In this small window of time, with these kind words, with the understanding that we'd both come out of our shared past alive and whole—this was the thing that let us let each other go.

We sat quietly together for a moment, looking at each other, and then, almost simultaneously, he started to say something about needing to go back to work and I began to say that I should check on Honor. We both petered out and laughed, wry and sad and finished with each other.

We stood up at the same time. Shaking hands would be too strange, and so I stepped into his arms. I breathed him in. Even under the cologne, he smelled wrong. He'd changed, or I had forgotten his scent so thoroughly that it was no longer familiar. Neither was this older, softer version of a body I'd once known so well. I held it close, but briefly. It wasn't mine.

He stepped back and said, "I hope we can be friends."

I smiled. "We are friends." I meant it, but we weren't the kind of friends who met for drinks or emailed until nostalgia caught them. We would be the kind who remembered each other with affection and a little sorrow, and who wished each other well.

As he turned away and left, I was hit with new regret. The James I'd always love a little bit was twenty years gone. Not real. Cam might have been real, and Cam was now. I'd sent him away.

I sank back into my chair and drank the chilly dregs of my coffee. I checked my phone. No texts from Honor. She was probably still sleeping. Before I could think too hard, or at all, I navigated to Cam's message window. Some breakup. I hadn't even taken him out of my phone.

I sent him three little words: I'm an idiot.

Then I stared at my screen, my knuckles white on the phone. No answer came. Not even dots to tell me he was typing. Maybe he was with his son, or driving. Or maybe I'd blown it, and he was done.

I sent another. When you come back through Atlanta for your flight, can we talk?

Still nothing. After a minute I started another text, and it got long. It turned into the overshare of the century.

Do you have a way to sign back into my doorbell app? If you can, you'll see Marker Man. He came into my building yesterday and trashed Cooper's place and wrote threats on his wall. So maybe you'll think I want you to come back just because I'm scared, and this is Damsel shit. That's not it, Cam. I promise.

Except maybe being this scared pushed me to figure out what I want. My wayward head keeps circling back to you. Of course I'm terrified of Marker Man, and I'm also terrified of dating. (Joke. Mostly.) But I'm not scared of us.

Anyway. If you still want to try, I do, too, and I'm not saying "Maybe." I'm saying, "Yes."

I hit send without so much as rereading it, and what I felt then was a huge sweep of relief. Then hope. Then maybe—joy? So that was good. I sat for another minute staring at the screen. No little dots. He was probably really busy having sex with some fantastic woman he just met. She had huge, natural boobs and she ate bread and she wasn't as messed up or egotistical as me.

I got up and headed to the exit that let me directly back into my building, my eyes and attention mostly on my phone, looking for those dots. As I pushed open the door, I banged right into another person, coming in. I grabbed his arm to steady both of us, and my phone dropped from my hands. We both stooped and reached for

it, but he got it. We straightened, and I was smiling, already apolo-
gizing and thanking him when our eyes met. What I saw in his was
avarice. And ownership.

I knew him, then. I knew him.

He'd been right in front of me, or, no, right behind me. My
mouth stopped working. My breath stopped, too. He saw the recognition blooming on my face. He smiled.

"Hello, Meribel," Marker Man said.

30

HONOR WOKE UP disoriented, blinking. She sat up and kicked at her covers pile until it got off her and all slithered to the floor. She fell asleep! How? She snatched her phone up to check the time, and it was way past noon.

There were also many messages from Sheila. Honor? Is it time? You didn't say when? Hey, HONOR! WEIRDO! WHEN! NOW? The last was an hour ago.

That flattening feeling, like she was rising up inside her skull to press against the dome, started happening again, immediately. She had missed her window to check on Cat. Her mom was hard to trick, and Marker Man burning up Cooper's apartment had made her extra careful. It was all ruined!

Sheila probably already went down and saw Cat was fine and made best friends with her and not Honor, who let her down by sleeping. Or Cat was or hurt or dead and Sheila saw it and would never be okay again. Maybe Marker Man got Sheila, too. Honor's body rocked as she floated up and up, so very calm. She had to help her friends, though, so she pushed her thumbs into her bruises. The space around her eyes was already sore. She only had to press a little to hurt enough to feel it. The pain yanked her floating self down. As soon as she was okay to make her hands work, she texted Sheila.

I FELL ASLEEP WHAT HAPPENED

She scrambled out of bed and shucked her pajamas to pull on shorts and a clean black T-shirt that said, YO, MEDUSA, STOP OBJECTI-FYING PEOPLE! She jammed her feet into her Toms.

She left her room and crept quietly down the hall to peer around the corner. It was quiet. The den and kitchen were empty, and her mom's bedroom door was open. The balcony door was open, too, and the pretty weather was in the house. Maybe it was still okay. She went into her mom's empty room and no one was in the bathroom or on the balcony. Honor came back to the den and looked at the table and the hooks by the door. Her mom's purse was gone and her mom's keys were gone.

The meeting was still going. That was good. She could still check on Cat if—a text landed, and it was Sheila.

NOTHING. I was scared. I am worried about OUR CAT. Are you ready to go? Did you get the THING?

So that was all right. She texted for Sheila to meet her in the stairwell in five minutes. All she needed was the gun and—the office door opened behind her. She froze and turned around to see Cooper's head poked out. She was still disoriented from her long daytime sleep. She had forgotten him entirely.

His head was smiling and full of questions that all came out of his mouth in a row: Was her nap good and did she want juice and did her bruises bother her and did she need ibuprofen?

"No," she said to all the offers. "I'm grumpy. I want to be quiet and read books."

Instead of leaving her alone, his whole body came out. "Do you want company?"

Honor wanted zero company. She wanted to leave. Thinking of Cat hurt or dead all night had left her stomach upset and sour. She had to make him go back in his room so she could slip out and go see, but she was bad at lying. She had to make him go away without lying, then.

"My mom wants me to have a shower today." This was true. Her mother always wanted her to have a shower. "Do you know my mom has three spigots in her shower?" True. "You can stand in it and put all three on 'Jet' so it pounds down on you. Mom says it's like being in a hot storm." Also true. What was also true was that she hated it.

Cooper helpfully jumped to the conclusion that she'd come out to use that fancy shower. "That's a good idea. After all, an ounce of water prevents a pound of smell."

Now he was trying to play clichés. She liked that, but not right now. Her mom could be back any minute. Honor told Cooper sternly, "I need privacy to shower." True! A person did need privacy to shower. "You should go in your room and let me have time to myself." True true true.

"Okay. Your mom should be back any minute. I have a work call anyway," he said.

"You have a job?" she asked, by accident, because she was surprised.

"Oh, yes," Cooper told her, and then he told her things about his job. It was hard to stand quiet and wait for him to be done, staring between his eyebrows, which was a trick you could do so people thought you were listening when they were being boring.

"Cooper," she said sternly the second he paused, "can we talk about this later, or not today?"

"Sure," he said.

She said, "I'm going to go in the bathroom now and put on music. I like loud music. And privacy. When I take a shower. So go in that office and work on your job."

That made him laugh for some reason, but he went back into the room where she was pointing. She hustled very loudly—bang stomp slam!—through her mom's room and into the master bath.

She turned on the shower, all the jets, and set them to the tightest setting so they drummed into the walls the loudest way they could. Her mom's laptop was on the bedside table, and she started up Pandora and turned the volume up.

It worked. He stayed in the office as she crept past to the kitchen to ease the pot-and-pan drawer open and take out the gun box. She was almost out the front door when she remembered that Cam had installed the new doorbell that would see her leave and show her to her mom and Cam and maybe the police (she was not clear on this). Her mom for sure would see her going down the hall with the gun box, live and in real time.

That was not ideal. She needed duct tape, but Sheila had gotten it. She had none. They kept a roll in the junk drawer at home, but they had accidentally left it in LA, even though her mom had a joke about it that she liked to say to Wallace: "Duct tape can fix anything, so I keep it in lieu of a husband." Wallace laughed like that was funny. It wasn't funny, and duct tape couldn't fix anything. Sheila took some down to Cat, and look what happened.

She looked around and saw a movie script with a yellow Post-it on the cover that said, *Looking at you for the middle sister. Any interest?* in Mom's agent's writing. Honor peeled it away and went to the front door. She eased it open, quiet, quiet, and then she sent her hand around and slapped the Post-it over the camera's eye. Now she could go. She slipped out and hustled into the stairs. She knew Sheila was there waiting because she could smell the steam from her Juul coming up the stairs. She hurried down and found her on the next landing. She stood up very fast when she saw Honor.

"You took forever. Is that it?" Sheila asked. She was eyeing the gun safe. Honor nodded and sat down by her friend with the box in her lap. Sheila touched it with one finger, and then she tried to make it open. "It's locked."

"It's okay. I heard the code," Honor said, and then she sang, "*Beep boop bah bah.*" Her mom said Honor sang flat, but she didn't. She could hear notes perfect in her head. She poked at the buttons to hear the sounds. She cocked her head as she punched one through nine and then a zero, trying to hear which number matched the first tone. One time through and she was sure it was 6533.

It wasn't. That pattern was right, the intervals were right, but she was off on notes. Maybe she *was* flat? She went up a note and tried 7644. That was it. The box opened and there the gun was, black and thick and heavy.

Sheila blew out all her breath through pursed lips, but not a whistle. "You know how to use it, yeah?"

"Probably," said Honor. "I've never seen this kind up close." True. She'd never seen any kind up close.

She picked it up and looked at it. It was loaded, Mom had told Cooper. There was no hammer part like on a cowboy gun. It was sleek and plain, almost square, like the shape of gun Detective Abbie Mills had on *Sleepy Hollow*, so she held it out now like Abbie did, arms stretched forward using two hands. It was really heavy. She pointed it down the stairs, at nothing. She squeezed the trigger, but only barely, only a little, not to shoot it, but to see if it would go. The trigger felt stuck. She squeezed harder, cautiously, and then she really squeezed, and it didn't shoot.

She turned in her hands until she saw a plain lever near where her thumb touched. It looked like a little clicker, so she moved it. Under was a red dot, painted on in what looked like Mom's favorite nail polish. The one called I'm Not Really a Waitress. Click, no red dot. Click. There it was.

"This is the safety and it will shoot now, with the red showing." She said it with authority, not like she was guessing. But she was guessing.

"Should I carry it?" Sheila asked.

Honor shook her head. It was her responsibility. She had to make good choices. "I'm only going to shoot it if we see Marker Man."

If they found him down there, and Cat was hurt, she would shoot him. She thought shooting him was good to do. He was terrible. He was dangerous for Mom. She would definitely shoot him, even though thinking about it made the bees start filling up her blood again.

They started down the stairs, Honor in front, pressing on her bruised eye with two fingers. It would be hard to shoot him. But it was what a paladin would do.

31

"HELLO, MERIBEL," MARKER Man said.

I looked up, and up, and up into his face, he was so tall, and—
He smiled, his face shadowed by his Georgia Tech ball cap. He had
on a Tech jacket, too, props that rendered him near invisible this
close to campus. He was gawky and storky and spotted.

How could this be Marker Man? This kid. This child. But it was
him. It had been him, all along.

This boy was at Wild Waves on Honor's birthday. He stood in
line for the Dragon Drop behind us, angling his body so it seemed as
if he was with the older couple behind him. He rolled his eyes and
shuffled while that pair discussed *Dancing with the Stars*. He stared
past me, as if watching Sheila, but holding me in his peripheral vision. He climbed into my boat and rode with me, his legs stiff and
pressing. I bought the damn picture of us riding it together! I had a
picture of me and Marker Man riding down a log flume in my phone!

How could this kid be the monster that I'd feared so deeply, so
long? But it was. This was Marker Man, and I was old enough to be
his mother. He looked eighteen, or at most twenty. All at once, I
wanted to laugh. He must weigh 140 pounds, for all he had a foot
of height on me. I thought, *I should grab him and yell for someone to
call 911 so the police can take this boy to get some kind of help.*

I opened my mouth and pulled in breath, but he was faster. He stepped in toward me, and I felt something hard jammed into my ribs. I looked down. Between us now there was a scant six inches. And a gun. The call for help stuck in my throat. The gun was short and thick and brutal, close between us, mostly hidden by our bodies.

I felt a power shift as immediate and physical as if we were on a teeter-totter. He went up as I was sinking. My body seized and went as still as any rabbit in a road. I did this when I was afraid. The response was hardwired into my brain stem. Some animals fought, some fled. I was a freezer. How did I know this? I had never been this scared, had I? But in my cells, I felt a dreadful déjà vu; I'd been this powerless before. I couldn't breathe. My vision narrowed to a pinhole. Behind me, in the coffeehouse, generic jazz was playing. I heard people talking, laughing, eating, like they were all at some happy gathering. I was near them, but not with them. I was alone in every way that mattered.

Marker Man casually dropped my phone into the trash can by the door. He put his hand under my chin. Tap tap. Like he was chucking it? Like some kind of creepy uncle? He wanted me to look up higher than the gun. He wanted me to look at him. I got my gaze up as high as the little wasp, Tech's mascot, that was embroidered on his jacket. It stared back at me, both silly and merciless.

If I looked up any higher, I wouldn't be able to see the gun. I wanted to watch it. It was as if I believed it could not hurl a bullet through my soft abdomen, all my organs, if I kept my eyes on it.

He tipped my chin up anyway, pushing harder with his hand as he bent down close. At the same time, finally, I sucked in air. His breath smelled like old ham, a metallic, aging lunch-meat smell. I thought, *If he kisses me, if this is some big movie kiss in a doorway, I will throw up all this coffee in his mouth.*

He didn't try, though. He stared into my eyes. I felt the gun's cold press into my guts, but I looked at his face: big-eyed, soft cheeked, dotted with acne. That sad fringe of mustache, pale and downy. My vision wavered. I ought to be telling him to eat his peas, not be terrified that he would shoot me. He was closer to Honor's age than mine.

Honor! The thought of her made my spine go straight. I couldn't freeze here, and I couldn't let him shoot me. My eyes went right back to the gun, and he tutted and slipped it into his jacket pocket. I could still see the shape of it. It jutted at me like a finger aimed as a joke.

I thought, *Is that a gun in his pocket? Yes. Is he happy to see me?* I felt weird bubbles in my throat that might be a laugh or screaming. All that came out of my mouth was a small exhale.

"Sweetheart," he said. His voice was high and breathy. His eyes were bright, so excited. "Sweetheart, I got you. It's okay."

He did have me. It was not okay. The room was full of people close enough to call, but none of them could act fast enough to keep him from shooting me if he decided to. I understood this. I understood how fast it could be done. You freeze, they act, it's over.

He took my arm and pulled me all the way out the door. I didn't want to go, but my feet obeyed, shuffling out of the coffeehouse. To my left was the glass room with elevators up to my place. Where my exhausted child was holed up, healing.

"Your place or mine?" he asked me.

A movie line. He tried to purr it like some seventies porn version of James Bond. I hated his gun and his clunky, fake delivery. I had a gun of my own, upstairs, and he was offering to walk me toward it.

I said, "Yours," though, my voice faint and shaky, because I would let him shoot me dead before I took him up to Honor.

If I went with him, though—Wallace and I had taken a self-defense class when Marker Man starting stalking me in earnest. The instructor told us, "If they say, 'Come with me, or I will shoot you,' let them shoot you. Statistically you have a better chance of surviving the bullet than the second location. If you go with them . . ." He shrugged wryly, like, *Oh, well, you just got yourself raped and tortured, mutilated and killed.*

I could still hear generic jazz toodling through Java House's closed side door. I knew, didn't I, that if they said, "Come with me," and you went, then whatever happened was on you. You went, didn't you? Into the van, or out of your building, or up some stairs, if you went, then you got what you got. You deserved it.

I still let him lead me out of the building. I felt like a balloon on a string, being toted along to the second location to be killed slowly instead of being shot here by this gun. At the same time, every step out of the building was a step away from Honor, and this was right, and this was good. Outside the building that was sheltering my kid, I would breathe better. I would think better.

"You're so quiet," he said.

I finally got words out, and they were not the words that I expected. "How old are you?"

He laughed. "Too old for Didi, old enough for you." I could feel his greedy gaze sliding sideways, up and down me, his damp clutch on my arm. I felt the gun still trained on me, invisible but present. He said, "Do you know she almost drowned? Your kid, at the water park. I saved her. And her friend. I did it for you."

I had no idea what he was babbling about. He'd put his hands on Honor? I felt a small, cold trickle of something new, something stronger than my fear. This cold voice thought, *I'm not going to die. I'm going to kill you.* I almost couldn't hear it over my pounding heart. But it was there.

When he turned us into the alley, I felt a spark of hope. The homeless girl. Was she camping here? She had pepper spray, and she was cagey and fast. She even got the drop on Cam. As we came close to her alcove, I felt my body trying to coil, to gather itself. I was finally unfreezing. Thinking. If she—

She wasn't there. Her trash bag was gone, too. In her place was a small motorcycle with two helmets locked on. The second helmet was hot pink. With cat ears.

"Didi's favorite color!" He let go of my arm and got his keys out of his jeans. He handed them to me, then pulled his Georgia Tech cap off and shoved it in the other pocket of his jacket. The one with no gun in it.

"Baby doll," he said, relishing the words. "Put mine on me?"

His helmet was black with flames licking at the sides. Both looked like toys, both were clichés, but not ones even Honor could enjoy. The helmet cast *me* as a toy, something soft with animal ears, not truly human. His said he was the badass, powerful, a force straight out of hell. My hands were shaking so hard it took me three tries to get the lock open. He stooped to let me put his helmet on, and even then, I had to stand on tiptoe. As I settled it over his head, his face became a blank, black window. I could feel his gaze eating me alive even through the shield.

I stepped back and he said, "Such a sour, pouty mouth it has!" Was he talking baby talk to me with a gun trained at my center mass? He was. "Ooh, it so mad. I know. I meant to give you time. But fate decided it was now. Our time. Now put on your helmet, hide that little pout mouth, ha. By the time you take it off I want to see a smile, because I'm about to be so sweet to you. Get on."

I did it, exactly what he said. It was easy for that man to say, *Oh, let him shoot you. Don't obey*, to a self-defense class full of girls mostly in their twenties, earnestly trying to learn how not to get sex-murdered for real. Many of them had auditions later, to see if they could do it in pretend. If I disobeyed, I really could die here. Now. Did Marker Man understand how final and decisive it would be, if he pulled the trigger? Some things can't be taken back or fixed. What person this young truly understood that? This boy was so deep in delusion he could hold a gun on me and call me baby doll, as if we were in love. If I tried to fight or run, and he killed me, here, what would stop him from going straight upstairs to Honor? He had seen her, met her—saved her?—interacted in some way, at the water park. She might see him through the peephole and let him right on in, if he could remind her who he was.

I swung my leg on over, and he settled behind me. "I wouldn't ride bitch for just anyone. But I will for you, because I know you like to drive 'em. Motorbikes." He knew everything about me. His letters always said so. "You ready to feel some power between your legs?"

His voice sounded hollow and weird inside the helmet. The words were gross and crazy, and they sounded practiced, as if he had heard them in some snuff film and had been saying them to himself in the bathroom mirror for months. He was excited to be saying them out loud at last to a Didi-shaped woman with no face, a woman who was now crying quietly behind her helmet.

He pressed in close. I could feel his erection in the small of my back. I thought, absurdly, *I am at a high school dance. I should drive to a police station. No, a hospital. Straight to the ER, screaming. Then when he shoots me, at least I am right near all the doctors.*

I felt the blunt hard end of the gun, softened by the thick cloth of his jacket pocket. He pressed it directly into my spine, and I knew I would do whatever he said to do next.

"Start the bike." I started up the bike. The man who taught the class would tell me, *You are in control.* But if he pulled the trigger, I'd be paralyzed. Or dead.

"Go right," he hollered over the engine. I didn't yell for help or purposefully crash the bike or hurl myself off sideways or try to talk to him or trick him. I felt the gun pressing between two of my vertebrae. I didn't want to be shot. I didn't want to leave my daughter orphaned. I followed his directions, crying, mind a blank. Time skipped and churned.

We were almost to the highway when it occurred to me that this storky young person was not the short, thick-built figure my doorbell camera had caught going into Cooper's place to wreck it. I wobbled, and the bike zigged. I had to fight it back under control. Who had I seen staring up at my building? Who had watched me have coffee with Cooper? Who had burned up his bed?

That stocky figure in the London Fog–style raincoat . . . I remembered pushing out into the rain to try and chase my watcher down. I realized I'd seen the real Marker Man then, too, this boy with his gun and his erection both pressing my back. I'd run out to find the person in the coat, and God, I'd put my hands right on my real stalker. I'd shoved past him when I ran out the door. He'd mixed himself in with a gaggle of high school boys.

So who the hell had been across the street watching? Who had the doorbell camera caught? Who had done those awful things to Cooper's place? I was letting this armed child, dangerously crazy, steal me away, but someone else had been in our building. Someone else had been watching the whole damn time.

Honor, I thought. *Oh, Honor. I'm luring him away from you. Have I left you at someone else's mercy?*

32

HONOR TOOK THE lead down the dim hallway lined with storage lockers. Because she had the gun.

It was quiet, so Cat was definitely dead, then. Nothing alive could be so quiet. Honor could hear her own soft footfalls, her breathing, her heartbeat. Her free hand pressed and pressed her bruises. The gun was so heavy. It wobbled and drooped. Sheila's family's storage locker was halfway down to the fire door. If Cat was dead, that was where the parts of her would be.

As they got close, Honor could see the combination lock was still fastened on the slatted door. Honor looked at Sheila, and then she pointed the gun into the locker. Sheila swallowed so loud it was like gulping, but she darted over, put in the numbers, and tugged. The lock clicked loud as it released. Sheila took it out of the latch and put it in her pocket. They stepped back, and the cheap door slowly swung itself open wide.

Nothing happened. No one spoke or came out or tried to kill them.

Honor said, "Hello?"

She said it loud. The hall was very empty and it had an echo. She hated that. The gun shook and wavered and she wanted to press her bruises but she needed all her hands now to keep the gun pointed into the darkness at the old sofa and the crates and boxes. She hated the shadows. She hated the dusty air sticking in her lungs. Most of all, she hated it when a figure rose up from behind the sofa, an amorphous person-shape in the dark space. She felt her stiff, cold finger tightening.

Then the shape said, "Shit, is that a gun?" and the voice was creaky with sleep, but it was Cat. No. It was Xena Warrior Princess. If she wasn't dead or cut up or ruined then it was fine for her to be a person.

The pistol sagged down. Honor's gun hand was cramping. She had to work to make her sweat-slick finger stop being on the trigger. Was Honor crying? She pressed her bruises with her free hand and the skin under her eyes was very wet. She peered down at the gun and her hands felt thick and clumsy as she put the safety on.

Sheila was rushing forward, climbing past crates and over the sofa to hug Xena. "Oh, my God! We thought Marker Man got you!"

Xena looked to Honor. "The stalker? Your mom's? Why would he want *me*?" She patted at Sheila's back awkwardly, and then they climbed back over the sofa and came out into the hall with Honor. Xena had peeled off her many, many layers, down to boy underpants like shorts and a plain black T-shirt. She was smaller without her layers, but still thick and tall for a girl. She still smelled like musty clothes, old sweat, and Lysol, a combination that was both mossy and astringent. Honor liked that smell now, because it was familiar and meant Xena. She put the gun in her waistband, in the back, which they did in movies. The safety was on, so she wouldn't shoot her butt off.

"Marker Man broke into the building, and he tore up our neighbor's house, and he put his poo on the walls," Honor told her.

Sheila was talking, too, their words running over each other. "He lit Cooper's bed on fire, can you believe?"

Xena stared at them for a long time with her mouth flat. Then she said, abruptly, just to Sheila, "Why didn't you ask to read my book?"

Sheila said, "What?"

Honor didn't understand the question. The gun was so heavy her shorts were sagging down. She hitched at them, and she pressed her bruises hard with her other hand.

Xena said again, "I told you I was writing a book, but you didn't ask to read it or—you didn't ask why I wanted to be inside."

Sheila blinked and shrugged. "I mean, inside here? Well, because of rain. And it's scary . . ." she petered out. "Why wouldn't you want to be inside?"

"Inside *this* building," Xena said, very loud. "Specifically."

Honor felt suspicions. "Are you two sometimes friends without me?"

It came out sharp. This was a thing she worried about sometimes. She didn't want it to be true. Honor and Sheila were tier-one friends, and Xena was the maybe friend. Honor didn't know if she was allowed to let Xena even be a tier-two friend like Mom was with Paul, because Xena was homeless and maybe dangerous and older and a secret.

Xena crossed her arms and pushed her eyebrows in toward each other. "They think—you all think Marker Man did that? Did Cooper think it was? Cooper thought some stalker—" She broke off, and her eyes rolled wild with white showing around the top like that mare, Trouble, when she was feeling bite-y.

Sheila said, "Yeah. Of course."

"No, but it was to warn him! If Cooper thinks it's Marker Man, he isn't even warned!" Xena hollered, and this made no sense.

Was Xena crying? She dashed at her eyes like there were tears there, but if so, she'd only had two, because no more fell. She stomped back inside to one end of the sofa and grabbed her trash bag. She dropped to a crouch and rummaged, hurling things out, then started pulling on more clothes, fast and jerky. First a longer-sleeved shirt, big and black, and then black jeans. Sheila made an unreadable face and mouthed something at Honor. Honor could only shrug, bewildered.

"How could he not know!" Xena said as she yoinked on even

more layers. Oh, she *was* crying, now, making a bray noise like a donkey, and snot came out. She wiped it away on her sleeve, then pulled on a bulky sweatshirt, then a cardigan. It was like watching a rogue pulling on a set of padded armor. "I finally was brave! I did a thing! I told him to stay away from Sheila, and he didn't even know that it was *for* him? I thought he would think of me, at least? I should have signed it, but, like, it seemed dumb to do a crime and sign it. Hell, I should have signed my mom's name, and my sister's. I should have written Gemma Hightower, and Ruby Hightower, both in five-foot shit letters."

Now Honor got it. She thought. She wanted to be sure. "You put the poo on Cooper's walls. You burned his bed."

Xena was still railing. "I want to burn *him* down, now. Not the bed. Him. But all I do is read and sleep and say, 'I'll make a plan tomorrow! I'll be brave tomorrow.'"

Sheila understood now, too, because now she got very red in the face and yelled back, "Why! Why would you do that!"

Xena threw her hands up and hollered at Sheila specifically instead of just hollering at the walls. "You should have asked to read my book. You should have asked me any damn thing. Like, why do you think a girl my age is living in an alley? Just for fun? This isn't fun!"

Well, because Xena was homeless, that was why. A lot of homeless people were here, but then Honor realized they were mostly men, and old. When Mom took her to Little Five Points, to the Nerd Store (which was what her mom called it; it had games and all kinds of crystals and dice and cards), that was where she saw the younger homeless people, panhandling with green hair. Still, Honor didn't like being yelled at about it.

She asked, "Why are you pulling on all those clothes? It's really hot outside."

Xena turned to her. "I'm not going outside. I'm going upstairs, and there are cameras." Honor knew the elevator ones were faked, and she had taped over the doorbell one, but she didn't interrupt to say so because Xena was talking so upset and loud. "I don't want my face on camera because I am going to—I am going to do something. For real. I'm going go right up to him and say, It's me, Maxene Hightower—that's my whole name—and then I am going to do something. Really. Finally."

She pulled on her big raincoat over all her layers. It was gray. A man's long London Fog gray raincoat. When they were at Wild Waves and her mom and Cooper were asking about Cat, she told them Cat's coat was gray, and that was a joke because cats have coats and Maxene had a coat, too. Xena's shape in this outfit now was less like a girl and more like the shape of Cam, the man with the gun who had slept on her mother's sofa. Before she learned the smell, the shape of her in this coat was the best way she had to recognize Xena Warr—no, Maxene. Maxene, Maxene.

Maxene dug deeper and got out a fisherman's cap. She jammed it down low on her head. She was a very thick person, taller even than Sheila in her steel-toe boots, and now she looked very broad and thick and mighty and mysterious in all her layers. Assassin rogue. Revenge module.

Sheila was shaking her head and muttering, "That's crazy. You are crazy."

That might be true, Honor thought. A lot of homeless people were extremely crazy, though her mom said that was wrong to say. Honor should say they were unmedicated, or mentally ill.

Honor ignored Sheila, trying to make it all be sensible. "You wanted us to let you be inside so you could burn down Cooper?"

"You bet your ass," the man-shape said. "Cooper Hayette killed my sister."

"Oh, my God," said Sheila, loud. "What the actual f—"

"Yes," said Maxene Hightower, even louder. Maxene, Maxene, Maxene.

They both stood puffing loud breaths at each other.

Sheila said, "I'm going to leave. I am going to tell. I'm going to get my mom," but she stayed there, breathing more.

Honor said, "I'll read your book."

She offered because Xena wanted it so bad, and might be a friend. Also, the book seemed like where the answers would be. It was like in Dungeons and Dragons. Before you had the fight with the BBEG—the big, bad evil guy—you found a scroll or a book or an NPC who told the story of why he was so bad, so you would know it was okay to fight him.

Maxene Hightower stopped buttoning the coat, and now she looked at Honor, not Sheila. Now she said, "Okay. Okay, I'll show you."

The book was in her bag. It was a blank one, like a notebook, but with a leathery red cover, and she had filled a lot of it with notes in crabbed handwriting. Sheila didn't leave. Instead, they all three climbed back over the sofa and sat in a row with Maxene in the middle. Honor leaned in, snuffing at Maxene's shoulder just a little because familiar smells, even bad ones, helped her not have bees.

It took an hour to read the book, because even though Maxene talked fast and very flat and loud, she kept stopping to do crying. Then she would go back and say more of the story. She told them all of it. It all. She had things that could be held: a plastic eye, some keys, the book itself with all her notes. By the middle, Sheila was crying, too. She started interrupting to say, *No no no*, and *You are lying*, but Maxene wasn't lying, and Honor told her sternly to be quiet.

Then she just cried, and Honor asked, "Why are you still crying?"

Sheila said, "Because I think I believe her. I think it might be true."

Honor nodded. It was definitely true. Honor knew this, even though she was a very bad liar. Mom said when Honor told a lie, she would do a good job saying it, but then her whole face would become a question, like she was checking to see if Mom believed her.

Honor wasn't great with expressions, or what Mom called "tone," either, so that wasn't how she knew what Maxene said was the truth. All DND modules had NPCs who lied to you, and in play-by-post, reading those stories, there was no tone at all. To find out who was bad, Honor had to look for clues and evidence. Maxene had more than just a story. She said she'd been following Cooper for weeks now, trying to make a plan to get him. She had all the places she had been to track him, so many notes in her red book, all in different inks and different amounts of faded. She hadn't faked this book up in a week. The plastic eye was cracked and very old. The keys were old, too. Maybe these things wouldn't prove things in a law way, but Honor looked at them and knew: Maxene had told the truth.

Honor asked her, "Do you need my gun?"

Maxene said, "Yes."

Honor showed Maxene exactly how the safety worked, and then she passed it over.

33

COOPER SAT ON the white love seat facing the door of Meribel's office so that if Honor came in, she wouldn't see his laptop screen. He might not hear her coming, even though she was a stomper, because he had his headphones on. He was watching a compilation video of all the "Not Even Once" anti-meth PSAs on YouTube.

The headlines were all about the opioid crisis these days, but honestly, meth struck him as more correct. A stimulant, not a depressant.

What would happen, he wondered, *if a person took meth and didn't know they took it? Once. Then twice. Then every day for a week. Then every other day for a month? Or what if it was more determined, and they took it every day they were a bitch to their mother?*

Fascinating question. Would she instinctively start looking for a way to reproduce that high, like a newborn rat creeping toward a nipple? Would she get meaner to her mother for the chemical reward? He needed to choose a method before he played it out in real time. It was exciting, thinking about outcomes and odds, starting a new game with a girl who deserved it.

On the "Not Even Once" reel, he watched a boy whore out his girlfriend, a different boy punch and rob his mother, a bunch of kids dump a dying girl onto the road beside the ER, and two girls turn to whoring together. Well, Sheila was halfway to that outcome already, and she was drug-free.

He was using the Tor browser so as not to leave a record of his research; while he had it open, he searched for a recipe for meth that could be taken orally, then for a description of the taste. Bitter and chemical. Well, he could refill her Midol capsules with it. Then her extreme mood swings would match up with her periods. Interesting, but damned if the next page he opened didn't tell him how to flavor it. Strawberry meth was sweet and popular—and pink, which felt amusing and thematically appropriate. He'd painted Sheila's room pink for her two years ago, and now she said it was babyish. She should have stayed the kind of girl who liked her room.

There were a lot more factors in play here then there had been with Lizzie. Lizzie had been a disappointment, really. Looking back, he regretted betting on her allergies. It was true that the house always won in the end, but Lizzie still felt a little like a gimme, a sucker bet.

His idea for Sheila had a lot of promise, as many paths as he had gotten out of Ruby Hightower. He remembered Ruby shrieking at Gemma while he stood silently by, and when Gemma was wrecked, Ruby would go stomping off in her cowboy boots, her butt hanging out of her cutoffs, heading to her swim hole at the edge of the property to smoke weed. Her dad had hung a knotted rope there years before he left. She'd swing out fearlessly over the small, deep hole, flip, and dive. Maxie, quieter, more cautious, jumped off the side. When her sister goaded and teased her, she would swing back and forth on the rope, clinging, then eventually plop in feet first. Toward the end, Maxie hardly went down there at all. It became Ruby's place, really. Cooper suspected she was meeting boys down there and spreading it; Gemma wasn't ready to be a grandma, much less raise her daughter's baby.

When sweet, cute Ruby changed into that stompy, nearly naked vixen, he was already having a bad year. He'd moved into Gemma's

isolated farmhouse off Highway 29 because he'd made some invest-
ments that did not pay off the way he hoped. Not that he'd put it to
her that way. He was a better boyfriend than that—he made it sound
romantic. The truth was, he couldn't afford both his apartment and
his office space in Austin until he turned things around.

That spring, every time Ruby was a bitch to Gemma, he stole a
cinder block off a construction site near his office. Then he stopped
by Ruby's swim hole on the way home, and if no one was around,
he plopped it in.

He and Gemma had swum there themselves a few times. He'd
jumped in plenty, and once or twice, he'd felt his toes scrape the
silty bottom. It was deep, but not that deep. The chances that the
cinder blocks would actually hurt Ruby were slim. Cooper understood the odds, but each block bought him the same kind of high-
yield fantasy as a dollar lotto ticket—and it didn't cost him a dollar.
That year, as the stock market bounced around, there were days a
dollar mattered.

All spring, the Texas honeysuckle that grew around that swim
hole reminded him of Barely's Jean Naté. By summer, its sweetness
was replaced by the strange oily scent of the lantana, a little like
orange peel that was going off, a little like urine or a woman. A dirty
woman, in between her legs. In August, he jumped in one day and
scraped his foot so badly that he bled. Heartening. But Ruby was
light and lithe, and she never seemed to sink that far. Or her fat
tits, falling out of her bikini top, made her too buoyant. Nothing
happened.

The cooler the weather got, the lower he got. He was a happy
person, an optimist at heart, but that fall, nothing he invested in
paid off. The temperature took a dog-day bounce up in September, so at least Ruby was swimming on the daily. As he watched his
portfolio full of this high-risk investment and that one fail and fall
and molder, throwing in those cinder blocks felt like his brightest
moments. When he thought ahead to October, he got low. He actually needed the money from his animations now, which made the

work less fun. His credit cards were close to maxed. He couldn't get through a bleak winter where Ruby did no headfirst flips into the opaque green water. Not when he already had heartburn every day, watching Ruby sass and smart-mouth. She was thoughtless in a thousand little ways, the kind of girl who ate the soft part of the French bread right out of the middle and left a hollowed crust in the bag. She took endless baths, the water running long after the tub would have filled. He knew what she was doing in there, and he suffered icy showers for it.

Every little cold snap swung him toward depression. Two days after the Weather Channel proclaimed they were about to hit last good heat wave of the year, he was heading home when he passed a Chrysler, rusted through in places, with an old vanity plate that said BIG STUD. It had been abandoned on the side of Highway 29 no more than six miles from home.

The next day, it was still there, and he only went a mile past it before he pulled off the highway, himself. He'd been thinking about it all day. He parked and sat weighing his options for a good long while, and then he decided and walked back. It appeared truly abandoned. Windows down, keys in the ignition, even. He was about to pop the hood when, on a whim, he got in and tried the key. The Chrysler roared to ugly, coughing life.

Lucky, lucky, lucky. He felt the moment as a sign, a whole-life shift. He would rebound.

The swim hole was closer than the house, but the damn car almost overheated twice. Each time, he pulled over and stopped the engine and sat, letting it tick and cool. His luck held. No Samaritans stopped by to look full into his face and ask if help was needed. He texted Gemma to say he really wanted to finish his current project and would be home late, not to wait dinner on him, he would cook the trout tomorrow. No pushback. She cheerily said she would order pizza.

He worried then that the old heap wouldn't make it across the meadow or fit through the trees to the swim hole. He was sure it would stall out, or the tires would rut into the soft earth and mire it. But no. He had to flatten a huge butterfly bush, but he got the car right to the water's edge. He turned the engine off, pocketed the keys, got out, and walked around to the back. It was a beast to push the old car in, what with its heavy steel body, but he was strong, and the slope was on his side. In it went. As it blubbed and sank, he was sick with nerves, thinking the hole would not be deep enough and the Chrysler's ass would stick out. But no. It slid in like it was going home, disappearing entirely beneath the deep-green water.

He stood at the edge for a moment, wondering how much time he should spend obscuring tire tracks. He decided not to bother. To leave it up to wind and weather and Ruby's self-absorption. It made the whole bet sweeter, and anyway, he wasn't trying to create an outcome. He merely wanted to create a situation where Ruby's own poor choices might have the consequences she deserved, the little whore. In the end, he only fluffed the filaments of the butter-fly bush. He left it up to Ruby, really. She could stop acting like a bitch, grow up, pay attention, show some caution and respect—and see the winter.

He bet that she would go right in, though. Swing out on the rope, release, flip, headfirst. He bet she'd be no more cautious with her body in the pool then she was with it aboveground with the boys, no more careful with her dive than she was with her old, sweet, soft, sad mother's tender heart.

In the end, he won his long-odds bet. Shame Maxie had been with her. Shame the kid had to be the one to lower herself in at the edge when Ruby didn't come back up. She was the one to swim down slowly and cautiously and thrash in the green water until she found her dead, open-eyed sister and dragged her out into the mud. Hard on a kid, that. Unlucky.

Cooper was the one who beat the odds. Always had been a lucky bastard, and the bet on Ruby turned his bad streak. Three days later, some shit tech stocks he'd held on to for no reason blasted right out of the mire and up to stellar heights. Tech was like that, some days. As his father used to say, *You pay your money and you take your chances*—now there was a cliché Honor might not know. He was reminding himself to try it on her when he realized that the shower was still going.

How long had it been? He'd lost track, what with all his plans and research, his fond reminiscing.

He carefully closed out his anonymous browser and listened. Still music. Was the shower still going? He left the office and tapped at Meribel's door, calling, "Honor?"

Nothing.

He got louder. "Honor!"

He pushed the door open. Taylor Swift was warbling about bad boys, bad love, and the bathroom door was wide open. He poked his head in, feeling embarrassed, but there was no small form behind the smoked-glass shower wall. The kid was gone.

34

THE MOTORBIKE ROARED powerfully beneath them as he pushed himself in close to Meribel. He was happy. He was. But also he was thinking about Captain, his old hamster. When his mom died, he was sad and he forgot about Captain. No one gave it water for a while and then he started smelling it. It made him so mad then that his mom had died. Because of that, no one reminded him about Captain or gave Captain water, and look what happened. Just look.

It still made him mad every time he thought of it, except today. Today, he was back with Meribel at last, and now everything would be perfect. He should have insisted on her place, though. The Roadtrek Ranger wasn't ready for her, quite. He thought about Captain, wondering how many days it took. Hard to say. He was grieving his mom real hard back then. Anyway, it was quiet in the camper now. Anyway, they'd been broken up. It was not Meribel's business. Meribel herself had kept having coffee with different men and made out in an alley with that dickhead from California.

It was good she was already crying. He could feel sobs shaking her body as he pressed in close behind her on the motorcycle. Her tears helped him believe that she was sorry. Maybe not sorry enough to cover the breakup, leaving LA without him, the other men, but she would be.

As they finally turned into the campground, slowing down, his free hand wanted to rummage around her body. He let it. Her little breast was like a small bird, but she shrieked, "Stop it!" loud enough for him to hear.

She was ruining it. And pissing him off. He could put his hand anywhere. Anywhere. She loved him and her body was for him, he knew, but as he squeezed, the motorcycle wobbled and veered, and he realized she was too turned on. Her attraction to him was so very great and electric that she might wreck. Then he was less mad. They would be alone so soon. He could wait. He put his hand down.

"You like it," he told her, quietly. "You know you do. Go to the fifth road and then left."

They were going to be alone so soon, and happy. But first, she had to be sorry. He would help her. He would help her be so sorry. After she was fully sorry and begged him, he'd do it to her and she'd love it. He hadn't ever done it to anyone. But he'd seen a lot of porn and he knew how.

She was going slower now. The road was built wide for campers, but it was old and pitted, so slow was smart. He was still impatient, though. They passed the turnoffs for the cabins, then the one for the playground and the rec center, then first one and then the other entrance to the U-shaped road of full hookups for campers and RVs. He had gone farther in, to the small clearing where there was only water and electric. That meant he shat and peed in the woods a lot so as not to have to dump the tank. Even with these precautions, there was a smell starting. But it was better to be on the smaller road with only five old no-sewer hookup spots in a line. The only thing past his section was tent camping, and that was very far along.

So far, he'd had the row of five all to himself, but when Meribel took the last turn, he saw with instant fury that another vehicle had come. Worse, they had taken the middle place. It should be like urinal rules. He was on one end, and the next person should take the other end. If a third came, they could use the middle. That seemed obvious. Just regular courtesy. But no, the trailer was jammed into the middle spot, only one lot down from his.

His teeth gritted and pressed. They needed privacy. She might be loud. Girls were loud when they were crying and sorry and then fucked correctly.

Now there was a campfire. Four people around his age sat around it. They were in two couples, boy, girl, boy, girl, and they had a big yellow Lab with them, hairy and sloppy. He could smell weed and hot dogs through his helmet. The Black girl was hastily tamping out a joint and tucking it away. The white girl lifted her hand all friendly as Meribel pulled up beside the Roadtrek Ranger. They all smiled and looked. The sloppy dog stood up and wagged and looked, too.

He lifted a hand back, and Meribel got off. She stood by him, quiet. He knew she was furious that these stupid people were ruining the privacy. But he had the gun, which helped her be calm. Then she pulled her helmet off. Her hair was sweaty and flat. She had cried all of her makeup off and her eye skin was crepey and tired. He was pissed she had taken off the helmet, but seeing her so sorry already made him feel very tender and sweet to her. She still had to say she was sorry, though. She had to say all the things she did wrong, correctly, on her knees. He had to be stern about that.

"Go in," he told her, really quiet.

"Hey, man," the boy who was not white called after them. He wasn't Black, either. It was hard to tell what he was. He had an arm around the white girl. "Sorry to be close, but the hooks are broke on that end."

He lifted a hand back, like, *Sure, sure whatever.*

"Oh, my God! It's her," the Black girl said, looking right at Meribel, who was already pulling the door open. "It's Didi from *Belinda's World.*"

Now they were all looking at Meribel, who froze in the doorway, and the white boy asked her, "Hey, are you okay?"

Meribel was tearstained and trembling, overcome with sorriness, and probably excited, too, to be alone with him. These kids were going to ruin it. Behind his dark face shield his mouth flattened and got so, so thin. The other campers looked back and forth at each other. They were around his age, like nineteen or so.

"Holy crap, it really is, though," the second girl said. "It's her, it's you. You're Meribel Mills."

Well, shit. Now he was definitely going to have to kill them.

35

THEY CAME OUT of the stairs in order of height: Sheila, Maxene, Honor. Then they spread into a line to walk down the hall with Honor in the middle. Honor wanted every door they passed to open. Some adult should poke a head out and say, *Girls, girls, are you armed? Is one of you homeless and possibly dangerous and also are you walking toward a man who has killed girls like you? That's bad to do, girls. Go sit down and wait for mothers.*

But her mother hadn't come back. All the doors stayed closed. The eye of the only camera in the hall had a yellow Post-it over it.

Sheila whispered, loud for a whisper, "I'm still not sure he—he can probably explain it." She was crying again, but only a little.

Honor was sure. She had no sister and she didn't want a sister, but she kept imagining her mom, open eyed in the green murk.

The worst part was that it was on purpose, and Maxene Hightower hadn't known. Not for years. After he put the car into the water, Maxene hugged him and was his friend and didn't know. Even at the funeral. She cried when he and her mom broke up. She never knew at all until she had to leave her house with only one suitcase because her mom had no car by then to carry more. Maxene wanted to take a thing of Ruby's, and her mom had put all the things of Ruby's in the attic because it made her sad to see them.

Maxene wanted to see them. She spent a lot of time up here when her mother wasn't home. She went up there and got her sister's old bear, Vita. There was a box of clothes there, too, labeled *Cooper*. Just clothes, because she had rooted around in it before, a little. That day, she dumped it out.

When Sheila asked, "Why? Why did you dump it out?" she was crying so hard the word "why" had three syllables. *Why-high-high*.

Maxene told them, "He was Mom's last boyfriend who was nice to me and not a drug person. Me and Ruby liked him, and we thought he would marry Mom. I wanted to take a thing that was his, too. Like a big shirt to sleep in, and I dumped it all out to leave a mess for whoever took our house because I hated them. The key chain fell out of a pocket when I dumped the box, and it said exactly what the car's plate said. BlG STUD, with a one for the 'I.' I remembered. I saw it when I swam under when Ruby didn't come up from her dive. I dream that plate still, sometimes, because her face was right by it. Her eyes were open and her hair floated across the words like weeds."

When Maxene put the key chain in her hands, Honor saw it had four keys. One of them was for a Chrysler. Honor knew it was all true, then.

"I didn't understand it then. I was just a kid. I didn't want to see it or know," she said. She kept the key chain, though, hiding it like a shame until she couldn't not know anymore. "He has his own business, with a website. I used to look him up in libraries, sometimes. On their computers. I missed him or I was curious or maybe I really did know, but I wouldn't let myself. I wanted to write him a letter. I wanted to ask him to come back because we had to stay in shelters and I missed the way it was when he was with us. So I had his address in Hattiesburg. I knew he'd left there for Atlanta, but I went to Hattiesburg first. I asked around near where his business used to be. It's not, like, a big town."

Cooper dated a single mom there, too, with two boys and a girl. The girl, Lizzie, had had bad allergies. A woman at the library branch near his old office space said she had known the girl. She tutted and said that it "was just so tragic."

The second dead girl made even Sheila think it might be real, but she didn't feel it as strongly and truly as Honor did. It made her agree to come up the stairs with them. Just to ask. Sheila was still snuffling, but Maxene Hightower wasn't crying at all as they walked down the hall, and Honor realized it was very easy to remember the name of a person who had a gun. If everyone carried guns, the world would be terrible and everyone would be afraid all the time, but she would never forget names.

Honor believed Cooper had killed this girl and then that girl, but the hardest part to believe was that Maxene thought the next would be Sheila. Sheila especially didn't believe it, until Maxene asked if she had had any accidents. Recently. That made Sheila get real quiet because of Wild Waves. She shook her head, though. It was easy to look at proof and know he was a BBEG who killed two girls, but not very easy to know you would be next.

Honor understood this part wasn't easy because Maxene said that when Sheila was dead, Cooper would have sex on Honor's mother and then kill Honor, too. Maxene had watched Mom and Cooper having coffee. Like a flirt coffee. Like a date.

Mom was not a person who would have a date, much less do sex things with Cooper and let Honor be killed. That was all impossible. Both her book about sex and her mom said Honor shouldn't have sex now, and to not be in a hurry, which was great, but her mother and the book also both said that grown-up people liked it. Yuna's mom confirmed, telling Yuna that even mothers liked it, and both their books told them about orgasms. Last month, Yuna said she had one. An orgasm. Yuna was pretty sure, she said. It happened at her riding lesson. Honor never had one, and she'd taken a lot more riding lessons than Yuna.

Her mom, after she made Honor have a sex talk, asked if Honor had questions. Honor had zero questions, then. Now she had a lot of them. Now Honor wanted her mom really really bad; she was so full of bees. She started drifting up inside her skull again as they got close to the door. She could feel herself flattening. It was possible that she was very, very angry because Cooper had tried to hurt and drown her friend. It was possible that she was scared because she wanted the gun back in her hand or Mom. Mom said she would be at the coffeehouse for only just a little, but she had not come back.

Maxene and Sheila had lost their breath coming up fourteen floors, but Honor hadn't. She went to the gym most days and also didn't smoke or even Juul much. But now her breath started puffing and her heart banged fast. She unlocked the door and reached for the doorknob, and Sheila gasped and made a breathy howl sound.

"Be quiet," Maxene said. "He deserves it."

"Deserves what?" Sheila asked, her eyes rolling around this way and that.

Honor knew. "For her to shoot him. Maxene is going to shoot him."

Sheila made a worse sound, like a person throwing up, but at least no throw-up came out. "I thought you would point it at him. Make him confess!"

"He won't. He won't confess or stop," Maxene said. She pointed at Sheila. "You see that he won't stop."

"Why can't we put him into prison?" Honor said. She was weighing the options in her head. Shoot him was safer, but prison was more legal.

Maxene had the gun in two hands, holding it in a way that seemed better than how Honor had held it. "He's so smart. Sheila even doesn't believe me. A girl breaks her neck. A girl has an allergic reaction. A girl drowns at a water park . . ." Sheila was sobbing and snotting again. Maxene shrugged. "He's rich and white and a man. I'm some homeless girl with a junkie mother. My mom didn't believe me. My own mom. I showed her the key chain. Before I left to go to Hattiesburg. She slapped it out of my hand and cried and said no, no, no."

Everyone was breathing so hard. Maxene huffed and Sheila puffed. Honor blew out all her breath and opened the door.

Somewhere inside there was a Big Bad Evil Guy. They didn't see him in the den or sitting at the dining room table or in the kitchen. The door to the office was open, and he wasn't in there. Her mom's door was open, now. She had left it shut. He must have gone into her mom's room, so she pointed. She started forward and Max came too. So did Sheila, but behind them.

Honor had never seen a person get shot for real. Only in movies or TV. Only in games. There, someone pulled a trigger, there was a bang noise, and another person fell down. On *Buffy*, even if you died, you might come back. In D&D, Honor's paladin had died twice. Once he was dead for three months of play, adventuring inside the Shadowfell. But Cooper was real. If Maxene Hightower shot him, he would be dead forever. So was Maxene's sister, though, so it seemed fair.

Honor realized she was floating in the air now six inches above her head. She had flattened up way even past her skull. Her body kept walking with her friends, hands clenching and unclenching. She followed her friends and her own body back to her mother's room. The music was off. The shower was off.

The French doors to the balcony were open, and there was Cooper. He was all the way out by the rail with his back to them, peering down at the street with his head going back and forth. They walked to the open double doorway and stopped, standing in a little row. He was no more than a dozen steps away, but he didn't hear them. Honor had to clear her throat very loud before he turned around. He saw her first, and he put his hand on his heart and said, "Oh, thank God! I was worried sick. Where did you—"

"Where is Mom?" Honor asked him really loudly. She wasn't back from coffee. What if Cooper had done a bad thing to her? She had asked if Sheila took drugs. Maybe she was suspicious and he knew it.

He didn't answer. He was busy looking from Sheila to Maxene

to Honor and back while his mouth came all the way open and said nothing. Honor wasn't good at facial expressions. She couldn't say what all faces he made in a row then, only that he made a lot of them. His eyes opened and shut and opened. His mouth twisted and yawped and he backed up a step until his back hit the railing and he had to stop.

"Max?" he said. "Maxene?" He sounded like a person who was choking. He recognized Maxene, even in the coat and hat. He knew her face, and that made what Maxene told them feel even more true. "Good God! What's happened to you?"

He started to take a step toward them, and Maxene Hightower lifted up the gun and pointed it at him. That made him stop. He rocked back.

"You killed Ruby. Now you're going to, going to, going to hurt Sheila," Maxene said. Her teeth chattered and she shivered, but it was hot outside.

Sheila cried even harder. So much crying. It grated. Her breath sounded like whooping. Donkey sounds, bray bray.

"No. No," Cooper said. "No, I loved Ruby. I loved your mom. I would never hurt your mom." This is exactly what a BBEG would say, Honor decided, if he was talking to a gun. "Honey, what happened to you? Are you—are you living on the street?"

Maxene's eyes got full and very glossy, and then two tears dumped out. The gun shook and wavered. Cooper looked like he was about to start crying, too. That surprised Honor. So many feelings all in a swirl. It was terrible. Why.

Maxene already said that Cooper wouldn't go to jail or stop, already decided she was going to shoot him. Why did she cry and not make it be over? Cooper kept talking, and she didn't shoot him. He was saying a lot of very soft words, *Girls* this and *Honey, I would never* that. Honor was floating so far above her body now that all his words were far. The sounds of talking ran together in a mush. Honor took both hands and pushed fists hard into her bruises, and when she got back close to inside herself, Shelia was talking.

"—*I almost drowned.*"

Cooper said, "It's crazy to even think it. You must have had a little stomach flu. You were sick this morning."

So much talking. So much crying. He had tears on his face now, too. Sheila was crying so hard she was struggling to breathe. Maxene cried harder, too, horking like a cat, but she wasn't a cat, and she wasn't a warrior princess. She was an upset girl with a gun drooping lower and lower. Honor should have kept it.

"Maxie," Cooper said. He spread his hands out. "The police must have given that key chain back to your mom. I loved you guys. You know I loved you all. Like a dad. I wanted to be your dad."

Now the gun hung down from Maxene's one hand. She had to wipe at her face with the other, and Sheila had her face hidden in her hands. Cooper looked at Honor. He made a wink at her. A wink like her mom made to tell Honor whatever she was saying was a joke. Was it a joke on her friends as they snotted and cried? Honor was very rocking but very calm, very up high against her own skull. She could think clearly, for all her body was spasming and wanting to slap and flop. She looked at Maxene and she knew then: Maxene was never going to shoot him. Sheila hadn't wanted to at all, anyway. What they both really wanted, so badly, was to believe it wasn't true.

It was true, but they refused to know it, so he was never going to stop. He wasn't even stopping now, and her mom was late and missing. Honor thought of Sheila at the birthday, paddling downward, downward in the terrible wave pool. The boy said she was *tripping balls.* Now Honor thought this must be drugs put in by Cooper. Her mom had asked if Sheila did them.

"It's okay," Honor said, and she was lying. It was not okay. "It's fine." It wasn't fine at all. She wasn't a great liar, and she wasn't in her body, and her voice was small and shaky. She looked to see if he believed her. Her mom would not believe her, but he nodded.

"Yes. Listen to Honor. It really is okay," Cooper said. "We'll help you, Max, won't we, Sheila? Won't we, Honor? I am so sorry that Gemma has had problems. I had no idea. You shouldn't be on the street. I'm going to fix that."

"It's good if we can help Maxene," Honor said. True. "She had a bad time." True. "I know you are a real good person who will help her." Lie. She was bad at lying, but Cooper didn't know her well. He didn't know her at all. He nodded, and she said, "I'm going to hug you."

She stepped toward him, and he let her. He wanted her to hug him, because then it would be harder for Max to shoot him. This was called line of sight, in D&D. He wanted her between him and the gun and for Honor to believe that he was not a terrible, bad person who killed girls. He looked at Sheila, looked at Max, opening his arms for her. He was watching to be sure Max wouldn't shoot him. She wouldn't, though, and Sheila was being useless.

Yuna was wrong and Honor was right. There wasn't a way to split the Fates into three things. Honor had to spin and measure and cut.

She didn't walk. She dashed. He was close to the rail and the rail was too low. She darted fast between his open arms. Instead of hugging him she put her hands flat on the taut meat of his belly, and she pushed. She pushed hard. Hard as she could.

His body rocked back and the middle of his spine hit the railing. She felt his body bending backward under her pushing hands. His spread hands flailed and then grabbed for the railing instead of her and his head snapped back.

He didn't tip over, though. He didn't fall. She scuttled back three steps. He reared up, and she saw so much eye-whites all around his eyes. He grabbed the rail behind him with both hands. She'd failed.

"Jesus, Honor!" Cooper said.

She had tried to be all the Fates, and she had failed. Cooper's face was very white now and his lips were so white, too, like how books sometimes described a vampire with no blood in him at all. Honor looked at him, and she wanted her mother.

"You should go to jail," she told him. "Maxene says you won't."
She meant to say it very firm, like her paladin might. It sounded
whistly and weak, though. Maybe she was crying, too. She hadn't
noticed.

"He never will," Maxene echoed.

"Of course I won't," he said. He let go of the rail, but still the
gun kept him from coming closer. He was watching it again, looking from it to them. "You're being—you girls are being crazy. A
homeless girl. Sheila, you are troubled. Honor is autistic. You are
crazy, and you've made this up. Better to never talk about it." He
looked at Maxene now. He knew she wasn't Xena Warrior Princess.
He said, "Who would ever believe you?"

That was a mistake. To say all those things was a mistake.
Maxene made a sound like a mad animal.

Sheila said, "I believe her."

Sheila moved, then, and Honor heard the gun thunk to the
ground as Maxene dropped it and came with her. Sheila barreled
fast up by Honor, so that Honor felt gathered, carried forward by
the wind of them. Maxene was on Honor's other side, thick and
strong, bending, reaching for his legs as Honor's hands hit his chest,
and Sheila's, too. A wave of three girls, all moving as one.

36

SOMETIMES MY DAUGHTER, Honor, said, *I'm full of bees.* I clambered off the bike, and even though I was so grateful to create a small but necessary empty space between his body and mine, I felt as if ten thousand bees had crawled inside me and were seething in my veins and scrambling along the inside of my skin. Who had been watching me in the rain? Not Marker Man. Who had been in Cooper's house? Not this boy. Was Honor safe? I wasn't, and almost worse, I had no way to check on my kid. I was dizzy, sick at the thought, and I needed air. My buzzing hands reached up and pulled my helmet off, unthinking.

Almost immediately, one of the girls at the neighboring campsite jerked up straight and tall in her chair and said, "Oh, my God! It's her. It's Didi from *Belinda's World.*" Beside me, Marker Man stiffened, his spine elongating. They all looked over, started asking questions and talking at me in a blur of sound.

It was surreal to be recognized in the middle of my kidnapping by four kids sprawled in camp chairs under a pullout awning. They looked like a United Colors of Benetton Scooby Gang, arranged in couples around a smokeless firepit and a big beer cooler with s'more ingredients piled on top. They even had a dog. They were no more than thirty feet distant, so normal and so cute. A world away, I stood by a crazy man-child with a gun clutched inside his jacket pocket. This person had stolen me to hurt me, and yet he looked like he should be over with them, roasting hot dogs on sticks. I should be at home. With Honor.

The kids were beginning to make concerned faces the longer we stood frozen. I glanced at Marker Man, and thought, *He's panicking.* I couldn't see his face, but it was in his body language. He was so tense he felt coiled, and his hand was back in his pocket. With the gun. I knew from his letters how deluded he could be, how very far from what was real. If he shot them dead, he would probably be sorry that they had made him. If he shot them, it would be their fault.

All the way here, I told myself, *Drive off the highway into that tree!* And then, *Smash into that car!* A wreck would bring police. I had to get to Honor. But my body was so frail on the motorcycle. I didn't want to be dead or paralyzed or lose a leg or have brain damage.

In my head, I could imagine a thousand voices asking me, later, *Why didn't you just . . .* One of those voices was mine. As if it was so easy to make a plan with a gun grinding between your vertebrae. Time skipped and rocketed past me while I obeyed his instructions to exit here, turn there. I drove exactly where he said, metronoming between fear for me and fear for Honor, swamped in helpless rage. My thoughts ran in a circle, and on that loop, they kept coming around to something new: *This isn't on me. If I am scared or imperfect or hopeful or frozen and a person hurts me, if they hurt me—that's on them.*

Somewhere on the highway, circling back to this thought again and then again, I stopped crying. Now I manufactured a smile, small and shaky, but present. "We just came from a funeral." I spoke loudly, as if volume could fix stupid and illogical. Why would Meribel Mills be staying in a shitty camper in rural Georgia to go to a funeral? But like most actors, I was a good liar. When I said it, I let my childhood accent out, thick and sweet. They blinked at me. Marker Man's inhuman, faceless helmet turned toward me.

Finally one boy said, "Oh, hey, sorry."

"Yes. Um. Sorry for your loss," the girl who had recognized me first chimed in. She was questioning her recognition now. I didn't sound like Meribel Mills, and death was awkward, the grief of strangers even more so.

"*Go inside.*" It was a whisper behind the helmet for me alone.

I didn't want to go inside. Nothing good was waiting for me there. He could make me, though, with his gun, with the four young lives in front of us. I thought again, *Anything that happens inside is on him, his fault, even if I go there now on my own legs.* Every time it came around, the thought felt louder, truer, stronger. I headed toward his camper, and I felt both relieved and horrified when he turned away from the kids and followed me in. It was worse to hear the door click shut behind us.

The camper was small, cramped. To my right, a little table angled like a diamond had one point jutting between the driver's chair and the passenger seat. To my left was a slim passageway with a kitchenette on one side and a closed-off space that smelled like a bathroom on the other. The whole place had a tangy, rancid scent: cat urine and Febreze and mildewed upholstery. Beyond that, the back half of the space was filled entirely by a flat, low bed. The mattress had a seam running horizontally across the middle of it. There were two pillows, side by side, both listing and deflated. My stomach lurched. I did not want to go that way.

He yanked off his helmet. His greasy hair stood up in tufts and his mouth pulled itself into a frown so deep it looked like a parody. "Shit! They know who you are. They'll call the paparazzi, and it's all going to be ruined."

He took the gun out of his pocket. Whenever his gun was visible, it was hard to look at anything else. Even he looked at it instead of me. He was doing math. I could see it: Guns were loud. But they had recognized me. But guns were loud.

"They won't call the—" I was going to say cops. But he was so deluded. I finished with "—press. They're high. They—" As soon as I started talking, all his attention came to me, and I felt myself shrinking back, my whole small body trying to retract itself into something even smaller.

Marker Man would rape me and hurt me. He would probably kill me, too, because I wasn't the right Meribel. I wasn't the one he had invented. When I was dead, he could fold me into the shapes he liked, or cut me into pieces to fit his ideas of me. He'd been drawing my body as a thing he owned, a thing he had invented. I'd invented a Marker Man in my head, too. This real one was a dangerous child with no impulse control.

He said, "Telling them we went to a funeral was a good idea. We still have to move, though."

I hated how the compliment made me happy. I hated how I wanted to please him because then he might hurt me less, but I still complimented him right back, saying, "Moving is a good idea, too."

It made my gorge rise, and so I thought, deliberately, *I'm not trying to befriend you. I'm going to stall you.* It was the same new, wiser voice that had told me all of this was his fault. Then that voice had a better thought. That small, wise voice said, *No. I'm going to kill you.*

"I'll get the bike in and unhook us, and we'll go," he said.

It felt like a reprieve, and hope leaped high in me. He would go outside, and I would—what? Scream for help? He'd shoot the kids. Hide? It was so small in here. There was a bathroom, and I thought the seam in the stained mattress meant the platform could hinge up into a storage chest. There were no other spots where I might fit. He'd find me in seven seconds, and he'd be mad. I had to get away, get home to Honor. I had to help my kid. Someone had been watching me, our building, someone in a gray raincoat, and it wasn't Marker Man, or Cam, or James. Who?

"Whatever you want," I said. "Baby."

His eyes lit up at that. I could see he was excited, and I felt a sour excitement, too. I could work him, maybe. I could be sweet and put him off his guard. Or so I thought, until he said, "The thing is. We really have to hash things out. Before it is okay between us."

I heard myself swallow. I told him, "We can do that."

He nodded, and I didn't like the weird light in his eyes. "I need you to be sorry."

"I am. I am so sorry," I said, instantly. Girlish. A little baby voice that I was much too old to use. I was too old to be here with him at all.

"Maybe while I get us moved, you should be still and quiet and really think. About being sorry. Be still and think of how to make it up to me." He opened one of the tiny drawers in the strip of kitchen and lifted out a roll of silver duct tape.

I instinctively stepped away from him, farther down the narrow galley kitchen. It put me closer to the bed. I did not want to go closer to the bed. "You don't have to do that," my gross little girl voice said, now rising even higher, toward hysteria. "I can be still. I will think. I will be sorry."

He followed me, and I stepped back again in spite of myself.

"It won't hurt you." He had the tape in one hand, the gun in the other. He set the gun down on the kitchen's strip of workspace. My eyes went to it. He stepped past it, pulling off a long strip of tape. It made a horrible grinding sound as he ripped it free. Now my eyes were flicking back and forth. Gun. Tape. Tape. Gun. I wasn't sure which scared me more, to be shot and killed or to be bound and helpless.

"Please, don't," the baby voice said.

His eyebrows came down. "I need you to show me you are ready to be sorry."

The backs of my legs touched the bed. I blinked. "I am. I will sit here. I will be still and quiet. I'm really, really sorry."

A flash of temper. "Don't be a little bitch, Meribel. It's just duck tape."

"Duct," I said, unthinking. Automatically. Duct not duck. Shades of Honor, who was so exact.

I had a full half second to see his face change. To know correcting him had been a bad mistake. His mouth twisted, and he snatched up the gun and came at me. I tried to get my hands up, cowering back, but he was so tall. The gun came whistling down at me and banged hard and cold and sharp into my temple.

I had time to feel myself falling. Time to feel the hot red wash of blood spilling down my face. Then I slammed into the wall, and my body started sliding down. I went with it, down into a long gray moment when I wasn't there at all.

37

COOPER HAYETTE HAD fourteen floors to change his luck.

He flipped as he went over the railing, spun twice, like a coin. Some animal instinct made him try to go horizontal, try to spread his arms wide, as if he could catch the wind and fly, or slow, or hover. But he spun, unable to control it. Wind, created by his own velocity, roared in his ears. He saw the sidewalk rushing up to meet him.

There was time to scream, though it took less than four seconds. There was time to be surprised. There was time to think one thought, or feel remorse, or make a promise, and he wasted it.

All he thought was *Call it. Call it in the air.*

As if that could help. As if there was still a way to win this.

Then he was pointing like an arrow, facedown. His lips and eyelids flapped and pocketed.

Heads, he thought. He even got that wrong.

38

IT WAS HARD to get my eyes open. Fast-congealing blood had gummed them up. I lay on the thin, deflated mattress, my feet pointed at the back of the camper, my head close the edge. I was mostly on my side, and my arms were pulled so firmly behind me that it hurt my collarbones. My wrists were taped together, and so were my ankles. I was barefoot. He'd knocked me right out of my shoes. The bindings were so tight that my toes and fingers tingled, and I was sick and dizzy. The bed smelled like laundry that had been left to mildew in the washer for days and days.

Marker Man sat on the edge, his ass by my head, holding a dirty washcloth full of ice against the oozing cut beside my eyebrow. He saw my eyes were open, and he smiled and set the makeshift ice pack aside. He put his hand on my chest between my breasts. I thought my skin would peel itself right off my body at his touch.

"Your heart is going so, so fast. Like a little bitty bird heart," he said reverently. He took his hand away, but only so he could tear off another, smaller bit of duct tape. He smacked it over my mouth, like a slap, and my headache bloomed and pulsed. "Stay."

He stood up, and every step he took away from me felt like a blessing. I craned my neck to watch him. He took the Tech baseball cap out of his other jacket pocket and put it on, pulling it down low to hide his hair and shade his face. He'd brought the motorbike into the kitchen area, where it took up almost all the room.

"I'm going to go get us unhooked. Then I'll move us," he said. "You stay there, and work on being sorry. Think of what you need to say to me. So I don't have to punish you too much. You know I love you." I stared at him through my bloody lashes. Whatever I said, it would be wrong. The way he lingered on that word, "punish." He wanted to hurt me. Tears welled up in my eyes. I couldn't help it. Crying made my nose stuffy, and all at once, it felt very hard to breathe. I started panicking, sure I would drown and smother in my own tears and mucus, my mouth clamped firmly shut by the duct tape. He liked that, liked watching me writhe and cry and be afraid. He stood there for a long thirty seconds, enjoying my struggle to breathe, and black hate rebloomed in me, under the fear.

"Sit tight, baby." As if I had a choice! He worked his way past the motorbike, turning sideways and half climbing it to get to the door. Out he went.

The second the door clicked shut behind him, I started jerking at my hands, rolling, kicking with my legs, trying to get my wrists or at least my feet free. I could tell almost immediately that it was hopeless. I was bound so tight. That made me cry harder, which made breathing worse. I fought to be still, to calm my heart, to concentrate on getting air in.

Outside, I heard voices. One of the Scooby kids had come over and was talking to him. The one I would cast as Fred, I thought. I couldn't make out the words, but the tone was very friendly. Even so, it horrified me. *Please*, I thought, *Please don't shoot that poor, dumb kid.*

He would be back here any second. Would he rape me before he drove me off into a deeper wilderness to "punish" me and rape me more and kill me? If "second locations" were almost always fatal, what the hell would a third location be like?

I was dizzy from lack of oxygen, but I could still hear whimpering and crying. Was that my voice, so small and dry and muffled in the tape? I sounded pitiful and beaten. I had to stop. For Honor. Was she safe? If I drowned here in tears and snot—I couldn't. I would find a way to get home, to my girl, and make sure she was safe. I jerked at the tape, fruitlessly, rubbing my face against a flat, musty pillow, blowing my nose into it, and somehow, I stopped crying. For just a moment.

I still heard it, though. Sad little mewls. I was so disoriented, and my head hurt. It took me a long, wasted moment to make sense of it.

The sounds were coming from underneath me. I stilled, every nerve vibrating, ears straining. I felt a soft thumping vibration through the mattress. It was so faint that my own shivering had hidden it.

I looked at the seam bisecting the mattress. I was right. The front half of this bed was the lid of a chest. I pressed my ear down. A soft thump. A whimper. Something, someone, was alive in there.

My heart was not a little bird. It was a jackhammer. I kicked and rolled and wormed until I could lower my bound feet and stand in the scant space in front of the bed platform. I crouched and saw it was a chest. It had a push latch that locked it automatically when it was closed. I turned my back and scrabbled at it, trying to work the latch and turn the small knob and then pull the lid up all while blind and facing backward and hampered by the binding tape. My hands tingled, sausage-fingered and thick from lack of circulation.

As I struggled with it, I heard the scree of the old doorknob turning. I froze. No time to get back in. Marker Man would catch me being bad and hurt me. *I have to be good*, I thought, even though I knew that there was no good that was good enough. He wanted to hurt me. He had taken me to hurt me.

As the door cracked open, I heard a girl's voice calling. "Hey, wait! Can you—"

It snicked shut again. The Scooby gang, again. Oh, he was going to kill them if they didn't stop. He really would. But they were buying me a precious minute. My heart was thumping so loud. How did he not hear it from outside? I closed my eyes and concentrated, fumbling with the latch—

I felt it catch and turn. I rose up pushing, opening the lid behind me, and instantly I started gagging behind the tape. If I threw up, I would choke to death on my own bile, but God, the smell. I closed my streaming eyes and concentrated on not puking. I'd smelled the tang of human waste and terror-sweat under the mildew and ammonia, blaming the bathroom. Now this smell came out of the box like a living thing. It stung my eyes, and the whimpers and the mewls were louder. I knew what I would see even before I turned around and looked down at the woman in the chest.

She was small and folded, gagged with a dirty red bandanna instead of tape, her hands bound in front of her. She was younger than I was, but not by much. I almost couldn't believe she was alive. She didn't look alive, except for her blazing, desperate eyes. She was gaunt, her eyes bugging, her neck corded. Her lips were so dry and cracked they'd bled and scabbed onto the gag.

"It's okay," I tried to tell her, but the tape muted my words to a horrified hum. It wasn't okay, actually. I tried to beg her with my eyes to help me, so I could help her. Her own gaze back was crazed and feral.

I turned my back and crouched to jam my hands down into the storage space, searching for her own bound hands. Instead, I felt her neck and chin. Too far up. Her skin felt papery, arid. I scooted down in a crouch, reaching until I felt her scrambling fingers on my wrists. I felt her fingers picking at the tape. She was helping. She was trying.

She was so weak. It was so slow. Outside, voices buzzed and warbled, rising and falling. Her hands plucked and worried at my binding as I tried to pull my hands apart, or out, desperate. I had to get free.

So I could freeze again? So I could bend? No. So I could live. So I could get to Honor.

One hand popped free. I felt blood rushing into my fingers in a painful tingle. I left the rest of the tape as a floppy bracelet on my left hand and bent to rip the tape off my ankles. The woman in the chest made desperate noises, squirming in the filth.

I pulled my gag off, leaving lip skin on the tape, tasting coppery blood, then turned to try to help her stand. She was tiny, but she was also weak. I tugged and pulled at her. God, the smell of her. Surely he would notice? He hadn't seemed to notice the cat pee and the toilet or the mildew, but this was worse. She pushed with her legs, clinging to me, and together we got her upright. I pulled her out of the chest, clasping her to me, and tried to set her on bound feet. He'd used clothesline. Her ankles were chafed and bleeding, and without my support, she could not stand.

"Get in the bed. Be me, be me," I told her. I was already shoving her down. She was too weak to fight me. I pushed at her, pointing her feet away, turning her on her side.

She was tiny and we had the same color hair, but even as I pushed her into position, I knew it couldn't fool him. She was wearing a short dress, gray, like a waitress uniform, unspeakably stained now. I wore an aqua tunic, bright and belted. I pulled her gag down, though, and picked the knot that bound her hands.

"Water," she said. It was a croak, a rasp.

God, her lips were so pale and cracked. She could die of dehydration before he came back and shot us both. I turned to the kitchen. The motorcycle was blocking the door of the mini fridge and the low cabinets that might have a cup.

"Water, water," she begged.

I could not get in there without major movement and—oh, the ice pack. He'd pressed a dirty washcloth with ice in it to my face. Where he had hit me. There it was, lying crumpled in the bed. I opened it and found four square cubes of ice, the kind that comes out of a tray, melting into the cloth.

I grabbed one, slippery and cold, and put it to her mouth.

"Suck on it. Slow, or you will puke. There's more in here." I pushed the little bundle with the other cubes close to her hands.

She puled and licked at the ice with a tongue so desiccated it was dead white. I saw she had a nametag on, and it said her name was Margaret.

"Just a little, just a little, do not chew it, slow," I was whispering, and she sucked it out of my fingers into her mouth. Her dry tongue felt pebbled on my fingers. I'd started crying again, out of fear and horror, out of pity. She moved the cube around her mouth, moaning, so desperate and greedy.

Again, the doorknob moved. Again, I froze, and inside I was screaming. I'd been too slow! She stared at it, too, big-eyed, but she had no tears at all.

The door stayed closed, rattling a little. I realized he was locking it, not coming in. Was he preparing to drive off? I heard his footsteps moving, heading around the back, and I understood. Yes. We were leaving. He would walk around to the driver's side and get in and look back, and he would see us. I had to hide. The motorbike blocked the bathroom door. She was lying in the bed over the trunk lid. There was no place I could go.

I forced my tingling feet into motion, slithering and climbing over the bike, heading toward the front of the small camper van. To what? Attack him? Try to grab the gun? He hadn't left it on the counter. It must be back inside his pocket. Outside, he was ahead of me, walking to the driver's side. What would I do when he opened the door? Scream? He'd kill the kids. And her. Then he would hurt me again, hurt me more, and likely kill me, too, when he was done; and back at home, someone in a gray raincoat had been watching. I'd left Honor there. I could not be killed; I had to get to her.

As he reached the door, I dropped into a crouch and scooted forward, wedging myself under the tiny table that sat on the diagonal between the driver's seat and the passenger one. I bent my knees and clutched my legs close to my chest, my spine pressed into the back of his chair.

I heard the door open, and I closed my eyes, as if this would help him not to see me. I stopped breathing. I mashed myself so small.

I felt the driver's-side chair shift as he climbed in, heard it creak as he settled and slammed his door. Then he craned around to check on me, looking back toward the bed. From my hidey-hole, I could see the top of her head, her feet pointing toward the back. She had bright hair, like mine, but an inch-thick stripe of dark roots ran down the middle. Her slight figure was in gray, not aqua. I could smell her. I knew again that there was no way this would work.

He called out, "Good to go, babe, good to go!" in happy tones. He turned forward and started the big engine. I felt him seesaw back and forth and heard the zip sound as he put his seat belt on. I blinked in disbelief as he called back, "You rest, doll baby. I know exactly where to take us. Soon, so very soon, we will finally be alone."

The engine started up, mercifully loud. I took a small sip of air in through my mouth, silent, and I understood: I was fungible, to him. There was a woman where he had put one, wholly helpless. Good enough. It could be any woman, really, as long as he could call it Didi, dress it up, and kill it.

39

CAM REYNOLDS WAS having lunch with his son and his son's new girlfriend when Meribel's text landed. Sadie was charming, if a little overearnest, and clearly head-over-heels with Marco. Cam was warm and polite with her, but yeah, he had some sour thoughts running. Cam was in love, himself. Bowled over with it, actually. He'd tried to stop, and failed, so he'd taken a big gamble and gone to check out Atlanta. It was a good little city. He could see himself there, sure, but Meribel said no. She was out.

Okay, then. That was that. He was pretty damn busted up about it. The young, fresh, doe-eyed adoration happening across the table was bittersweet.

When he got up to hit the gents', there was Meribel's number, back on his phone. He felt his blood speed up, a little zing. He'd taken her out of his contacts, but he knew those digits. He stopped in the hall to read her chain of texts, starting with I'm an idiot, and then some truly worrying information about her stalker. And then—I'm not saying "Maybe." I'm saying, "Yes."

He rubbed his eyes and tried to keep from grinning like an idiot at no one and nothing, and failed. Failed utterly, and didn't care. He texted back: Hell, yeah. OMW.

By the time he got back to the table, he'd decided Sadie wasn't overly earnest at all. No such thing. Cute and sweet, and Marco was nuts about her, too, that was obvious. Now this all seemed adorable. She was having a hard time picking a dessert, so he ordered all five for the table, saying, "Why pick?" His grin was still too big, embarrassing, unfaded. Marco had his eyebrows up.

When Sadie went to the restroom, he told his son how much he liked her, and was rewarded with a gush of information about all the ways that Sadie was a wonder. Cam was forty-three years old, but he looked at his son's young, happy face as he gushed on about a girl, and he thought, *Christ, I am no different.*

He flashed his phone and told his son a text had landed that meant he had to get back to Atlanta early. He apologized, and meant it, but a man in love gets texts like that? Nothing on this green earth could stop him from galloping toward her. Marco was okay with it. When he slipped the kid a couple hundred to take his girl out somewhere wonderful instead of hanging with his dad, he was more than okay.

Cam had to go back to his hotel and fast-pack and check out. She still hadn't answered when he was ready to get on the road. His response had been terse, but she knew he texted short. The fact that he was he getting in his car ought to tell her he was in. He felt a ping of anxiety, thinking of the stalker in her building. He paired his phone up with the rental car, a pain in the ass that took ten minutes of digging in the manual, so he'd know when she hit him back. She didn't, and the longer he drove, the more this struck him as off brand. She always had her phone close. She should have answered by now. The feeling only grew.

About an hour outside of Atlanta, he had to stop for gas. While the car filled, he re-added Meribel to his contacts and remembered he never took her off his FIND MY app. His phone told him that hers was currently turned on and at her home address. Okay, so, she was probably asleep or on a long work call with Liza, but it was still worrisome. Marker Man had gotten in again. Cam had a bad feeling. He put his foot down and pushed up exactly nine miles past the speed limit; he didn't have time to get pulled over. He rode it tight like that, all the way back to Atlanta.

The scant visitor spaces in the garage that served her building all were full. He had to circle twice, cussing softly, getting more and more anxious, which on him always looked pissed. He finally found a spot on a side street and hurried back toward Meribel's place. He was moving very deliberately, even at speed, eyes hard and mouth tight, ready for something. Or, he thought he was ready. He was shocked as hell when Meribel's neighbor, Cooper Hayette, came hurtling out of the sky, screaming, and smashed into the pavement right in front of him.

Cooper landed on his belly, his face in profile. The left side of his head caved in instantly, spattering bright crimson, the body landing so close to Cam that droplets hit his shoes. Cam recognized the sandy hair and the hipster glasses and the pricey Italian shoes. He looked up before most other people on the sidewalk started screaming and grabbing for each other.

Was that a flash of movement, up on Meribel's balcony?

On Tenth Avenue, traffic was backed up, but even so, three cars lost control and swerved and banged and jostled into one another, and then two banged into the mess from behind. The pileup called attention away from the building, but it didn't look serious; Atlanta's notoriously slow, miserable traffic was for once working in someone's favor.

Cam went dead calm, the way he always did when things got violent. His mind snapped into an attentive slo-mo while his fast body was already hurrying past the corpse. More fluids, darker, thicker, were already sludging out of Cooper as Cam sprinted toward the building's front door. A chorus of pissed-off horns began from cars too far back for their drivers to see what had happened.

He bulled his way inside, weaving through the people who were pushing out, asking questions. As soon as he got clear, he sprinted toward the glass elevator lobby. He passed the entrance to the CVS, where a couple of people were still shopping, calm and oblivious.

He punched in the new code to let himself in, then pressed the elevator call button and stood waiting for a thousand years.

Outside, people would still be gathering around the body, pressing in too close, filming and yelling at each other to call 911. They had no way to know what floor Cooper had fallen from. He should have yelled *Fourteen* at them. But he hadn't. He was shakier than he knew. Because this wasn't combat or a job. This was personal. This was Meribel. He should have—

But no. *Not* a mistake, a decision. He hadn't yelled the floor because he wanted to get to Marker Man before the cops. He could end this for her, now. Fast and forever.

Anyway, telling the crowd or the cops that the body had fallen from Apartment A up on the fourteenth floor was not going to help Cooper. Cooper was past all that. The elevator doors finally jerked open.

The ride up was agony. Every second was the longest of his life. He had his backup gun out and down by his leg as he waited, in case Marker Man was there when the doors opened, dragging off Meribel in a choke hold.

When the car finally arrived, the hall was empty. Cam believed he had moved fast enough. Marker Man couldn't have killed Cooper and already have Meribel in another elevator. Anyway, any smart person doing an abduction would use the stairs. Cam would loop through the apartment and then go down them at a gallop if she wasn't there.

His panic pressed him down lower and colder, made him hyperobservant. He saw the Post-it note slapped over the doorbell's camera and felt his teeth grinding together. He'd taken the feed off his phone after Meribel broke up with him. He'd blocked her on every bit of social media, too, because he loved her, and she'd said no. He had respectfully taken her out of even his peripheral vision. This was right, but why had he done it so fast? Hair trigger. Now he desperately wanted the lost footage.

He charged the door like a battering ram, because Marker Man must still be inside. With Meribel. With Honor. Cam couldn't fuck around with knocking. He was still ten feet out when the door opened. It was hard to draw up short, but there was Honor peering out, red faced and sweaty, a tufty crest of cowlicks stuck up from the back of her head like a chicken tail. He stopped dead, even though he heard crying behind her. Female crying. Meribel? At least two women were weeping their guts out. He needed to understand the situation. Hostages? Would busting in there do more harm than good?

"Oh, hello," Honor said. It sounded calm, but she generally talked a little flat. Meribel said she wasn't great with facial recognition, but she knew him, he thought.

His gun was pointed down, and now he slid it back behind his leg. She was rocking faintly. Her face looked oddly set. He saw as he got closer that the skin around her eyes was bruised and swollen, and after she greeted him, she reached up and casually ground two fingers into the purpled flesh, pressing so hard he flinched. She didn't.

"Is that your mom?" he said, quiet and collected. He meant the crying. She looked back over her shoulder, as if checking, then shook her head, no. "Where is your mom?"

"I don't know," Honor said, and now she did seem flustered. "She never came back from having coffee with a person. I want her, please. I want her."

He couldn't make sense of it. Meribel not home, but her phone was in the building? Oh, right, there was a coffeehouse downstairs. That would be his next stop, but first—here was Meribel's kid, alive, in front of him. Cooper mashed to pudding on the sidewalk. "Is he in there?" he asked. Now Honor looked confused, and Cam said, low and urgent, "Marker Man?" He was right outside the door now.

Honor shook her head in another stoic no, fingers pressing the bruises. He wanted to pull her hand away from her poor face, but he knew enough about her to feel cautious about touching her when she was shaken. Honor swung the door wide, and behind her he saw the red-haired neighbor girl and a stocky young brunette wearing way too much dark and layered clothing for the season. These two had their arms around each other, weeping themselves to death. He felt a ping of shock as he recognized the third one as the homeless girl, from the alley. He'd given her his pepper spray gel.

"Did Cooper jump?" he asked the older girls. They sobbed and clutched each other. "Did you see what happened?"

"We did a thing," said Honor. She shrugged. She pressed her fingers to the bruises. "We did something on the balcony. Cooper is bad. He's bad. He's very, very bad, and I want my mom."

That . . . was a lot to process. That would take some thinking, some conversation. Definitely he had questions. This was not the time.

"Where's *your* mom?" he asked the redhead. Then back to Honor. "How long has that been covered?" He pointed back to the doorbell camera.

"Sheila's mom is at work," Honor said. Sheila didn't seem capable of answering anything right now. "I put that Post-it on before I went to get Sheila. Then we went downstairs to check on Maxene."

"This is Maxene, huh?" Cam asked, and Honor nodded. "Maxene? You okay?"

The girl from the alley met his eyes and nodded, slowly, like she was deep underwater.

He asked all three of them, "Did the camera see you girls, any of you, coming in or out of the apartment?"

Honor shook her head, immediate and definite. Good.

Out in the street, far but getting closer, he heard sirens. They would figure out which floor to check pretty damn fast, if Cooper had his wallet on him. They would come to Meribel's, perhaps right after Cooper's, because only the largest units had balconies. He had bare minutes to make some pretty big decisions.

These girls. Someone had to talk to them. Find out the facts. He already knew he didn't want cops in charge of that conversation.

He thought it should be Meribel. She should lead it, get the story. Meribel and her money and her fame and her lawyers could get between Honor and, well, anyone, if these girls really had "done a thing." He looked at them, two weeping, one stimming, and he thought, *Oh, yeah. They did a thing, all right.* He thought of Honor saying in her forthright way, *Cooper is bad.* So . . . shut this down?

Yes. He was still in crisis mode, so the second he decided, he was moving. As he stepped forward, Honor melted out of his way, so he walked straight through Meribel's room to the balcony. He stayed as close to the French doors as he could, and couldn't see the street, so he assumed the street could not see him. He took down the small camera he'd installed and pocketed it. Unlike the mass-market doorbell cam, this feed had audio, and it went right to Meribel's computer. She'd know exactly what had happened, and then she could decide how best to handle it. He pulled the Leatherman off his belt and removed the mount for it, as well. He left the doors open and went back out into the living room. The older girls had subsided into snuffling, still clinging to each other.

"Come on. We're going to, um, Sheila's place," he told the girls. "We'll wait there for your mothers. We have to go right now."

They shuffled forward, happy to have a grown-up taking charge, asking zero questions. Good. He checked that the hall was clear, then fast-hustled them down it, leaving the Post-it to cover their retreat. He checked around the corner. Empty, so they speed-walked around and down to Sheila's place. They got inside without running into anyone. Cam closed the door, locked it, and then the two older girls plopped onto the leather couch, side by side. Honor stood over them, patting at them with her dry little hands.

He stayed on his feet, looking down at them all, very calm and serious. "Here's the story. When Meribel left to get coffee, Honor, you covered the camera so your mom wouldn't see you sneaking out to go to your friend's house. Sheila? Sheila, are you with me?" The redhead looked up, her face blank and tearstained, but he held her gaze until she blinked and nodded. "Honor came right to your house. You don't know what happened after that. Cooper was at Meribel's, and you two were here. That's all you say. You don't have to explain why Cooper was at Meribel's. You don't have to explain, period. Just shrug and say you don't know if anyone asks you to explain 'why' anything."

No one would ask, he thought. No one would get the chance to so much as lay eyes on these girls, if he could help it, not until Meribel had seen the footage, asked some questions, and decided what was best for them.

"What do I say?" Maxene asked. She looked to him like she might not be a minor.

"Not a damn thing. Not to anyone. You weren't ever here." No reason for the cops to know she'd so much as been in the building. The girl had clearly had a run of bad luck to end up where he'd met her and now at what might be a murder scene. Still, Meribel's daughter was patting at her with great solicitude. Whatever kind of bad Cooper had been, this girl was at Honor's side when things went south, which meant she'd have Meribel's money and fame and will behind her. He thought Maxene's bad luck might be about to change.

"We good to sit quiet here a little?" he asked.

Honor said they were, and he could see she got it. The girls on the sofa nodded, but their faces stayed blank and dazed. It was okay. He could go over it again, and then again, as many times as needed, now that they were safe at Sheila's.

Cam went to the open kitchen and dug around, looking for cocoa or packets of hot chocolate. No such thing, but he found tea and made it for them, adding an exorbitant amount of brown sugar and milk to counteract shock.

While he was making it, Honor said something to the others, and then she came to the kitchen, carrying his gun in a careless, wrongful way that almost stopped his heart.

"Maxene dropped this on the porch. I picked it up."

"Good thinking," he said. Christ, what had happened here? He took the gun and checked the safety. It was off. He clicked it on. Honor started to explain, but he held a hand up, and they all froze. He eased silently to the door to look out the peephole. The girls all went as still as little rabbits tucked in a warren, big eyed, shaking. Cam watched as four cops made their way past this door and down the hall. They disappeared around the corner, heading for Meribel's.

Good enough.

40

I STILL DIDN'T know the name of the man prepping to drive me away from my kid, my life, forever. Why would he tell me? In his mind, we were desperately in love, so of course I must know it.

Would he feel my heart pounding through the driver's seat? I was hyperaware of his terrible presence, keyed to his every little shift and twist. I hated being close enough to feel his movements, even through a chair. The gun must now be back in his pocket. I wanted to reach one sneaky hand through the crack between his seat and the door and try to get it, but what if he caught me? I tried to remember which pocket he'd put it in before. Was he right-handed? I had no idea.

The woman on the bed moaned, a weak, harried sound.

"It's okay!" Marker Man called back to her, to me—who cared? His empty reassurances were for any bright-haired female shape that he had laid out hurt and helpless on his bed. "We'll be alone soon. I know where to go. I just have to set the GPS up."

There was a pocket in the back of his seat. Lumpy. My busy fingers tucked down into it, exploring. The first thing I pulled out was an ancient Nacho Cheese Doritos bag. So crinkly! I stopped breathing again. Froze for an endless heartbeat. Two.

"Got the directions," he called back. He sounded so cheery,

like a dad in some Disney Channel family vacation movie. I felt a thready bloom of red rage leaking into my fear. He put the RV in gear and began maneuvering it away from the hookups. I hoped the shifting of the vehicle hid my movements as my hands crept desperately back into the pocket, seeking anything that might help me. Anything.

The lump was a lighter. Not a small one, for cigarettes. The long kind with the clicky trigger, meant for grills and campfires. In my crazy head, I thought, *Can I light him on fire?* I didn't think his clothes or the upholstery would burn fast enough to kill him or even hurt him enough to stop him. He would put the fire out and get to me, burn me back, or worse.

He kept right on seesawing the camper back and forth, slowly working its cumbersome length free of the space, talking loudly. "You need to show me you are sorry. I need to believe you really, really are." God, he was so chipper, practically ready to whistle as he demanded my subjugation. "And you know I'm going to have to kill that asshole in the alley for how he put his hands on you, right?"

I put my hands all the way down in the pocket, hoping for anything, anything else at all, and came up empty.

I was so screwed. I bit back a sob; sobs were loud. I ran my hands up and down my body, as if I might discover that I actually had a gun or a knife or a magic power in my pocket that I had forgotten. What my hands found was my belt. Slim and leather, it looped twice around my soft, light tunic, giving me a waist.

"I'm madder at him than you. Even though I was faithful to you. Always you. Only you. I've never been with anybody else, I hope you know."

It was something. My fingers fumbled at the buckle, and I took it off as smoothly as I could, trying not to shake his seat, trying to be silent. I tested the strength of it in my trembling hands. Too thick to be a garrote, but—if I could cut off the blood flow to his brain—

I'd been killed like this before, once. On a prime-time detective show. Crazy to think about pretending to be murdered, to remember how I decided to kick my feet in a panicked tattoo, thinking, *This is what my feet would really do if I was dying.* Another actor, in a black ski mask—my friend Jeremy Johnick—fake-choked me. I had to struggle in a way that wouldn't break my body tape and let my boob pop out of my nightgown. It was a good guest spot, even though my character was dead before the theme song. She was the estranged sister of a main character, so I had flashback scenes as well. The scene I remembered now, as I shivered and my small, weak hands clutched at my belt, was the one in the morgue: Me laid out on the table wearing nothing but modesty patches, my body blued and bruised, ligature marks layered onto my neck with greasepaint and rigid collodion. It was chilly in the studio, so they'd brought in space heaters to keep me from shivering while dead.

"Honestly, the murder scene is bullshit," the consultant told Jeremy and me later, at craft services. "They had you struggling far too long, but I suppose it makes good drama." He was a Canadian fellow, a doctor, and he knew a lot about murder. "You'd actually be knocked out in seconds, maybe seven, maybe ten. Also, Jeremy let you go too soon. He'd need to keep on wringing your neck for minutes after you were unconscious, to be sure. Otherwise, when the blood flow to your brain restarted, you would pop back up, as right as rain."

I told him, very arch, "I'll keep that in mind next time I need to strangle someone."

So funny, then. Oh, how we laughed.

The doctor said, "Little thing like you? Much more likely to catch than pitch, I'd say."

We laughed at this, too, Jeremy with his ski mask pushed up to gulp a sparkling water because he was on a fast, all three of us amused that I was so much more likely to be choked to death than they were.

I wasn't laughing now.

I had one shot at this, and I was small and shaking, with nothing but my own slim leather belt and hopefully surprise to help me. If I messed this up, what would he do? He would be so angry, so fake-hurt by the betrayal of his fake, invented love. I thought, *Well, he can't kill me twice*, and then had to fight down a bubble of insane, panicky laughter. I told myself, *Let him try*. I was done freezing and bending and thinking I deserved anything I got. If I was going to go down, I'd do it fighting. I loved my child. I loved my life. I would go to war for these things, even if it hurt, and if I lost, it was all on him.

The woman in the bed moaned faintly. My head throbbed where Marker Man had slammed his gun into the side of it. The whole left side of my body was busy bruising, throbbing from where his blow had banged me into the wall, especially my face and shoulder. Three of my back teeth felt loose on that side, and coppery blood was still slow-weeping from a molar, nauseating me. It didn't matter. It had to be now, before the camper got up to speed. I spread the belt out between my fists. I didn't want to die in a crash, or be shaken off from strangling him by some violent impact.

The camper paused as he moved it out of reverse into drive, and then he leaned forward to turn on the radio. "Sugar, We're Goin' Down" burst out of the speakers, jaunty and raw. He cranked it.

With the relentless drums as cover, I stood up. I was quick and quiet, but he saw me in the rearview. Our eyes met. His widened, flicking past me toward the bed, seeking the woman he had put there. He still didn't understand she wasn't me or how I could be in both places. I saw all this in his dazzled eyes. It bought me two good seconds, and I used them.

His hands were still on the wheel when I reached over the seat to loop my belt over his head. I crossed the strands to make an X between his neck and the seat back, and then I dropped. I dropped hard, and I hauled. The belt jerked tight, so tight, yanking his head back against the seat. I pulled and pulled, one knee deep into the seat back, using my weight, practically hanging.

He didn't make a sound. I wasn't sure he could. I felt his hands, first as a vibration, scrabbling at the leather and then they came flailing over the seat at me. His feet kicked out a drumbeat, just as mine had when I pretended to be strangled for a camera, and I thought, *There, you see, I got that right.*

His kicking foot came off the brake, and as he flailed he hit the pedals randomly. The camper shot forward in a jerky surge-stop-surge. He stretched his body long and one reaching hand disappeared. A second letter, the hand was back, holding the pistol. He was trying to point it down at me with his head clamped to the seat, hampered by the angles. I screamed and tried to bend myself away from the dark eye of the weapon.

The gunshot was huge in the enclosed space, and I heard or felt or just imagined the bullet thumping into something behind me. The woman on the bed started screaming, too, as the radio blared out bass and drums and angst. I spun, twisting the belt as I jammed my back against the seat, flattening and crying. The gun swung about wildly, his hand twisting, trying to get a bead on me, and he rapidly shot two more times. The first bullet burrowed into the floor right by me, making me scream again, even as the kickback jerked his hand up. The second shot shattered a window. Over the music, I heard a dog barking. My ears were ringing, but I still heard it when he shot again. This bullet pinged hard off the motorcycle and ricocheted at least twice around the camper.

The woman in the back reared up on all fours, moaning, crawling to get off the bed and into cover. I hauled on the belt, and my scream had turned into a word, the same word over and over: "No, no, no!" He thrashed, surging against the belt, and he must have jammed a foot hard into the gas. The short nails of his empty hand tore at my wrist as we lumbered forward. In his other hand the gun waved wildly.

The camper canted left, so sharply that we almost tipped in a surge of momentum. I clung and braced my feet and pulled and the song ground on in stretched slow motion, a cacophony. I hauled as hard as I could and now the sobbing words coming out of me changed to "Die, just die, please die."

"Yes, fucking die!" the woman rasped. She'd already thumped heavily off the bed, but when she spoke, he shot again. His bullet hit the mattress where she'd been a breath ago.

Each second felt like a forever, but now, finally, I felt him slow. His hand spasmed. The gun dropped, hitting me in the shoulder with bruising force, then thunking to the floor. The camper kept careening left, and I thought, *I am winning!*

I *was* winning. My words devolved into a wordless howl, an animal sound, all victory and terror. The waitress howled with me, a shriek so dry it was like tearing metal. Her head and shoulders popped up from behind the motorcycle. She looked dead already, but her eyes blazed hope and fury.

Both his hands now flapped and tore at me, weaker and weaker. I felt blood running down my wrists from where his nails had scratched my skin open. Then I was hurled away from the seat, my feet losing traction. I kept my grip on the belt as I swung out and then banged back painfully into his chair. I bit into my own tongue and my hands slipped down, the thin belt tearing my palms open. The camper had smashed into something, but I kept my grip.

The engine ground and roared against whatever had blocked its progress. My voice felt lost in drums and bass and the roar of the engine, and then his foot fell off the gas. Now I could barely hear my shrieks and hers over Fall Out Boy. The camper still tried to push itself through something, but with much less force. I dug in and pulled. His feet stopped kicking, and I pulled. His hands stopped scratching and flailing, and I pulled. His hands fell entirely away. Still I pulled.

I had to make myself stop howling. She stopped, too, and then we both heard the voices of upset young people, yelling, and the endless, upset barking of the dog. *Scooby Gang,* I thought. I had my feet back under me by then, still holding the belt tight, tight as I could, though the leather was now slicked with my blood. I pressed up with my legs, craning my head around to see out the window. We were bashed into a big tree near the turn. I held the belt, so tight. In the rearview his eyes were half open and glassy, no one home. His mouth was open, too, and his tongue showed, almost lolling, like an actor's might, like this was fake, a movie.

I looked back at the woman, and she nodded at me, then slumped back to sit on the bed. Her dehydrated shriek of a voice told me, "Don't stop."

I thought, *If I let go, his eyes will blink and kindle. They will. He will get back up, and I will never get to Honor.*

"End him," she said. "End him." I understood the waitress perfectly, though her voice was the desiccated howl of a monster. We were fungible, this woman and I. I could be in her place, and she could be in mine. I nodded to her. We were the same to him, and we both wanted him dead. I pulled, even as I heard the driver's-side door scree open.

I yelled to whichever of the kids had come, "I've been abducted. I'm Meribel Mills. I'm Meribel Mills, please call the cops. My kid might be in danger."

From the bed, the nightmare version of me yelled again, "Keep pulling."

Outside the kids were saying *What*, and *Shit*, and *Oh, my God*, in an overlapping tumble. The dog was going crazy, barking loud, sharp barks. I was hollering over all this and the radio, and the girl I'd cast as Velma—it was always Velma—yanked the passenger-side door open and clambered up into the cab where I could see her. She clicked the radio off and then poked her head between the seats to look at me. She was so young, this Velma, only a few years older than my child. A quiet voice inside me said, *So is Marker Man. So is he.*

"There's a gun on the floor, back here, past me," I said, and with the music off, it was so loud. "Get it. Get it."

Velma climbed over the diamond-shaped table and found the snub-nosed pistol. She backed away from me with it, triumphant, unlocking the camper door and practically falling out into the arms of her boyfriend. I stared into the rearview at Marker Man's face and his wispy baby's mustache. Silent. Still. So very young.

My hands let go of the belt. No, I decided. I let the belt go. I leaned over the seat to loosen it, even, then peered out the open driver's-side door, past Marker Man's still form. The boy I'd cast as Fred, the one with the dark curls flopped over his eyebrows, was the one who'd yanked it.

"No! Oh no, no, no," the woman on the bed gibbered. "No, don't stop."

I didn't blame her for it, not a bit. But I already had stopped.

"You have to tie him up," I told Fred as Marker Man pulled in a long, slurping gurgle of a breath. "Use my belt." It was still hanging loose around his neck.

"Holy shit!" said Fred. He stepped up and grabbed Marker Man by his shoulders and then pulled, yanking his limp body out to crash bonelessly into the ground. I hoped it hurt. I hoped it bruised him. Fred rolled him facedown and sat on his back while he fought his way toward consciousness. The big goofy dog circled, quiet now, ruff up, anxious. By then the other boy, the one with the Shaggy soul patch, had come around. He yanked Marker Man's arms tight behind him and began to bind him with the belt.

I was babbling, words falling out in a torrent. "He's dangerous. Tie him more. Don't let him get up. There's a woman in the back, and she might be dying; she needs water. Please call the cops, and Fred, stay sitting on him. Please call the cops. I'm Meribel Mills. I was abducted."

"Oh my God, it's really her," said Daphne.

Velma climbed back into the cab now and took the driver's seat. She shut the engine off.

"Duct tape," I told her. "In the kitchen. Give it to the boys. That belt is not enough."

I staggered to the side door and by the time my torn hands, rope-burned from the wreck, got it open, Daphne was standing there, telling me, "I can help her. The woman. I'm in nursing school."

"Give me your phone," I said. "I have to call my daughter."

She did, pausing to unlock it for me, and I came out and she went in, heading back toward the waitress, who was dry-sobbing in rasps into her hands. Velma was already clambering over the diagonal table to get the duct tape as she called police on her own phone. I could hear her talking to an emergency operator.

I leaned against the outside of the trailer. Marker Man was on the other side, saying awful things, threats and racial slurs to the boys. Awake. Alive. Not through any choice of his. He was alive because I had decided.

My fingers fumbled to press numbers.

It rang twice, and I was fighting not to fall apart. "Answer," I said. "Answer."

If she could, she would. My girl loved rules. Memorizing them, anyway, obeying them to the letter, uninterested in the spirit, enamored with finding loopholes. She loved systems, and consistency, and she always answered her phone. Always. Even when she didn't know the number, even though all those calls were from scammers or the car warranty people.

Her line rang a third time, and each of those unanswered rings took a year right off my life. Then I felt the connection open, going live. I felt it all the way to my bones. She spoke in that formal little way she had when she was not sure who was calling.

"Honor Mills."

"Hi, baby," I said. I sounded strange and raspy, like the woman in the back. As if I was the one who had been strangled.

"Oh, good. Oh, good, it's you," she said.

Through the phone, I heard a voice behind her. "Honor. Who is that?"

"It's Mom," she said, and I knew who was asking. Cam. I knew his voice. She was with Cam, and half my fear ran right out of my body. There were a thousand things I didn't know, and I had at least two thousand questions, but I damn well knew this: If Honor was with Cam, then she was safe.

"Hi, baby, yes, it's Mom. How are you? How are you?"

A pause, as she seriously considered this most pro forma of questions. I knew that she would say the truth.

Finally, she answered. Very quiet. Very serious. "I'm good."

I sagged against the camper, half laughing, with tears falling down my face. She was good. She was. She was. She was good, my little paladin, so very good, all the way down to her bones, and nothing I learned later changed that fact.

"Me, too," I told my girl. "Me, too."

ACKNOWLEDGMENTS

FIRST, ALWAYS, I thank you—Reader, Librarian, Bookseller—ye who bought, stocked, and recommended my work. You are a gorgeous creature individually, and as a group your radiance is blinding.

Thank you, Book Paladin Emily Krump and all the story-passionate adventurers at William Morrow who have given my work such a supportive home. Gratitude to: Liate Stehlik, Jennifer Hart, Tavia Kowalchuk, Kelly Rudolph, Maureen Cole, Christine Edwards, Andy LeCount, Mary Beth Thomas, Ashley Mihlebach, Carla Parker, Rachel Levenberg, Virginia Stanley, Eric Svenson, Michael Morris, Ploy Siripant, Tessa James, and Greg Villepique.

Deep gratitude to my longtime friend and agent, dog lover Caryn Karmatz Rudy, who has never even once told me that I have to get a boob job. God bless the brilliant writers who did early chapter or whole book reads for me: Abbott Kahler (hoofs!), Anna Schachner, Ginger Eager, Lydia Netzer (OTG 4Ever), Reid Jensen, and Sara Gruen.

I love you, Scott. I love you, Sam and Maisy Jane. I love you, Betty (and Bob, always), Bobby, Julie, Daniel, Claire, El, Henry, Erin Virginia, Julian, Magda, Jane, and Allison.

A chain of small groups who love justice and Jesus formed my morals (such as they are) (to the best of their loving ability): NRSDC (the Brown and the Brownings, the Garbers and the Myers), STK, Slanted Sidewalk, small group, and Julie and Amy, who let me sit at the popular girls' lunch table in Chuck's class.

Love and gratitude to all who work with and support Reforming Arts.